W9-DAV-200

"D.C. lawyer and spy novelist Allan Topol must be sitting by the phone waiting for a call from Hollywood. His fast-paced novel, *Dark Ambition*, is a big-budget spy movie waiting to happen. . . . In this tightly written novel, Topol captures well the quiet neighborhoods of Washington, D.C., and the occasional ruthlessness of its people. . . . The moment of revelation is terrifically drawn, and Topol gives the reader just enough denouement to satisfy."

— *Legal Times*

"Topol might be the most riveting spy-adventure writer in America today. *Dark Ambition* is his second novel, and it continues the pacing and excitement of *Spy Dance*, his first novel. The masterful plot moves seamlessly between Washington, China, Zurich, London, and New York, while at the novel's core is the American process of honest, courageous people battling bureaucracy to ascertain the truth. I found myself solidly immersed in Topol's multifaceted conspiracy and am eagerly anticipating his next work."

— Newt Gingrich

Spy Dance

"*Spy Dance* opens with a haunting echo of recent events. . . . Topol, making his literary debut, displays a knack for this sort of story."

— *San Francisco Chronicle*

"The hero of Allan Topol's new novel is about as compelling as they come. . . . *Spy Dance* is all about the thrill of the chase, strength in the face of fear and enmity, knowing whom you can and can't trust. . . . A smart, cohesive, passionate novel about a tangle of foreign affairs and industry. A truly thoughtful and relevant spy novel—that may teach its readers a good deal as it entertains—is relatively uncommon, and it couldn't have come at a better time."

— *The Montgomery County Gazette* (MD)

"The story takes off at warp speed . . . extensive descriptions of each locale show that Topol has done his homework. . . . *Spy Dance* has the potential for mass appeal because of its readable pairing of romance with action and politics. It's a guilty pleasure."
—Washingtonian Online

"A superb first novel . . . very persuasive premise. . . . This is both an enjoyable book and a useful book in suggesting new thoughts about a country that is important but may be on the edge of substantial change."
—Newt Gingrich

"*Spy Dance* is a cloak and dagger novel about an ex-CIA agent forced into hiding for five years. Living in Israel under an assumed name, someone has discovered his identity and is trying to force him back into service—against the United States. Sounds like the stuff paperbacks are made of, but Topol's book has a message."
—*The Jewish Chronicle*

"An intriguing book that you will have a real tough time setting down. . . . Renegade CIA agent Greg Nielsen . . . is clearly better than James Bond in escaping bullets, traps, countertraps, etc. A smooth and exciting ride . . . I was sorry the story stopped."
—*Carnegie Mellon Magazine*

"The fabric of Topol's fiction is woven from the threads of real events and real-life concerns . . . the result of careful research."
—*Legal Times*

"In superbly suspenseful fashion, first-time novelist Allan Topol . . . weaves an intriguing tale through the lattice of actual events. . . . Topol has done his homework, exhaustively painting the scenes of the action, which spans from Israel to London, Geneva, Paris, Saudi Arabia and other locales. As a senior operative who has gotten rusty in the ways of the cloak and dagger. . . . Ben Aaron is a believable character. *Spy Dance* is a must-read for fans of espionage thrillers, and deserves a place on the bookshelf alongside the works of Tom Clancy, Robert Ludlum, and even John Le Carre."
—*Hadassah Magazine*

ENEMY OF MY ENEMY

Allan Topol

AN ONYX BOOK

ONYX
Published by New American Library, a division of
Penguin Group (USA) Inc., 375 Hudson Street,
New York, New York 10014, USA
Penguin Group (Canada), 10 Alcorn Avenue, Toronto,
Ontario M4V 3B2, Canada (a division of Pearson Penguin Canada Inc.)
Penguin Books Ltd., 80 Strand, London WC2R 0RL, England
Penguin Ireland, 24 St. Stephen's Green, Dublin 2,
Ireland (a division of Penguin Books Ltd.)
Penguin Group (Australia), 250 Camberwell Road, Camberwell, Victoria 3124,
Australia (a division of Pearson Australia Group Pty. Ltd.)
Penguin Books India Pvt. Ltd., 11 Community Centre, Panchsheel Park,
New Delhi - 110 017, India
Penguin Group (NZ), Cnr Airborne and Rosedale Roads, Albany,
Auckland 1310, New Zealand (a division of Pearson New Zealand, Ltd.)
Penguin Books (South Africa) (Pty.) Ltd., 24 Sturdee Avenue,
Rosebank, Johannesburg 2196, South Africa

Penguin Books Ltd., Registered Offices:
80 Strand, London WC2R 0RL, England

First published by Onyx, an imprint of New American Library,
a division of Penguin Group (USA) Inc.

First Printing, February 2005
10 9 8 7 6 5 4 3 2 1

For my wife, Barbara, for everything

Chapter 1

Robert McCallister was terrified. He was more frightened than he had ever been in the twenty-five years of his life.

His prison cell was smaller than the closet of the bedroom he had had as a boy in Winnetka on Lake Michigan's Gold Coast, north of Chicago. The stone walls were cold, and coated with a green mildewlike substance in which a myriad of insects crawled. The stench from the toilet bucket was overwhelming. The rusty shackles were cutting into his wrists and ankles.

Sitting on the dirt floor, he strained his ears as he heard the sound of men's voices approaching in the corridor outside the cell. There were two of them laughing and talking loudly in a language he couldn't understand. For the past day, only a single soldier had brought his food. Something different was happening. A round of torture after all?

He lifted up his knees in a protective position. His whole body tensed from fear. Two rodents scurried across the floor and disappeared into a hole. Even they were taking cover.

He didn't know how long he had been living this nightmare. Without a window to the outside world and minus his watch, which an angry mob had torn from his wrist when they pounced on him before he had a chance to extricate from the parachute, he had no sense of time. He rubbed his hand along his unshaven cheek and chin, trying to gauge how much stubble had accumulated. The scratches on his face were healing and scabs had formed. He guessed that he had been captured two days ago. Maybe three.

The mob had been hysterical. Some were tearing and scratching his face; others kicking his body, while chilling guttural cries spewed from their mouths. The words were incomprehensible to him, but the venom in their voices was apparent.

Initially, he had been relieved when soldiers had pulled him away. Quickly, his relief had given way to a new terror as he had faced his interrogator. Abdullah was how he had introduced himself to Robert. Dressed in a brown military uniform, he was powerfully built, with a thick, bushy black mustache, a sadistic smile, and small, beady dark eyes. The instruments of torture hanging on the wall behind Abdullah's desk—electrodes, rubber batons, and metal poles with multiple thin, sharp, pointed objects at the end—were what Robert was staring at when Abdullah told him, "You have twenty-four hours to decide whether we do this the easy way or the hard."

Waves of fear had shot through Robert as he heard those words. With an incredible effort of self-control, he had kept his body from shaking or losing control of his bladder, as he recited, "Robert McCallister, lieutenant, United States Air Force," in response to each question Abdullah asked about the location and strength of American forces in the region.

Two soldiers had dragged him from the room, away from Abdullah's contemptuous sneer and his threatening words: "You'll talk. Sooner or later, they all do." Robert had wondered how long he would be able to hold out. How long it would be until he disclosed everything he knew.

From his position on the dirt floor, he stared at the one-foot-square barred window on the metal door of the cell, waiting for the next hate-filled face to appear on the other side of those bars. When the door opened, he saw the two soldiers who had dragged him from Abdullah's office after his interrogation the first day. One crossed the room, moving toward him with bold, deliberate steps. Robert tried to pull himself to a standing position, but the soldier lifted his leg and smashed his boot down hard on Robert's shoulder, keeping him in place. Then he unsnapped the leather holster on his hip and removed his pistol. He began laughing, gesturing to his comrade with one hand while he gripped his gun tightly with the other. He pressed the hard, cold steel against the side of Robert's head. "I kill you, fucking American pilot," he said. "Now I kill you."

Robert wanted to pray, but he didn't know how. Brought up without any religion, how do you pray?

Resigned to his death, Robert didn't plead for his life like a sniveling coward. He didn't cry. His body was taut. He closed his eyes. His hands clenched into fists. His knees were shaking despite his effort at self-control. He held his breath.

The soldier pulled the trigger. Robert waited for the explosion. Nothing happened. The gun must have malfunctioned.

The soldier aimed the gun again. He pulled the trigger. Nothing.

Then he burst out laughing. "No bullets in gun. You lucky, American pilot."

Relieved, but furious that it had all been a sadistic joke, Robert didn't say a word. He wondered what they would do to him next.

"Maybe not so lucky," the soldier said. "We take you to Abdullah."

As they dragged him upstairs, Robert tried to steel himself for what was coming next. "Robert McCallister, lieutenant, United States Air Force," he muttered under his breath. No matter what Abdullah did to him, that was all he would say.

When he entered the office, Abdullah said, "Are you ready to tell me about American military deployments in the area?"

"Robert McCallister, lieutenant, United States Air Force," he said in a voice that tried lamely to express the courage he didn't feel.

Abdullah turned around and pointed to the instruments of torture on the wall while giving that cruel smile. "Would you like to choose or shall I?"

"Robert McCallister, lieutenant, United States Air Force."

Before Abdullah could respond, the telephone on his desk rang. As his interrogator listened, Robert watched the expression on the officer's face. The smile gave way to an angry, surly frown, his tone subservient as Robert guessed he was responding, "Yes, sir . . . Yes, sir," to whatever orders he was receiving.

He hung up the phone and stared hard at Robert. "Someone powerful believes that you're worth more to us alive than dead."

Chapter 2

Jack Cole sat at his desk in Tel Aviv with a puzzled expression on his face as he studied the computer screen. The e-mail from Monique, his secretary in Paris, was terse: *Daniel Moreau from the SDECE (Service de Documentation Extérieur et Contre-Espionage) came to the office today to see you. I told him that you were out of the country, and that I didn't know where you were, how to reach you, or when you would return. He said he will be back.*

Jack had never met Moreau, but he knew the Frenchman from reputation. He was the assistant director of SDECE charged with investigating espionage that took place on French soil. Jack wondered whether he was still pursuing the 1981 Osirak affair, or the recent assassination in Marseilles of Khalifa, a Palestinian terrorist. Jack didn't think either of these could be tied to him, but he couldn't be positive there wasn't a leak somewhere. It seemed impossible that Moreau could have found Francoise in Montreal or wherever she was now, after all these years.

This was a dangerous situation for Jack. The purpose of Moreau's visit had to be interrogation, arrest, or expulsion. He would have to find a way of dealing with Moreau, or Jack's entire life—so carefully constructed with France and Israel at the center—would come crashing down.

Jack thought about calling Moshe to report this development, but decided against it. He rationalized that he needed more information before he alarmed the director of the Mossad, but his real reason was something different. Moshe might pull him from Paris. Jack didn't want to run the risk of that happening. France was now a hotbed for Arab activity. That was where the action was.

Jack's worries about Moreau were interrupted by the buzzing of the intercom. "Ed Sands at Calvert Woodley in Washington is calling," Rachel, his secretary in Tel Aviv, said.

Jesus, this is not what I need right now, Jack thought. He wanted to concentrate on Daniel Moreau and sending back a message to Monique, but he had no choice. He had to keep his wine business afloat, to maintain his cover. Then there was the problem of what he should say to Ed Sands.

Stalling until he picked up the phone, Jack turned around and looked out the window of his office on the fortieth floor of the Azrieli Towers, one of two side-by-side gleaming skyscrapers, the highest buildings in Tel Aviv, at the sprawling city below. He had loved Tel Aviv the first time he had seen it as a boy in 1968. Not being religious, he chose to live here rather than in Jerusalem. For Jack, secular Tel Aviv was the cultural and economic heart of modern Israel. Writers and musicians thrived on the cutting edge of their art. A burgeoning high-tech industry burst forth and rivaled others around the world. It was a city, like New York, that never slept, where boutiques, discotheques, and buses were crowded late at night.

Jack had been dreading this call ever since he had sent the e-mail yesterday advising Ed that he couldn't deliver the fifty cases of the special Cuvee Chateauneuf du Pape that Ed had ordered and paid for six months ago, because Jack's supplier had welshed on him. Jack had made his deal for the wine with Claude DuMont, a broker in Lyons, before he sold it to Ed. Yesterday, DuMont had returned Jack's payment with a note that read, *Impossible to supply.* Jack knew exactly what had happened. With the wine in great demand throughout the world and the price soaring since Jack and DuMont had made their deal, the thief DuMont had found a customer willing to pay a lot more than Jack. That left Jack stuck in the middle. He had no doubt that Ed had already resold the wine to his retail customers. If Jack followed DuMont's lead and returned Ed's money, Ed's customers would raise holy hell when they couldn't get their wine.

Jack picked up the phone and held it away from his ear in case Ed shouted.

"I'm not a very happy man," Ed said in a low grumble.

Jack took a deep breath. "I didn't expect you to be."

"We've been doing business a long time."

Jack knew Ed's vocal inflections well enough to determine that he was furious, as he had a right to be. "I'm really sorry. I sent you a copy of the note from Claude DuMont."

"And should I send Claude DuMont's note to my customers?"

Jack was running through the options in his mind. There were only two: Stick Ed the way Claude had stuck him. Jack's guess was that Ed would probably not go to the expense of suing. Jack might lose the Calvert Woodley business, but Ed might eventually come around. Or Jack could offer to go out into the open market, buy the wine at the market price, and supply it to Ed as promised, taking a financial beating in the process. Jack grimaced, his face looking as if he had bitten into a lemon.

Due to the world recession, Jack's company, Mediterranean Wine Exports, with offices in Paris, Milan, and Barcelona, was less profitable this year than last. As he crunched the numbers in his mind, he realized that he would be taking a serious hit if he had to cover, but he had no choice. Ed had been one of Jack's earliest customers.

Twenty-three years ago, when he had started the business and dropped into Calvert Woodley on a marketing trip to the United States, Ed had been willing to give him a chance. Besides, covering was the decent thing to do. He had made a commitment. He had to honor it.

"I'll find the wine for you," he said to Ed. "The price stays the same. Give me thirty days."

Before Ed could respond, Jack's secretary burst into his office with a note in her hand. "Hold on for a minute," he said to Ed.

Jack reached out his hand for the note. *Your brother, Sam, is here,* Rachel had typed.

Jack shook his head in disbelief and hit the mute button on the phone. "This is one hell of a day," he muttered.

Rachel looked at him sympathetically. "Anything I can do to help?"

"Yeah, tell him to go back to London and break his engagement."

She cracked a tiny wry smile.

"Since you won't do that, tell him I'll be off in a couple of minutes."

Jack activated his phone. "Okay, I'm back," he said to Ed. "What do you think?"

"You're an honorable man. That's what I think. I like doing business with you."

"Our relationship means a great deal to me as well."

Ed cleared his throat. "As long as I've got you on the phone, what are you hearing about last year's burgundies?"

"I tasted some of them in the cask," Jack said, trying to sound enthusiastic. "It may be the best vintage in a hundred years."

Ed laughed. "You guys say that about every two years."

Jack laughed with him. "Yeah, well, this time it really is."

"Anyhow, send me a price list and I'll fax you an order

for some of those wines from the small producers you're working with."

"Thanks, Ed. I'll look for it."

When Jack hung up the phone, he breathed a sigh of relief. His profit on Ed's new order would make up some of his loss from DuMont's crummy behavior. Now he had to turn to the surprise visitor in his office. If Jack could fly, he would open the window and take off. Anything to avoid talking to his brother.

Sam was more than Jack's only sibling. For all practical purposes, Jack had no living relatives other than Sam. Back in Chicago, where they had grown up, Jack, ten years older, had been part father and part brother to "the little guy," as he affectionately referred to Sam. Their father, a newspaper reporter at the *Tribune*, had worked long hours. Their mother was immersed in charity work. Left alone, the two of them had developed a close bond. Jack had expected it to last forever, and it would have, but for one fact.

About a year ago, Sam, living in England as the head of the London office of a large Chicago-based international law firm, had begun dating Ann McCallister. "Don't get started with that family," Jack had admonished Sam, to no avail. A month ago, Sam called Jack to announce his engagement. Viewing it as a personal betrayal, Jack had slammed the phone down on him.

There could be only one reason Sam had come to Israel now without any warning: to tell Jack he had set a date to marry Ann. *Well, you're wasting your time if you think I'll stand up with you and those people during a wedding ceremony,* Jack vowed to himself. *I'm not even sure that I'll be there.*

The more he thought about it, the angrier he became. Sam had done him a favor by showing up in his office. Jack would be able to deliver the message in person. He hit the intercom. "Send him in, Rachel." *Deal with this unemotionally,* Jack cautioned himself.

As the door opened and he saw Sam, a glass of Coke in his hand, Jack was struck by the fact, as he always was, of how little resemblance the two men bore. Jack had gotten their good-looking mother's genes. Sam was a dead ringer for their father.

Sam, who was five-eight, with a protruding waistline, worked too hard and couldn't find time in his busy schedule for exercise. He had a bald spot in the center of his dark brown hair. Jack was an inch over six feet, thin and in good shape from running and using an exercise bike five or six times a week. Jack had thick, wavy sand-colored hair and sparkling blue eyes. Sam wore wire-framed glasses over tired bloodshot brown eyes.

Sam was wearing the Savile Row double-breasted suit that was the uniform of his trade, mergers and acquisitions. He was a specialist who crafted transactions for the world's most powerful businesses. Jack was dressed in his normal Israeli garb of slacks and a sport shirt open at the neck. No one would have guessed that Sam was the thirty-eight-year-old, the way they looked.

The picture Jack still had in his mind was of the two of them in shorts and T-shirts. Jack was on his way to play baseball or football with his friends. Sam, thrilled to be Jack's sidekick, held on to his brother's hand as they made their way to the park. There, Sam hung out with the older boys as a sort of mascot. Jack loved the little guy tagging along, looking up at him with great admiration. All of that changed when Jack went off to Michigan for college.

"This is a surprise," Jack said. "You down here for business?"

Sam took a sip and placed his glass on an end table. "Nope," he said. "I just wanted to see you." Sam's voice had a nervous edge.

"Quite a gamble on your part. I might have been out of the country." As soon as the words were out of his mouth, Jack remembered the phone call he had received last night around midnight. When he had answered and said, "Jack here," the caller had hung up. That had to have been Sam, checking that he was at home.

"This must be about your great romance," Jack said.

"I want—"

Jack cut him off. "I'm not interested in hearing about it." Breaking his vow to remain calm, he was raising his voice. Sam knew damn well what Jack thought of the idea of his dating and then becoming engaged to Sarah and Terry's daughter. Apparently, the legal genius with the Harvard Law School education who crafted billion-dollar deals couldn't get this simple fact into his head.

"You can do whatever you want with your life," Jack said.

Sam stepped forward toward Jack. "Why do you always have to interrupt people? At least let me finish a sentence."

"I know what you're going to say."

Sam pulled a wad of bills out of his pocket, extracted a hundred-pound note, and smashed it down on Jack's desk. "Looky here, I'll bet you don't. I'll bet—"

"Oh, c'mon, you're going to tell me you set the date to marry that girl." He refused to mention Ann's name. "And you want me to join you at your wedding."

"You just lost a hundred quid. I am going to marry her, but we haven't set the date yet."

Feeling chagrined at his outburst, Jack lightened up. "Don't act British with me," he said in a jocular tone. "You've only been there two years. They're called pounds. Not quid."

Jack came out from behind the desk and pointed to two chairs around a coffee table. When they were both seated, he said, "Okay, what gives?"

"It has to do with Ann."

Jack felt his anger rising again. He clutched the arms of his chair. "Yeah, go ahead."

"Her brother Robert's plane was shot down over southeastern Turkey."

Jack's eyes widened. "Is *he* the unidentified pilot they've been yapping about on CNN?"

Sam nodded. "Washington hasn't wanted to go public with his name. The Turks are claiming that the Kurds are responsible. The Kurds are blaming the Turks. Both of them say they have no idea who the pilot is or what happened to him."

"What are Terry and Sarah saying about it?"

The question annoyed Sam. "What do you think they're saying? It's their son. But looky here, that's not why I came. I don't give a shit about Terry or Sarah. It's Ann I care about. She and her brother are close." He raised two fingers pressed together for emphasis. "Like you and I were once."

Jack let the comment pass.

Sam continued. "Ann's been going through hell since she heard the news. Can't eat. Can't sleep. Can't work."

"What's the American government doing?"

Sam held out his hands. "Not much . . . so far. Terry's using all his clout as a big contributor and fund-raiser for President Kendall and the Republicans. Leaning hard on Kendall to do whatever it takes to win his son's release, and you can't blame—"

This was too much for Jack. He cut Sam off again. "Good old Terry, always a man of action. Leads a charge up a hill even though he's got no idea whether there's anything at the top worth taking."

Sam sighed in exasperation. "I know that something happened with you, Sarah, and Terry when the three of you were at Michigan. I've been trying to get you to tell me about it ever since you went into orbit once I started dating Ann. But you refuse to talk. So what the hell can I do?"

"You could have stopped dating her," Jack said, his eyes blazing. "It's called loyalty."

"If we're such a team, then tell me what happened with the three of you."

Jack waved his arm. "I won't talk about it."

"I didn't come all this way for another round with you."

Jack was on the edge of his chair. "Then why did you come?"

"Yesterday President Kendall sent a private message to both the Kurds and the Turks. Either find and return Robert or suffer serious consequences."

"Yeah, that'll produce Robert's release," Jack said sarcastically. He looked away from Sam at the red ball of fire setting over the Mediterranean. He wouldn't wish this on anyone. Not even Terry and Sarah.

Jack turned back to Sam. "So that's what you came to tell me? Fine. I know it. Now that you're here, I assume you'll stay with me overnight. We'll go out for some dinner."

"You don't understand. I want your help."

Jack wondered what was coming next. "My help with what?" he asked warily.

"Rescuing Robert."

A long, low whistle flew out of Jack's mouth. "That's a hell of a request of someone who runs a wine-exporting business."

Sam was not to be put off. "Looky here, you've lived in Israel a long time. The Israelis have a close relationship with the Turks. You must know people in the Israeli government. People who . . ."

His brother's plea astounded Jack. Sam couldn't possibly know about Jack's Mossad connection unless he had let something slip out. But he had always been so careful. Hoping that Sam was shooting in the dark, he decided to tough it out. "Hey, I've got an idea. Maybe the Turks and the Kurds will take a few cases of good French wine in return for Ann's brother. Suppose I make it Haut Brion or Margaux. Something extraordinary like that."

Sam bristled. "One of those two groups probably captured Robert and is holding him prisoner. You know what those people are like. This is no time for smart-aleck comments. Have a heart, for God's sake."

"I can't help." Jack stood up to signal the end of the discussion. "I'm really sorry."

"Damn it, Jack!" Sam cried out. "I'll bet that kid's in a prison somewhere being tortured. He's the brother of the woman I love. This isn't about Sarah or Terry."

At the sound of her name, a tiny smile appeared on Jack's face. Life was funny. If you lived long enough, anything was possible. "Well, well, isn't that nice. So now Sarah needs Israel, and she sent you."

"Sarah doesn't know I came. I didn't even tell Ann."

"I can't help," Jack said in a tone of finality.

Sam shot to his feet and moved in close to Jack. "You could if you wanted to!" He was shouting. "You're such a hard-ass. No wonder you've never had a relationship with anyone."

Afraid he might strike Sam, his face red with rage, Jack retreated to the far corner of the office. It was true that Jack had never had a serious relationship with any woman in the three decades since he'd broken up with Sarah, but he certainly hadn't lacked for women and romance.

Sam was contrite. "Look, I shouldn't have said that. Regardless of what happened between you and Terry and Sarah, I don't think it's right to hold the children responsible for the sins of their parents. You have to agree with that."

Angered by Sam's words, Jack picked up a white china ashtray from his desk and moved it around in the palm of his hand. "Tell you what," he finally said. "If old Terry, the world's biggest hypocrite, flies over here, gets down on his knees, and begs me to help, then I just might do it. Otherwise the answer's no."

Sam refused to stop. Tenacity was the key to his success in law practice. "Terry will never know you did it. He has no idea Ann and I are even dating."

"The answer's still no. Terry's so important now. Let him do it himself."

Sam had one more card left to play. "Have I ever asked you for anything before? You moved to Israel and left me holding the bag for Mom and Dad. I never complained about it. I know you sent money, but that wasn't the issue."

Sam paused to take a deep breath before continuing in an emotional voice. "Even when Dad was dying after his heart attack, and then Mom from cancer, you were never there. You came to sob at their funerals. Big fucking deal. A couple of cameo appearances by the prodigal Israeli son. You didn't have the vaguest idea of what goes into watching two parents die from day to day."

Sam's words bothered him more than Jack would ever admit. Being away from Chicago for those horrible two years and unable to visit more often was something he had always regretted. But that was the critical period for the Osirak operation. Sam didn't have a clue about it, and Jack couldn't explain, even after all this time. Sam had no business hitting him with a huge guilt trip. "I'll forget you said that," Jack replied, feeling his anger rise close to the boiling point.

"I don't want you to forget it. Now for the first time I'm asking you for something, and you're turning me down. When it comes to family, you were a shit then; you're a shit now."

Sam's words were too much for Jack. He clutched the ashtray tightly in his hand. With a look of fury, he raised it and threw it at Sam. The white rectangle was flying on a line

straight for Sam's forehead. "What the . . ." Sam blurted out as
he ducked to one side in the nick of time. The ashtray smashed
against the wall and shattered into hundreds of pieces.

"You bastard!" Sam shouted. "Keep your fucking dinner.
I'm going back to London." He turned and bolted from the
room, slamming the door so hard it nearly tore the hinges
out of the door frame.

Jack shook his head, frustrated and upset that the conversation had ended this way. For several minutes he agonized
over what had happened, knowing that he could never explain anything to Sam. *Ah, the hell with him,* Jack finally decided. He closed the door to his office and turned back to his
computer. Monique's e-mail about Daniel Moreau's visit
was ominous. Here was something he had to deal with immediately.

He was usually good at compartmentalizing different issues in his mind and shifting gears mentally. But the conversation with Sam had thrown him. It took several minutes
for Jack to begin thinking clearly about Daniel Moreau.

The Frenchman might come back again and search the
office. He thought of the materials he kept in there. Was
there anything he should ask Monique to destroy? Anything
troublesome that could tie Jack to his Mossad activities?

He closed his eyes and visualized every file, every drawer
in his office. There was nothing, he decided. He had been
meticulous about confining what he maintained in the office
on Avenue de Messine to the wine business.

Monique didn't know a thing about his other life. He had
never involved her in his work for Moshe. Travel arrangements and logistics for those trips were handled by a contact
in the Israeli embassy in Paris. Still, Monique was in the line
of fire with Daniel Moreau. He had to get her out of there.

Quickly he punched in the number of his office in Paris.
"Monique," he said. "I saw the e-mail about Daniel Moreau."

"It was terrible." She sounded distraught. "He's an awful

man. He kept pressing me about what you do and where you go. He wanted me to let him look through all our documents."

"What'd you tell him?"

"That he'll need a warrant before I show him anything. I remember that from school." No longer on her own, Monique was now sounding stronger and pulled together.

"How did he react?"

"He tried to lean on me, but I wouldn't back down."

Jack remembered that Monique's former husband had been a brute who whacked her around from time to time. She had learned to hang in with intimidating men. "Good for you."

"He'll be back," she said. "With a warrant."

Jack knew Moreau would return—not with a warrant, but when the office was empty. He didn't tell Monique that. There was no point alarming her any further.

"Don't worry about Daniel Moreau," he said, trying to sound reassuring. "It's nothing. I'll make a couple of calls and deal with it. Meantime, since everything's quiet, I decided to give you a well-earned vacation."

"You did? Thank you."

"You know how you always wanted to take a trip to Australia?"

"Yes," she replied with enthusiasm.

"Go for the next month. Put the airplanes and hotels on the company credit card. Maybe you could even check out some of the producers while you're there, as my emissary."

"Oh, my God! Are you sure?"

"Absolutely."

"Anything I can do before I take off?"

"Not a thing," he said. "Just lock the door."

He was prepared to do battle with Daniel Moreau.

Chapter 3

Shrouded in heavy fog that rose from the Potomac River, the black Lincoln Town Car moved cautiously along the GW Parkway in the gloom of the predawn. It was mid-March. Spring should have been bursting forth, but Washington was still in the grip of one of the nastiest winters in memory, which prompted the pundits to say, "What global warming?"

Behind the driver, an exhausted Margaret Joyner looked out of the window into the abyss and closed her eyes. She couldn't doze. The pain in her back was killing her. One of the orthopods had recommended surgery, but the head of the world's most powerful intelligence agency was afraid of going under the knife. And many people said back surgery never worked anyway. Joyner decided to live with the pain as long as she could.

She rested her weary mind, mustering her strength for the long day ahead. The three hours of sleep she had gotten each of the last four nights were taking their toll. It had been the worst week Joyner had in her six years as CIA director. Ever since Robert McCallister's plane had been shot down, she had been on constant call for President Kendall and that asshole Jimmy Grange, as Terry McCallister kept turning up the heat.

When Kendall had defeated Harry Waltham for the presidency two years ago, she should have packed up and gone back to California. But the president-elect had pleaded with her, "I don't know the intelligence business. Without you, the congressional committees will crucify me. I'll be dead in the water."

Faced with a presidential plea like that, Joyner had found it impossible to say no. Acting against her better judgment, she had told President-elect Kendall, "Four years, but only four." She had done it for the country. Not for Calvin R. Kendall.

It was dark outside, but Joyner's corner suite on the top floor of the Company's headquarters in Langley was fully lit. Two secretaries were typing furiously, while an extraordinarily handsome man in his mid-thirties with curly black hair, a soft, winning smile, and sparkling dark eyes that pulled the gaze of people in the room like magnets, sat stiffly in a leather armchair along one wall. He was sipping coffee from a Styrofoam cup and reading the morning *Washington Post*.

The minute she walked into the office, he sprang to his feet. "Good morning, Mrs. Joyner."

"Sorry to bring you in so early, Michael. After I called you back to Washington, the McCallister matter exploded. This is about the only time that we have a decent chance of not being interrupted."

"Not a problem. Anything that's good for you works for me. Besides, my body's still on Moscow time."

"Well, mine isn't. I need a boost to get started." She nodded in the direction of one of the two secretaries. "Carol here brews a great cup of coffee, and it's already in my office. Right, Carol?"

"Absolutely, Mrs. Joyner."

Michael Hanley picked up the attaché case at his feet and followed Joyner toward the heavy mahogany door that led to her corner office. As she walked, from the corner of her eye she watched Carol watching Michael, who was Carol's age. She wasn't surprised. He had a sensual look that turned women's heads. When he was seated at the circular conference table in the corner of her office, Joyner kicked the door shut and poured them each a cup of coffee.

Michael had been in the director's office only once before. That was when Joyner had given him this assignment. Then, like now, the thought that kept popping into his mind was, If only the walls could talk. So many intrigues against foreign governments. So many operations concealed from Congress and the White House had been hatched in this room.

Joyner took off her glasses and tossed them on the table. The rest of the world couldn't stop because Terry McCallister's kid was shot down. Then she said to Michael, "What you're doing is one of the most important projects this agency has going. I want a personal briefing."

"Certainly, Mrs. Joyner," he said in a courteous voice.

He reached into the attaché case, pulled out two copies of a report in a blue folder, and handed her one. "I prepared this for you last night on my laptop."

"Any other copies?"

"None. The disk is inside the cover of yours. The message from your secretary was that you wanted to meet alone with me. That no one else was to know about it. I've followed that instruction, of course."

"Good." She liked this young man. She was glad she had handpicked him for the project.

"Power Point or paper?" he asked.

Joyner smiled. "I'm from the generation that has to hold papers in their hands and make notes. If I can't touch it, it's not real." She walked over to her desk and hit a button that dropped a screen from the ceiling. "Do your high tech thing," she said, "but leave me a hard copy of the report."

He nodded and began pushing buttons on his laptop while

she walked around the room in order to alleviate the pain in her back.

On the screen the words flashed:

Assignment: Determine whether Russia was the source of nuclear weapons recently acquired by Pakistan and North Korea.

Michael pulled out of his pocket a silver pointer that emitted a red laser beam.

He hit a button on the computer. The next image flashed on the screen. Following the beam of the pointer, Michael read the words:

The most serious problem now facing the world.

- Over 20,000 nuclear warheads exist in Russia from the former USSR stockpile.
- Despite ten years of American subsidies, safeguards are still minimal.
- Soldiers providing protection are underpaid, demoralized, and subject to being bribed.
- Opportunities exist for theft, particularly of the smaller tactical nuclear weapons.

Impatiently, Joyner glanced at her watch. The White House could be calling any minute to reassemble the McCallister crisis team. She interrupted Michael. "I know all of this. That's why I gave you the job. Cut to the guts of what you've learned."

For an instant Michael was flustered. His first-ever presentation to the director, and he was blowing it. He took a deep breath, swallowed hard, and said, "Bottom line is that your hunch was right. Nuclear weapons of the former USSR, supposedly being guarded by Russia, are being sold."

"You're sure?"

He nodded. "And I know who's doing it."

Michael now had Joyner's undivided attention. He skipped ten slides and put up on the screen a photograph of a man with a coarse-looking face, dressed in a suit and tie. He had short gray hair and hard, cruel eyes. He was missing his left ear.

"Dmitri Suslov," Michael said. "More precisely, Gen. Dmitri Suslov."

"Russian army?"

Michael nodded. "Retired five years ago. He lost the ear in Afghanistan. Caught some shrapnel. He was one of the major strategists of their war in that country."

"He must be a brilliant tactician."

Laughter or a smile was called for, but Michael was briefing the director herself. He was too serious for that. "Then Suslov led the crushing of rebels in Chechnya. Commanded his troops to kill everything that moved—even the animals. They were delighted to comply. It was a waste of ammunition, but it sent a message."

"Sounds like a nice man."

Michael moved to the next slide. A series of bullets appeared on the screen. He stopped talking and slid the red pointer from top to bottom, letting Joyner read it herself.

- Resigned from the army.
- Went into business.
- Corporate headquarters of Dmitri Suslov Enterprises is former KGB operations center.
- Incredible success as an entrepreneur.
- With strong-arm tactics, took control of the third-largest Russian bank, which he uses to dispense money to friends starting up businesses in return for a piece of the action.
- With threats and intimidation now controls 60 percent of all pulp and paper production in Russia.
- Has much of his own money out of the country in Switzerland, Cayman, and Gibraltar.

- Has a private militia of former army officers, who served under him, as enforcers.

She finished reading and resumed pacing around the office, holding her back, thinking about Dmitri Suslov. "So he's one of the handful of robber barons who now control the Russian economy."

"Exactly. I think of them like J. P. Morgan, John D. Rockefeller, or others of that crowd who dominated American industry at the turn of the century."

"With a big difference. Over there, all they had to do was grab pieces of the industrial pie with the breakup of the Communist state and the absence of law."

"Agreed." Michael nodded readily. "I suppose, too, that Suslov and the other new economic Czars in Russia are more like thugs. They'll use force to get what they want. One thing is clear, though: Suslov's not happy with the billions he has. He wants more money."

"Sounds familiar," Joyner said. "During the dot-com bubble years in the U.S., a reporter asked one of those captains of industry, 'How much money do you want?' To which the answer was, 'Just a little more.'"

"Well, for Suslov the answer would be, 'A lot more.' Anyhow, he saw a pot of gold waiting for him to snatch."

"Nuclear weapons?"

"Exactly. He knew that most had been moved into Russia from the former Soviet republics at our request and with our money, but that's as far as any real safeguards go. The level of security at storage facilities is a joke."

She stopped on a dime. Her eyes bored into Michael. "You're telling me that Suslov made the sales to Pakistan and to North Korea?"

Michael met her gaze without flinching. "Absolutely, and it's only a question of time until the next one."

Joyner took a slug of coffee, then picked her glasses up

and fiddled with them while standing next to the table. "Damn," she muttered. It was worse than she had thought. "How reliable's your information?"

"My main source is Vladimir Perikov, a member of the Russian Nuclear Control Agency."

"The distinguished physicist?"

Michael nodded. "He's frustrated because his agency has no real power . . . appalled by his government's lax control over the nuclear arms that have been moved to Russia from various Soviet republics after the breakup of the USSR. So he's willing to work with me, though he knows Suslov will kill him if he finds out."

"Are we paying Perikov?"

"Refuses to take a cent. The only honest Russian I've met in the eight months you've had me on this project."

"There's one in every crowd. What other sources do you have?"

He shuffled his feet anxiously on the floor. Michael had hoped to avoid this topic, but he wouldn't lie to Joyner. "I've developed a relationship with a woman, Irina, who works as a secretary in Suslov's office. She confirmed that North Koreans and Pakistanis came visiting at about the right time period."

Something in Michael's voice told Joyner there was more to this than he had just said. "Tell me about Irina."

He briefly closed his eyes. "She also sees Suslov from time to time. Socially, you might say. She doesn't really like him, but he's supporting her family. You know how that goes."

Joyner frowned. "And you're seeing Irina from time to time, socially, as you just put it. I know how that goes, too."

He looked down at his hands resting on the table. The nails were manicured. Michael cared about his appearance. He didn't dare tell Joyner that Irina excited him in a way other women did not. To impress Irina when he returned to

Russia, he had stopped at a Washington hair salon yesterday to get a decent cut. In Moscow they were all hacks. "Not yet, but hopefully I'm headed in that direction. I may also be helping to support her family, too, if I can set it up."

"Company funds?"

"If it's okay with you. She would be a valuable asset."

Michael was charming, and he had the looks of a magazine model for high-priced Italian suits. "You're playing a dangerous game."

Michael appreciated her concern for him. She was not only smart, but she cared about her people, which wasn't always the case for someone atop a huge bureaucracy like the Company. Still, he shrugged, brushing aside her cautionary note. He was in the process of extricating himself from a bad marriage with Alice, a dull, whiny woman, and his relationship with Irina was a heady ride. It was like being on a giant roller coaster. Swept up in the exhilaration, nobody ever remembered that the structure was built on a bunch of wooden sticks, rotting and aging, that could come crashing down at any time.

He was soaring with Irina. Alice, on the ground, seemed small and remote. He wondered what he had been thinking three years ago when he married her. She knew that he traveled a lot in his position with the Company, which he couldn't talk about. Then she had said, "Gosh, that's exciting." Now it was, "Why can't you get a job as the director of security at a company in Philadelphia so we can move up there and be near my parents?" There was no way he would do that. He loved the thrill and excitement of being a spy.

Then, Alice couldn't get enough of him in bed. She had one of the most talented mouths he had ever encountered. Now the only tubular object she placed in that mouth of hers was a cigarette. Fortunately, there weren't any children. He had hired a lawyer a month ago. The divorce papers were winding their way through the court system, clogged with similar divorce filings by others who had found that what they got wasn't what they thought they had bought.

"Sometimes it's worth living on the edge," he said glibly.

"Being reckless won't help anybody," Joyner shot back sternly through a tightly drawn mouth.

"Sorry," Michael said. "I didn't mean to convey that impression."

"You ever hear of Clint Darling?" Michael shook his head in bewilderment. "One of our top people in the seventies," Joyner said soberly. "Constantly putting his life on the line."

"And?" Michael said nervously.

"He ended up dying a fiery death in a car with an East German scientist we wanted to get our hands on. Clint tried blasting his way through an armed border crossing. His recklessness did more than cost him his life. We desperately wanted what that scientist knew."

"I get the picture," Michael said.

He sounded chastened, but Joyner's guess was that it was an act for her benefit. Still, she softened her expression. "Okay, let's move on. Use Irina if you think it'll help. I'm willing to do just about anything. The goal has to be to assemble enough evidence to take to the Russian president and have Suslov arrested."

Michael nodded his head up and down. "The only way to do that is to catch him in the act on his next sale. He's paying off too many people. Unless we catch him red-handed, Drozny will never move against him."

"Is another sale planned?"

"Not yet. I don't think so."

"Then what do you think we should do?"

Michael's eyes lit up. He was ready for this one. "My sources claim the Pakistan and North Korea sales brought in a small fortune. Estimated amounts are laid out in the folder. It's as good as printing money. I say we set up a sting. Bring someone to Suslov pretending to be a buyer. Say from a Colombian drug cartel. Or from an international terrorist organization. Catch Suslov when the exchange takes place, and hold him until the Russkies come."

"Which means he goes off to jail, and you get Irina."

Michael blushed. "That's not why I suggested it," he protested.

She didn't like his proposal. "Bad idea. From what you've told me, Suslov will do his homework on the buyer. There's a good chance he'll kill both you and Irina."

"Do you really think—"

"Don't be in such a hurry. Keep your eye on him. Your cover as an oil company development official is a good one . . . if you don't mess up with Irina. Sooner or later he'll slip; then Kendall can call Drozny. We'll move in with them."

Michael was preparing to argue with her when the buzzer rang on the intercom. "Kathy just called from the White House," Carol said. "The president wants you over there ASAP. That was her term, not mine."

Bristling at the idea of being summoned like a schoolchild, Joyner grabbed her glasses and stood up. "Sorry, Michael. It's back to McCallister. Is there anything else you want to tell me?"

He leafed through his copy of the report. "We've covered the essentials. If you have any questions from the document, please call me."

"You can be sure I will. Keep me informed with calls and messages on that cell phone the agency technical people gave you. Better yet, use a secure phone in the embassy in Moscow. If the bean counters downstairs give you any trouble on your expenses, send them directly to me. Meanwhile, I'll brief the president, vice president, and a couple of key congressional leaders on what you reported today. We'll have a team ready to move as soon as you tell me we have a chance of catching Suslov in the act. We can't let him make another sale under any circumstances. The risks to the world and millions of innocent people are too great."

"I understand." He loaded the report and pointer into his attaché case and started toward the door. Then it hit him. He should tell her how he felt. Michael pivoted and looked at Joyner shuffling papers on her desk. "I appreciate the opportunity to do this project. I really do, and I like working directly with you. I'll do my best to—"

She smiled. "That's enough of that stuff. Just get out of here and do your job. Don't forget that with Irina, you're playing with a grenade. Make sure Suslov doesn't pull the pin."

Joyner's coat was on. In her hand was the battered thin burgundy briefcase that Ken had given her on her last birthday before he died, the victim of a hit-and-run when he had been chaperoning the prom at the Washington suburban high school where he taught. Suddenly she heard the distinctive *ping . . . ping . . . ping* from the red phone on her desk that connected her to the director of the Mossad in Jerusalem. They'd have to wait for her at the White House. Moshe called only if it was urgent. He might have information about Robert McCallister.

Standing, she picked up the red phone. "Joyner here."

In his usual gruff manner, with little time for small talk, Moshe said, "I learned that the pilot they shot down is the son of one of the president's big-shot money men, Terry McCallister."

She was startled. "We were trying to keep a lid on his identity. How'd you find out?"

"Our air force people talk with yours. Life must be miserable in Washington right now."

"That has to be one of the great understatements of all time. You can't believe the heat in this town."

"So why haven't you called? You know we can be of help finding young McCallister and getting him out. We have good relationships in Ankara and strong assets on the ground in that whole area of southeastern Turkey."

"Which is more than I can say."

"Remember, it's easier for us. We can send people who speak the language and blend in."

Joyner was well aware of that fact. She took off her coat. Slowly and painfully, she eased down into the straight-backed, hard wooden desk chair. "I proposed calling you and asking for your help, but . . ." She paused and sighed.

Before she could continue, Moshe broke in. "Don't tell me. Let me guess. Terry McCallister doesn't want those heavy-handed Israelis complicating the chances of his son's release. He's afraid if they find out we're involved, they'll kill young McCallister for sure. So he's convinced his good friend the president to reject your recommendation. 'It's my boy' and all that."

She laughed. "How'd you get to be so smart?"

Of all the CIA directors he had worked with over the years, Moshe liked Joyner the best. She never forgot that the United States and Israel sometimes had different interests on specific matters, but she always leveled with him. There was never any deception, and she had a sense of humor, which was rare in their business. "My dear friend Margaret, I'd be stupid if I couldn't fill out the picture after forty years of working with your government. And, of course, the father's fooling himself. If they want to kill his son, they'll do it whether we're involved or not."

"You can't believe the pressure Kendall is feeling from Terry McCallister."

Moshe was eager to learn what Washington's next move would be. "Are you sending troops into the region to rescue him?"

"At this point, we don't even know whether it was the

Kurds or the Turks who shot down the plane. They both have the capability in that area. Right now all of the options are on the table. That's all I can tell you."

Moshe grumbled. He understood that Kendall was indecisive. He wasn't surprised that Washington hadn't developed a clear course of action. "Let's come back to the reason for my call. Suppose, just suppose, a little birdie flies in through my window and drops some information on my desk about young McCallister. Do you want to know about it?"

Joyner was hesitating. Moshe's offer of clandestine assistance was tempting. The trouble was that Kendall had been adamant: "No Israeli involvement." Usually she was willing to take heat from the White House to do what was right. Here, her dislike for Terry McCallister overrode that impulse.

"Don't do anything, Moshe," she cautioned.

"Do you really mean that?"

"Without any question," she said bluntly, letting him know by the sharp tone in her voice that she was serious. "If your people become players and Robert McCallister ends up getting killed, we'll both have hell to pay for it."

By the time Joyner entered the cabinet room at the White House, President Kendall, seated in his usual place at the center of the polished wooden table, facing the thick bulletproof glass picture window, looked at her irritably. "We've been waiting for you to start."

"Traffic on the bridge was insane."

"You should have used a chopper." He made no effort to conceal his annoyance.

"Next time I will," she responded without apology.

It was Kendall who had informally dubbed the assembled group "the McCallister crisis team." On the president's right sat Jimmy Grange, an undistinguished Washington lawyer, who had no official position. He had earned his place as the president's adviser and counselor by being Kendall's drinking and golfing buddy ever since they had been roommates at Yale thirty years ago. Across from the two of them sat Chip Morton, secretary of defense, red faced, with a large, veiny, bulbous nose, another longtime pal of Kendall's who had been CEO of Morton Industries, one of the nation's largest defense contractors, before coming into the government. Next to him in air force blues was Gen. Harry Childress, chairman of the Joint Chiefs, with a thin, narrow face and short-cropped, bushy gray hair.

At one end of the table sat the vice president, Mary Beth Reynolds, former Texas governor, an attractive woman with a warm, winning smile and poised manner, whose accomplishments were a tribute to her brains, hard work, and determination to succeed. That was what it took for Reynolds, born into hardscrabble poverty in Odessa, Texas, to propel herself on scholarships through Stanford and the University of Texas Law School, where she had been the editor in chief of the *Law Review*, to a position in one of Houston's mega law firms, which elevated her to managing partner before she entered politics. Reynolds was ending her term as governor of the Lone Star State when Jimmy Grange had paid her a visit during the convention to offer her the second spot on Kendall's ticket. "Don't expect to play a major substantive role," Grange had said.

Reynolds immediately knew what this was all about. "Why don't you just say that you want me because I'm a woman and I'm from Texas, which has all of those electoral votes, not to mention the rest of the South, where Kendall is weak?"

The odious Grange had sneered and replied, "Give that girl a prize."

Despite all of that, Reynolds took the offer because she loved her country, and she saw the post as a stepping-stone

to the White House. Her husband, a medical researcher at
Rice in the forefront of novel cancer treatments, was eagerly
welcomed at NIH. Then a funny thing happened. The press
and public liked her so much that Kendall, albeit reluctantly,
had to make her seem like a part of his team, or risk having
her take the nomination away from him at the end of his first
term. So here she was sitting at one end of the table.

At the other, with a thin pair of glasses resting halfway
down on his nose, was Warren Doerr, the secretary of state,
who viewed the job as a great learning experience that
would make him a better teacher when he returned to
Princeton. Reynolds, who had a sharp tongue, referred to
Doerr as "the professor" in her increasingly frequent one-
on-one conversations with Joyner.

Joyner nodded to the others and sat down next to the vice
president.

"Chip, you wanted to open this up," Kendall said, looking across the table at the portly defense secretary.

"Yeah. There's a new development," Morton replied, his
voice brimming with enthusiasm.

Joyner wasn't surprised that she was hearing about this
for the first time in the meeting. Ever since McCallister's
plane had been shot down, Chip had been engaged in a turf
battle with Joyner to take charge of the rescue effort. Arguing that the life of a military man was at stake, Chip, with
the tacit acquiescence of General Childress, contended that
DIA, the Defense Intelligence Agency, should take the lead,
and Joyner's CIA should merely provide assistance when
asked. For the first two days Joyner had fought Chip tooth
and nail. She didn't give up the battle until the president had
taken her aside after one of the team meetings. With Grange
standing next to him, he told her, "Back off, Margaret. Let
Chip and General Childress run with the ball. It's one of
their boys who's down."

All eyes were focused on Chip. He paused, coughed, and cleared his throat, drawing out the suspense.

"For chrissake, spit it out already," Kendall said.

Undeterred, Chip began speaking slowly. "We have been carefully analyzing satellite photos and communications Lieutenant McCallister had before his plane was shot down. Those all clearly point to the Turks being the perpetrators."

Kendall leaned back in his chair and gave a deep sigh. "Jesus, they're our ally."

"It's possible," the conciliatory Doerr interjected, "that one of their guys with his finger on the button in a SAM battery got trigger-happy."

Kendall ignored the words of his secretary of state, as he often did, and turned back to Chip. "Do you have any information about the pilot?"

Chip coughed again. "Following the decision at yesterday's meeting, we put a six-man special-ops unit commanded by Major Davis on the ground in the area where the plane went down. It's remote, mountainous terrain. Lots of caves. Very little vegetation. Only a couple of small, isolated villages, one with a name I can't pronounce, in the immediate area. Davis has been interrogating people."

"Any confrontation with Turkish or Kurdish forces?" the president asked.

Chip turned to General Childress, who picked up the briefing in a heavy Alabama accent. "No engagement as of an hour ago, sir."

"Good. What have they learned?"

Childress reached down to the floor and brought up a cylindrical silver tube. From it he extracted a map, which he spread on the table. "Outside of this village," he said, pointing, "is where Major Davis and his men found pieces of the plane. What they've learned is that Turkish soldiers seized Lieutenant McCallister. They had to pull him away from an angry mob. After that, they drove him off in an army truck."

"Bastards," Kendall muttered. "How do we know all this?"

"Major Davis has bought an informer from the area with cash and a promise to fly the man out of the country when this is over. Ishmael's his name. He agreed to go with Davis and help us find out where they took Lieutenant McCallister."

The president was pleased. Finally they were making some progress. "If Major Davis finds out where the Turks are holding McCallister, I assume that he'll go in and try to rescue the pilot?"

"Your orders were no engagement until you personally approved it," Childress said. "You can change that if you want. It's your decision, Mr. President."

Kendall looked around the room. "Anybody see a downside to my giving Major Davis a blank check? Letting him go in with whatever force he thinks is needed to get our pilot out?"

Jimmy Grange responded in a soft voice: "Lieutenant McCallister might get killed in any rescue effort. Maybe we should run it by Terry first."

Kendall looked at General Childress. "What are the chances of losing Lieutenant McCallister in any rescue effort?"

Childress tried to be patient. It was the kind of ridiculous question the general had grown accustomed to hearing from civilian leaders in Washington over the years. "Major Davis has an elite unit specially trained for this type of operation. They're the best we have."

The president tapped his fingers on the table. "Terry McCallister's been leaning hard on me to do something. If the military people think this makes sense, Terry's got no basis to bitch. Besides, he's not running the country."

Grange was preparing to respond, to remind Kendall how much money Terry had raised and contributed in the last campaign and how valuable he would be the next time around. As his mouth opened, he caught himself. That would be a mistake. He knew Kendall well enough to realize his words would only irritate the president, who wanted to believe that none of his decisions were politically motivated.

Before Kendall could decide, the secretary of state spoke up. "As you said before, Turkey's an ally. I can't believe that Ankara authorized this. That means they have renegades in their military who pulled this off. People who hate the United States because of the war in Iraq. It's only fair that we give the Turkish government the opportunity to deal with this matter themselves."

Doerr's haughty manner, as he looked over those little glasses of his, annoyed Kendall. Putting him in the job of secretary of state had been a mistake. But he did have a point here. Giving Ankara a chance to deal with it wasn't a bad idea. Also it would be a way of avoiding the decision authorizing military action.

Kendall shook his head in frustration. "God, what a mess."

Joyner looked away from the table and through the window at the trees struggling to bloom. She was no longer unhappy about being a bit player in this drama. For now she was willing to wait in the wings. Her gut told her they weren't about to rescue Robert McCallister. They would need her before this was over. She wasn't burning any bridges.

Meanwhile, the president closed his eyes, pondering the decision he had to make. If anyone thought that being the governor of a state prepared a person for this job, they were kidding themselves. It was Kendall's first foreign-policy crisis. No matter which way he went, the press would second-guess him. No one made a sound. The tension was heavy. Finally, Kendall opened his eyes and pointed to his secretary of state. "I want you to summon the Turkish foreign minister to your office as soon as you leave this room. Chip should be at that meeting. Tell the ambassador that we now have irrefutable evidence that the Turkish military shot down the plane, and provide it to him. His government has twenty-four hours to return our pilot, or we intend to take appropriate action. . . . Don't tell him any more than that. Do you understand?"

Doerr and Chip nodded.

Kendall turned to General Childress. "If we don't have Lieutenant McCallister back in twenty-four hours, give the order for Major Davis to mount the rescue effort."

Chapter 4

Standing on the center of the stage, in front of the orchestra, Gil Shaham moved the bow across the strings of his violin with confidence and intensity. The glorious music of Bach's Violin Concerto in A Minor that emerged testified to the young man's genius. No other sound was heard in the Mann Auditorium in Tel Aviv other than Gil's playing until the Israeli Philharmonic picked up and joined him, meshing perfectly. In the sold-out, richly wood-paneled auditorium, everyone in the audience sat spellbound, entranced by the music. Well, almost everyone.

In row K of the center section, Jack Cole wasn't hearing a sound. Unable to shake off Sam's visit, his mind had taken him thousands of miles and years away to the north side of Chicago, to a block of simple middle-class homes, the Coles on the corner, and the Goodmans, Sarah's family, next door. To his hardworking father, Joe, who covered the metro beat, which usually meant crime and corruption stories for the *Trib*. To his mother, Miriam, raised in a Zionist family, who never tired of working for Jewish charities. To Friday-night dinners, the only night that his father would come home for dinner on time, no matter what crisis was breaking over at city hall. Sometimes relatives joined them, but usually it was just the four of them, Joe at one end of the table, Miriam at the other. On the sides, sitting across from each other, Jack and the little guy, Sam, the miracle child who was born years after doctors told Miriam there was no chance. Sam was the brother Jack desperately wanted during all those years he had been an only child. All his friends had siblings. He had given up hope by the time his mother became pregnant. From the minute they brought Sam home, Jack had loved the little guy so much.

Now Joe and Miriam were gone. Other relatives had perished in Europe in the Holocaust or were scattered throughout the American West. Jack had never seen or heard from any of them since his mother's funeral. It was just Jack and Sam now. Jack and the little guy.

"Damn you, Sam," he muttered under his breath. "How could you have put me in this position?"

There was a pause in the music before the orchestra began the last movement of the Bach, the final piece of the evening. Next to Jack sat Chava, the world-renowned opera singer, whom he had been dating for a year. Chava, tall and sensuous, with coal-black hair, was dressed in a low-cut red dress that showed off her striking décolletage. Chava whispered in Jack's ear, "Isn't Gil marvelous?"

But Jack didn't hear her. Nor did he respond when she put one hand around his back and rubbed his thigh with the other. The orchestra began playing again. Jack wasn't with them.

He was deep in thought. Anger and guilt vied to dominate. He was furious at Sam for not appreciating the raw nerve he had struck. It was unconscionable that Sam didn't accede to what Jack had asked and back off.

It wasn't merely Sam. Jack was still bitter at Sarah and Terry—even after all these years. Terry had been such a patently obvious phony, and she a ridiculous fool for not seeing it.

Despite all of that, Jack couldn't repress the guilt that he felt. Sam had pushed the right button. He kept hearing in his mind his brother's bitter rebuke: *When it comes to the family, you were a shit then; you're a shit now.*

The words had stung yesterday. They stung even more this evening. *Well, you're wrong, Sam. I'm not like that at all.*

The orchestra moved toward the crescendo in the last movement. Jack began to wonder whether his anger toward Sarah and Terry had pushed him to an irrational result. Ann and Robert hadn't done anything to him. He had no score to settle with them.

Thinking about Robert made Jack feel horrible. He knew what had happened to Israeli soldiers who had been captured, how cruelly nations in the Middle East treated their prisoners. He could imagine the tortures that they were inflicting on Robert. If there was anything he could do to help the young man, shouldn't he do it?

Besides, it was his brother, Sam, who was begging him for help. Not Sarah or Terry. He wouldn't be doing it for the McCallisters. Whatever he did would be for Sam. Only for his brother, whose happiness was now tied up with the fate of Robert McCallister.

The music reached its final pitch. As it did, Jack stripped away the emotional baggage he carried with him. Seen in that light, the issue looked much different. He had to do whatever he could to help the little guy.

The concert was over. The audience rose to its feet, applauding. That brought Jack back to reality. He put an arm around Chava's shoulder and said to her, "Incredible. Absolutely incredible."

As they made their way out of the hall, people came up to Chava and greeted her. "I saw you in December in London. Your Dona Elvira in *Don Giovanni* was fabulous . . . your Golda in *Rigoletto* last month in Tel Aviv was the best ever. . . ."

Jack loved being with her, and the admiration she received. She was fun and the sex was great, although with her career, their relationship wasn't going anywhere. He knew that when he was in the country, she viewed him as someone enjoyable to be with on her intervals at home in Israel between demanding performances on the road. That was enough for Jack.

On the concrete plaza outside of the concert hall, with Chava on Jack's arm, a photographer for the popular newspaper, *Yediot Aharonat*, took their picture. Jack smiled broadly.

When they reached his car, he said, "It's a beautiful evening. Let's drive over to Yafo and eat outside."

"Actually, I had something different in mind." She winked at him. He knew what that meant.

"I asked Alexandra to leave us a cold supper at my place. I've got an early plane to New York tomorrow to start rehearsals at the Met. Besides, I'd like to get out of these clothes and into something more comfortable."

She rubbed a hand on the back of his neck, lest he had any doubt about what she had in mind. But Jack didn't. He knew her.

"You seemed so preoccupied at the concert," she said.

Unwilling to share his concerns with her, he tried to brush them off. "Just business. Same old crap. A Frenchman cheated me, so I'll have to cover an order for an American."

"Ah, the French. Why do they hate us so much?"

Jack laughed. "This wasn't politics. Just business."

"With them it's always politics. I haven't had a role in the Paris Opera in years. You tell me why?"

Jack was silent. The nature of their relationship was such that he didn't share his personal thoughts with her.

Once they reached her apartment, Chava said, "Why don't you see what wine I've got chilled? I'll put on that little Dior number you brought for me from Paris. The sheer pink one."

"Sounds great," Jack said, feeling himself become aroused as he imagined what she'd look like in it.

In the refrigerator, he found a bottle of Corton Charle-magne by Latour he had given her, and opened it.

The phone rang. "My agent in New York," she called. "I'll just be a minute, honey."

Waiting for her, Jack thought about Sam again. His con-clusion at the concert had been right. He owed it to his brother to do what he could. Now determined, Jack yanked the cell phone out of his jacket pocket. From memory, he di-aled Moshe's home telephone number in Jerusalem.

The director of the Mossad sat at the desk in his study in the old stone house he had occupied in the Rehavia section of Jerusalem since 1943. Inside it was a time warp. His wife, Leah, had furnished it in the early fifties. That was the way it still looked.

He moved his pen swiftly across the pad, preparing his statement for the cabinet meeting tomorrow morning at eight. The prime minister would be grilling him about Robert McCallister. Moshe knew that the Israeli leadership was split. Some were hoping that the Americans responded militarily. Others were afraid of creating further instability in the already tumultuous region.

Though Moshe had slept little since Leah had died last year, he didn't intend to spend too much time tonight wor-rying about this matter. For Moshe, the issue was simple after his conversation yesterday with Joyner. He scribbled, *The Americans don't want our help. Joyner has made that crystal-clear. They will do what they want to do, and we'll have to live with the consequences as best we can because this is our neighborhood. It's their pilot. It's their decision. We should stay out of it.*

Moshe expected a stormy debate, but in the end he was confident that the prime minister and the cabinet would accept his recommendation. The fate of Robert McCallister was an American problem. Israel would be willing to help, if that was what Washington wanted, but Joyner had told him Kendall was adamant about going it alone. Right or wrong, that was Kendall's decision. Moshe was convinced the Israelis should respect it.

He closed up the pen and stood at his desk. Then the telephone rang. "Who's calling, please?" Moshe asked.

"It's Jack Cole. I have a matter I want to talk to you about. It involves—"

Moshe cut him off. He had no idea how secure Jack's phone was.

"Where are you, my boy?" Moshe asked.

"Tel Aviv."

"We should talk in person. You can come here tonight, unless it can wait until tomorrow."

Jack thought about Chava in that pink negligee and decided it wasn't even a question. "Tomorrow will be good."

The cabinet meeting was scheduled for two hours. "My office at eleven in the morning," Moshe said.

"I'll be there."

As Moshe hung up the phone, he wondered what in the world this mysterious call was about. Though Moshe liked Jack and the work he did for the agency, Jack had never called Moshe at home unless they were in the middle of an operation. He hoped that there weren't repercussions from the Khalifa assassination. The last thing Moshe needed right now was a new crisis with France.

Chapter 5

A smartly dressed middle-aged secretary with large tortoise-shell glasses ushered Jack into Moshe's office. She handed them each a cup of Turkish coffee and rapidly departed.

With Moshe, there was no small talk. Before Jack could get settled in a chair in front of the large, empty wooden tabletop desk, the Mossad director said, "You did a good job on Khalifa in Marseilles."

Pleased with the compliment, Jack smiled. "If people transport explosives in their cars, sometimes they get blown up."

Moshe returned Jack's smile. "That's what I told the French when they called to chew me out. Since they refused to extradite him to Israel despite all the evidence we presented of his murders, they should be grateful for what we've done. He would hardly be a law-abiding citizen in their country. Have you heard anything about it in France?"

Jack thought about Moreau's visit to his Paris office. The Frenchman hadn't mentioned Khalifa's assassination. "Not a word," Jack said. He didn't want Moshe to pull him from Paris.

"Good. I was worried that's why you came to see me."

Jack glanced at his watch, not wanting to take too much of Moshe's valuable time. "I have something quite different to talk with you about. Perhaps you can help me . . . and it may be in Israel's interest as well."

Jack's words hooked Moshe. "Okay. Talk, my boy," Moshe said in his typically no-nonsense, brusque manner, while lifting the small cup to his lips.

Jack took a deep breath. In the hours since he had made the call to Moshe, he had thought long and hard about where to start. The story began back in Chicago forty-three years ago, when he was five and the Goodmans, Sarah's family, moved in next door, but Moshe didn't need to know any of that. *Begin with the present,* he had decided. The words tumbled out. "An American pilot by the name of Robert McCallister was shot down over southeastern Turkey."

Moshe put his cup down with a thud and looked squarely at Jack. "How do you know that?"

"It's been on CNN and in the papers."

"Not the pilot's name. The Americans have kept it a secret. No one else has released it."

So Sam was right about the lid that both sides had placed on the identity of the pilot, Jack thought. He shifted in his chair. "My brother's living and working in London. He's engaged to Robert McCallister's sister, who's a student there."

Moshe nodded in recognition. Now he knew why Jack had come. "You want me to use the Mossad to help rescue the pilot for your brother's sake."

"Yes. That is why I wanted to talk to you." Jack felt defensive. "But it isn't only for me. I thought it would be in Israel's interest as well."

Jack was met with a hard, cold stare. He began to wonder if this had been a good idea. "Now that you have the question, what's the answer?"

"In a word: no."

"Why not? You would earn a great deal of gratitude from President Kendall if you could free their pilot."

Moshe took a deep breath. He had no hesitation sharing

confidential information after what Jack had done with him over the years. "Because the Americans don't want our help. They've told me to stay out of it. It's that simple."

Jack was astounded. "But that's insane! You have a deep network of intelligence assets in the area, and you're well connected with some key Turkish officials."

Moshe smiled. "You were born in the United States. You spent eighteen years of your life there. At my request, you kept your American passport. I don't need to explain to you how Washington operates."

"Is Kendall afraid that if we help, it'll show how close our relationship is with Washington, and he'll lose his standing with Egypt and some of the other Arab countries?" Jack was incredulous. "Thinking like that prompted Washington to fly wounded Americans to Germany rather than Israel when the American embassy in Beirut was bombed. It cost American lives, as I recall."

Moshe shook his head. "If it were just that, I think they'd have given us a green light."

"Then I don't understand."

"Do you know this Terry McCallister, the father of the girl your brother is engaged to?"

Jack lifted his cup and took one final sip. No matter how sweet Turkish coffee was at the beginning, it was always bitter at the end.

"I know him," Jack said curtly, not wanting to explain.

"Then it may not surprise you to learn that Margaret Joyner wanted our assistance, but Terry McCallister leaned on the president to turn it down."

Jack snarled. "That anti-Semite wouldn't want Israel to help. What's his rationale?"

"Our involvement will inflame the situation and lead to Robert's death."

Jack shook his head in disbelief. "What an asshole. Nothing Terry McCallister does would surprise me." Jack's eyes sparkled with hatred. He was raising his voice. "Terry's brain is still clouded from all that dope he smoked back in college."

Moshe was stunned by the information and the intensity of Jack's response. "There's obviously a personal history here. You want to tell me about it?"

Jack pretended not to hear Moshe's question. His competitive juices were flowing. Now that he knew Terry was opposed to Israeli involvement, he wanted it much more. "Why should Terry McCallister be able to make the decision on our participation?" Jack asked.

"You'll have to ask President Kendall that."

"Suppose you ignore what Joyner said, and move in anyhow? Suppose—"

Moshe raised his hand, signaling Jack to stop. "I have a relationship with Margaret. I won't jeopardize it by flouting her request. I also have a second reason to keep out of it."

"What's that?"

Moshe sighed deeply, remembering how sharply he had been interrogated at the meeting this morning before his recommendation was accepted. "When I briefed the prime minister and the cabinet about McCallister, I told them that Joyner wanted us to stay out. They decided that I should comply. It's the Americans' problem."

Jack shrugged. "They're politicians. What do they know?"

Moshe grinned. Jack was throwing one of his own favorite expressions back at him.

"No, really," Jack continued with zeal. "Go ask any of our air force officers. You know what they'll tell you."

"You're a tough man, Jack." Moshe wasn't sure whether he was annoyed or fascinated by Jack's determination.

"The last time you told me that, you were happy about it. I was doing what you wanted." He paused. "You know I'm right."

Moshe wrinkled his forehead. "Of course you're right. However, I won't cross Joyner on this. Also, despite what some people in this city and in the press say, I don't go out of my way to disregard orders from the cabinet."

Jack decided to keep pushing. "Think about the pilot. If it were one of our boys down, you'd do everything humanly possible to rescue him." Jack felt himself growing emotional as he thought about what was happening to Robert McCallister.

Moshe shook his head. "But he's not one of our boys. Is he?"

"So what?" Jack fired back, raising his voice again. "An innocent man's life is at stake. We have a moral obligation to—"

Jack had gone too far. Moshe was furious. Jack Cole had no business coming in here and lecturing him about morality. He didn't care whose brother the American pilot was. "You're way out of line." He pointed a finger at Jack for emphasis.

Jack knew the rebuke was deserved. He backpedaled. "I'm sorry, it's just that—"

Moshe cut him off. "I don't want to hear any more about it." His tone was sharp and crisp, with a ring of finality. "I won't use the Mossad to rescue Robert McCallister. The issue's closed."

Jack was angry at himself for handling the discussion with Moshe so poorly. Wanting to cool down, he left Moshe's office and walked along the tree-lined thoroughfare toward the main campus of Hebrew University. The buildings, all constructed of gray stone torn from the Judean hills, gave a sense of peace, tranquillity, and permanence to one of the most hotly contested pieces of real estate in the entire world.

The sun was bright in a cloudless blue sky, which made the Middle East a photographer's dream. It was a spring day for young lovers losing themselves in each other, not for middle-aged men worrying about pilots being held hostage by an implacable foe.

Jack didn't think about the path he was following. His legs automatically carried him toward the university sports complex and the tennis courts, where he had spent many hours as a student, some in glorious victory, others in the anguish of defeat. The tennis team was practicing. Jack walked into the complex and sat down in a corner of the stands that ringed center court.

He was there only five minutes when a tall, thin, gray-haired man dressed in tennis whites, walking with a decided limp, the result of a bullet he took in the leg from a Palestinian sniper in the intifada, came up and stood next to Jack.

He shouted to one of the players: "Motti, get the racket higher on your serve. All the way up."

He watched, then grimaced. "Follow through. Whatever happened to the follow-through?"

Same old Dov Landau, Jack thought. He and Dov had played on the university team together. Dov, the star, made tennis his career, playing in international competitions, then coaching Israel's finest players.

"Jack Cole," Dov said as he sat down. "I haven't seen you in ages. I read about you in the papers. The gossip columns. You and that dish of an opera singer."

"Chava. She's a nice person."

Dov smiled. "Yes, I'm sure that's the only reason you date her. What brings you to Jerusalem?"

"Business."

Dov laughed. "That tells me a lot."

"I'm selling wine."

Dov cupped his hands around his mouth and shouted, "Run, Noah. Run. That's why God gave you legs."

He turned back to Jack. "I was sorry to hear about your knee surgery. Have you resumed playing?"

"The doctor said I'll never be any good again. I gave away my rackets."

Dov frowned. "That's the trouble with people our age. We're still young enough to do whatever we want, but we listen to people who tell us we can't. You should have told the doctor to stuff it."

"Well, it's too late for that now."

Dov patted Jack on the back. "You had a good run. For someone without much talent, you did okay on the courts."

Jack winced. "Not much talent? Ouch. That hurt."

"I meant it as a compliment. People were always telling you that you couldn't beat this guy or that one. You never gave up. Often you found a way to win when you should have lost. I admired that."

Jack smiled. Coming from Dov, who rarely gave compliments, the words raised Jack's sagging spirits after the discussion with Moshe. "Fair enough. You redeemed yourself."

"You want to stay in Jerusalem and have dinner with me and Naomi?"

"Thanks, but I have to get back to Tel Aviv. . . . Just wanted to say hello."

On his way out of the stadium, Jack thought about what Dov had said. When Jack was younger, he often found a way to do things that people told him weren't attainable, whether it was tennis matches or projects for Moshe. Sheer grit and determination were two of Jack's main characteristics. He was afraid he was losing those now. He had gone to Moshe with a proposal—rescue Robert McCallister—and Moshe had turned him down. He had readily acquiesced. Well, that was ridiculous. He would find a way to do it.

He needed someone who had spent time working in Middle Eastern countries and had sources of information in the area. He had to find out where they were holding Robert and what his condition was. After what Moshe had said, Jack couldn't contact anyone working for the Mossad. But that didn't preclude people who were retired from the agency.

He tried to recall the names of Mossad people with whom he had worked or who had recently left the agency. There was Yheuda Neir, but he had left Israel to work in Mexico as a consultant to the government there on antiterrorism measures. Ditto for David Allon in China. Then the name Avi Sassoon popped into his mind.

The Osirak project had been a long time ago, but Jack remembered every detail as if it were yesterday. Avi had been the Mossad point person in Baghdad who was relaying information to Israel from Iraq at the same time Jack was forwarding it from Paris. He had never actually met Avi, but he knew the man had a reputation for courage and for being a bit of a firebrand, which Moshe usually didn't tolerate in career Mossad people. He also knew that Avi had conducted operations in Syria, Iran, and Turkey as well as Iraq. About a year ago, one of the Mossad agents passing through Paris told Jack at dinner that there had been a big brouhaha over a failed operation in Jordan. Avi had taken the blame, and Moshe had sacked him.

Jack retraced his steps to the Mossad headquarters, but not to Moshe's eighth-floor office. This time he slipped down to the basement to the finance department, where Gila, affectionately nicknamed Miss Moneypenny after the character in the James Bond books and films, supervised payroll and expense reimbursement. Jack always called her when there was a delay in the checks he received, which was often, because Gila tried to hang on to money as long as possible.

He knew Gila liked him. That should be enough to get what he needed.

"What do I owe you now?" she said with a twinkle in her eye when he walked into her cluttered office. Papers were piled on the desk, the bookshelves, and even the chairs.

"Actually, you're up-to-date, but Avi Sassoon owes me for a bet we made on a basketball game last year. Since I was in the building today, I figured that I'd collect. I was told he retired."

"You didn't know?"

Jack feigned ignorance. "Know what?"

"About the Aqaba fiasco. It was a mess, and Avi took the fall."

"That's too bad."

She shook her head. "We all liked him. Even though he was a maverick." Loyalty asserted itself for Gila. "Still, the old man had a point. He had to do something to placate the king of Jordan."

"Now I have to locate the deadbeat. You must be sending him pension checks."

She moved over to a computer behind her desk and began punching keys. "He lives on Moshav Avahail." She wrote a number on a piece of paper and handed it to Jack. "His home phone. He's working for Koach, the big arms manufacturer, selling weapons systems to foreign governments. I don't have an office number."

"Don't worry. I'll find him."

Once he was outside of the building, Jack dialed Avi on his cell phone. It was late Friday afternoon. He expected to find Avi at home if he was in the country. Jack wasn't disappointed.

"This is Jack Cole," he said. "We've never met, but—"

"Osirak," Avi immediately said. "You were the guy in the wine business in Paris."

Jack was pleased he remembered. "There's something I want to talk to you about. I need your help."

"Where are you?"

"Jerusalem."

"Good. Come up to the Moshav tomorrow at one o'clock. You can have lunch and meet the family. Avahail. Just outside of Netanya."

Jack was pleased. He had made a start on rescuing Robert.

Chapter 6

To pass the time, Robert, sitting on the dirt floor, doodled on the ground with one finger, tracing and retracing the letters *USA*. He listened for sounds, but there were none. The other cells in the building must be vacant, he decided.

Following that session in Abdullah's office, when the phone call came, the guards, who had repeatedly slapped Robert, didn't lay a hand on him. Prior to that time, the food he had been given was a thin, watery fluid with a couple of suspended solid objects that he was afraid to eat. After that, food became ample and tasty. There were no more rounds of interrogation with Abdullah.

Robert could guess what had happened. They had found out who he was—or more precisely, who his father was.

That thought didn't comfort him. As he closed his eyes, a cold fury surged through his body. He knew why he had been pulled out of his air force unit at a base in California and shipped to the Middle East: Terry McCallister had made a call to Chip Morton, the secretary of defense, urging Chip to give Robert some flying time where it mattered, to build his résumé for the political career Terry had planned for his son. Robert knew all of this from his unit commander on the base in Saudi Arabia, who grumbled about having been ordered to use an inexperienced pilot on reconnaissance flights that sometimes turned lethal.

Robert still wasn't sure what had happened. Had his F-16 strayed off course? Where did the missile come from? He had been in contact with air control at the base. How had he missed it?

All of those issues were fuzzy. But one thing was clear: It was all his father's fault that Robert was here. No, that was wrong. It was Robert's own fault. He was the one who was constantly striving so hard for his father's approval. He was the one who had rejected the offer from Brown University for their combined premed–medical school program, giving up his lifelong dream to be a doctor. He was the one who agreed to attend the Air Force Academy because it was part of the blueprint for his future that his father had drawn. He could have simply followed Ann's lead and gotten as far away from the man as possible, but Robert wasn't Ann.

When this ends, Robert thought, *I'll go back to school and take the science courses I missed for medical school. Then I'll start over. I'll live the life I want to lead. To hell with him.*

For a few minutes that thought buoyed Robert's spirits. Then he opened his eyes and looked around the dingy cell. Despair snuffed out hope. What was the point of thinking about the future? He didn't have one. He would never leave this hellhole alive. Robert heard the sound of several men approaching the cell. Sliding backward, he moved himself into a corner. He tensed, waiting to see what they wanted.

The door creaked when it opened. Abdullah was standing there, accompanied by four soldiers.

Abdullah pointed to two of them. Without saying a word they pulled Robert to his feet, then hoisted him onto their shoulders. That was the way they carried him out of the cell.

"Where are you taking me?" Robert cried out.

His question evoked a grunt from one of the soldiers. They hauled him up two flights of cracked and splitting stone stairs, through a door that led outside into bright sunlight that momentarily blinded Robert after so long in the dark cell. He squinted, trying to see where he was, where he was being taken.

They loaded him into the back of a truck, open on top, which was empty except for bits of fruits and vegetables. Two of the soldiers climbed up and sat down on the floor with him. A heavy dark green vinyl tarp was pulled over the top. Then the truck began to move. "Where are we going?" Robert asked.

No one responded.

The air was stifling under the tarp. Robert strained his eyes to see through a rip in the plastic, but he was too far to the side. One of the soldiers pointed a gun at Robert. The other took a pack of cigarettes out of his pocket and lit one. In a matter of seconds the pungent aroma of Turkish tobacco filled the air. To Robert, the odor was disgusting.

He wanted to remain awake and alert, to observe everything he could about where they were taking him, maybe even to escape if he had the chance. But his body betrayed his mind. Ever since he could remember, he fell asleep in a vehicle when he was tired and he wasn't driving. He felt himself drifting in and out of consciousness.

The truck slammed to a stop. Robert opened his eyes and saw a worried look on the face of the soldier who was smoking. He crushed out the cigarette with his boot and peeked out of a corner where the tarp was loose. His look of concern turned to amusement. He said something to his comrade, which Robert couldn't understand. They both laughed. From his pocket he removed a grease-stained cloth, covered Robert's eyes, and tied it behind the prisoner's head. Robert smelled another cigarette being lit.

The wheels of the truck started rolling again. Robert, sitting and leaning back against one of the wooden planks on the side, found a haze descending over his mind. He could no longer think clearly. He closed his eyes. He wanted to believe that it was good he was being moved, that his father had found a way to win his release. More likely, he thought with grim bitterness, his father had somehow managed to make Robert's fate worse, as he usually did.

Sarah McCallister stared into the bathroom mirror in the suite at the Four Seasons and was horrified. "My God, I look like a mess," she announced to the haggard, wrinkled face with bloodshot eyes that stared back at her. It had been another long night of anguish—the third since her Bobby's plane had been shot down—tossing and turning in bed, her chest and stomach muscles tightening to the point of agony when she tried to imagine the horror confronting poor Bobby. Twice she felt she was on the verge of a heart attack. And all the while Terry was in the same bed sleeping soundly, secure in the belief that the president, who owed him big-time, would secure Bobby's release. Finally, at four-thirty, she had moved to the other bedroom in the suite.

She couldn't stand to be with him in bed any longer. How could he sleep? He was the one who was responsible for what had happened to Bobby. He was the one who robbed Bobby of his childhood, who constantly raised the bar so high that no accomplishment was ever enough, who latched on to the absurd idea that his son would have a career in politics and one day become president, a blueprint that Terry would dearly have wanted for himself but was unable to achieve because of what he had done in his youth.

"Leave him alone, Terry. Let him live his own life," she had pleaded.

"Stay out of it," he had snapped back.

He had brushed her concerns aside and increased the

pressure on Bobby, who didn't have Ann's courage to dis-
obey him.

The idea of Terry's living vicariously through Bobby's
accomplishments infuriated her, but she was helpless to do
anything.

Terry had been stupid to drag them both from Chicago to
Washington once he learned that Bobby's plane went down.
He could have pressured Jimmy Grange and the president
by telephone. They were no closer to Bobby in Washington
than in Chicago.

Finally, around six o'clock in the morning, alone in her
own bed, she had begun dozing off, sleeping fretfully, until
the sound of Terry's voice woke her. He was on the phone
barking orders to assistants in the private equity firm he had
founded in Chicago. "Sell that interest. . . . Buy that. . . .
Straighten out that company. . . . What am I paying you
for . . . ? We're not running a charity, for Christ's sake."

Even now, he was on the phone as she was splashing cold
water on her wrinkled face. When the second line rang,
Sarah raced across the room. It might be somebody with
news about her Bobby.

"It's Jimmy Grange, Sarah."

She held her breath.

"There's been a development," Grange said. "I want to
come over and brief you and Terry."

Her heart was pounding. "Good or bad?"

Grange hesitated. "We'd better talk in person."

"Don't do this to me, you bastard," she screamed. "Tell
me whether it's good or bad."

Terry broke into the conversation from the phone in the
living room. "Who is this?"

"It's Jimmy Grange. I want to come by and update you."

"Good or bad?" Sarah wailed hysterically.

"Come now," Terry told Grange.

The line went dead.

"Pull yourself together," Terry shouted from the living room. "Don't make an ass out of yourself."

She dressed in a black skirt and black blouse, prepared for mourning, and tried to comb her long brown hair. When that failed, she grabbed a rubber band from the living room desk that held Terry's business papers and tied it up in a ponytail, the way she had worn it when she was a student at Michigan. Thinking about Michigan depressed her even more. Terry had worn *his* hair in a ponytail then, too.

She was certain that her appearance—and especially her hair—startled Terry, but he didn't say a word to her about that or anything else. They sat on separate sides of the living room in plush chairs covered with burnt-orange velour. In silence he read the *New York Times* while she stared out of the window at M Street in Georgetown below, watching carefree tourists go in and out of little shops while she agonized over how much pain her Bobby was in now.

When the bell to the suite rang, she remained in her chair, grabbing the sides tightly with white knuckles, letting Terry answer it. She was bursting with anxiety to hear what this man she detested had to say. During the long presidential campaign two years ago, she had referred to Grange as the bagman. Terry raised money from wealthy people and corporate executives. Then he gave it to Grange, who periodically came to Chicago to collect the checks, hear about the contributors, and return to campaign headquarters in Washington.

"Okay. What do you have for me?" Terry said gruffly when the three of them were seated around a glass-topped coffee table with a vase of red roses in the center. Grange was on the sofa, Terry and Sarah at each side.

In the White House limousine on the way to the hotel, Grange had decided that he'd better mask the optimism he felt about Major Davis's rescue effort. The last thing he wanted was to build Terry up, only to have to deliver bad news if something happened to make the operation go south.

Grange began in a slow, hesitant voice. "We believe that a renegade unit of the Turkish military shot down Robert's plane. The Turkish government has failed to meet our deadline for dealing with the matter themselves. So we put a special-operations unit on the ground in the area where we *think* Robert went down. We *believe* that the rogue Turks are holding him in a small prison in the locale."

"How did you learn that?" Terry demanded.

"From an informer."

Sarah felt a sudden burst of excitement. This was the first confirmation they had that Bobby was alive.

Terry bored in on Grange. "How good's the informer?"

Grange shrugged. "Major Davis, who's in charge of the unit, is prepared to rely on him. That's good enough for the president."

"But Kendall's son's not the one down there, is he?"

"True."

"How many men in Davis's unit?" Terry was cross-examining Grange as if he were a trial lawyer confronting a hostile witness.

"Six. All highly trained."

Terry shot to his feet. "Six?" he said, raising his voice in incredulity. "Six fuckin' men? That's it?" He shook his head in exasperation. "There could be a whole division of Turkish soldiers guarding that prison."

"Listen, Terry," Grange said, now losing patience himself. Sure, he was sorry that it was Terry's kid, but he didn't need a tongue-lashing, no matter how much Terry contributed to the campaign. "It's a military action. We've got General Childress personally involved. He's air force too. He was a pilot himself. He knows what it's like. They're the experts. We have to trust their judgment. You wouldn't tell a surgeon how to operate, would you?"

Terry sneered. "I would if he wanted to cut me open with a pocketknife!"

Grange started to fire his own nasty retort, then choked back the words. Terry was pacing around the room like a caged predator. Grange glanced at Sarah, who was leaning back in her chair, her eyes closed. One of the buttons of her blouse was undone. She wasn't wearing a bra.

She opened her eyes and caught Grange leering at her, as he frequently did. *The pig.* She looked down and rebuttoned her blouse, then glared at Grange, who turned away.

She had first heard about Grange from Lucy Preston, Senator Preston's wife, in the ladies' room during one of the parties on inaugural weekend two years ago. Lucy had said, "Did you see how Jimmy Grange was looking at us when we walked by? He thinks he's superstud. Jesus, what a scumbag. Always on the make. And our distinguished new president isn't much better."

Lucy's words had made Sarah's blood run cold. Her own marriage with Terry had been less than ideal for years. *Separate lives* was an apt term to describe it. She knew that he slept with other women, younger ones, from time to time. Once she had confronted him with it. "That's what I do," he had said, not sounding the least bit contrite. His attitude was, *Stay if you want. Leave if you want.* She had stayed because she couldn't face herself after severing her ties to her family when she had decided to marry him.

His face red with rage, Terry stopped pacing and turned toward Grange. "We should be sending in a thousand troops, for Christ's sake." He was shouting. "Supported by bombers."

Grange stood up. He refused to be a whipping boy. Terry had lost his sympathy. "The order's been given. The operation's under way." In fact, it wasn't, but Grange figured this was a good closing line as he beat a path to the door.

He was almost there when Terry cut him off and moved

in tight, his hands gripping the lapels of Grange's expensive suit jacket. "If this doesn't work and you guys manage not to get Robert killed, which will be a miracle, I insist on being consulted before the next move is planned. Tell the president that."

Grange pulled away. "I'll let him know immediately. Meantime, stay here by the phone from seven on this evening. I'll call you the minute we know something. I hope to be able to tell you that your son is safe and in our hands."

"The way you clowns have planned this, that'll never happen," Terry yelled at Grange as the president's buddy was outside in the hall, beating a path toward the elevator.

Sarah couldn't remember the last issue on which she had agreed with Terry. On this one she did. In her mother's heart, she believed that Major Davis and his unit were never going to rescue her Bobby. Something awful was going to happen to him.

Maj. Charles "Butch" Davis looked up into the sky and gave a silent prayer of thanks. There was only a sliver of a moon. Even that was almost completely concealed behind dense cloud cover. Darkness was what he wanted. Darkness was what he had.

Butch Davis was thrilled to be on this mission. He had never known his father, a marine captain who had died as a POW in 'Nam, when Davis was only two. If there was one assignment he had yearned for in his fourteen years in the army, much of it recently spent attacking and searching caves in Afghanistan, it was rescuing an American held captive by an enemy. That was his own way of doing something for his father's memory, something no one had ever done for Capt. Warren Davis.

The six members of his special-operations force, an elite counterterrorist unit, were dressed in civilian clothes Ishmael had supplied, their faces colored with charcoal to simulate beards. Each of them was armed with an automatic pistol and a submachine gun. They were moving in two old battered cars along with Ishmael, who sat in the back of the lead car next to Davis, stroking his thick black beard.

The cars bumped over the pockmarked roads cutting through rough mountainous terrain. "How much farther?" Davis said to Ishmael.

"About two miles."

"We'll go the last half mile on foot," Davis said. His voice was calm. "Tell us where to stop."

Up in the front, next to the driver, Lt. Buddy Burns was peering out of the window, his eyes moving rapidly from side to side. "I don't have a good feeling about this, Butch," he muttered to the commander he had served under for two years in a Ranger unit in Afghanistan.

Davis shared Burns's anxieties. The car windows were open. Outside it was still, deathly still. This could all be an elaborate ambush, with Ishmael leading them into it like pigs to slaughter. There was something that bothered him about Ishmael. At some point they might have to cut and run. It would be up to him to decide when that was.

He took the revolver from the holster at his hip and pressed it hard against the side of Ishmael's head. In Turkish he said, "If you've lied to me and it's a trap, you will be the first to die."

The mountain air was chilly, but sweat was running down Ishmael's cheeks. "No trap," he said. "No trap," he repeated for emphasis.

Following Ishmael's instruction, the two cars pulled off the road near a large boulder, which concealed both vehicles. The five, other than Davis, jumped out of the cars, their eyes scanning the area, automatic weapons gripped tightly, ready to begin firing. Davis walked along the road, now dirt, and moved slowly, his gun trained on Ishmael, his eyes constantly roaming over the hostile mountainous terrain. The instant he saw anything suspicious, he would begin firing.

High on a hill, above the left side of the road and behind a rock, crouched Abdullah, an AK-47 in his hand. He had a straight shot at the American walking next to Ishmael. He'd like nothing better than to rip that American apart with bullets, even if the others killed him, which they probably would. But opening fire wasn't an option. He had been given strict orders. He knew what he had to do.

Ishmael had told Davis that there were only six guards in the small prison compound now, in addition to Lieutenant McCallister. Most of them would be asleep.

Davis was fifty yards from the compound. Straining his ears, he couldn't hear a sound. He raised his hand up over his head, signaling for the others to join him.

The plan was to encircle the small stone building and rush it from all sides. As they moved closer, Davis began getting a queasy feeling in the pit of his stomach. There was no noise at all emanating from the stone structure.

Once his troops surrounded the building, Davis turned Ishmael over to one of the others to guard. "C'mon Buddy," he said to Burns. "You and I are going in. Cover me with a gun. Gimme some light with your flashlight."

His automatic weapon tightly in his hand, Davis raced toward the front of the building. Burns was two steps behind, lighting the way. Uncertain where McCallister was, Davis was afraid to open fire.

The front door was wooden. Davis lifted his leg. With a powerful kick he smashed it open. The ground floor of the building was deserted and empty, devoid of furniture or any object.

On the right side Davis saw a staircase leading down. *Bastards could be hiding there,* Davis thought. He shouted down the steps in Turkish, "Anybody here?" All that he heard was the echo of his own voice. Cautiously he started down the stairs, squeezing the handle of the gun. From behind Burns lit the way.

Davis didn't see a thing. Didn't hear a sound. Nothing. Total silence.

He followed his nose—and an awful smell—to one of the three empty cells, where a toilet pail that hadn't been emptied stood in one corner. A prisoner had been here not long ago, he realized.

As Burns joined him in the cell and shone the light around, something on the dirt floor caught Davis's eye. "Gimme that," he said to Burns, reaching for the flashlight.

Davis moved the beam across the floor until he found what he was looking for. There on the ground, someone had scratched in the dirt the letters *USA*.

McCallister had been in this cell recently. Davis was now certain of that. "Go up and bring down Ishmael," he said to Burns. "I want to look around some more. Tell the others to watch the hills around the building. They could be up there, waiting for the best time to attack us."

Minutes later Burns pushed Ishmael roughly down the stairs and into the cell with the initials carved into the dirt. Ishmael was whining and sniveling.

"You lied to me," Davis shouted. "The pilot isn't here."

Ishmael was squatting down, cowering in a corner.

"You were part of a scheme to set this up so they'd have time to move the pilot. Isn't that right?" His voice had a sharp edge. He was furious.

"I know nothing," Ishmael wailed. "I saw them bring the pilot here. I had no idea he would be moved."

Davis shone the torch directly on Ishmael's face, into his eyes. Ishmael couldn't look at Davis. He turned away. The major had interrogated enough prisoners in Afghanistan to know when one was lying to him.

"Where did they take the pilot?" Davis demanded in a menacing voice.

Ishmael shrugged and held out his hands.

"I'm going to give you one more chance," Davis said as he handed Burns his automatic weapon and removed the pistol from a side holster. He pointed it at Ishmael's right knee. "You tell me where the pilot is, or I'll shoot your knees."

Ishmael cried out in fright. He couldn't say a word. That vile Abdullah had forced him to play the role of an informer to trick the Americans. His men were in Ishmael's house now, holding guns against his wife and children. A blood-curdling cry of anguish poured out of his mouth. "Please, American. I don't know a thing."

Davis wasn't moved. "First one knee. Then the other. You'll never be able to get up the stairs and out of this building. You'll die here in this cell. Just you and that bucket of shit."

Ishmael's face was white with terror. "I don't know," he screamed. "I don't know."

Davis was convinced Ishmael was lying. The man knew far more than he was telling them. He gave Ishmael ten more seconds. When all he heard were more wails, he raised his gun, aimed, and fired twice into one knee, shattering bone and muscle.

"Ah! Ah!" Ishmael screamed out in pain. He rolled over onto his back, holding his blood-soaked knee and continuing to scream in pain.

"Now I shoot the other knee," Davis said, angry that Ishmael had deceived him, "unless you tell me where they took the pilot."

Burns was shining the light on Ishmael's face. Tears were streaming out of his eyes. Davis could tell the man was close to passing out. "Here goes the shot," he called out in a loud, booming voice to make sure Ishmael heard him over the man's cries.

Ishmael stopped screaming. "Istanbul," he mumbled in a barely audible whisper. "Istanbul."

Davis was down on the ground, his face close to Ishmael's, the man's beard brushing against his cheek. "What do you mean, Istanbul?"

"They move the pilot to Istanbul," he whispered. "No more shooting."

Now Ishmael was telling the truth, Davis decided. The Turks had transferred McCallister to Istanbul, where it would be damn near impossible to locate and to rescue him.

Davis turned to Burns. "Get a couple of men. Carry Ishmael upstairs and tie up his leg so he doesn't bleed to death. Then place him on the road we came in on. He'll survive until tomorrow morning. Somebody will come by then, and we'll be long gone from this hellhole of a country."

He removed a satellite phone from his jacket pocket. "I have to call Washington and tell them what happened." He sounded despondent.

The veins on President Kendall's neck and forehead were protruding and pulsing with rage when he finished listening to General Childress's report of what had happened to the Davis rescue effort. It was clear to him that the Turks were playing games . . . with his pilot and with the United States.

Kendall may have been uncertain what to do next, but not Jimmy Grange. Before any other members of the crisis team had a chance to offer a suggestion, Grange fired away. "I say we send the Turkish government a note and tell them that they have seventy-two hours to return Robert McCallister. If they don't do that, we'll bomb them back to the Stone Age."

Joyner, sitting next to Mary Beth Reynolds, shook her head in disbelief. The country couldn't possibly go to war with Turkey over a downed pilot, regardless of who in their country was responsible. Grange was such an idiot. How did Kendall tolerate him? But she knew the answer to that question. She had learned long ago that when people had a good friend, often they would be blind to their faults and follow their advice, regardless of how irrational it was.

She glanced around the room to see if anyone supported Grange's idea. When she saw Chip Morton nodding vigorously and repeating the words, "The Stone Age," she wrote on the pad in front of her, *The testosterone level in this room is off the chart*. Then she slid the note over to the vice president, who smiled and responded in writing. *Boys will be boys*.

Kendall wasn't eager to accept the bellicose proposal. "Do we have another alternative?" he asked.

From the other end of the table, Reynolds raised her voice in an unmistakable West Texas accent. "Why not have the professor draft a note for you to Ankara threatening specific actions and giving them a ten-day deadline to return Lieutenant McCallister? For example, we could threaten to cut off all aid to them, and we could threaten a measured and surgical military action, such as the destruction of several of their planes at one of their bases. That's at least a credible threat. Then, during the ten days, we use all our available intelligence resources to try to find out where they moved McCallister, in Istanbul or somewhere else. If we get that information, we mount another rescue effort."

Kendall was furious. He didn't like Miss Texas—which was how he referred to his vice president, who thought she was smarter than any of the men in the room—trying to usurp his role. He had the perfect response to Reynolds's comment: to dump the issue back on her great buddy, Joyner. He looked at the CIA director. "Do you have the intelligence sources in Turkey to do that, Margaret?"

Kendall knew damn well it was a rhetorical question, Joyner thought with disdain. Having been pushed aside up until now, she refused to be defensive. "We don't have solid assets on the ground to get that information, but the Mossad does."

Kendall snarled. "I've told you more times than I can remember that we're not involving the Israelis."

Reynolds rallied to Joyner's defense. "Why should Terry McCallister dictate this country's foreign policy?"

Kendall was seething. It was time he began following the approach of other presidents, who didn't invite their vice presidents to key meetings. Freeze her out, regardless of the political consequences. He ignored the question and looked in the other direction at the secretary of state. "After this meeting, send the note to Ankara. They have ten days to release Robert McCallister, or we take the actions that were discussed." He refused to attribute them to his vice president.

Worried he hadn't been firm enough with Joyner, Kendall turned to her again. "And don't call your pal, what's his name, who runs the Mossad."

"Moshe."

"Yeah. No calls to Moshe."

The president rose, signifying that the meeting was over. As he walked back to the oval office, Grange fell in alongside. "Terry wanted a few minutes of time with you."

"What the hell for? I'm busy running the country. Holding his hand is your job."

Notwithstanding their friendship, Grange knew that Kendall had a strong independent streak, and that he turned on Grange from time to time. Grange trod softly. "Perhaps you can invite Terry and Sarah over here and explain to them your approach and how much a priority their son's release is for you."

Kendall was hesitating. Worn out from the pressure and lack of sleep, he didn't want one more meeting this evening. He didn't even want to talk to his wife. He wanted to go upstairs, have a sandwich with some straight scotch, and go to sleep.

"If we start bombing," Grange said, trying not to push too hard, "they might hack his son to pieces."

"Yeah, well, I haven't agreed to do any bombing, and we're giving them ten days to avoid any consequences at all. If you want to explain it to Terry, you can go over to his hotel and do that."

Grange was tired of being beaten up by Terry. That was one option he didn't like. He persisted. "The Hundred-thousand-dollar Club Terry chaired during the campaign raised a hell of a lot of money for you." Grange could tell by Kendall's face that he was wavering. "You'll need him again in two years when you go for another term."

Kendall sighed in resignation. "Call and invite them over. Bring them upstairs. That always makes people more malleable."

President Kendall's prediction turned out to be half-right. Being in the president's living quarters did a great deal for Terry. It did nothing for Sarah.

Two hours later, the long black limousine pulled out of the White House grounds and turned toward the west, returning Terry and Sarah McCallister to the Four Seasons. With the thick glass partition that separated them from the driver, Terry was confident he could talk and that his words wouldn't get back to Kendall or Grange. In fact, the White House limos had hidden recording systems, but no one saw the need for activating this one to overhear the conversation between Terry and Sarah.

"Tonight I felt good about the fund-raising I did for Kendall in the campaign," Terry said, sounding charged. "The president certainly gave me a lot of respect."

Sarah groaned. "Oh, for God's sake. It's not about you. It's about getting Bobby out of there and back home."

He shot her an irritated look. "I know that, but Kendall's doing the right thing, giving them a ten-day ultimatum." Terry had been impressed by the president's living quarters and was willing to accept Kendall's representation: "The Turks will knuckle under and put pressure on the renegade group to release Robert rather than risk a cutoff in American aid and an attack on one of their air force bases."

Enthusiastically, Terry added, "And look at what Robert is gaining. Being a prisoner like this will be an advantage for him. It'll enhance his political career." Sarah didn't respond. "You're not sold?" he said.

She couldn't imagine how anyone could be such a fool, particularly the man she had married. "The only useful thing I heard was about the letters Bobby traced in the dirt. He's still alive. That's something. The rest of it is wishful thinking on their part and yours. By inviting you upstairs in the White House, Kendall bought your support. Can't you see that?"

Sarah had no sense of how the real world operated, Terry thought. Derisively he shot back, "Oh, horseshit. Stop playing the antiestablishment seventies radical. The rest of us grew up. Isn't it time for you?"

It was a frequent lecture he gave her. Usually she screamed and called him "a fucking hypocrite," but this evening she was too drained emotionally from worrying about Bobby to argue. "We have no idea what their agenda is in Turkey. They don't think the way we do."

The car stopped for a red light. Terry tried to absorb her words. "Then what do you think we should do, since you're such an expert on world affairs?" He made no effort to conceal the sarcasm in his voice.

"Recognize that it's out of our hands, and it's hopeless. We'll never see Bobby again. At least not alive. You should go back to Chicago and run your business."

"And you?" he asked flabbergasted. "If I go, you're not going with me?"

"You're right. I'm taking an early flight tomorrow morning to London."

"To be with Ann," he said choking on the name.

"As I remember, she's your daughter as well as mine."

"The way she acts toward me, you can have her all to yourself."

Sarah looked away from him, facing the window, not wanting him to see the tears running down her cheeks. The family she had tried so hard to build was a sham. Terry and Ann detested each other. And she was convinced after talking to President Kendall that she'd never see Bobby again. At least not alive.

Chapter 7

Jack turned off the highway and up the narrow road that ran into Moshav Avahail. The first thing he saw were two steel watchtowers with armed soldiers on top looking east. Nearby was an Arab village, quite close enough to reach the Moshav with a rocket. An armed guard stopped Jack at the gate that marked the entrance to the Moshav and asked to see his ID, while inquiring about the reason for the visit.

Satisfied, he gave Jack directions to Avi's house, in the center of the Moshav. Driving along tree-lined streets, passing well-kept houses with grassy lawns, Jack felt as if he were in a suburban subdivision, rather than an agricultural collective community. Prosperity was visible, with many late-model cars. Avi's house, on a corner lot, the largest on the block, had an older gray-stone core and two recent additions, judging from the different colors of the weathered rock.

Alerted by a phone call from the guard, Avi was waiting for Jack in the front, dressed in khaki shorts and a print shirt unbuttoned on top. His chest was covered with salt-and-pepper hair. On his head it was thinning. His nose had been broken and poorly set, leaving a bump in the center of the bridge. He was smiling amiably, showing nicotine-stained teeth. With heavily creased leathery skin, his face had a light olive color that placed him as being from the Mediterranean. His eyes sparkled with a devil-may-care look.

Avi came forward to greet Jack in the driveway. "At long last I get to meet the infamous Jack Cole, who saved my ass in the Osirak operation."

Jack laughed. "That's hardly an accurate version, but I won't argue."

"Oh, but it is. I couldn't get the information we needed in Baghdad. You supplied it from Paris. After it was over I wanted to come up and thank you."

"But Moshe insisted on keeping our parts of the operation separate and compartmentalized."

"Yeah. And in those days I didn't have the guts to defy the old man."

There was an edge to Avi's voice when he referred to Moshe. Remembering what Gila in the finance department had said, Jack guessed that it had to do with the Aqaba fiasco. He decided not to pursue it.

"Everybody's in back," Avi said, "waiting for you."

As he led the way, with Jack walking alongside, Avi said, "Actually, I saw you about five years ago at the Israel Tennis Center. You were playing for the men's forty-and-over championship."

"And getting killed by Amos in straight sets, six-two, six-one. Were you in the tournament?"

"Just a spectator. I once played, but that's a sad story for another time. You still play?"

"I wish. That was the zenith of my amateur tennis career, such as it was." Jack smiled and patted his right knee. "This one decided to quit on me a few months later. Haven't picked up a racket since the surgery. You should have come over to me after the match."

"Are you kidding? You definitely did not want company."

Jack cracked a smile. "Was I that bad?"

"Worse."

"I play to win."

"Is there any other way?"

Jack liked the comment. Avi was his kind of guy.

In the grass-covered backyard, a large wooden table was set with grilled chicken, colorful salads, bottles of soda and fruit. Avi introduced Jack to his wife, Dora, and his three teenage children, two girls and a boy.

"My friend here is in the wine business," Avi announced to the group.

Nurit, his fifteen-year-old daughter with freckles and braces, thought that was neat. "Did he bring any samples?"

Avi chuckled. "I don't think so. He's not dealing in wine today. He wants to sell me something else."

"Will you buy it?" Nurit asked.

Dora was shooting Avi a look full of daggers. Last year when he left the Mossad, she had finally begun sleeping soundly at night for the first time in their eighteen years of marriage. She knew him so well that she had no trouble reading the meaning of his response to Nurit. This Jack Cole had come to recruit Avi for a dangerous intelligence project. She hoped that Avi stuck with his promise to her and turned it down.

Avi knew exactly what Dora was thinking. "I'm not sure," he replied to Nurit, while looking at his wife.

During lunch they kept the conversation to small talk about the Moshav, what the children were doing, and how good the food was. Once the meal was over, Avi said to Jack, "Let's take a ride."

Before they left the backyard, Jack looked longingly at the table. Avi had the kind of family Jack had hoped to have one day when he had moved to Israel. So what happened? He couldn't blame it on Sarah. He had gotten over her long ago. There was the army, then the Yom Kippur War, and after that his recruitment by Moshe and his life shuttling to and from Paris in the service of the Mossad. It was easy to say he had never met the right woman, but he had never given himself a chance. Life moved on.

They set off in an old battered pickup truck that coughed and wheezed when it started. Avi drove down a hill to a small orange grove, where he parked, and the two of them climbed out.

"We don't grow many oranges here these days," Avi said. "Most of the residents work in the cities in computers and other high-tech jobs. And it's just as well, because we've had to import workers from Thailand to take care of even the small crop. Certainly a far cry from the old days, when my father settled on this Moshav and built the house I live in now."

"When was that?"

" 'Forty-nine. He came from Shanghai."

Jack raised his eyebrows. "Funny—you don't look Chinese."

Avi rolled his eyes at the bad joke. "His great-grandfather, David, went there from Baghdad in the middle of the nineteenth century to buy silk. He liked Shanghai so much that he decided to bring his wife and stay. The family made an enormous amount of money for about a hundred years. My grandfather even did well during the Japanese occupation, because the Japanese left the Jews alone, contrary to Hitler's orders to kill them all."

"I didn't know that."

"Yeah. But when Mao and the Communists took over in 1949, all the Jews left Shanghai. Many came here. Others went to the United States, Canada, or Australia. By then my father had become an ardent Zionist. He didn't have a question."

"Does he still live on the Moshav?"

Avi shook his head sadly.

"He died in the Sinai in the Six Day War in a tank that the

Egyptians hit near the Mitla Pass. He was the commander of a reserve unit. A horrible way to die."

"I'm sorry," Jack said. "Was your mother from China too?"

"No. She was a Sabra. Traced her roots to Jerusalem for at least six generations. She died in a suicide bomb attack in a Tel Aviv restaurant during the intifada."

"I think I'll stop asking questions."

Avi's eyes burned with intensity. "It's the price we pay to live here." With a pack of cigarettes and a lighter in his hand, Avi climbed onto the hood of the old truck and stretched out his legs while leaning against the windshield. He lit up a cigarette and blew out the smoke. "Okay, now tell me why you came."

Jack described Sam's visit and his plea for help. He followed that with a report on his meeting with Moshe.

Avi was mystified. "So what do you want with me?"

"I need someone who isn't in the Mossad but has contacts in Turkey. Someone who could find out the fate of Robert McCallister. I remember hearing that you spent some time there after Osirak, which finished you in Iraq."

"And then what? You thinking of rescuing him?"

Jack nodded. "Yeah. I might try to mount an effort, depending on what we find."

Avi gave a long, low whistle. "That's a tall order."

"But first I need information. Are you willing to help?"

Avi wasn't ready to move on. "You really care that much about what happens to your brother's future brother in-law?"

"Let's just say that the family situation with my brother is complicated."

Avi gave a wry smile. "Aren't they all? My father had two brothers in Australia he never communicated with."

"So will you help me?" Jack repeated anxiously.

The response to Jack's question was stony silence. He decided to push Avi. "All I'm asking you to do is get some information."

Holding a cigarette, Avi jumped off the hood of the truck. He paced around, thinking, while he blew smoke circles in the air.

Jack added softly, "Just to make a couple of calls."

Avi stopped walking and wheeled around, his dark brown eyes boring in on Jack. "C'mon. You know damn well how these things unfold. It's never that simple. One thing always leads to another. You've got a reason . . . with your brother and all that . . . for putting your own ass on the line. But I'm different."

"You can bail out on me at any time."

"Easier said than done."

Jack stopped talking and held his breath.

"Dora would be furious," Avi said, thinking aloud. "I told her last year when I left the Mossad that she'd never have one more night of worrying whether that was the night she'd get the call telling her that I'd taken a bullet, that I'd never be coming home again."

Jack was convinced Avi intended to turn him down. Then Avi kicked one of the tires on the truck. "Oh, what the hell, I feel as if I owe you from Osirak. Besides, selling weapons may be lucrative, but it's boring as hell. I need some action—like I used to have in the Mossad."

Avi's words alarmed Jack. He wondered if he'd be able to control the former agent whom Gila had called a maverick. For now, the important thing was he had agreed to help. "I really appreciate it, Avi. Thanks."

As he climbed into the truck, Jack decided not to tell Sam what he was doing. Nothing might come of it. Also, he still had his cover to maintain.

"Give me a little bit of time to make contact with some former sources in Ankara and Istanbul," Avi said, starting the engine. "A day or two. Then I'll get back to you. After that, we'll decide how to get that kid out."

Chapter 8

General Kemal, the director of Turkish military intelligence, stood at the window of the building that housed the prime minister's office, and wiped the perspiration from his forehead. Kemal gazed at the park below, and at central Ankara filled with nondescript cinder-block buildings. It always amazed him that a nation as rich in history and culture as Turkey could have such a boring capital. But perhaps it was fitting for a country that in the last few centuries had been forced from its rightful place in the top tier of the world by the Christian nations of Europe and was being maintained there by the upstart, arrogant Americans.

That thought grated on Kemal so badly that he had decided to take a giant step to assert Turkey's independence from foreign dominance, a bold move to shape its own destiny.

For it was Kemal who had given Colonel Abdullah the order—in a clandestine meeting at night on a deserted hilltop—to shoot down an American plane. It was Kemal's plan. And no one other than he, Abdullah, and a handful of troops loyal to Abdullah knew about it. No one else had to know.

The course of events from that point forward should have been simple. Kemal would claim that the Kurds had shot down the plane, which would create a rift between the Americans and their new friends—the despicable Kurds. Abdullah would interrogate the pilot about American military plans, then kill and bury him where he would never be found.

It was all so straightforward. Then Kemal had learned from an agent attached to the Turkish Embassy in Washington that the pilot was the son of a powerful American named Terry McCallister with close ties to President Kendall. That had led Kemal to instruct Abdullah to take good care of the pilot. He might be a valuable bargaining chip, although Kemal didn't know how he could be used.

Now the Turkish politicians were in the act. As usual they were anxious to suck up to the Americans. It was disgusting. The call summoning him to this meeting had come from the defense minister. One terse sentence: "You have some serious explaining to do."

Everything was in danger of unraveling, but Kemal refused to bend. He refused to be sacrificed at the alter of Turkish–American relations. He wiped the moisture from the back of his neck, then put the handkerchief away and looked at his watch. The defense minister had asked him to come at two this afternoon. It was already 3:25. It was as if they thought his time was of no consequence. That infuriated him further.

Finally the thick wooden door opened and the defense minister came out of the cabinet meeting. "We're ready for you now."

Kemal followed him inside, passing the two guards armed with AK-47s who stood at the entrance of the inner sanctum.

At one end of the long wooden table sat the prime minister. He was a short, squat man who was overweight. Thick black-framed glasses were pushed up on his high forehead, exposing tired, bloodshot eyes. The six other top cabinet officers were spread out, three on each side of the table.

The prime minister pointed to the chair facing him at the other end and nodded toward Kemal, who realized that this was his cue to sit down.

He was confronted with a hard, cold stare. "You told us that the Kurds fired the missile that brought down the American plane." The prime minister's words were spoken with a cold, white anger.

Keep calm, Kemal cautioned himself, while he clutched the sides of his chair for support. "That's what I have been advised by our troops in the area, and I have pressed them hard."

The prime minister snarled. "Obviously not hard enough. The Americans have now supplied us with proof, by satellite photos and other evidence, that our forces are responsible."

Kemal considered asking to see the evidence, but he quickly banished that thought. The Americans were good at this kind of technology. Focusing on what they had would only dig him deeper into a hole. Instead he straightened up and looked indignant.

"The Americans have no right to call us liars. Why would we shoot down their plane?"

"You're the head of military intelligence. You tell me."

The defense minister tried to help Kemal out. "Perhaps one of our men made an error. He mistook it for an enemy aircraft. Not our ally's."

"That's certainly possible," Kemal said quietly. "I'll fly to the area immediately. I'll personally conduct an investigation."

Kemal rose, hoping he could leave.

"Not so fast," the prime minister said. "The situation is even worse than that. The American pilot's father is Terry McCallister."

Kemal feigned bewilderment. "The name means nothing to me."

"He's one of President Kendall's top supporters."

Kemal swallowed hard.

"As you might imagine," the prime minister continued, "the Americans are threatening very serious repercussions if their pilot is not returned within ten days. They say that they'll cut off all aid and attack one of our air force bases."

Kemal remained standing. "Let the Americans try it," he replied softly. "We're not the Iraqis. We have powerful anti-aircraft batteries in place at all our bases."

The prime minister shook his head in disbelief. "Is this what you want? A war with the Americans?"

"We don't have the pilot," Kemal said, shifting his ground. "How can we return him?"

The defense minister interjected: "They have evidence that he parachuted out over our territory. He couldn't have disappeared."

"It's hilly, wild terrain with lots of caves. He could be hiding in one." Kemal shrugged. "He could have been injured when he landed. The plane hit rocks and broke into millions of pieces. I had our troops check the area of the wreckage. They didn't see any sign of the pilot."

"The Americans want to inspect the wreckage of the plane themselves."

Kemal was looking at the defense minister, playing toward him as the most hopeful audience. "It's our land. We'll report to them. They have to respect our territorial integrity. I'll look at the plane. If any portions are salvageable, we'll return those to the Americans. They're always trying to dictate to us."

The defense minister was sympathetic. "Let General Kemal visit the area himself and report back. Then we can decide on our next steps."

The prime minister was watching Kemal closely, gazing

at him suspiciously. "There's more to this than meets the eye."

Kemal straightened up and looked indignant. "I resent the insinuation." Even as he protested his innocence, Kemal felt moisture spreading under his arms.

"Then disprove it," the prime minister said. "Find the pilot and bring him here so I can deliver him to the American Embassy."

Now in the back of a car on the way to a military airport, General Kemal closed his eyes and focused hard on the jam he was in. There had to be a way out. As they were reaching the air force base for his flight to southeastern Turkey, he had a possible answer. He yanked the phone out of his pocket and dialed the cell of Maj. Gen. Husni Nadim, the deputy director of Syrian intelligence. Since the United States had attacked Iraq, Kemal and Nadim had increasingly coordinated intelligence activities.

"Where are you now?" Kemal asked.

"In Damascus."

"Can you meet me in Van tonight? It's quite important."

"I'll be there."

"Check into the Buyuk Urartu and wait in your room. I'll call you."

The Syrian, Major General Nadim, was trembling with excitement as he waited in his hotel room for Kemal to call. He didn't know precisely what Kemal wanted, but his guess was that it concerned the American pilot who had been shot down over southeastern Turkey.

Though it was almost midnight, Nadim was dressed in a perfectly pressed military uniform. He was tall and suave, with a thin mustache he thought gave him a debonair look that appealed to Parisian women. When he wasn't in Damascus he was in Paris. Nadim despised the Syrian capital, which he viewed as a cultural cesspool lacking in the pleasures of life. But then again, how many other places in the world could rival Paris in that regard?

Nadim had fallen in love with the city of lights when he had been a student at the Sorbonne. His good looks concealed a keen intellect. They also concealed a hard, cruel streak that enabled him not only to survive amid a multitude of intrigues, but to plan many of the recurring bloodbaths aimed at purging their foes. When Syria had tightened its control over Lebanon years ago, it was Nadim who eagerly assumed the role of strongman and implemented a program of systematically executing any Lebanese leader or private citizen, Christian or Muslim, inclined to oppose Syrian control or to make peace with Israel. The flow of Lebanese blood, for which he was responsible, earned Nadim the nickname "the Butcher of Beirut."

Nadim, who hated the Americans because of their support for Israel, had cheered when he had heard an American plane had been shot down, though he had no idea who was responsible. What surprised him was that the Americans hadn't released the name of the pilot the way they usually did. So he activated some very good sources in Washington. To his pleasant surprise, he found out that the pilot's father was one of President Kendall's big supporters. Nadim, who had spent three years attached to the Syrian Embassy in Washington, knew how the Americans worked. This incident had to be getting a lot of top-level attention at the White House.

The phone rang. It was Kemal. "I'm in front of the hotel in a black car. Come now."

Nadim moved swiftly from the hotel entrance to the car. He wasn't surprised that Kemal was in the back of a bulletproof vehicle. Van was a focal point for the Kurdish separatist movement, and violence was a daily occurrence. Nadim got into the back with Kemal. Up front next to the driver a soldier clutched a machine gun tightly, his eyes darting in all directions.

They drove for about fifteen minutes until they reached a hospital surrounded by armed soldiers.

Kemal climbed out. With Nadim at his side, he led the way to a staircase, then two floors underground. The armed guard from the car was following right behind.

Midway along a deserted corridor they reached an empty room with a table and two chairs, used to interrogate prisoners who happen to be patients. Kemal told the guard to wait outside. Once he and Nadim were alone, he kicked the door shut.

This was an odd place for their discussion, Nadim thought, but he decided not to say anything. It was Kemal's show. The two of them had increasingly cooperated since the Americans had brought down Saddam Hussein's regime. Kemal and Nadim had developed a mutual respect.

"Thank you for coming on short notice," Kemal said when they were both seated.

"You told me it was important. That was enough. I assume it concerns the American pilot."

Kemal nodded. "It was my idea to shoot down one of their planes and say the Kurds did it."

Nadim raised his eyebrows. "Very creative."

"But now it's all turning to shit."

"Because of the identity of the pilot."

"How do you know?"

"I have my own sources in Washington. What are the Americans telling your government?"

"They know we did it, and they're all worked up because it's Terry McCallister's son. Initially I thought it was good that the pilot had an important father. Maybe he'd be valuable to swap for something."

Kemal paused and shook his head in disgust. "Now I realize I got a bad break. If it had been some ordinary kid, they wouldn't be going berserk in Washington . . . and turning my prime minister into a wild man." He took a deep breath and repeated. "A bad break. I need your help, my friend."

Nadim's mind was racing. An idea was taking shape—something that was at once brilliant, daring, and sinister. Something that could radically change the course of events in the Middle East and propel Nadim to control of the government in Syria.

"Perhaps it's not a bad break at all," Nadim said softly. "Perhaps you got lucky."

"I don't understand."

"Where is the pilot now?"

Kemal raised his hand and pointed a finger to the right. "We're holding him in a room at the end of the corridor . . . sedated and unconscious. He has no idea where he is or how he got there. He's being carefully watched and monitored by a doctor and a nurse. But I can't keep him here much longer. I'm under tremendous pressure from my government to find him and return him to the Americans. That's why I called you. I was hoping you'd be able to take him secretly to Syria. That way I could say he's not in Turkey. Even if the Americans came here with a whole army, they wouldn't find him. You could kill him and dispose of the body however you'd like. I can't do that any longer because they'll interrogate people, and some frightened bastard will talk. But they'll never think to focus their attention on Syria. If you do this for me, I will be in your debt."

Nadim couldn't believe he was hearing this. It fit perfectly into his own idea.

"Well . . . will you do it?" Kemal asked nervously.

"I'll do more than that," Nadim said, letting the excitement bubble out in his voice. "I have an idea that will make you a hero for all time in your country, because Turkey will finally be able to control the Kurds. They'll bow down to you in Ankara—the prime minister and all of the other top people in the government."

"I'm listening," Kemal said, still apprehensive.

Though he was acting on his own, Nadim was ready to forge ahead. Ahmed, that imbecile of a president Syria had, would never understand the plan even if Nadim explained it to him a hundred times. The Syrian president was an optometrist by education. When he had been handpicked by his father as a successor to punish his power-hungry uncle for plotting to capture the presidency, the streets had erupted with laughter. The man was no leader.

But when Nadim succeeded, he would be able to rally the army behind him and oust Ahmed. He would know how to run the country. They would finally be able to strike back at the Israelis for the 1967 and 1973 humiliations.

"The first thing we have to do," Nadim said, "is move the American pilot to Syria, but not for execution, as you suggested. Instead, for safekeeping. I have the perfect place to hold him."

Kemal was troubled. "But if he's alive he can create problems for us. If my prime minister finds out—"

Nadim held up his hand. "Hear me out first. Then you decide."

"Okay. Tell me your idea."

Nadim began talking, and as he listened to the Syrian for the next half hour, Kemal, too, became excited by what he was hearing. A smile formed at the edges of his mouth.

"If we can pull this off," Kemal said, "both our countries will be so much stronger and more dangerous. You'll be better able to deal with the Israelis, and we with the Kurds."

"Exactly." Nadim nodded vigorously. "It will change the entire political situation in the Middle East. And we will succeed." Nadim said it with confidence.

Kemal became nervous again as he thought about one of the aspects of Nadim's plan. "But we need the miserable Iranians to participate. They're unpredictable. And they hate us because of our secular government. They'll never go along."

Anxious to gain Kemal's unqualified support, Nadim placed a reassuring hand on the Turk's arm. "They despise the Israelis even more. They won't pass up an opportunity to weaken the Israelis and their position as the dominant military force in the region. Besides, they'll be able to gain some concessions from the Americans."

Kemal was mired in thought, weighing the risks and benefits to himself. Deep furrows appeared on his forehead.

Nadim pressed the Turk. "When we succeed, you'll be a hero in your country."

"And if we fail . . ."

"We won't fail," Nadim said. "You can count on that."

Kemal was coming around. Whether or not Nadim's plan succeeded in the long run, Kemal would gain an immediate advantage: He was getting the American pilot out of Turkey and across the border into Syria. "I'm in," Kemal finally said.

When Kemal left the room to make the arrangements to transport the American pilot, Nadim pulled the phone from his pocket and dialed a Paris number. There was no answer. He decided to leave a message.

"Layla, my dear," Nadim said, "I'll be back in Paris in a couple of days. I want to schedule a date with you for dinner."

Chapter 9

Michael Hanley waited for Irina in a blinding snowstorm in Moscow in front of the Pushkin Memorial Museum on Prechistenka. Night was falling over the city. Two hours ago Irina had called. "Dmitri's going out of town on a business trip." She had giggled. "We can have a date tonight."

This could be the break he had been waiting for with Suslov. He wanted to shout, "Where has he gone?" but he controlled himself. If things broke his way, he'd end up getting that information.

He glanced at his watch as large, wet snowflakes pelted him. She should have been here fifteen minutes ago.

A new dark silver Mercedes SL500 turned the corner and spun to a stop. Through the windshield he spotted Irina—beautiful Irina with skin as white as the falling snow and long blond hair spilling over her eyes. The car must have been a gift from Suslov, Michael decided. God only knew how much it cost in rubles, with expensive foreign imports priced to the sky. But if you were virtually minting money, as Suslov was doing, price was no object. Hell, maybe he had his goons extract it from a car dealer as a "protection fee" if they wished to stay in business.

Michael was still closing the front door on the passenger side when she gunned the engine. The car glided over a patch of icy snow, then shot forward. For the next several minutes Irina, nervously glancing into the rearview mirror while biting down on her lower lip, didn't say a word. Michael watched her. Her short black skirt had ridden up high on her thighs, showing him lots of beautiful soft, pale skin. While her right foot was pressed tensely on the accelerator, her left leg, encased in a long black Ferragamo boot, was shaking from fear.

Once she was satisfied they weren't being followed, she relaxed.

"I'm glad you could meet me, Micki," she said in Russian, which was what they always spoke. She had studied English in school, but retained little of it.

"I'd meet you anytime," he said.

Irina loved calling him Micki because she said Michel and Michael were too formal. Though he hated that nickname because it reminded him of his childhood in a rough part of ethnically divided Boston, where it was still the Dagos against the Micks, he was willing to tolerate it. There was a lot he was willing to tolerate with Irina. He was going for the gold.

Don't forget your priorities, he reminded himself. *The gold is not between her legs. The gold is what she can tell you about Suslov and his nuclear arms operation.* He remembered Joyner's words: "You're playing a dangerous game." *Sometimes the prize is worth it,* he thought. The idea of nuclear weapons falling into the hands of an outlaw regime or an international terrorist organization was too horrible to contemplate, and North Korea was already claiming membership in the nuclear club. Even without them, Al Qaeda had been able to wreak havoc on the United States and the world.

Without a signal or any other warning to following cars, she turned right sharply, narrowly missing a parked car.

Jesus, the woman drives like Dale Earnhardt, he thought. He gripped the grab handle on the car's roof for support.

"Where are we going?" he asked.

She pushed the hair away from her eyes. "A small inn outside of town. Very few people know about it."

She raised a hand to her lips, kissed it, then waved it in his direction.

"Touch me, Micki," she said.

He rubbed his hand along the arm of the black leather Ferragamo jacket that matched the boots.

"Not there, silly." She giggled while pushing up her skirt. "Give me your hand."

When he held it out, she took it and pressed it between her legs. Jesus, she wasn't wearing any panties under the black suede skirt. "Surprise," she cried out. Her bush was soaked. He pressed his hand against her soft folds of skin.

When she braked for a red light, he pulled his hand away.

"Now lick your fingers," she said. As he followed her command, she reached across and touched his penis, stiff and hard, jutting forward in his pants.

"That's what I like. Take it out," she said in a devilish voice.

The light turned green. "Not now. Later," he said.

"Boo-hoo," she feigned crying.

He laughed. *She's twenty-four years old,* he thought. *Immature. A baby.* Michael had met her when she was shopping in a store that had small French and Italian boutiques. Though he had followed her to the store because he knew that she worked in Suslov's office, he pretended that their meeting was coincidental. With his looks and charm she readily agreed to have coffee with him. On their second coffee date, she had explained that about a year ago Suslov had seen her picture in a magazine when she was modeling clothes. He had decided that he had to have her. So he had told one of his goons, "Find that girl and pay her whatever it takes to get her to come and work as a secretary in my office."

As she had told him that, Michael had thought, *My God, I know that some people order the clothes they see in an ad. I never heard of anyone ordering the model.*

The road was opening up. The snow was tapering off, which greatly relieved Michael. The last thing he wanted was to get stuck in the snow with Irina. Her being rescued by the police might come to Suslov's attention.

"How did you find out about the inn for this evening?" Michael asked.

"One of my friends is dating an older married man. Somebody important whose name I won't mention, who brings her here so his wife won't find out about it."

Suslov didn't have that problem, Michael knew, because he didn't have a wife. He had killed her about five years ago. Strangled her with his bare hands, although Michael didn't know why. Large payoffs to the prosecutor, coupled with intimidation, precluded any charges from being filed. It was Russian justice at its finest in the post-Communist era. Michael often wondered, if the Russian people were given a choice, would they prefer the new system of freedom or the old Communist regime? His guess was that many would opt to turn back the clock, although certainly not Irina and her friends.

"Aren't you afraid that you'll see one of Dmitri's buddies at the inn?" Michael asked.

She smiled. "I took care of that. They only have three rooms, plus a dining room where they serve meals. I rented all three for the night."

"That must have cost you a bundle," he said.

She giggled, that silly girlie laugh of hers he liked. "Actually, it'll cost you a bundle. You're paying for it."

Her words didn't bother Michael. He touched his pants pocket and the wad of American bills he had brought with him; all Company money, of course. Whatever he paid to the proprietor would mean there would be less to give Irina. Her father, an old Communist bureaucrat, was now out of work, and her mother had breast cancer. In reality he doubted whether any of that money, his or Suslov's, ever reached them.

It was seven o'clock when they arrived at the inn. An old man with one crippled arm carried in Irina's gigantic overnight bag, which to Michael looked as if it had enough clothes, makeup, and God knows what for a week. All Michael had was the clothes he was wearing. The proprietress, a heavyset woman with forearms resembling bowling pins, followed them up to their room with a tray that held English biscuits, a pot of tea, two cups, a bottle of Johnny Walker blue label, glasses, and ice. "Dinner will be whenever you want it," she announced, and departed.

Michael looked around. The room was decorated in belle epoque style, with heavy red curtains and a king-size wooden four-poster bed that dominated the room.

"Tea or scotch?" he asked Irina.

"Tea now. Scotch later." She poured two cups, handed him one, and dropped three cubes of sugar into her own.

He took a sip. It was a fine jasmine tea that was rarely found in Russia.

"Are you hungry?" he asked.

"Not for food," she said, enticingly. "Dinner can wait."

With that she pulled off her powder-blue angora sweater and tossed it on a chair. She wasn't wearing a bra. He had never seen her naked before, and he was stunned. Though she was almost six feet tall, she was perfectly proportioned. Her breasts were round and full, with sharp, pointed pink nipples. Her skin was snow-white. Her broad shoulders tapered to a tiny waist. Michael wasn't a religious man, but what kept running through his mind was, *God, you got it right this time.*

He was still staring at her when she walked across the room and unbuttoned his shirt. She tossed it onto the floor, then pressed her naked chest against his. Kissing him hard, she shoved her tongue into his mouth. When she pulled away, she whispered into his ear, "I've never fucked an American before. Will I like it?"

"You'll love it," he whispered back. With his hand he reached under her skirt and stroked her velvet pelt as she moaned softly.

"Jesus, I'm hot," she said as she unzipped her skirt and let it fall to the floor.

"Eat me, Micki. Eat me," she cried out, spreading her legs. When he dropped to his knees, he placed one hand on her round, sloping buttocks and pulled her close to his face. With the other he opened her up while he pressed his mouth against her soft, moist skin.

"There," she cried as he licked her clit, which swelled to the size of a grape. "Right there. Oh, God, right there."

He kept licking and eating her until her whole body shook.

"You're good," she moaned. "You're so fucking good."

"You haven't seen anything yet," he said. With the taste of her in his mouth, he led her toward the bed. As they walked, she unzipped his pants and pulled out his engorged member, red and veiny, ready to explode. "That's what I want," she said, wrapping her long slender fingers around it.

He dropped his pants and kicked them off with his shoes. Michael was standing on the floor, and she was on the bed on all fours with her gorgeous rear end thrust out when he entered her soft, wet vagina from behind. He slipped in and out slowly and rhythmically while cupping her breasts in his hands. She was playing with her clit and moaning with pleasure. "Your finger," she cried out. "Put it in there. The other hole." He removed one of his hands from her breasts and did what she wanted. Her whole body bucked and shuddered as she came again. "You too," she shouted, but he held back.

Still standing next to the bed, he flipped her over on her back and lifted her legs up on his shoulders. Then he raised her bottom into the air before shoving his hard and pulsating cock into her wet vagina. In that position he found the sensitive G-spot deep inside her. Her response was immediate. "Oh, God, yes!" she shouted. "Oh, God, yes!" as he moved in and out. "Now, dammit! *Now!*" she screamed. This time he came with her, both of their bodies shaking together.

He fell onto the bed and collapsed next to her heaving body. She was on her back, gasping for breath. "Nobody ever did that to me before. That position. Nobody. If that's how they do it in the United States, I'm moving there tomorrow."

He laughed. "You're funny, my little bird."

She ran her hand over his chest. "I like when you call me that. It makes me think that you care for me. You want to protect me. You're not just taking me for the sex, like most men."

Her words made him feel guilty. She was so vulnerable, and he was using her. He had to be careful that she didn't become a victim in his game with Suslov.

"Let's have some scotch," she said. "If you fuck me like that, I'll be your slave. I'll serve you anything you want."

She fixed two glasses of Johnny Walker on ice and brought them back to the bed. When she handed·him one, she said, "After dinner when we come back up here, I'm going to pour scotch all over your cock and balls and lick it off. What do you think of that?"

"Sounds to me like a great use for Johnny Walker. Can we spend the night here, or do we have to go back after dinner?"

"Dmitri won't be back until six tomorrow evening."

He was itching to ask her where Dmitri had gone, but he

bit his tongue. He decided to wade into the quicksand from another direction. "I'll bet I'm a better lover than he is."

Her entire body tensed. "You don't want to know," she said, dropping her voice to a nervous whisper. "For your own sake you don't."

That only whetted his appetite. "Tell me."

"I shouldn't, but I feel as if you're someone I can trust. Someone who will help me one day when I need it, and I know I will."

"Absolutely," he replied without hesitation.

She climbed out of bed, walked over to the door, and checked to make sure no one was hiding there and listening. After refilling her glass, she returned to the bed. She sat down with her back against the headboard, her knees curled up against her body. "Something happened to him in Afghanistan," she said. "He was wounded down there"— she pointed to Michael's genitalia—"with some shrapnel. The same time he caught some of it on his ear. Down there," she repeated, still pointing, "it hit a nerve. So he can't get hard. You know what I mean?"

Michael nodded. "Never?"

"Never, but he likes to do other things to me. Horrible things." She was choking back tears thinking about it. "He refuses to tell anyone. Once I foolishly told him to go see a doctor, and he slapped me hard. He said they know nothing. Besides, he said, they will talk and everyone will know. He explained to me that his wife went to see a doctor about it secretly. When he found out, he killed her."

"Jesus."

"That's why he needs the relationship with me."

Michael rubbed his hand along her leg, to soothe her, to keep her talking. "I don't understand."

"His friends see him with me, and they think he must be virile, a man in his fifties, to keep me satisfied. He fuels that by telling them lies about what we did together. He says things like, 'God, am I bushed. Four times last night. She can't get enough of me. My thing will fall off if I do it any more,' and all that."

She grabbed Michael's wrist and clutched it tightly, digging her nails into his skin. "You know how you men are with each other."

"So why do you keep seeing him?" Michael asked.

She shook her head. "You can be so stupid, Micki. He made it clear that if I break it off with him, I'll end up like his wife. He'll hunt me to the ends of the earth if he has to, and he has the stooges to do that. I don't even want to imagine what he'd do to you if he found out about us."

The game had now gotten far more dangerous than Joyner could ever have imagined. But Michael refused to turn back.

Irina grabbed her glass and took a long sip of scotch. She began trembling, and pulled up the blanket around her body. "I don't want to talk about it anymore," she said. "Tell me about your oil development business. What you do and all that."

Her words stunned him. He had told her that was what he was doing in Russia, but why was she asking about it now? Again, Joyner's words popped into his mind. It was a dangerous game he was playing. Was Suslov using Irina to get information about him?

He tried to remain calm. "A new discovery was made in Uzbekistan. I may have to go there."

"And leave me all alone in Moscow?" She sounded annoyed. "You men are always leaving me for your business trips."

This was the opportunity he had been looking for. "Where did Dmitri go?" he asked, trying to sound casual.

"Volgograd. Do you know where that is?"

Michael knew exactly where it was: seven hundred miles south of Moscow. Volgograd was better known by its pre-

1961 name, Stalingrad. It had been the scene of one of the bloodiest and most decisive battles of World War II. Michael lied to her. "I have no idea." He was afraid she'd become suspicious if he knew too much about Russia.

"Me neither," Irina said, "but then again, I didn't do well in geography in school." She rolled her eyes. "Or any other subject."

Then it hit him. Volgograd was on Vladimir Perikov's list of locations where large quantities of nuclear arms were being stored following their collection from former Soviet republics. Suslov must be thinking about another clandestine sale of nuclear arms. *Okay, here we go*. This time Michael would stop him.

Chapter 10

"We have to talk," Avi had said to Jack on the phone. "Let's meet in an hour at the Café Eden on Dizengoff Street in Tel Aviv."

What in the world could have happened so soon? Jack wondered.

It was a balmy night, with a breeze blowing in from the sea. Jack parked a few blocks away and walked in the salt air. The streets were crowded, the restaurants mobbed. He used a pedestrian bridge to cut over the circle, Kikkar Dizengoff, with its trendy shops and boutiques.

Arriving at the café before Avi, Jack took a table in a corner on the patio and ordered a cappuccino. Intense discussions were raging about literature and politics. A young woman with a shrill voice was defending A. B. Yehoshua's latest novel. The man she was with was tearing into it.

A few minutes later Avi walked into the café, dressed casually in a print shirt and khaki slacks, with a poker expression on his face. Avi nodded to Jack and pointed to the back of the café. "We need privacy," he said as they settled into a booth.

Avi waited for the owner to deposit a Maccabee for him and another cappuccino for Jack. He lifted the bottle of beer to his lips, took a long pull, and put it down.

"He's not in Turkey," Avi blurted out without any opening.

Jack was stunned. "Who's not in Turkey?"

"Robert McCallister. Isn't that who we're—"

"You sure of that?"

"Positive. I've communicated with two different military intelligence people I've worked with in Turkey, one in Ankara and one in Istanbul. Both told me the same thing. Shooting down the American plane was a rogue operation conceived by Kemal, their chief. Some members of the Turkish government are starting to catch on. They may even be happy about it because there's a lot of animosity toward the United States. But the prime minister's still in the dark and raising hell with Kemal to get to the bottom of what happened. To save his own hide, Kemal moved the American pilot out of the country."

As Jack stared at him in incredulity, Avi sipped his beer and grinned. "It just goes to prove you can't always rely on CNN."

Jack was trying to absorb Avi's information. "But if he's not in Turkey, then where is he?"

"I thought you'd never ask."

"Well?"

"He's been moved to Syria."

Jack's jaw dropped. "What? That doesn't make sense."

Avi shrugged. "I told you . . . Kemal did it to save himself. No body . . . no crime."

That explanation didn't ring true for Jack. "I can't buy it. Why would the Syrians take him if that's all that was going on? The United States has been looking for a chance to hit them. Why present it to Washington on a silver platter?" Then the answer to Jack's question popped into his mind. "Unless Syria's planning to use Robert McCallister in some type of blackmail scheme."

Avi was right with him. "And Kemal's a part of it with the Syrians."

"My God," Jack said. "The stakes have just increased enormously for us. If the Syrians are involved, you can be sure that we're a target of what's being planned. Not just the United States."

"Precisely. Don't forget what we read every Passover. While Pharaoh wanted to slay only the firstborn Jewish males, Laban, the Syrian, wanted to kill all of us. Nothing's changed in twenty-five hundred years. Before 1967 they loved firing down on our villages from their bunkers up in the Golan. They'd do it again in a minute if we ever gave the land back."

"I guess I'd better tell Moshe."

Avi tapped his fingers on the table. "You can do that if you want. But then you can forget about helping free Robert Mc-Callister. I know what Moshe's like when he makes up his mind that an operation can't be undertaken. There's no way to convince him."

Jack looked pensive. He had the same opinion of the Mossad director. With the Syrians now a part of the action, Jack had no intention of backing off. An idea was starting to take shape in his mind. "How good are your contacts in Syria?" Jack asked.

Avi wondered where Jack was going with this. "I have one and only one good relationship. He's in Damascus."

Wide-eyed, Jack was looking at Avi.

"Don't get too excited," Avi cautioned. "I haven't seen him in about eighteen months."

"Tell me about him."

"Yasef's his name, a midlevel official in the Syrian intelligence agency. You remember back in March of 'eighty-two, when Ahmed ordered the total destruction of the town of Hama because there were some political dissidents?"

Jack nodded. "How could I forget? They leveled the town. Killed twenty thousand residents. All Syrian citizens."

"Exactly. Well, anyhow, then–Colonel Husni Nadim, now

a major general and deputy director of Syrian intelligence, implemented the plan. Yasef was on his staff. He was outraged at what he saw. The killing, raping, and burning. The murder of so many innocent people."

Jack was on the edge of his chair. "How'd you get him to come over?"

"He was a walk-in at our embassy in London. Wanted to do what he could to topple Ahmed and destroy Nadim."

"Has he been useful?"

"Very. I've gone in from time to time. He's fed me hard information that permitted us to thwart Syrian border attacks and cut off the movement of military supplies into Lebanon."

This is just what I need, Jack was thinking. "Will you call this Yasef and see what he can find out about Robert McCallister and what they're planning to do with him?"

Avi shook his head. "I can never use the phone that way with Yasef. The government frequently listens in on calls of its low- and midlevel intelligence people. It's one of the routines they established after they found someone else passing us information a few years ago. If I call Yasef like that and they're on the line, he's a dead man."

Jack thought about what Avi had said. He had only one possible move at this point. *You're going to owe me big-time, Sam.* "Can you get me into Syria?" Jack said. "And tell me how I can get in contact with Yasef once I'm there?"

Avi was taken aback. "You can't do that."

"When I start something, I like to finish it."

"It's insane. Yasef may not even be in the same job any longer. Nadim may have found out he was working with me and killed him."

Jack wasn't deterred. "I'll take my chances."

"You ever been to Syria before?"

"I fought there in the 'seventy-three war."

Avi was stunned. *This guy's more of a wild man than I am.* "That doesn't count. You have any idea how dangerous it is for a lone Israeli there? Not just the top leadership, but the people on the street hate us. They'd give anything to avenge 'sixty-seven and 'seventy-three. They'd kill any Israeli they could get their hands on. You know damn well I'm right."

Jack couldn't argue. "There's no other way," he said stubbornly.

Avi took a pack of Marlboros out of his pocket and offered one to Jack, who declined. He lit up, blowing the smoke into the air. "There's a tire company based in Milan, Angelli, with whom we have good relations. I've gone into Syria from time to time over the years with an Angelli executive ID— Mario Leonardo, group vice president. Angelli sells there. They could put a new plant in Syria if they wanted to. You'd be surprised how the possibility of jobs eases entry and movement restrictions even in a totalitarian regime. If you're really hell-bent on this lunacy, I could get the two of us Angelli papers."

Jack grimaced. "I didn't say anything about your going. You've got a wife and family. There's no way I'm letting you come with me. All I want is a letter I can hand to Yasef. I'll take it from there."

Avi pulled back and shook his head. "It's too treacherous for you to go alone. If we're right that they're planning a joint operation with Turkey, security will be even tighter than usual. It'll take two of us—one to watch the other's back."

Jack was now feeling guilty about involving Avi. "If our cover's blown, we'll have a hell of a time getting out. I hate to see you putting yourself at risk for that scumbag Terry McCallister's son."

Avi shook his head. "I'm not doing it for the pilot. That's between you and your brother. For me, the gut issue is Syria's involvement. Nobody hates us as much as Ahmed. And Nadim's capable of anything. We have to find out what they're scheming. As you said earlier, the stakes have now changed. They're huge."

Jack was persuaded, though he felt very uneasy about Avi coming. "Okay," he said reluctantly. "We'll both go." He shifted in his seat. "You've done this before. What are the logistics?"

"We fly to Milan in the morning and from there to Damascus. In the evening I'll try to contact Yasef."

Avi finished his beer with a large gulp, belched, and rose to leave. "I have to get our plane tickets tonight and make arrangements for the papers we'll need. We want to make an early plane in the morning."

Jack put his hand on Avi's arm. "A few more minutes won't kill you. There's something I want to ask you."

Avi sat back down. "Sure. Shoot."

"Yesterday you said that you had a story to tell me about your playing tennis. You piqued my interest." Avi sighed, took another cigarette out of the pack and lit it up. Jack could tell he didn't want to talk about it. "Sorry I asked."

"No, it's not such a big deal." Avi looked at the empty bottle on the table. "If I'm going to talk about this, I need another one. How about you?" he asked Jack.

"I'll pass."

"I don't trust people who don't drink."

Jack smiled. "You're safe with me then. But only good wine."

Avi wrinkled up his face. "Snob."

"What can I tell you? I'm in the business."

Once the owner deposited another Maccabee for Avi, he began talking softly. "When you were a kid, did you ever have a dream for the rest of your life?"

Jack thought about his plan to marry Sarah and move to Israel. "Sure," he said without explaining.

"Well, my whole childhood I wanted to be a fighter pilot. And I made it. I came through training with distinction. Then they sent me to Alabama to fly with the Americans, where I got the highest grade in the class. For about a year, I was flying an F-4 Phantom and having the time of my life. The Egyptians or Syrians would put planes up in the air, and we'd shoot them down. When I was home on leave in the summer, I went out and played tennis with a pal. He had a strong serve, and the court surface was a little rough, to say the least." A glum expression covered Avi's face. "Well, anyhow, one of his serves took a freak bounce and struck my eye. Tore the zonules in the eye and dislocated the lens. It was repaired with surgery, but my flying days were over." Avi sipped some beer.

"That really sucks," Jack said.

Avi took a puff on his cigarette and shook his head. "It's life. You worry about one set of dangers, and wham." He smashed his fist into the palm of his hand. "Something else comes out of nowhere. My mother had a great-aunt Rivka who survived Auschwitz. She and her husband. They came to Israel. Had one child. A son. He made it through four years in the army, including one war. A year after his discharge, when he was a student at Haifa University, he died in an auto accident. Go figure."

"So how'd you get mixed up with Moshe?"

"I was spending my time at home picking oranges, whining and feeling sorry for myself after the eye operation, when Moshe paid me a visit and recruited me. Dora says I'm reckless, that I have a death wish, that's why I drive so fast, and that was why I joined the Mossad when I couldn't fly anymore. But she's wrong about that."

Avi paused before continuing. "I was ten in June of 1967. Before my father was mobilized in his reserve unit, he taught me how to shoot a rifle. My mother already knew. She had been in the army. We also had my two-year-old sister at home. The Jordanians were part of the Arab armies that were tightening the noose around us. If they broke through our line of defense, which was thin, we and the other residents of the Moshav were all that was stopping them from reaching the sea. They were so close we could see them getting ready to attack with binoculars."

Jack thought about what he had been doing then. He hadn't developed his passion for Israel until the 1969 trip. In early June 1967, he was caught up in "Cub fever," as the usually pathetic Chicago Cubs were in first place in the National League before their annual "June swoon" brought them back to mediocrity.

Avi shook his head somberly. "It's not for the excitement and the danger that I joined up with Moshe. *Ein Barera.* We've got no alternative to self-defense if we want the state to survive."

Avi's words hit home with Jack. "We're similar in that way. I didn't come to Israel to spy and kill terrorists. I wanted to be part of the new Jewish state. I saw this as an ideal place to live. To raise a family. The society was rich intellectually and culturally. There was an excitement about trying to fulfill a two-thousand-year-old dream. But our neighbors don't see it that way. So we do what we have to do in order to survive. As you put it, we've got no alternative."

"What about Moshe? When did he recruit you?"

"I came here from Chicago in 'seventy-three," Jack said. "Fought in the Yom Kippur war in an infantry unit on the Syrian front."

"Two citations for bravery," Avi interjected.

"How did you know that?"

Avi gave him a broad smile. "It's amazing what you can learn on the Internet."

"After the war the army assigned me to a new elite unit that hunted and killed terrorists. I was planning to make a career of that when Moshe came to visit me one day. He said he was looking for an American-born Israeli to set up in the wine-exporting business with offices in Paris, Milan, and Barcelona. The idea was that I would be available to do jobs for the Mossad from time to time in Europe. He thought the cover of an American in the wine business was perfect. When I agreed to do it, he sent me to Hebrew University for an economics degree and to learn Arabic. In the summers he arranged for a French Jew in Burgundy to teach me the wine business and to speak colloquial French. Over the years I paid back the Mossad's initial investment. The business is mine."

Avi put his cigarette out and lit another. "What jobs did you do for him?"

"At first, mostly small stuff relaying info between Israel and Europe, primarily on terrorist activities. Then a big job came along."

"Osirak?"

Jack nodded. "Yeah. I located a metallurgist named Jean Pierre, who was working for a firm in Lyons that had a large piece of the project. Jean Pierre thought it was an outrage that his country was helping the lunatics in Baghdad develop nuclear weapons. So he was willing to assist us."

Avi's eyes opened wide. "How'd you use him?"

"I set him up with this good-looking woman I knew in Paris. Francoise Colbert was her name. Gentile. A struggling actress." Avi didn't need to know everything about Jack's relationship with her—just the operational facts. "In return for Mossad funding, she agreed to see the engineer whenever he came to Paris, which was quite often. He brought plans and copies of progress reports with him in his briefcase. We had a team follow Jean Pierre from the train station to Francoise's apartment on the Left Bank to make sure he wasn't being followed. The team stood guard out in front when he went inside. I installed several copy machines in her apartment. While Francoise kept Jean Pierre occupied in the bedroom, our people copied documents."

Admiration was visible on Avi's face. "Now I see why we knew precisely what to bomb and when—immediately after they finished construction. It would have been horrible for the entire world if the Iraqis had gotten nuclear weapons. You should have been given a medal for what you did."

Jack looked down at the table. He didn't like talking about the prime minister's award he had received, which hadn't been publicized. "Yeah, well, things got a little dicey at the end. The SDECE caught on to Jean Pierre. We got a tip that they picked him up in Lyons. We scrambled and shut everything down. I hustled Francoise off to Montreal with a new identity and a large bank account."

"What happened to Jean Pierre?"

Jack felt guilty about this part of it. "Supposedly hung himself in a French prison. They made it look like a suicide. My guess is they tortured him to talk. They couldn't get much, though. He didn't know my real name or Francoise's."

Avi shook his head. "None of that's surprising. It was a huge embarrassment for them. What have you done since for Moshe?"

"For a long time, smaller stuff again. Relaying information obtained from French government people willing to defy their leadership and supply material to us. Then in the last couple of years we began focusing on Arab terrorists in France."

"Was Khalifa in Marseilles your kill?"

Jack nodded. "The French refused to extradite Khalifa after we gave them clear evidence of his involvement in three suicide bombings and other murders. Then Moshe called me. I went down to Marseilles and made the arrangements. For money, it was easy to find locals to help. They all hate the Arabs."

"From what I heard, it was a clean job."

Jack thought about Daniel Moreau's visit to his office. "I hope so." Right now he couldn't worry about Daniel Moreau. If he didn't make it back from Syria alive, what happened in France would be immaterial.

Chapter 11

Daniel Moreau should have felt tired and jet-lagged. Only a few hours ago he had gotten off a plane from Paris and arrived in Montreal, which was still in the grip of winter. The frigid, moist air cut through Moreau like a knife. None of that mattered. The surge of adrenaline he was feeling easily overcame his weariness and the weather. After years of intensive investigation, he was finally closing in on his prey.

Jack Cole must be very pleased with himself, thinking that he outfoxed me by closing up his office in Paris and sending Monique away. He underestimated me. There's no way I'm buying into his phony cover. In a few hours I'll have the proof I need to nail him.

Moreau was traveling on a passport in the name of Simon Prieur, businessman. Canadian police never liked it when law-enforcement people from other countries, especially the United States or France, operated in their country. In his suite at the Queen Elizabeth, he ordered dinner from room service and then waited for ten o'clock to come, passing the time by rereading for the umpteenth time Camus's *The Stranger*. He didn't have with him the extensive dossier that he had compiled on Francoise Colbert, including every report card she had received at her Catholic girls' school in Paris. All of that he had committed to memory.

At ten o'clock he put on a suit and tie, making himself look like a visiting businessman. Then he set off on foot, heading toward the river. Periodically he stopped and pretended to be window-shopping to make certain he wasn't being followed.

Two blocks from the river he found what he was looking for: an open-air drug market. Sensing that he had cash, three vendors hustled over to Moreau. He waved them away and continued walking until he reached the building with the number twenty on the dilapidated brown-brick exterior. In the doorway stood a large, beefy man with a red face marked with blemishes. His right hand was concealed in the pocket of his black leather bomber jacket.

Moreau stopped and stared at the man. *"Duc,"* he whispered, using the code that had been arranged. When the man nodded, Moreau reached into his pants pocket. As he did, the beefy man pulled out his right hand with a plastic bag containing a white powder. In the flash of a second, he exchanged the plastic bag for a roll of Canadian dollars. Moreau moved away.

It was a mile to Le Club. Moreau covered it on foot, again making certain he wasn't being followed. He had been in Montreal only once before, but he had committed a street map of the area to memory.

Le Club was a dingy, sleazy bar in a seedy part of the city. The walls were covered with red velvet wallpaper to make it look like a bordello. The material was stained and peeling away from the wall. Next to the bar was a small raised platform. On it, an emaciated blond woman gyrated and unhooked her bra to disclose a set of improbable breasts.

A couple of the dozen male customers leered. Most looked bored and sipped exorbitantly priced beer. Off on one side of the room, a couple of other men ignored the show and shot darts into a board on the wall.

Two women in short, skimpy brown skirts and white halter tops, a redhead and a brunette, sitting together at a table, eyed Moreau when he walked in and let his eyes adjust to the dim light of Le Club.

He headed toward the bar, overpaid for a Molson, and carried it to a booth in a corner, isolated from other patrons. The redhead got up and walked over to him. "Will you buy me a drink?"

"I want to see Roni," he replied.

She gave him a contemptuous glare that said, *You'd be better with me,* but Le Club had its protocol. She moved away and nodded to the brunette.

Watching her approach, Moreau, who grew up in a well-off Paris family, thought of an expression his mother frequently used: "shopworn." As Francoise moved closer, he changed his characterization. "Down and out" seemed more accurate. The former actress had short hair and bloodshot eyes. She swung her hips in an undulating motion. Heavy makeup was caked on her face, covering bruises.

When she slid into the booth across from Moreau, he noticed the tracks on her left arm. "I drink champagne," she said. He smiled. He knew how the game was played. She'd get a glass of colored water, he'd pay twenty bucks or so, and she'd get a cut from the house.

He reached into his pocket and pulled out a thick wad of bills. "I was hoping we could go somewhere more intimate."

She looked at him warily, trying to decide whether she could trust him. That German who had treated her like a punching bag two weeks ago said something similar. Her gaze went from his face to the money in his hand. That made up her mind.

"A hundred," she said. "And you wear a condom. The whole time. Even if I blow you. You got that?"

He nodded.

"We'll go to my place."

She got up, grabbed a fake-fur coat from a hook in the

back, and headed toward the door. Moreau was two steps behind.

"What are you doing in Montreal?" she asked as they walked two blocks to a dilapidated twelve-story building that reminded Daniel of public housing built for Arabs in Marseilles.

"Trying to make some money."

That was good enough for her. "Tell me about it."

When they got into the elevator, heavy with the stench of urine, she pressed the number twelve. "I have the penthouse," she said, cracking a smile.

She was missing a tooth, but it didn't matter. That smile lit up her face and confirmed what he had known from the dossier: Twenty years ago she had been a beautiful young woman. The apartment was a chilly, tiny mess—a kitchen and two rooms with a balcony that ran along the outside of both rooms.

Once they were inside she held out her hand. He peeled off a hundred dollars, which she placed in a cabinet in the living room. In a couple of seconds she stripped off her halter top, skirt, and underwear. Around her neck she was wearing a tiny gold cross. She had shaved all of her pussy hair. She had small breasts that sagged and an incision across her stomach from the cesarean. He knew from the dossier that the baby had been born with a heart problem and died at two months. She returned to the cabinet, where she had stashed the money, and pulled out a package of condoms.

When she saw that he wasn't undressing, she said, "Let's go. Speed it up. I don't have much time. I have to be back for my next shift."

Without responding, Moreau reached into his pocket and extracted the bag of white powder. Her eyes bulged. Her whole body began trembling.

He opened the plastic bag and held it up to her nose so she could smell it. Perspiration dotted her forehead.

"Let's do some business," he said.

"All I have is the hundred you just gave me. You can have that back, and I'll do whatever you want." She was pleading with him. "You don't have to use a condom. You can come in my mouth."

He looked at her with contempt. He hated junkies.

"Or anywhere else . . . I'll do Greek."

"I want information," he said. "You give me what I want and the whole package is yours."

She eyed him suspiciously. "You didn't come here to fuck me, did you?"

What he wanted to say was, "There's no way I'd put my cock into that sewer," but instead he said, "Let's talk first, Francoise Colbert. Later we'll fuck."

At the sound of the name she had been given at birth, she looked at him in stunned disbelief. She hadn't used that name in years. She had legally changed it shortly after coming to Montreal, hoping to start a new life. Suddenly a light went off for her. "You're a cop. Aren't you?"

"Not exactly," he said.

"The accent is from Paris. I had trouble picking it up. Now I know."

He nodded.

"You bastard."

He looked at her with indifference and stuffed the plastic bag back in his pocket. "If you don't want to talk, that's okay with me." He turned toward the door.

"Don't go," she begged, desperate for the white powder.

She grabbed a threadbare blue terry-cloth bathrobe from the sofa and pointed to a table in the living room. He sat down across from her with the plastic bag on the table in front of him. *Let her look at it,* he thought.

"How do you know my name?" she asked.

He shook his head. "I ask the questions."

"What do you want to know?"

"In 1981 you were seeing an engineer from Lyons by the name of Jean Pierre. Weren't you?"

She was shaking. It had been more than twenty years, and she had heard nothing. She and Jack had been so young. She was certain it was ancient history. Now this man came out of nowhere.

"Maybe I was, and maybe I wasn't," she said in a hostile voice.

As he studied her face, he knew that she was the woman he had been looking for all these years.

"Why do you care?" she asked.

He ignored her question. "Did you know that valuable French government secrets were given to the Israelis by Jean Pierre each time he came to Paris to meet you?"

She looked down at her veiny hands without responding.

"You can help yourself," he said, trying to gain her confidence. "Tell me what you know, and I won't charge you with being part of the conspiracy."

When she still didn't answer, he said, "What's the matter? The sisters taught you not to lie at Sacred Heart?" He smiled broadly. "That's rich."

"Go fuck yourself," she said.

"They also taught you not to use foul language."

"What do you want?" she said, now concluding that her chances of getting any of the white power were between slim and none.

"The name of the Israeli agent who put you up to it, how the operation worked, and how much he paid you. Let's start with the name."

"He never told me," she said.

Her answer was truthful. When she had first met Jack Cole, he called himself Gregory Walsh. She had fallen in love with him, and not just because of the money he was giving her. He had been so idealistic and so mysterious about his life. Once, after they had made love and he had fallen asleep, she had rifled through his wallet and found the French driver's license in the name of Jack Cole. She had laughed to herself. He was so new at what he was doing that he had kept his identity with him. She never told him about it. A month later, when he had asked her help with Jean Pierre, she had done it to please him because she loved him. She hoped he would marry her.

And there was something else. She was an innocent in those days, a holdover from the youth culture of the seventies, a believer in the dream of world peace along with free love. Jack had a dynamic personality. He was inspiring. When he explained to her that the point of this operation was to block the proliferation of nuclear weapons, she was enthusiastic. Then there was the sense of danger. It was the most thrilling thing she had ever done. The excitement was intoxicating. In bed with Jean Pierre, she went through the motions each time while Jack copied documents in the next room. The next night she and Jack made passionate love, intoxicated by "her role in history," as Jack explained it.

Once the operation was over, she knew that Jack would never marry her. But he was wonderful and concerned about her. He gave her all of the papers she needed to resettle in Montreal under a false name, and enough money to last for ten years. He had been good to her. She had loved him. She couldn't betray him.

"You're lying," Moreau said sharply.

"I don't lie. He never told me his name."

Moreau extracted a picture from his wallet: a five-by-seven black-and-white. It was an older version of Jack.

"Is this the man?"

She didn't respond.

"How did the operation work?"

She stared at the ceiling with a sullen expression on her face. This cop was like a hungry dog with a bone. He'd never let go. She was in deep trouble.

"Suit yourself," Moreau said in a hard, cold voice. "I'm taking you back to Paris with me. I think you'll talk there."

She knew exactly what he had in mind. When he got her to France they'd put her in a prison cell and withhold the heroin until they broke her and she talked.

They'd force her to testify against Jack. Afterward they'd put her in jail for life for her role in the operation. Never mind what this bastard said now.

A great wave of depression enveloped her. She was disgusted with herself, with what she had become. She remembered those days of glory. She knew what she had to do.

"I kept a notebook," she said, sounding reluctant, "the whole time of the operation. It lays out all of the details. Exactly what you want. I thought I might need it one day to save myself."

Moreau was elated. This was what he had hoped for. "That day has come. If the notebook's as good as you say, you could escape with your freedom."

She nodded.

"Where's the notebook?"

She pointed to the bedroom. "In the dresser. Third drawer down on the right. Under my lingerie."

"Get it," he ordered.

She gave him the finger. "Do it yourself. I'm not your slave."

Thinking about the notebook, Moreau was too excited to argue with her. "Don't move, bitch," he barked. "I'll be right back."

She watched him jump up and run into the bedroom. Then she crossed herself for lying, took a deep breath, slipped off her robe, and ran toward the door leading to the balcony.

As she hoisted herself up onto the waist-high, ice-cold wrought-iron railing, finally she felt joy. At least this way she would be saving Jack. Without her testimony, this prick of a detective would never have a case against him. That was why he was practically wetting his pants at the thought of the notebook.

Long before this French detective had arrived, the reality of her situation was smacking her in the face every day. She had squandered her life, which had turned to shit. By doing this now for Jack, she would at least be doing something useful with what meager little she had left. Salvation for Jack. Redemption for herself.

The railing was cold on her bare feet. Using what little strength she had, she willed herself to stand up. For an instant she was precariously perched, her arms spread out for balance. Then she closed her eyes and leaped into the void. "I love you, Jack Cole," she cried out. "I love you."

In the bedroom Moreau cursed as he searched frantically through the drawer, tossing her smelly lingerie to the floor. There was no notebook here. He raced back into the living room. Then he stopped in his tracks and gaped at the open door to the patio. By the time he reached the railing, she was already splattered on the street below.

Furious at himself for leaving her alone, Moreau left the building quickly through the rear, before anyone could see him. Disheartened, he gained no solace from the fact that she had confirmed what he had deduced from reexamining the transcript of Jean Pierre's interrogation. He needed a live witness to testify against Jack Cole.

On the cab ride to the airport, Moreau became even more determined. If he couldn't charge Jack Cole with this crime, he'd redouble his efforts to charge him with another. Meantime, he had distributed Jack Cole's name and picture to passport control at all the French airports. It had been given to gendarmes who patrolled the Paris train stations, and it was pasted on bulletin boards there. Monique, Cole's secretary, had said he was out of the country. Sooner or later he'd come back to Paris. Then they'd nab him.

Chapter 12

Sam's eyes swung from Ann, seated on one side of the living room, to Sarah seated on the other. *These two are so much alike that it's scary,* he decided.

"Looky here," he said. "You have to eat. I'm taking the two of you out to dinner."

Ann raised her hand. "Leave us be. You go out yourself. We'll be all right."

Still frantic with worry about Bobby, but feeling better to be away from Terry, Sarah overruled her daughter. "He's right, Ann. We're not doing a thing for Bobby by starving ourselves. We need our strength to cope."

Ann smoothed down the side of her hair and gave a deep sigh. "Getting the two of you together may have been a mistake on my part."

Sam booked a table at The Square on Bruton Street off Berkeley Square, a restaurant at which he had clout because he frequently brought U.S. clients there. What he liked about it for this evening wasn't only the superb French cuisine and professional service, but the comfortable ambience of the high-ceilinged, wood-paneled modern room. The decibel level was low, and the tables were widely spaced.

Initially, when Sam had heard that Sarah was coming to London to stay with Ann in her flat, he was fearful that his effort to bring Ann out of the deep depression that had engulfed her was doomed to failure. He was pleasantly surprised to hear Sarah asking Ann about the status of the research in her postgraduate study at the University of London on the causes of the decline of British influence in the Middle East in the twentieth century. The relationship between mother and daughter intrigued him. Ann, who had always clashed with her father, had fought with her mother as a child as well, because she saw her mother as the agent who willingly implemented her father's arbitrary demands. Late in her teens she began to see her mother as a victim of her father, just as she and Robert were. With that reassessment, a close bond between mother and daughter developed. In Ann's mind, they were coconspirators with a common enemy. Sam had first seen the two of them together when he and Ann were already dating, and Sarah had come alone to visit her daughter. "Of course, I won't tell your father that you're seeing him," Sarah had said.

"If I thought you would, I would have never have told you," Ann had replied.

Under the overhead lights of The Square, Sam was struck by how wan and pale Ann was. When he had first met her, she had her mother's good looks, the soft brown eyes that sparkled, the wide smile, the wavy brown hair. Now for both of them all of those were eclipsed by a tightly closed mouth, a long face, and bloodshot eyes. Anxiety about her brother had taken its toll on Ann as well as Sarah.

During cocktails Sam tried to steer the conversation to topics other than Robert, including Ann's work at the university, his own law practice, and the London theater. By the time their first course arrived, a fabulous foie gras with rhubarb that all three had ordered, Ann had turned the conversation back to her brother. "What's so frustrating is the helplessness of it all. There has to be something else we can do for Robert. Somebody we can talk to."

Sarah shook her head in disbelief. Ann's speech was one she had heard frequently from Terry before he decided that they should go to Washington. Trying to help her daughter cope, she said, "Believe me, honey, we tried everyone back home. Your father and I have met twice with the president himself and three times with Jimmy Grange, his close adviser."

Ann rolled her eyes. "Father probably pissed off everyone so badly they won't lift a finger."

Sarah smiled despite herself. "That's true. There was some of that."

Ann's face lit up. She turned to Sam. "Hey, I've got an idea. Your law firm has an international practice. There must be one of your clients who does business in Turkey."

"I've already made those calls," Sam replied, sounding sympathetic. "I came up empty."

"We're not thinking creatively enough," Ann insisted.

A waiter clad in a black jacket was clearing their first courses.

"There must be something you can do," Ann pleaded in a way that tore at Sam's heart.

He paused to sip some wine. He loved her so much and wanted her to know he had done everything he could. He realized that telling her about his trip to Tel Aviv meant walking into a minefield, but he had to do it.

Sam sighed. "I even went to Israel to talk to my brother, Jack, in the hope that he might know somebody there who could help."

Sarah, who had been slumped in her chair, shot to a straight position, her back rigid, her facial muscles tense. "What did he say?" she asked before Ann could respond.

Sam didn't want to tell them the truth. "There's nothing he can do. He said he was sorry."

Sarah snapped at Sam. "He wasn't sorry at all. You were

nice to try that approach, but I could have told you that Jack will never lift a finger to help."

Sam felt the need to defend his brother. "I'm sure if he could—"

Sarah cut him off with a short, sardonic laugh. "Ha! C'mon, I know Jack a lot better than you do. In everything he did, he played to win. Losing was something he would never accept. So the idea of him helping Terry McCallister's son is preposterous."

Sarah's tone upset Ann even more. "Mom, what's wrong? What exactly was the deal with you and Father and Jack?"

Sam was fidgeting in his chair. Though he had always wanted to know the details of what had happened between Sarah and Jack, he was now sorry he had opened this can of worms. Miraculously, a waiter arrived with their main courses on a tray under metal domes. As another waiter removed the dishes from the tray and placed them on the table, turbot for Ann and Sarah, roast squab for Sam, he tried to change the subject. "What I like about this restaurant is—"

Ann cut him off. "What exactly was the deal with you and Father and Jack, Mother?" she repeated.

"He was the boy next door," Sarah said, trying to recover and brush her off. "We dated in high school. We both went to Michigan together. Freshman year I met your Dad. Jack moved to Israel. End of story."

Ann was smart and knew her mother too well to believe that was all there was. "C'mon. The details."

Ann didn't make a move to lift her fork. Sarah took a deep breath. They were both weakened emotionally. "Leave it alone, Ann."

"I want to know."

Sam's eyes moved from one to the other, as if he were watching a Ping-Pong match.

"This isn't the time."

"I want to know now. I *need* to know."

Sarah didn't have the strength to resist Ann's demand. She knew that her daughter wouldn't give up until she was satisfied. In desperation, she looked at Sam for help, but he knew how strong-willed Ann could be. He wasn't about to try to block her in her current state.

With a sigh, Sarah yielded and began talking in a slow, halting voice. "From the time we moved in next door to the Coles, Jack and I were inseparable. He was not only the first boy I ever dated and kissed, he was the only boy until I got to Michigan."

She turned to Sam. "I'm sure that you don't remember, because you were only three at the time, but I went with my parents to Israel with your family for Jack's bar mitzvah. He and I slipped out of the hotel at night and explored the city. It was a marvelous time to be in Israel in 1969, two years after the 'sixty-seven war. Euphoria was the mood. Peace seemed likely. Everything was possible. Jack fell in love with the place. He wanted us to move there after high school, go to Hebrew University and spend the rest of our lives in Israel."

"You were only thirteen at the time," Ann said.

"I know, but we assumed, both of us, that we would get married one day. Although I have to admit I was less than enthused about the living-in-Israel part. So compromised. First we'd go to college in the United States. After graduation we'd get married, try Israel for a year, and see if we liked it."

Ann was surprised. "You were so young. How could you be talking about marriage with any man?"

Sarah took a bite of her fish, remembering how magical their relationship had been in high school—the high school prom at Senn, where she had been selected prom queen and Jack was class president. Ah, the promise of youth.

"It was a different time, Ann. We were in love. The sexual

revolution was just starting. Your generation knows a great deal more about sex then we did. A lot less about love."

"So then what happened to this great love affair?" Ann asked. She and Sam were staring at Sarah, who needed a good slug of wine before she could continue.

"In the fall of 'seventy-one, we went off to the University of Michigan together, Jack and I. We both enrolled in the R.C., a small liberal-arts college within the university made up mostly of liberals, which we were, and intellectuals, which we wanted to be. In the first couple months I met Terry and got caught up in the radical politics of that time. I became an officer in the new left student movement. We were activists. Our focus was not only on the campus, where students wanted a greater say in running the university, but on national issues. The goal was to avoid the 1968 debacle of Humphrey and move the Democratic party to the left at the 'seventy-two convention in Miami Beach."

"What about Jack?" Sam asked. "Was he involved, too?"

"Not at all. He tried to discourage me. We had some huge fights. All he cared about politically was Israel, which I thought was ridiculously narrow."

Sam looked startled. "He was religious in those days?"

Sarah smiled. "Jack didn't even believe in God. He believed in Israel and the Jewish people. He was studying Hebrew and heading up a group of pro-Israel Jewish students."

Ann raised her eyebrows. "Did you guys ever go to class?"

Sarah laughed. "Not very often. Most of us were too busy for that. Besides, we were convinced that we knew more than the teachers. But Jack was different there, too. He refused to miss classes. He did homework, wrote papers, and studied for exams. Other students laughed at him. He didn't care."

"So where did Father fit into all of this?" Ann asked.

Sarah did her best to conceal the pain she was feeling. The decisions you made when you were young, you had to live with your whole life. "Terry was a senior when Jack and I were freshmen. He was the president of the new left student movement."

Ann picked up her fork and smashed it against the plate, causing everyone in the dining room to stare at them. "You mean to tell me that Mr. Right-wing Republican Investment Banker was a pot-smoking pinko? How hypocritical can you get?"

Sarah didn't respond. She, who had never abandoned the liberal leanings of her youth, had often asked herself the same question. She had no desire to defend or justify Terry.

Ann was now nodding her head up and down. "I can probably fill in the rest of the picture. I bet Jack was wonderful, just like Sam. You ditched the nerdy geek for the older, charismatic rabble-rouser."

Sam interrupted. "Hey, I'm no nerdy geek."

Sarah didn't hear what Sam said. Ann's words sliced through her like a knife. "You have a wonderful way of expressing yourself."

They had eaten so little that a waiter came by to inquire, "Is there something wrong with the food?"

Sam waved him away. "We're just talking. The food's superb."

"How would you put it?" Ann asked her mother.

"I had never dated anyone other than Jack. I was swept up in passion with your father. I thought we had a lot in common."

"Not religion."

"Obviously."

"Did Grandpa really sit shiva for you when you married Father?"

Ann knew how to cut to the core. This was the hardest part to recall. Neither her nor Terry's parents had come to their wedding. "Let's just say that they liked Jack, and they didn't like the idea of my marrying outside the faith."

Ann pushed on. "So why'd you marry him?"

"Well, in August we went off to the Democratic convention in Miami Beach."

"You and Terry?"

Sarah nodded. "Once the school term was over, Jack went to Israel to live. Terry and I hung out in Ann Arbor for a while. Then we flew down to Miami, where we met other left-wing student leaders from around the country. It turned out to be a big dud. Nothing exciting, like the 'sixty-eight convention. In the auditorium, the delegates were nominating George McGovern. On the sands of South Beach at midnight, surrounded by hundreds of radical students, many of whom were stoned out of their minds, a campus chaplain from some university I can't remember married your father and me."

Ann pulled back as if she had been shot. Her mouth was agape. Her arms flew up involuntarily above her head. "What did you say?"

"Oh, my God," Sarah said, realizing immediately the dreadful slip. The horrible, horrible mistake she had just made. She had been thinking about Jack, remembering what had happened. She hadn't been paying any attention to what she was saying. She wanted to die. She didn't know what she could do to rectify it.

As Sam looked from daughter to mother, one face more contorted in pain than the other, he knew something serious had happened. At first he didn't realize what it was. Then he did the math in his head. Ann's birthday was March fifth.

"So you lied to me all these years," Ann said in an accusatory tone. "You celebrated your anniversary in April because you didn't want me to know that you were pregnant when . . ." Ann's face turned deathly white. "Oh, God. I ruined your whole life." She sprang to her feet. "I think I'm going to be sick." Covering her mouth with her hands, she raced toward the rest room, past the entrance to the restaurant, with Sarah two steps behind.

At the table, Sam wanted to cry for both of them.

A few minutes later Sarah returned. Sam jumped up. "How is she? What can I do?"

"She'll be okay. She wants to be alone for a while."

"Maybe I should go to her."

Until he began dating Ann, Sarah hadn't seen Sam since he was seven years old, during winter break her first year at Michigan. That was the last time she had ever set foot in her parents' house. Despite all the baggage, she had to admit that she liked Sam. He had Jack's concern and sensitivity. Terry would have been eating his dinner right now. "That would be a little difficult. She's locked in a stall in the ladies' room. Leave her be."

A waiter was hovering around. "You can take this food," Sarah said to him. When he was gone, she refilled her glass with wine, emptying the bottle. "I think we need another one, Sam."

He motioned to the sommelier, then sat quietly, leaving her alone with her demons while she drank.

Somehow Sarah would have to make Ann understand that she had ruined her own life. Not Ann. It wasn't only politics that drove her into Terry's bed. She felt she had outgrown Jack's limited world.

Then there was sex with Terry. Experienced at "the art of making love," as he called it, he not only initiated her in sexual acts that she couldn't even have imagined, but he made her feel things that were mind numbing. *No, Ann, you didn't ruin my life. I did it myself.*

She looked at Sam, unsure what to say. "Don't you want to know what happened after Terry and I got married?" *Not particularly,* he thought, but to be polite, he nodded. "I dropped out of school. We went to live on a commune near Big Sur. That's where Ann was born."

She emptied her glass. Sam refilled it. "How's Jack?" she asked, her voice quavering.

"He's still based in Israel."

"Based?"

"Yeah, he started and operates a company called Mediterranean Wine Exports. He has offices in Tel Aviv, Paris, Barcelona, and Milan. The business is pretty successful."

Sarah cracked a smile. "You're such a corporate lawyer. I mean, is he married? Does he have children? Is he happy?" Sarah asked wistfully.

Sam shrugged. "Happy—who knows? He doesn't have children. He was married once for a year or two to an American who thought she wanted to live in Israel, but then she realized what it was like. Decided it was too tough for her. Jack refused to move back to the U.S." He snapped his fingers. "That was that."

"Personality-wise has he changed?"

Sam grinned. "Same old Jack."

"The original straight arrow."

Sam nodded. Family loyalty was now raising its head. "Jack's still decent and hardworking, but he's made a glamorous life for himself. Because he's in the wine business, he moves in the fast lane socially. Last year he dated this Italian movie star. He made the papers when he showed up with her at the Marbella Club for a weekend."

Sarah was taken aback. That wasn't the Jack she remembered. "Suppose I were to go and meet him in one of his offices. Do you think he would try to find someone in Israel who could help rescue my Bobby if I asked him?"

"You'd be wasting your time. Like I said, I already tried that. Jack made it clear to me that there is nothing he can do."

The more Sam thought about it, the more convinced he became that Jack had to be lying to him. Hatred had been driving Jack. Sam's initial instinct had to be right. There was something Jack could do.

Chapter 13

His wife and three daughters were asleep, but not Yasef. In his tan military uniform he sat on a chair with frayed navy-blue material and padding bursting out of the arms, staring at the television set, which was broadcasting the late-evening news. Having helped with the scripts for the news-people on many occasions as part of his job in the intelligence agency, Yasef knew very well that what was called "news" in Syria was nothing more than government propaganda. Still, if someone with Yasef's background listened carefully, he might pick up hidden meaning between the lines. That was what he was doing this evening.

There was something big going on, being run by Major General Nadim. Yasef had learned that much in the corridors of the intelligence agency headquarters today. However, his own section, military intelligence, had thus far been frozen out. Only the Office of State Security seemed to be part of the action. An order had been given to check and recheck passports of any visitors at airports and border crossings. Hidden video cameras were being operated at each arrival point to take pictures of foreigners. A tail was being placed on questionable foreigners. In the state security section they were paranoid about Israel, and Syrians spying for the Israelis. The thought made him tremble. Anything was possible.

Yasef was listening so closely that he didn't hear the phone until the third ring. Then he jumped up with a start and raced across the room. It was past ten. If the people from State Security were onto him, they wouldn't be calling. They would sweep down and haul him in.

"Yes," he answered in a hesitant voice, trying to conceal his pounding heart.

"Is this the Damascus Coffeehouse?" a man asked in Arabic in a voice that was unmistakably Avi's.

The Israeli's words were part of a code he and Yasef had developed. They meant that Avi was in Damascus. He wanted to meet in one hour at Abu, a small café outside of town. It had been a year and a half since he had heard from Avi.

Racing through Yasef's mind was the thought that Avi's visit must have something to do with whatever Nadim was planning. With the high-security alert, it was an incredibly dangerous time for Avi to be in Syria. An even more dangerous time for Yasef to meet with him. What he wanted to do was warn Avi, "It's too risky for us to meet now. Get out of the country fast," but he couldn't do that. Someone from State Security might be listening in on the call right now. He could simply say, "I'm sorry, sir. You must have the wrong number." That was the signal that Yasef couldn't meet Avi in an hour at the café. Then he wouldn't answer the phone when it rang for the next day or so, and he would instruct his wife and children not to answer. That would leave the Israeli on his own to fend for himself. Yasef couldn't bear to do that.

"You have the wrong number, sir," he said, leaving out the words, "I'm sorry." His response told Avi he would be there.

He tiptoed into the bedroom, moving quietly to avoid

waking his wife, who was bundled in the blankets, snoring loudly. He gently slipped open a bureau drawer and searched under his clothes until he found the Russian pistol. He loaded it and placed it carefully into his briefcase.

Then he went into the bathroom. From a cabinet he pulled out a bottle marked *Aspirin* which everyone in the family was forbidden to touch. He poured the capsules in his hand until he found what he was looking for. Several of the round objects were slightly larger than the others and didn't have the word *Bayer* etched on top. He wrapped two of the cyanide capsules in a tissue and stuffed them into his pocket.

With Jack beside him in the green Renault he had rented at the airport, Avi drove slowly and cautiously from the At-Tal hotel on Al-Marjeh Square to the Abu Café.

"Watch our six o'clock," he told Jack, who kept glancing behind to make certain they weren't being followed. They traveled on poorly maintained, narrow back roads with very little traffic, along a route Avi had committed to memory. They rode for forty minutes in a northerly direction toward Ma'Alula. They were only twenty miles from the Lebanese border on the west. About a hundred yards from the café, Avi pulled off the road into a clump of trees.

Satisfied that the car was concealed, Avi grabbed a pair of binoculars from the glove compartment, and his briefcase from the car seat. Then he and Jack climbed out. They kept their bodies low, shielded by the car, until they ducked behind a deserted old wooden shed.

Peeking out around a corner, Avi had a good view through the binoculars of the road, the front of the café and its parking lot, while Jack kept out of sight.

In the next half hour only two cars passed their observation point. Neither turned off for the café. "He should be here by now," Jack said anxiously.

Avi wasn't listening. He was focused on an approaching

car, a dull gray Russian Lada that had slowed to a crawl. Avi watched it pull into the café parking lot. Yasef climbed out and walked into the café, carrying a briefcase in his hand.

"Showtime," Avi said to Jack as he handed him the binoculars. "Remember what I told you about the license plates of the State Security cars. They all start with the numbers nine-nine. If you see a car like that, we've got trouble."

"I'll hustle down to the café fast and warn you," Jack said tensely.

With the binoculars pressed tight against his face, Jack followed Avi until he entered the restaurant. Then Jack turned his attention to the road.

Five minutes later, another car passed. A black Lada. Jack stared at the license plates. "Oh, shit." The number was 9970.

The driver hit the brakes and veered into the parking lot.

Jack had to warn Avi before the security agent entered the café or called for backup. On foot, Jack raced along the dirt side of the road toward the café. As he ran, Jack's right hand went instinctively into the pocket of his black leather jacket and gripped the Swiss army knife he had packed in the luggage they checked through. It had been years since he used it for anything except opening bottles of wine, but he kept the blade sharp.

At the entrance to the parking lot, Jack stopped running and slipped behind a large bush. There was a chill in the air, but he was perspiring heavily.

Jack paused for a second to evaluate his options. The agent's car was parked between Jack and what appeared to be the only entrance to the café. The agent had the window rolled down on the driver's side of the car. If Jack dashed for the entrance to the café, the agent would see him and cut him off.

Jack studied the agent in the dim light that was coming through the windows of the restaurant. The man was look-

ing at some papers in the car with the aid of a flashlight. He
picked up a cell phone from the car seat. To Jack's horror, he
heard the agent say in Arabic, "This is Hussein. I've caught
up with the Italians."

At this point, Jack's choices narrowed to one. He had to
divert Hussein from his phone call before the agent disclosed their location. He remembered a trick he had learned
when he was in the elite antiterrorist unit in the seventies.
He ran across the parking lot toward the agent's car. At the
same time he pulled the knife out of his pocket and opened
the blade.

In Arabic, Jack screamed out, "Rape . . . rape." He circled
around to the back of the car and crouched down, his knees
just above the rough gravel surface.

Hussein put the phone down and leaped out of the car
with a .45-caliber pistol in his hand. Puzzled, he looked
around, trying to figure out what was happening. Jack
sprang at him from behind. He looped his left arm around
Hussein's neck, cutting off his wind. With a swift motion he
plunged the knife into Hussein's chest, going straight for the
heart while trying to minimize blood squirting, exactly as
the military instructors had taught him years ago. He was
out of practice. Some blood hit the sleeve of his jacket while
he continued thrusting the knife.

In a futile gesture, Hussein struggled to turn and use the
gun, but it was too late. The .45 fell harmlessly out of his
hand. His eyes were bulging, his body convulsing involuntarily.

When he was satisfied Hussein was dead, Jack pushed the
agent back into the car, then across the seat to the passenger
side. After taking a quick glance around to make certain no
one else was in sight, Jack picked up the gun, climbed into
Hussein's car, and drove it into a cluster of trees.

Careful to wipe off any prints, he extracted Hussein's

wallet and ID from his pocket. He pushed the body onto the floor of the car. Then he walked calmly into the café.

In the dim light he looked around. Seated in a corner, with cups of Turkish coffee on a battered wooden table, Avi and Yasef were the only patrons.

Yasef was alarmed to see someone approach them. Avi put a reassuring hand on Yasef's. "Meet Jack Cole. He's my friend."

"We have to leave," Jack said.

Avi noticed the blood on his jacket. Rising to his feet, Avi whispered to Yasef, "Let's get out of here."

His eyes blinked nervously, but Yasef accepted the order. "I'll meet you outside. I have to take care of him," Yasef said, pointing toward the owner of the café, seated behind the bar. He was a heavyset man in his forties with one wooden leg, the result of a mine he had stepped on in Lebanon when Syria had seized control of the country. Yasef paid him handsomely for the use of his café for what Yasef told him were secret government meetings, and for keeping his mouth shut.

Yasef was confident that the man had no desire to jeopardize their arrangement. For insurance, Yasef handed him a wad of Syrian pounds.

Once Yasef joined them outside, Jack quickly explained in Arabic what happened. He handed the Syrian Hussein's wallet and ID.

"You did the right thing," Yasef told him. "You also did a favor for the Syrian people. That bastard was determined to advance in his career on the corpses of those he killed."

"He must have followed us here," Avi said, feeling guilty.

"You can't blame yourself for not spotting him," Yasef said. "In the last year State Security has gotten more technologically sophisticated. They installed an electronic homing device under the hood on many cars that foreigners rent.

It permits them to follow without being detected by the driver."

Yasef's mind was racing. Undoubtedly Hussein had concluded that these foreigners had come to the café for a clandestine meeting. In the Syrian police state, foreigners were considered suspicious, or as enemies of the state. If Hussein had seen Avi with Yasef, they would have both been tortured until they explained why they had come to the café at the same time.

Yasef kicked at the ground in frustration. There was no good way out of this mess. He had to assume that Hussein had reported he was following the Italians, even if he didn't have a chance to disclose his location. If Yasef drove off and left the Israelis on their own, it would be only a matter of time until Avi and Jack were captured. He could take a chance that the Israelis wouldn't break under torture and reveal his involvement, but Yasef didn't want that to happen. Avi had always been a friend, bringing things that Yasef wanted for his family and couldn't get in the country. Yasef's sense of honor required that he return that friendship.

The Syrian now had a plan for what they should do. "Get in your car and follow me," Yasef said.

Avi was willing to trust Yasef with his life. Without questioning the Syrian, he said to Jack, "Let's go."

They drove for about twenty minutes in an easterly direction, the green Renault behind the gray Lada, until they came to an area where the road fell off sharply to the right. Yasef pulled over to the side and stopped. Avi was behind him, with Jack in the passenger seat.

"Leave the keys in your car and wait here," Yasef told the two Israelis.

They did as they were told while Yasef drove the green Renault down the side of the embankment and into a natural tunnel in the ground. No one could spot the car from the road.

Breathing heavily, Yasef climbed back up the rocky slope. Sweat streamed down his face, moistening his beard. "I have to get the two of you out of the country," he said grimly. "There's no other way of dealing with this." He turned to Avi. "You go in the front of the car with me."

Yasef opened the trunk. "Your friend rides back here."

A horrified Jack looked at Avi. The Syrian read his mind. "Don't worry about suffocating. Fucking Russian cars leak like sieves. There are plenty of holes back there and lots of airflow from the interior. I once kept someone there for two full days."

"I hope it won't be as long as this time," Jack said nervously.

"Not even close. We're about a hundred fifty miles from the Jordanian border crossing point at Dar'a. We'll stay off the main road and approach it from the west. In four or five hours you'll be safe." He gave a nervous laugh. "Either that or we'll all be dead. There's no way I'll let them take us alive."

Once they were settled in the car, Yasef turned on the ignition and began driving.

Avi pulled a pack of cigarettes out of his pocket, lit one, and handed it to Yasef. Then he lit a second for himself. Two more cigarettes later, Yasef explained to Avi in a halting voice that there was a State Security alert in the country.

"You're saving our lives," Avi said. "How can I ever thank you?"

Yasef waved his hand, blowing smoke out of the open car window. "Don't worry about thanking me. We just have to get out of this alive. All of us. That means whisking the two of you out of the country. I assume there's nothing you need in your hotel rooms."

Avi's mouth was taut. "If I needed it, I wouldn't have left it there."

Yasef was too tense to crack a smile. "Good. Then we don't have to go back to Damascus. At the border crossing I'll try to sneak you over with me. You can use Hussein's papers. Fortunately he didn't have a beard."

Yasef paused and glanced at Avi. "You look a little like him. The guards will be tired. It'll be dark. They won't care."

"You said that State Security was already on high alert. Once they find Hussein's body—" Avi stopped in midsentence.

Yasef looked thoughtful. "It's our only chance. We're racing against the clock."

Avi tried to consider alternatives. None was better. From Jordan he would have no trouble getting back to Israel, as Yasef knew.

"Why is your government on such a high-security alert?" Avi asked Yasef, who slowed to avoid hitting a small animal crossing the road. The old battered Russian car was wheezing and snorting. *I hope it doesn't die on us,* Avi thought.

"I don't know," Yasef said. "All I've been able to learn is that Major General Nadim is planning some kind of big operation. What or when is a closely guarded secret."

"How long has this high-security alert been going on?" Avi asked.

"Just now. A day or two. All very recent."

"What does that mean?"

"All foreign visitors are being carefully checked. You have to assume that they have your picture from a hidden video that was running at the airport when you arrived."

Avi was digesting Yasef's words, trying to decide if this operation of Nadim's related to Robert McCallister, and if so, how.

Yasef interrupted Avi's silent and inconclusive analysis.

"Back at the café I asked you why you came to Damascus. Then your friend burst in. Let's pick it up from there."

"Have you heard an American plane was shot down over southeastern Turkey a few days ago?" Avi said.

Yasef nodded. "There was a huge story when it happened. Then suddenly inexplicable silence. It's as if the pilot disappeared from the face of the earth."

"He hasn't disappeared," Avi said grimly. "He's been moved from Turkey to Syria."

Yasef's head snapped back in surprise. "Are you certain?"

"Very."

"Why did they do that?"

Avi was putting together what he knew about McCallister with what Yasef had told him in the car. According to Yasef, Nadim was planning a major operation. It had just happened. One of the maxims that kept Avi alive through his years in the Mossad was that for the spy there could be no such thing as coincidence. What Nadim was planning had to involve McCallister. Avi told Yasef, "The American pilot is the son of a close friend of President Kendall."

Yasef's eyes lit up. "Then Nadim must be planning to use the poor bastard as the pawn in some deal he's masterminding."

"Exactly what I was thinking. Suppose Jack and I stay in Syria, and you try to find out what Nadim has in mind? How close can you get to him?"

Yasef shook his head. "Nadim's already gone back to Paris. He likes to act as a solo player. My guess is that very few people, if any, in the Syrian government know what Nadim's up to. He's a firm believer that people can't tell what they don't know. His other maxim is that dead people don't talk."

Avi rubbed his chin. Yasef was right. With Nadim gone, he couldn't learn any more in Syria about Nadim's plan. But there was another possibility: If they could rescue McCallister, they could thwart Nadim's scheme.

"Do you think you could find out where they're keeping the pilot?"

Yasef looked terrified. "Surely you don't think you can take him out with you?"

"We would do it ourselves," Avi said boldly. "Just Jack Cole and me. It wouldn't get back to you."

Yasef couldn't believe what he was hearing. "I didn't save your life so you could throw it away. It would take me at least a day, maybe longer, to find out where they're holding the pilot. Remember, I'm with the military intelligence section. They isolated us from State Security. I would have to do it without arousing suspicion. Meantime, State Security will have found Hussein's body. Headquarters will know he was following you. They'll assume you killed him. Every policeman, soldier, and intelligence agent in the country will be looking for you. You know how long you'll last that way?"

They were approaching an intersection. Yasef stopped to consult a map in the glove compartment, then turned left. "Besides," he continued his thought, "even if you were able to break into the prison, or wherever it is they're holding McCallister, and you managed to get him out of there, the three of you wouldn't last three seconds on the street."

While Avi mulled over Yasef's words, the Syrian added, "I know what you did at Entebbe. I know how bold and daring you Israelis can be. But even for you, this would be too much. On further thought, I'd give you three minutes on the street, but it would be fun to watch." Quite inexplicably, Yasef burst out laughing.

"It's not funny," Avi said.

"Sorry, gallows humor."

For the next two hours they drove in silence. Yasef was

pushing the old car hard, at the maximum speed it would take.

In the trunk, Jack had no trouble breathing. He wasn't sure where the air was coming from, but Yasef was right: It was there. On the other hand, every muscle in his body ached from being curled up like an accordion. He cursed every time they hit a bump. The roads were rough, the shocks on the car worthless. *God, I hope we get there soon,* he thought.

They turned onto the main north-south road that connected Damascus and Amman. A slow-moving train chugged on the tracks parallel to the road.

Avi saw a sign that said JORDANIAN BORDER TWENTY KILOMETERS. He pointed it out to Yasef, who nodded and reached into his pocket, pulling out Hussein's wallet and his State Security ID. He handed them to Avi, who glanced at the dead man's picture.

"You really think this is going to work?"

"Absolutely," Yasef said, trying to steel his own courage. "You told me once that your family lived in Baghdad for eighteen hundred years until your great-great-grandfather moved to China."

"Yeah, but so what?"

"Before that your ancestors lived in Palestine. So you've been a neighbor. You look like one of us. You even speak Arabic."

"You're assuming Hussein's body hasn't been found yet."

Yasef was ready for Avi. He had weighed all the factors in his mind. "Or if they found it, they didn't have time to notify all the border guards and distribute your pictures."

"Either way, I'd better twist up my face to look like the miserable bastard Jack killed."

Yasef didn't want to talk anymore. He was looking through the windshield, squinting as he concentrated on the road and the task at hand. Five kilometers from the border he said to Avi, "Take the briefcase on the backseat and put it on the floor at your feet."

Avi followed Yasef's command.

"Inside there's a loaded pistol. Use it if you're in doubt. Dead is better than being Nadim's prisoner." Yasef said it in a grim voice.

Avi glanced over at Yasef. What he saw was a determined soldier sitting ramrod straight behind the wheel, his jaw firmly set as if he were made of iron.

It was still dark when Yasef slowed to a stop at the border hut. Two soldiers in Syrian army uniforms strolled out. The one in front was holding a flashlight. "Identification, please," he said as he approached the car.

Yasef handed him his ID. "Military intelligence," he said. "The car belongs to the agency."

The soldier yawned. It had been a long night on duty. "Where are you going?"

"To Amman to meet with Jordanian military officials on a top secret mission personally ordered by Major General Nadim."

Yasef figured that mentioning the name of the dreaded Nadim would stop the inquiry. Certainly no lowly border guard would dare try to call the major general in the middle of the night. He was right. The soldier shone the light on Avi while his colleague walked to the back of the car to check the license plates.

It matched the papers Yasef handed them. He tapped on the trunk.

Yasef hoped it wouldn't pop open, which sometimes happened after a hard knock.

Inside the trunk Jack was in a fetal position. Now that the car had stopped, he figured they were at the border checkpoint. He was holding his breath, ready to spring at anyone who opened it up.

Alongside the car, the soldier with the flashlight pointed toward Avi and asked Yasef, "Who's he?"

"From the agency, too. He's on the mission with me."

In his left hand Avi held Hussein's ID ready to hand it over. His right hand was on the edge of the seat, poised to go for the gun if need be.

The soldier didn't ask to see Avi's ID. He waved his hand with the light. "Go on, you two."

Fifty yards ahead at the Jordanian border control, Yasef, now breathing easier and more relaxed, repeated his story. Again they were waved through.

They reached the outskirts of Amman as the sun was rising. Yasef pulled into a combination gas station and restaurant. Once they were out of sight behind the building, he stopped the car and opened the trunk. Jack climbed out and tried to straighten his stiff body.

"You okay?" Avi asked.

Jack smiled. "Yeah, it was almost as bad as flying economy on El Al."

They all laughed from relief that the ordeal was over.

"Let's stop and eat something," Avi said.

Yasef shook his head. "I have to get home before they suspect me in Hussein's killing."

"You need food to keep going. We won't waste much time."

Reluctantly Yasef agreed. Inside the restaurant, at a table, they wolfed down sandwiches of diced vegetables in pita and drank bottled water and coffee. Avi leaned over and whispered to Yasef, "Don't go back. It's too dangerous. Go to Israel with us. We'll take care of you."

Yasef sighed. "I can't leave my wife and children. They'll be interrogated. You know what that means."

Avi nodded grimly. "They don't have any information.

After a couple of months we'll mount an operation and get them out. We've done that for Syrian Jews."

Yasef didn't want to tell Avi that the Israeli didn't fully appreciate Nadim's cruelty. His only hope was to return before he was missed. If he didn't come back, Nadim would torture and kill his wife and children whether they knew anything or not. It would be his way of gaining a measure of revenge over Yasef. The Syrian didn't want Avi to know how terrified he was. He put his hand on top of Avi's. "You're a good man, but you worry too much. I'll be okay."

The look in Yasef's eyes told Avi he would never convince the Syrian to change his mind.

On Hashemi Street, near the Roman Amphitheatre, in downtown Amman, Yasef dropped the two Israelis in front of the Grand Hyatt hotel. Before he pulled away, he got out of the car and embraced Avi. "Good luck, my friend," Avi said.

Avi watched Yasef's car pull away. Then, in silence, he and Jack walked six blocks to the Israeli trade mission. The receptionist looked at him with surprise when he entered the office. "Is Nir in?" he asked.

"Well, well. Avi Sassoon returns." She smiled. "I thought you retired last year. Couldn't take the boredom, eh?"

"I'm still retired," he insisted.

Nir, a Mossad employee operating under a trade cover, was even more startled. "What are you doing here?" he said in a sharp, hostile tone.

"Is that any way to greet a former colleague?"

"Who is he?" Nir asked, pointing to Jack.

"A friend from Tel Aviv. We went hiking and got lost. We need a ride home."

Nir shook his head in disbelief. He motioned to Jack. "You wait here. The girls will get you something to drink." Then Nir led Avi into a small conference room and pushed the door shut. "I thought you were selling weapons."

Relieved that he had made it out of Syria, Avi was feeling good, and in no mood to take Nir's crap. "I am. Do you want to buy some?"

"Look, comedian. Our relationship with Jordan has finally recovered from your Aqaba fiasco last year. We're trying to keep things quiet with them right now. You want to tell me what you're up to?"

"Negative. It's a secret arms deal authorized by the Defense Ministry. I can't discuss it with you. You're not on the approved list." Avi could tell that his words were pissing Nir off in a major way, and he was enjoying every second. "Besides, it doesn't concern Jordan. So your skirts will stay dry, which is all you care about."

Nir scowled at Avi. "What do you want, then?"

"Transportation to Jerusalem on the next green car out."

Avi was assuming that the old arrangement from last year was still in effect. Israel could move people from Amman to Jerusalem in an official car, the so-called "green car" that traveled across the Allenby Bridge with no papers required and no questions asked. Jordan could do the same from Jerusalem back to Amman. His assumption was right.

"Be back here in three hours," Nir said. "And don't make any trouble till then."

Avi looked at him scornfully. "You've got to be kidding. Me, make trouble?"

"Aqaba wasn't your finest hour."

"Mentioning my name to the Jordanian foreign minister wasn't yours."

The director of the State Security section at the Syrian intelligence agency knew that something was wrong as soon as he reached his office at seven in the morning, reviewed the reports from all of the agents, and learned that Hussein hadn't reported in since eleven last evening, when he had followed two Italians to the Abu café outside of town.

He dispatched two agents to the café, where the owner insisted he had never seen Hussein. In less than an hour they found the agent's car and his dead body, where Jack had left them close to the café.

When they reported that to headquarters, they learned that the Italians never returned to their hotel last night. A clear picture was emerging: Whoever had met the Italians in the café must have killed Hussein. Then they escaped.

That led to a second visit to the café owner. This time they showed him a photograph of one of the Italians, which had been made from the video taken on their arrival at Damascus airport. The picture of the other one was too blurred to be of use.

They threatened to haul the proprietor of the café down to headquarters unless he told them everything he knew. "We'll work on your good leg until you talk, or until it goes the way of the other one. Think about it . . . with one good leg you can still have a life in this country. Missing two legs you become a pathetic beggar."

Quite apart from the threats, the proprietor didn't think he'd done anything wrong. Yasef was a member of their agency. Yasef always insisted that his meetings were government business. The café owner looked at the picture of Avi and said, "He's the man who entered with Yasef. Another one came in later, but I didn't get a good enough look to identify him." The owner decided to omit the payments Yasef made to him. Besides, they never asked about money. Once they heard about Yasef, they were in a hurry to get to Yasef's house.

That was where they were, sitting in his living room, pointing guns at his petrified wife and his three wailing daughters, when Yasef called.

He was on his cell phone in a restaurant near Izra'a, a small town on the Syrian side of the border, where he had stopped for coffee to stay awake. His wife answered the phone on the second ring, which surprised Yasef. Usually it took four or five.

"Are you all right?" he asked.

The two State Security men had written down on a piece of paper the speech his wife should give if Yasef called. Ten different times they had made her practice it to make sure she got it right. They wanted Yasef to come home so they could capture him and find out who the Italians were and what they were doing in Syria. The instant the phone rang one agent herded the wailing daughters into another room and silenced them.

Yasef's wife intended to give the speech exactly as they wanted. Truly she did. She began in a voice that sounded natural. "Where are you? When will you . . ." The agent was gripping his gun hard, pointing it at her face with his finger on the trigger. The fear became too much for her. She couldn't go on.

When the agent pressed the hard, cold steel of the barrel of the .45 against her forehead, trying to intimidate her into continuing, the phone fell out of her hand. She began crying and moaning. The agent slammed the phone down, then pistol-whipped her across the face, breaking her nose and jaw. "You stupid cow," he shouted.

In the restaurant, Yasef held the dead phone in his hand for several minutes. He had no doubt that State Security was in his house. Even the words he had heard were ones his wife would never have used with him. *Those people are so clumsy and witless,* he thought with contempt.

Yasef looked down into the muddy brown cup of Turkish coffee and weighed his options. Saving his own life was no longer possible. By now they were aware that his wife and daughters knew nothing. If he went back and they captured him, State Security would make him watch his wife and children being tortured. They would suffer unimaginable horrors, and eventually he'd break. But if he didn't go back, there was a chance that they'd let his wife and children live.

He removed the tissue from his pocket. Without hesitation he put one cyanide capsule in his mouth, washed it down with coffee, and followed the process with the second one. He had no regrets. He had done what he could to remove those monsters from control of his country.

Robert McCallister was walking slowly along a stone path under a blue sky on a beautiful spring day as he evaluated his situation. He was being held prisoner in a large villa surrounded by a twelve-foot-high stone wall. It was comfortable inside, with finely made furnishings that were now frayed and tattered. His guess was that at one time it had been the summer residence of a wealthy man. No one was living there, at least not now. He was alone except for the servants who cleaned the house and cooked for him. It was good food—meats, fish, vegetables, and fruits. As much as he wanted.

There were armed soldiers, of course, each one carrying an AK-47. They rotated in shifts, but two of them watched him twenty-four hours a day: when he walked outside, when he ate, when he slept, even when he showered. Unwilling to give him a razor, they insisted on having a man shave him each morning. For recreation they permitted him to jog in the morning and to walk around in the afternoon, but always on the grounds inside the walls. They offered him books to read: novels in English by Mark Twain and Charles Dickens.

He didn't know where he was. The soldiers' uniforms were plain dark brown without any insignia or other identification. They looked like Arabs, but when he tried to talk to them in the few words of Arabic he knew, they refused to respond. From being outside in the air, he discerned that he was at a reasonably high altitude, but not above the tree line. The scent of fresh flowers of spring drifted over the top of the wall. Tall trees in bloom were visible.

Often he thought of escaping, but so far he hadn't been

able to come up with an idea for doing that. *Before long you'll find a way,* he reassured himself.

Everyone addressed him politely, as if he were a guest in the villa. Each morning they gave him clean clothes to wear—a shirt and casual slacks with the labels cut off, precisely in his size. Whoever was managing his imprisonment was intelligent and meticulous. They left nothing to chance.

He walked slowly along the path, studying the wall on all sides. There had to be a weak spot. Something he could exploit to escape.

From the front door of the villa a man was calling him in English: "Lieutenant McCallister, please come here."

He glanced at one of the soldiers, who motioned with his AK-47, signaling Robert to move back inside. He turned and headed that way.

The living room had been converted into a photographer's studio. A soldier he had never seen before asked him to sit in a comfortable leather chair that faced the lens of a camera. One soldier put a sign around his neck with large letters that said LT. ROBERT MCCALLISTER. Another one handed him a copy of the *International Herald Tribune* and asked him to hold it in front of his body. As Robert moved the paper around in his hands, he got a quick glance at the date, March 24. That had to be today's paper, today's date, he guessed.

"Please smile," a man's voice called in English from behind the camera. Robert couldn't see the photographer's face. He kept his lips pressed together on general principle, but no one seemed to mind. The photographer snapped away. Robert didn't know why they were taking the pictures, but he realized what they would portray: Robert McCallister fit and healthy. What the viewer would never see was the anguish and misery he was feeling inside. The conviction that was growing stronger with each passing day that he would never get out of this alive.

Think positive, he told himself. *The photographs must mean that they're using you in some type of blackmail scheme. So if Father antes up enough money, which he will, then I go free.*

As he walked back outside after the photography session, gray clouds were moving in that matched his mood. He realized this couldn't be a simple effort to extort money from his father. It had to be far more complex—an attempt at political blackmail. The price for releasing him had to be an agreement by the United States to take some action so repugnant to President Kendall that the president would never do it, regardless of who Robert's father was.

He knew from a class at the Air Force Academy how these things went. There would be endless discussions around the clock in Washington. Memos outlining options would be drafted, revised, and revised some more before they made their way to the White House. There would be incessant hand wringing at the Pentagon and the State Department. But at the end of the day President Kendall would decide not to submit to blackmail.

Robert wouldn't blame the president. In fact, he would be upset if the president made any other decision, even though his own life was on the line.

During those four years at the Academy, he had become imbued with the concept that there were times when people had to die for their country to preserve America's freedom. If this was that type of situation, then Lt. Robert McCallister was willing to die. He didn't want the price for his release to be a diminution in America's freedom.

That didn't mean he would go quietly. He intended to redouble his efforts to find some way to escape.

"Don't get in that car," Jack said as Avi reached for the door of the armor-plated black sedan that was scheduled to make the next run from Amman to Jerusalem.

Avi quickly moved away. Instinctively he thought that he would be activating a bomb if he opened the door. "What's wrong?" he asked Jack, sounding alarmed.

Jack pulled Avi off to the side to talk, while the driver of the limo looked at them irritably. "Going to Jerusalem's stupid," Jack said.

"We have to brief Moshe."

"That's why it's stupid. We're making progress now. If we tell Moshe, we run the risk that he decides to call Joyner at the CIA. Even if the Americans don't blow the whistle, he'll yank it away from us and use his own full-time people."

Avi nodded.

"Besides," Jack continued, "when I met with Moshe in Jerusalem before I contacted you, he told me that he couldn't be involved. Well, it's our baby. Now that we're getting somewhere, I don't want to lose it."

Avi liked working with Jack. He was not only sharp, but he shared Avi's independent streak. "So we go to Paris," Avi said, "because that's where Nadim is, and he has the plan for the American pilot in his head."

Hearing the word *Paris,* Jack remembered Monique's e-mail he had received in Israel the day of Sam's sudden visit, and he cringed.

The driver trudged over. "Look, Avi," he said, "I'm on a tight schedule."

Avi had no intention of letting word get back to Moshe that he and Jack were flying to Paris. "Then go."

"What will you do?"

"Drop down to Aqaba for a swim. They love me there."

The driver burst out laughing. "You're a funny guy."

"You'd better take off before Nir blows a gasket. Don't worry about us."

Once the limo pulled away, Jack said to Avi, "Let's walk. I have to tell you something." They were in an upscale commercial area of Amman near shops and restaurants. Jack looked around nervously. "I have a problem with Paris right now. The SDECE may be looking for me. You might have to go without me."

That stopped Avi in his tracks. "What happened?"

Jack described the e-mail Monique had sent about Daniel Moreau's visit to his office.

"You think they suspect you in Khalifa's death?"

Jack shrugged. "I don't think the locals I used in Marseilles know enough to help Moreau tie it back to me, but I can't be positive." He shrugged. "Moreau may still be trying to build a case against me for Osirak. I've learned from friends in Paris that Osirak's been eating him up inside for years. He won't let go of it. He may have caught up with Francoise in Montreal. So you don't want me with you in Paris right now. I could be a real liability."

Avi mulled over what Jack had said. "Does Moshe know about the Moreau visit?"

Jack shook his head. "You're the first person I've mentioned it to."

"What do you think?" Avi asked. "You'll be the one at risk. Do you want to take the chance?"

Jack began thinking aloud. "The boys from the SDECE play rough, but they're also loners. They rarely coordinate with the local gendarmes or with the authorities in other E.U. countries." He paused. "On the other hand, we have to assume that they'll have my name and a picture at passport control at airports. Maybe even posted at train stations."

"You might be able to get one more use out of the Angelli tire ID if you needed it."

"That's too risky. The picture on the Italian passport is still mine, and the Syrians may have forwarded our Italian names to the French. A better bet might be to fly to Brussels and drive down to Paris. The European border checkpoints are a thing of the past."

Avi evaluated what Jack had said. "You'd better avoid your office and apartment in Paris."

"That's what I was thinking. In Paris my official residence is behind my wine business in a building on Avenue de Messine. But I also have another place off Avenue Victor Hugo in the name of a dummy company in case I ever had to go underground."

Jack sounded sheepish. He felt defensive about owning a second costly apartment in Paris. He had bought it years ago with his share of the life-insurance money from his parents that he and Sam split before prices went out of sight.

"Would your secretary give you away?"

"I sent Monique off to Australia for a month's vacation when I heard about Moreau's visit. You can stay with me at the Victor Hugo pad."

Avi shook his head. "I don't want to impose. Besides, Koach, the arms manufacturer I work for, keeps a suite at the Hotel Pyrenees on the left bank. I can toss the wet towels on the bathroom floor. We'll use your place for our working headquarters."

"I'll make sure I've got lots of cold beer for you."

Avi laughed. "Sorry to disappoint you, but in France I drink Armagnac and smoke cigars."

"Lucky for you, I have plenty of both."

They took a cab to Queen Alia Airport in Amman. As they sat in a coffee shop waiting to board a plane to Athens, where they would connect to Brussels, Jack said to Avi, "How much do you know about Major General Nadim?"

"I never met the man, but I feel as if I know him well, he's been a nemesis of ours for so long. A couple years ago I asked our researchers and psychologists to do an indepth profile from all the information we've been able to gather."

"How can I get a copy?"

Avi leaned over the table, close to Jack. "Wait until we hit Paris. I have friends at our embassy there. One of them will pull it off the computer for me without getting any approvals."

"We have to act fast," Jack said. "Nadim has to be worried that Washington could begin a massive bombing, or take some other action in Turkey or Syria if they know he's moved the pilot. So we have to assume that he'll probably make his move in a matter of days."

Chapter 14

"Where is Jack Cole?" Daniel Moreau demanded of George, the building manger, who lived on the ground floor of the Avenue de Messine building that housed the office for Jack's wine business as well as his official residence. They were standing in the entrance to the building.

George stared hard at Moreau, his face registering defiance. "How the hell should I know? He doesn't report to me."

"Is he in Israel with all the other *Jews?*" He pronounced the word with contempt.

"I'm not his travel agent," George fired back.

Moreau, who had arrived with two agents of SDECE and flashed his ID, had expected that George wouldn't be intimidated. Before coming he had run a background check on the man. George would be eighty-five next month. Active in the resistance and captured by the Gestapo, he never cracked under torture, even after losing an arm. After the war he had worked as a real estate agent until the company had retired him, and then as a building manager. Since the Germans hadn't broken him as a young man, Moreau didn't expect to coerce him into talking now. But Moreau couldn't resist making one more try. "Jack Cole's a spy for the Israelis," he said sharply. "If I think you're concealing information, I can lock you up until you talk. You won't have the right to a lawyer or anything else."

George looked indignant. "Listen, Inspector, or whatever the hell you are. As far as I know, Jack Cole's an American in the wine business. I don't know anything about spying."

"I have proof that you're lying."

George held out his hand and locked eyes with Moreau. "Then arrest me."

Moreau knew there was no point in doing that. "What about his secretary, Monique? I met her the last time I was here. Is she upstairs?"

"I haven't seen her in days."

"How convenient," Moreau said sarcastically. He reached into his pocket and removed a small notebook and pen from his pocket.

"What about other employees of Cole? Where are they?"

George shrugged. "You'll have to ask Jack Cole."

Moreau knew he was banging his head against a wall. "Give me the key to his apartment," he said angrily.

"I don't remember seeing a search warrant. Show me one."

Moreau pointed to one of his men, who was eagerly brandishing a crowbar. "You're looking at it."

George had no doubt that this bastard was going into Jack Cole's office and apartment whether George gave him a key or not. There was no point letting him break down the door. George went inside to his desk and returned with a key. "I'll walk up and let you in."

"Wrong. You give me the key. You'll stay down here with him." Moreau nodded to the other man.

Reluctantly George handed over the key. "He has the fourth floor." George mumbled under his breath while Moreau and the man with the crowbar went into the lift.

From his prior visit, Moreau knew that the front of the apartment was Jack's office, where Monique and Jack had separate rooms. Slowly and systematically Moreau looked through every drawer and file cabinet in those two rooms, searching for anything related to Jack's activities for the Mossad. To his dismay all he found were papers related to the wine business. As he looked through each drawer and came up empty, he cursed and dumped the contents on the floor.

Moreau took the computer hard drive and all the disks from both computers, Jack's and his secretary's. He shoved them into his briefcase. Then he turned to his assistant with the crowbar. "Do your work."

As Moreau moved into Jack's living quarters, the young man used the crowbar to decimate the green leather top on Jack's Louis XIV desk. Then he smashed one end through the screens of the two computers. He turned over file cabinets.

Meantime, Moreau searched Jack's living quarters in the back. When he failed to find a single inflammatory piece of paper, he called for his associate. This time the young man cut Jack's suits and scattered them across the floor of the apartment. A glass lamp was smashed. Tables were turned over. The mattress was slit open.

"Fucking Jews," Moreau cursed in frustration as his assistant finished the job.

An hour later Moreau entered the office of the director of the SDECE to report what had happened in Montreal. He decided to omit his pointless search of Jack's office and apartment.

As Moreau spoke, he watched the director's expression turn from curiosity to disbelief and finally disdain.

"You idiot," the director railed with scorn. "How could you have let Francoise jump off that balcony?"

Moreau was livid. His chest muscles tightened. He didn't like being chewed out as if he were a schoolboy by anyone, particularly by the director. "It was a mistake. I told you that. Obviously I shouldn't have let her out of my sight."

"It wasn't a mistake," the director screamed. "It was a total fuckup. Your brain froze on you. Now we've lost our only witness."

Moreau sat in front of the director's desk, trying to keep his anger in check. He was the one who had decided to reopen the Osirak investigation after the recent death of Khalifa persuaded him that the Mossad was operating again on French soil. He was the one who had painstakingly read and reread every transcript from Jean Pierre's interrogation and then combed Paris directories from 1981 for actresses, which was all that Jean Pierre said about the woman he slept with, until he found Francoise Colbert.

Now Moreau began silently to count. If the director's tirade didn't stop by the time he reached twenty, he would turn in his badge and gun and seek a job in industry as a private security chief in some big company, where he'd make a lot more money.

Sixteen, seventeen, eighteen . . .

The director stopped. "I'm sorry," he said. "It's more than losing our only witness. I hate the idea of the Israelis operating freely on French soil. The Jews should stay in their own country, where they belong. All of them. Let them fight their battles with the Arabs somewhere else."

"I couldn't agree more," Moreau said.

"All right. Let's get down to business."

"How certain are you that this Jack Cole, with an American passport, is operating as a Mossad agent?"

Moreau had explained this to the director before he had gone to Montreal. Wasn't the asshole paying attention? He hated wasting time repeating it again. "In Jean Pierre's interrogation, all he said about the man who recruited him was that he was in the wine business. Someone who spoke French with what he thought was an American accent. Before I went to Montreal I searched every trade list of people in the wine business at the time. Jack Cole is not only the best candidate; he's the only one. Is that clear enough?"

"But now you're back to square one."

"Not quite. I've been busy since I got back."

The director leaned forward in his chair and put his elbows on the desk with anticipation. "Really, what do you have now?"

"Remember the explosion of Khalifa's car in Marseilles?"

The director's face lit up. "Yeah."

"I checked flight manifests in and out of Marseilles around the time. Jack Cole flew down from Paris a week before the incident. He returned home hours after it happened."

"That's pretty good work," the director said grudgingly. "Where do you go from here?"

"Back to Marseilles to try to find a witness who can testify against Jack Cole."

Chapter 15

Michael Hanley and Vladimir Perikov flew from Moscow to Volgograd on Volga Airlines in a plane scheduled to leave at 6:15 A.M., that took off four and a half hours late with no explanation. It was an old Russian plane, a discard from Aeroflot, that was filled to capacity. They separated to avoid having someone who recognized the famous physicist report that he was traveling with an American.

Perikov was in the second row during the choppy flight, while Michael was in the rear of the plane, sandwiched in a narrow seat between a wizened old Russian man with garlicky breath who kept taking slugs from a bottle of vodka, and a woman with two small, red-faced, runny-nosed children. They cried the whole way, while she alternated between slapping them and feeding them bread smeared with a greasy coating that looked to Michael as if it were a combination of butter and lard.

Midway through the flight the plane, buffeted by strong winds, lurched and dropped without any warning through several thousand feet before the pilot regained control. Everyone in the plane was terrified. Some gasped. Others cried out in panic. Was this it? The end?

The pilot managed to get the tired old plane under control. At the airport they rented separate cars. Anyone watching them would have no idea they were together. Driving through Volgograd, Michael looked up at the sword-wielding statue of Mother Russia, seventy-two meters tall, that dominated the landscape, a memorial to those who died in the battle of Stalingrad, one of the most decisive of the Great Patriotic War, where the Germans lost 350,000 soldiers. But Stalin fell out of favor, and, like many other places in Russia, the city had been renamed.

For nearly an hour Michael followed Perikov along a winding road that skirted the Volga River. Dodging the huge potholes was a challenge. It was late afternoon, though still daylight, when they reached the remains of what had been a plant to manufacture farm machinery, operated by the government during the Communist regime, on the edge of a small factory town. The company had been privatized with the advent of capitalism. It operated three years in that mode until corruption and theft forced it into bankruptcy, to the chagrin of the American investment bank that had put up millions to back the purchasers in the expectation of reaping a huge windfall from the new Russia. The last tractor had been made four years ago. Since then the plant sat rotting and decaying at one end of the town, whose inhabitants suddenly found themselves without their main source of employment. Not surprisingly, the sale of vodka became the town's leading business, while the more ambitious young people drifted away to larger cities in the north.

A light rain, a damp, dreary mist, was falling from a foggy sky when Perikov came to a stop at what had been the front entrance to the factory. The lock on the gate of a rusty chain-link fence had been broken months ago by thieves who ransacked the old plant for items that had value on the open market. While Perikov got out and kicked open the gate, Michael looked around. The fence had numerous holes that someone had made with wire cutters.

Back in his car Perikov turned right, passing through the

gate and into the plant grounds. Behind him Michael glanced in the rearview mirror to make certain no one was tailing them. Driving slowly on the road, which was slick with water and oil, he followed Perikov into the grounds of the deserted factory.

They drove past two cannibalized plant buildings to a brown wooden shed roughly the size of an airplane hangar. Michael recognized the Russian word for *warehouse* painted on the side in letters that had once been white, but were now a faded and peeling gray.

There was a single guard in front of the locked main entrance—an old Russian soldier who sat on a stack of pallets with a rifle on the ground leaning against the warehouse. He had a stubble of a gray beard, and the dark green coat that covered his uniform was stained with mud. To Michael, staring through the open car window, he seemed to be of some indeterminate age north of fifty. It wouldn't have surprised Michael if he had fought against Hitler in the battle for Stalingrad. Though he was facing the two cars that were parking close to him, he didn't react. His eyes had a dead, glazed look.

Michael got out of his car and stood next to it, while Perikov approached the soldier, carrying his briefcase. Straining his ears, Michael listened for any signs of life. All he heard was the cawing of a bird. He walked in the direction of the sounds, through mud laced with chemicals that created a sheen, while cursing his stupidity for not wearing a pair of heavy boots.

Twenty yards away, around the corner of the warehouse, he saw about a hundred drums of waste chemicals scattered about, rusty and leaking onto the ground. A bird had apparently landed on one of these drums. Its tiny legs sank into sticky goo from which it couldn't extricate itself.

Michael walked over and gently lifted the bird from the top of the drum. It made an effort to fly, feverishly beating its tiny wings for about ten yards until it collapsed and fell pitifully to the ground, landing on a rock. By the time Michael reached the bird, it was dead.

When he returned to the front of the warehouse, he saw Vladimir handing the guard a fistful of rubles and a quart of vodka, which he had been carrying in his briefcase. The old soldier stood up with an effort, extracted a ring of keys from his pocket, and unlocked the rusty padlock on the door to the warehouse.

Perikov waved to Michael to accompany him through the door, while the guard retreated to his seat on the pallets and unscrewed the top of the vodka bottle.

"What's his story?" Michael asked Perikov.

"Boris is his name. The government hired him about a year ago to guard the warehouse. They haven't paid his salary in four months, but they keep promising. I gave him one month's salary and a bottle of vodka. He doesn't care what we do in here or what we take."

Michael shook his head in disbelief. "You're not serious."

"Unfortunately, I am. Until a month ago, there were twelve soldiers assigned to this location, but right now he's it."

Michael was stunned. "My God, this can't be real. What happened to the others?"

"Someone came and paid them off to disappear."

"One of Suslov's people?"

"Probably. Anyhow, Boris was visiting his sister about twenty miles away at the time. Otherwise he'd have taken the money as well. Then there wouldn't be anyone here."

The warehouse was dark inside. Perikov groped around on the wall until he found a light switch.

"Holy shit," Michael blurted out once the lights came on. To his amazement and horror, he saw that the warehouse was filled with nuclear weapons and delivery systems. There were long-range and intermediate missiles, row after row, menacing-looking long black tubes. There were piles and piles of tactical nukes, short-range weapons such as torpedoes, depth charges, artillery shells, and mines.

Perikov wasn't surprised. He had known what they would find. He led Michael on a tour of the warehouse, pointing out in detail what was there. They had been brought here from several locations in the former USSR.

"I may never sleep again," Michael muttered under his breath.

"If you want to feel even worse, then I'll tell you that there was never any inventory prepared of what was placed in this building."

Michael stopped to rub his hand along a slick black warhead. "Which means that some items could already have disappeared, or . . ." He was thinking aloud. "Dmitri Suslov could come here and easily remove any of these toys he arranged to sell."

Perikov snorted. "Sounds to me like you don't have a lot of respect for Boris."

"That isn't funny."

"It wasn't meant to be."

They spent almost an hour inside the building. On a pad Perikov had in his briefcase, he made a list of the weapons he could identify. Michael followed along making his own copy, writing down the items Perikov called out and taking pictures with a small digital camera. He planned to report directly to Joyner as soon as he got back to Moscow and a secure phone at the American Embassy. Later he would transmit a report and the photographs.

When they were finished, Perikov turned out the lights and they exited together. Neither of them was surprised by the sight that was awaiting them. Boris was lying on the ground passed out. The empty vodka bottle was next to one of his hands.

Perikov shut the door to the warehouse. He closed the

padlock, then dropped the keys next to Boris's body on the way to the car.

"Can you get someone on your staff down here?" Michael said to Perikov. "A man you trust who can pretend he's a tourist in Volgograd? Have him keep his eye on this building and let you know if anything moves out of here."

"I'll take care of it. . . . You figure that Suslov's next shipment might be coming out of this warehouse?"

Michael thought about what Irina had told him at the Inn. "I know it, and I sure as hell had better find a way to stop that from happening."

Chapter 16

Jack finished reading the Mossad file on Major General Nadim and closed his eyes. From the other side of the living room in Jack's Paris apartment with its high ceilings and huge windows, which opened to the narrow street below, Avi sipped a glass of Jack's 1945 Chateau de Laubade and puffed on a Partagas from Jack's humidor.

"Well, what do you think?" Avi asked. It was the ultimate rhetorical question.

Jack looked down at the photo of Nadim that Avi had clipped to the inside cover of the folder. "He's a piece of work. Kills people by day. A womanizer and a high liver at night. Charming."

"That's an understatement. Now that you've read the profile, does that put our visit to Syria in perspective?"

"Like the target on a rifle scope."

"The question is, How do we get close to Nadim?"

Jack looked down into the glass of Armagnac on the table in front of him. "There's the answer," he said, pointing to the glass.

"Sorry. That's a little too cryptic for me."

"The profile says he's a connoisseur of wine; that he's a regular at the top Paris restaurants. Before all of this arose I accepted an invitation for tomorrow evening to a dinner with a vertical tasting of Latour that the owner of the chateau is giving at L'Ambroise. It's a tough ticket to get."

Avi puffed on his cigar, wondering where Jack was going with this.

"Anyhow, I'm good friends with Hubert, the manager of the château. Suppose he was willing to send an invitation to Nadim, claiming he had a last-minute cancellation?"

Between puffs, Avi said, "Then what?"

"At the dinner I'll be able to approach Nadim casually. I'll introduce myself as an American. Maybe he'll think that I'm with the CIA, and the wine business is a cover. Who knows where it'll lead, but it may be a way for me to get started with Nadim."

Avi saw the intensity in Jack's face. "Okay, let's give it a try."

Jack was on a roll. "I'll not only get an invitation for Nadim, but I'll fix it so he can bring a guest. Getting close to the woman with Nadim may be another way of moving up on him."

Jack's enthusiasm had lit a fire under Avi. "While you're doing that, I'll go see Yudi, one of Moshe's people working out of the embassy in Paris. He owes me a favor. I'll ask him to begin monitoring airplane reservations and manifests in and out of Paris. If our friend Nadim decides to take any sudden trips, I want to know about it."

"What are you looking for?"

Avi shrugged. "I have no idea, but I'll know it when I see it."

"You're very good at this intelligence work," Jack said in admiration.

"Thanks."

"So what happened with you and Moshe last year, if you don't mind my asking?"

Avi put the cigar down in an ashtray and drained the rest

of the amber liquid in his glass. "I'm happy to talk about it. He forced me out."

"Because of Aqaba."

Avi nodded. "It was a total fuckup. We had good info, or so we thought, that the *San Remo* sitting in the Jordanian port had arms for Hamas terrorists. We were told, also on supposed good info, that the Jordanian government preferred to have us destroy the ship rather than confiscate the arms and have a public brouhaha. Moshe told me to do the job, but it was to be off the books . . . in case it went south on us."

Jack remembered Moshe using the same expression when he authorized Jack to undertake the Khalifa assassination.

Avi continued. "So I blew up the *San Remo*. When it turned out to be loaded with nothing but steel for construction, the Jordanians screamed bloody murder. To placate the prime minister and the public, Moshe made it look like I was flying solo. I took the hit. Firing me was what it took to placate the Jordanians and our own politicians. Nice, isn't it?"

Jack was appalled. "That stinks."

Avi was seething as he thought about the session with Moshe when the director had told him he'd have to clean out his desk. "I know it's a part of the business, but I don't have to like it. I also don't like the double standard Moshe has applied over the years."

Jack had no idea what Avi was talking about. "What double standard?"

"The three girls he recruited, Leora, Yael, and Sagit, could get away with anything. Falling in love with Americans. Going to bed with targets. Getting pregnant. And he always forgave them. For the rest of us, bam, one mistake and you're out." Avi made no effort to conceal the bitterness in his voice.

*   *   *

The next morning Jack made the call to Hubert, told the Frenchman what he wanted, and held his breath.

"Impossible," Hubert said with the tone of finality that French people use when they don't want to do something that they are perfectly able to do. "The invitation list has been set for weeks. L'Ambroise can't hold one more person. It's quite impossible." He paused and cursed under his breath. "This is what you call me on my cell phone about in the middle of breakfast?"

Jack wasn't deterred. "If you're worried about space at the restaurant, I'll call Monsieur Pierre, the sommelier. He and I are good friends."

"I am in charge of the invitations," Hubert said, making clear it was his decision alone.

"Have I ever asked you for a favor before?" Jack was talking in the most plaintive French he could manage. He visualized the roly-poly Hubert next to the breakfast table in his hotel suite in the Crillon with a huge basket of pastries in front of him, butter and orange marmalade lavishly spread on a croissant ready to be savored. "When you told me I had to take a full quantity of the 'eighty-four to get the 'eighty-five, did I argue? In fact, every time you have a less than perfect year, I take a full supply."

Hubert chuckled. "Ah, you Americans. You're always trouble. Give me a name and address. I'll have an invitation delivered."

There was one more hurdle. Hubert didn't like foreigners—any foreigners—although he was willing to tolerate some Americans, like Jack Cole, and some Brits who had big money to buy his wines. Jack waded in slowly. "He's an important diplomat. A connoisseur of wine and food."

"Give me a name and address."

"Major General Nadim, Syrian Embassy, rue Vaneau in the Seventh."

"What, an Arab? I like the fucking Arabs about as much as the Jews."

"Your tact is admirable," Jack said sarcastically.

"Do you want to tell me why you're trying to suck up to this Arab?"

It was a tough question for Jack to answer without arousing suspicion. "We've been friends a long time, you and I, Hubert. I'm asking you to do it as a favor for me, no questions asked."

Jack heard a deep sigh of resignation at the other end of the phone that signaled Hubert's capitulation.

"Okay," the Frenchman finally said. "In return, you'd better come up with two tickets at center court for the men's finals in the French Open."

"They're yours. I'll even toss in the women's as well."

"No, make it the men's semis. The good-looking women never make it to the finals these days. If that Russian dish gets there, I'll be after you for the women's then, just to look at her. Otherwise it's the men's semis and finals."

Jack laughed. "It's a deal. And please, Nadim can't know I am responsible for the invitation."

"As you wish. Play whatever games you care to. That's not my affair."

Jack was relieved. "I can't thank you enough. I'm sure that Nadim and his guest will enjoy the tasting."

"Guest?" Hubert said indignantly. "I agreed to invite one person. Not two."

"But surely you wouldn't want a sophisticated gentleman coming to a savvy party like this alone?"

"This had better be the last time you ever want anything like this from me."

"Thank you," Jack said quickly, hanging up the phone before Hubert could change his mind. He looked forward to telling Avi.

Not right away, though. There was something he had to do first.

Margaret Joyner was finishing up dinner with the vice president in the director's dining room at CIA headquarters when her secretary, Carol, entered with a note that read, *Michael Hanley is calling from Moscow. He says it's quite important. Are you available?*

Joyner turned to Mary Beth. "Let's go upstairs. You know about this mission. If you have time, I want you to hear what he has to say."

"Nothing is more important."

Joyner put the call on a speakerphone.

"I'm on a secure phone in the Moscow embassy," Michael said.

"Okay. Go ahead. I have the vice president with me."

That rocked Michael back on his heels. Talking with Joyner herself was impressive. Adding Mrs. Reynolds to the conversation was almost too much for the young man. He began in a halting voice, intimidated by the positions of the two powerful women at the other end of the phone. "You told me to report any major developments directly to you."

"Absolutely. I want to know."

He gulped hard. "I've got the worst possible news."

"Suslov's getting ready to make another sale."

"That's how it looks."

He explained that he had learned about Suslov's trip to Volgograd without mentioning Irina as the source of the information. Then he described his visit to the warehouse with Perikov. "Looking at all those weapons and imagining what they can do is mind numbing. I'm planning to write up a detailed report on what we saw. I'm afraid it won't do the scene justice. I'll also send along photographs to you in the diplomatic pouch. But I figured you wouldn't want to wait."

"You were exactly right. What makes you think Suslov is

planning to make a sale of some of the weapons in this warehouse?" Joyner said.

"He's following the same MO he did in the other two transactions. First he gets rid of all the soldiers regularly on guard with hefty bribes. My guess is that within a week he'll be moving arms out of this Volgograd location."

Joyner's mind was racing to come up with a plan to deal with the situation. "I need you to stay in Moscow and keep tabs on Suslov. Can you send one of our people down to Volgograd to watch that place around the clock?"

"Even better. Perikov agreed to send somebody. Whoever he sends won't stand out. He'll let me know when he hears something."

"Good. If anything starts moving from that location, I want to know immediately. You have all my numbers. I'll wire it on this end so President Kendall will immediately call the Russian president once we catch Suslov in the act. You okay with all of that?"

"Absolutely."

"And watch your step with Irina, Michael."

"Yes, ma'am. I will."

When Joyner hung up the phone, she looked at Reynolds. "I wonder who Suslov's customer is this time."

The vice president thought about it. "I hope it's not Al Qaeda or another terrorist organization." Her eyes closed as she thought about that scenario. "The kind of damage they could do is too awful to contemplate."

"Regardless, you and I need time with Kendall to tell him what's going on in Moscow."

"It'll be tough. He's consumed by McCallister and the crisis with Turkey. There are only five more days left on our ten-day ultimatum. Kendall's stupidly painted himself into a corner. He says he'll do something when the ten days are up, but at this point, my guess is that he doesn't have the vaguest idea of what he wants to do."

Joyner wasn't deterred. "I don't care. This is more important than the life of one pilot. It's no exaggeration to say that millions of lives are at stake. If you're right that a terrorist organization is Suslov's customer, those nuclear weapons could be used against the United States. I'll find a way to get in and see Kendall. You want to come?"

Thoughtfully, Reynolds leaned her head on her hand and pondered the issue. "My presence might be a liability. You're better to do this meeting without me. I can tell that Kendall resents me, and I don't want him to think there's a cabal of women in his administration. Besides, Michael Hanley is your project, and you're not looking for a decision. It's just informational. You don't want Kendall to go to the Russian president yet. Do you?"

Joyner shook her head. "We have to catch Suslov red-handed before Kendall can call Drozny. That means we have to wait for Suslov to fall into the trap and start moving those arms."

Joyner's mind was focusing on another troubling scenario. "Suppose we get evidence that Suslov's moving the arms and Drozny won't act? Would Kendall be willing to send in American troops to block the operation?"

"You mean American troops on Russian soil?"

Joyner nodded.

Mary Beth shook her head. "It would be the right thing to do, but we'll have an uphill battle with Kendall on that one."

Everything had suddenly gotten more complicated, Moshe concluded. He sat at his desk and studied the bizarre message he had received from a Mossad agent in eastern Turkey.

"Major General Nadim of Syria was in Van a couple of days ago meeting with General Kemal. Reliable sources report that Nadim was trying to enlist Kemal's support for a project with Syria that somehow involves the downed American pilot, Robert McCallister."

The spy hadn't learned any of the details. Even this cryptic message was enough to alarm Moshe. If Syria was collaborating on something with Kemal, anything, it had to have an adverse impact on Israel. Robert McCallister's fate was no longer solely an American issue.

Jack took a cab to No. 65 Avenue de Messine in the eighth *arrondissement*. It was a gray stone five-story structure, built to last for ages. Jack had bought the entire fourth floor with a personal loan from Moshe when he started his wine business.

By making this visit, Jack realized he was taking a chance, but he had to know how serious Moreau was. The risk was manageable, he decided. The uncertainty unacceptable.

Jack knew there was no point trying to avoid George, who somehow observed every single person who entered and left the building.

Inside the front entrance, Jack paused to knock on George's door. It was unnecessary. The old gray-haired man had spotted him on the street.

"Aha. You're back. . . . I'm so sorry." George sounded ashamed, even shattered. "Maybe I was wrong to give them the key, but I thought they'd only break the lock, and—"

Jack raised his hand to cut George off. "Whoa . . . what happened?"

"Daniel Moreau from the SDECE came with two others. Real bastards, all of them."

"What did you tell them?"

"Not a thing." George looked irate. "They weren't going to intimidate me. I hate those people. They're no different from their fathers who participated in the Vichy government. When the war was over, they all pretended they had been in the resistance."

One reason Jack liked living in France was because there were lots of decent people like George, free spirits who resented authority and treasured their independence. "What happened then?" Jack asked.

"Moreau and one of his men went into your apartment."

"Did he have a court order to search it?"

"Of course not, but he was going in one way or the other." George looked down at his feet. "I could have called the police, but they always defer to those people."

Jack gave him the reassurance he was looking for. "You did the right thing. Did you go upstairs with Moreau?"

"They kept me down here. They were up there about an hour. Moreau had a briefcase. I couldn't tell if he took stuff away with him. After they left I went up there." He paused and let out his breath in a whistling sound. "They made a mess . . . a huge mess."

"Thanks for telling me," Jack said as he reached into his pocket. "Can I offer you something for your trouble?"

George shook his head. "Keep your money. I do what I do because I want to. I didn't like this man Moreau. He's a devil. As far as I know, you never came back to Paris."

Jack didn't take the lift. He climbed the stairs slowly, thinking about his conversation with George. Daniel Moreau was closing in on him. He'd have to be careful.

A blind fury gripped Jack when he opened the door and looked around. George's expression, *They made a mess*, was one of the great understatements of all time for the destruction that he saw.

"Merde!" Jack cried out.

His blood was boiling as he walked into the apartment in the back. While Jack was exploding with rage, one fact mollified him: Moreau hadn't found any useful evidence. He couldn't have. Jack had been meticulous to avoid leaving anything behind. Once Moreau realized it wasn't here, the Frenchman had become vindictive. Jack realized that all of this had been in frustration at Moreau's failure to find anything.

Jack returned to the office and stood in front of the floor-to-ceiling window that faced Avenue de Messine below with its honking horns and heavy traffic. It had started to rain, a light spring shower. As Jack watched pedestrians scrambling for cover, he considered his options.

He realized now that his situation in Paris was more precarious than he had imagined. Moreau was on a vendetta.

If Moreau ever caught him, Jack would wind up in a harsh French jail for a very long time. Whether Moreau had a case or not would be immaterial. Espionage would be the charge. There would be no way for Jack to escape, no way to get a public trial.

One choice was to get the hell out of France immediately. That was tempting. The Israeli government would never extradite him. On the other hand, what he was doing with Avi was vital for the country, and he was the one who had the entrée to Nadim. The whole McCallister business was on a short time fuse. That much was clear. Quite apart from Daniel Moreau, he and Avi were racing against the clock to find out what Nadim had planned before he succeeded or before the Americans began a military operation. Either way, it would all be over in a couple of days.

Jack decided to tough it out and hope Moreau didn't find him. What he had going for him was that Paris was a huge city. Also the SDECE didn't like to involve the police. They did their own thing. He'd have to take his chances.

On the other hand, he couldn't be foolish either. Before the Khalifa operation, Moshe had given him the name of a man to see in Paris if he needed to make a hasty exit from the country. Denis was an artist working in the French motion picture industry who could change a person's appearance and give him a new passport to match in a couple of hours. That was what he needed right now.

Chapter 17

Major General Nadim sat at his desk in the Syrian embassy in Paris and agonized. He should have been in a good mood. Half an hour ago the photographs of Lieutenant McCallister holding a copy of the *Herald Tribune* had arrived in the diplomatic pouch from Damascus in a sealed brown envelope marked PERSONAL AND CONFIDENTIAL—TO BE OPENED ONLY BY MAJOR GENERAL NADIM.

The pictures were clear. No one could challenge their authenticity. No one could reject the assertion that Nadim's government had possession of Lt. Robert McCallister and that the American pilot was healthy enough to be the pawn in the scheme Nadim had developed.

Nadim moved the photos around on the polished wooden surface, trying to decide which ones to use. He finally concluded that it didn't matter. They were all equally good.

No, the pictures of the American pilot weren't troubling Nadim. It was the contents of the second brown envelope in the pouch that was also to be opened only by Nadim. Inside was a report of the incident at the Abu Café involving Yasef, Hussein, and the mysterious Italians.

A photograph of one of the men was included, taken at the Damascus airport on his entry into the country. The other one was too blurry to be of any use. "Crappy Russian technology," Nadim cursed. *Now that the Russians aren't our great benefactor any longer, we should get all of their products out of the country.*

Nadim studied the picture of the one so-called Italian. He had thin hair and a broken nose. Nadim felt as if he had seen the man sometime in the past, but he couldn't place the face. That troubled Nadim. When he was younger, he never failed to match a face and a name. Growing older was a curse. Even his sexual prowess was declining, he had to admit, but only to himself. At least that could be overcome with the new wonder drugs, but he wasn't ready for them. Still, it was good they would be there when they needed them. If you couldn't fuck, what was the point of living? For Nadim, there was one other point to life: at long last, to get even with the Israelis for the 1967 and 1973 wars.

Nadim looked through the rest of the items in the envelope: a copy of the demand by the Syrian government's foreign office to Rome for the immediate arrest and extradition of Angelli Tire Company executives named Mario Leonardo and Paulo Pegnataro. There was a response by the Italian foreign minister: *We have discussed the matter with the Angelli Tire Company. They have informed us that they don't have employees with those names.*

So the men's passports and other identifying papers were false. Nadim wasn't surprised. It had all been done in a very sophisticated way. Even the items left in the men's hotel rooms had been carefully selected to be consistent with the story. An Italian novel. Articles from economic journals about the tire business. A brochure for the next year's season at La Scala.

There were only two intelligence agencies capable of doing that, which might have the inclination: the CIA and the Mossad. Nadim found one possibility more ominous than the other.

He had to assume that the timing wasn't coincidental.

Whoever had sent the men pretending to be the two Italians knew or suspected that Robert McCallister was in Syria. They had sent the phony Italians to find out where McCallister was in order to plan a rescue, or to find out what Nadim intended to do with the pilot.

All of that worried Nadim. What was good, however, was that the phony Italians had undoubtedly failed. Nadim was confident that Yasef didn't have either item of information. If Hussein had not followed the phony Italians and paid for it with his life, Yasef might have been able to obtain what they wanted. But Yasef was dead. From the statement of the guards along the Jordanian border, at least one of the phony Italians had crossed into Jordan. The other one could have been hiding in the car. Those guards were so incompetent. Even if the other one was still in Syria, the most he could do was find out where the pilot was being held. No one in Syria, even Ahmed, knew what Nadim had in mind for the pilot.

None of this should foil his plan, Nadim decided. He would view it as a good warning. He would have to be even more vigilant.

The intercom buzzed. "Your visitor is here," Nadim's secretary announced.

"Show him in."

Ali Hashim didn't simply walk into a room. The Iranian intelligence chief acted as if he owned the office and everyone inside, including Nadim. It wasn't merely that he was a large, powerfully built man with a bald head and a thick, bushy brown beard. It was how he carried himself. Notwithstanding his country's rule by clerics, Ali Hashim managed to find the money to shop at Turnball and Asser on Jermyn Street in London.

Nadim found the man's haughty arrogance unbearable, reflecting his country's view of itself in the region. Today Nadim had to endure it. What made it tolerable was his confidence that Hashim didn't like Nadim any more than Nadim liked the Iranian. Still, when Nadim had reached Hashim on the telephone in London, where he was conducting other business, and said, "I want to meet you about a matter of mutual benefit," the Iranian had agreed to stop in Paris on his way back to Tehran.

"Your words were enticing," Hashim said as he sat down on a chair facing Nadim. "What could you offer me that would be of mutual benefit?"

The implication to Nadim was infuriating. It was as if Hashim were dealing with an insect. What could a lowly Syrian offer one of Allah's select? Nadim stiffened. His eyes bore in on Hashim. "What do you most want from the Americans right now?"

Now the Iranian's eyes blazed with interest. Nadim knew that he had Hashim's attention. He should have suppressed the smile that was breaking out on his face, but he decided not to.

"Access to their advanced technology," Hashim responded immediately. "They've blocked us from obtaining their electronic and computer technology by a presidential order. Also other high-tech items. If we had those, we could modernize our economy. We have the money from oil. If we had the technology, we could become a real player in the global economy. Israel wouldn't be the only economic power at the crossroads between East and West." Hashim narrowed his eyes. "But why do you ask me this?" His tone was suspicious.

"Suppose that the American pilot shot down over Turkey were the son of an important—"

Hashim interrupted him. "I know he's Robert McCallister, and who his father is." Hashim detected the surprise on Nadim's face, and he sneered. "You think that you're the only one who does good intelligence work?"

Nadim didn't want to endanger his plan by goading

Hashim. He tried to retreat gracefully. "I didn't mean that. I simply wasn't aware that you knew."

"Well, anyhow, you were saying?"

"Suppose that you were able to get possession of Robert McCallister, and you could turn him over to the Americans. Would that permit you to obtain the technology you want?"

Hashim scoffed and shook his head. "Kendall would never submit to blackmail like that."

Nadim shifted in his chair. "Not blackmail. It would be a goodwill gesture on the part of your government. You would say that you obtained the pilot to help the Americans and defuse the situation. They're seeking a thaw in relations with your government. This would be a good way to begin. It could be subtly orchestrated so that you would obtain certain technology, but it would never be viewed as blackmail. There are ways of doing these things with Washington. You know that."

Intrigued by Nadim's words, Hashim wrinkled his broad forehead, thinking. "You don't need me. Let the Turks do this themselves."

"The Turkish government's not involved. Kemal was flying solo."

The comment evoked a smile from Hashim. "Why doesn't your government do the deal itself?" the Iranian asked suspiciously.

"Two reasons. First, the Americans don't respect us. They view us as a peanut of a country. Also, Washington's close relationship with the Israelis precludes them from doing anything that involves us without Israeli approval. You're different."

That made sense to Hashim. He nodded. "And the second reason?"

"You have money. To pull off my plan will take lots of it. Kemal obviously can't come up with it, and my government doesn't have that kind of hard, cold foreign currency."

Hashim looked distrustful. "If your plan's that good, let your president borrow it. There are plenty of people who would be willing to finance an operation like this. Yet you come running to me when you need money."

Nadim felt as if he had been slapped in the face. Hashim always made him feel like a poor relation. Did he dare trust his life to the Iranian? He decided that the benefits justified the risk. If he succeeded, the rewards would be great. "President Ahmed doesn't know," he said softly.

Hashim gave a wry smile and tapped his finger on the side of the chair. "Well, well. So you have personal ambitions."

"Don't we all?"

"You're living on the edge."

Nadim knew the Iranian was right. He tried lamely to smile. "Life in both of our countries is constantly on the edge. You and I could find ourselves in jail or worse at any time with no warning." Hashim nodded. "But if you convince your government to accept my plan," Nadim continued, "you will be a hero. You will be the one who obtained the American technology and other benefits."

Hashim raised his hand and pointed a thick finger at Nadim. "Only if it succeeds."

"Agreed. But it will succeed."

"Tell me what you have in mind. I'll decide for myself about the chances for success."

For the next twenty minutes, Nadim laid out his proposal in detail. Hashim's only reaction was a snort and two grunts. At the end, Nadim said, "Well, what do you think?" He was holding his breath.

"I don't like it," Hashim said coldly.

"Why not?"

"My government will refuse to pay money to you and to Kemal."

Nadim decided to try a different tack.

"That's a small part of the operation. If the plan succeeds, you will not only be receiving American technology, but we will be striking a mighty blow at Israel."

Hashim rose to leave. "Do it without us."

"But I want you to enjoy the fruits of this effort."

Hashim gave him a haughty smile. "I have a keen sense of the geography involved in the plan. Iran's participation is critical."

Nadim was trying to decide if the Iranian was merely bargaining in the manner of the souk, seeking to make the best deal he could, or whether he was really opposed to the concept. "We could come up with another alternative."

"With great difficulty . . . perhaps." Hashim said it in the arrogant manner of someone who knew he held a key card.

"At least take it back to your foreign minister in Tehran," Nadim said. "With what's at stake, let him decide."

"He'll laugh at me. I don't even have any proof that you hold the American pilot."

Nadim reached into one of the brown envelopes on his desk and removed a photograph of Robert McCallister. "Take it," he said. "That's your proof."

Hashim snatched the photograph from Nadim, studied it for a moment, then handed it back. "I can't risk being caught with this now. It would mean a death warrant for me." Hashim paused. "In the unlikely event the foreign minister is interested, I will need the photograph before we go to our president with your plan."

Nadim was worried that the Americans might find out where the pilot was and undertake some military action to rescue him before he could implement his plan. If that happened, it would all go up in smoke. "We don't have much time," Nadim said anxiously.

Hashim smiled. "I won't be rushed."

"Fine. I'll give you the photograph the next time we meet

about this. Call me when you're ready. I'll be there. Any time or place."

Hashim was walking toward the door. "I doubt very much there will be any more meetings on this subject. The foreign minister will throw me out of his office before I complete my presentation."

Nadim didn't respond. Inside he was thrilled. He was confident that he had hooked his fish. He attributed Hashim's negative words to his unwillingness to sound positive about something his government might not accept. Hashim would lose face with Nadim if that happened. And then there were the terms. If the Iranians agreed in principle, those rug merchants would insist on at least one round of haggling.

When Hashim left, Nadim told his secretary, "No interruptions," and he closed the door to his office. Time was short. He had to assume Hashim would bring his government around. The political benefits were too great for them, the costs too small in comparison. Nadim's plan was brilliant. Now he had to turn his attention to the next steps. Everything had to be plotted carefully. He began making notes on a pad. Later he would burn the page.

As he scribbled, he heard a gentle tapping on the door. "I told you no interruptions," he barked to his secretary.

She hesitated, trying to guess which way she would be more severely criticized—for disturbing him or for failing to alert him about the messenger. Knowing how deeply passionate he was about food and wine, she decided that the better course was to risk his wrath with the interruption. She opened the door a crack.

"A messenger's here from Château Latour," the cowering secretary said. "He has a note, and he needs an immediate reply."

At the name of the famous Bordeaux château, Nadim covered up the photographs with the morning *Le Monde* and held out his hand. The secretary breathed a deep sigh of relief. She had made the right decision.

Nadim ripped open the envelope and read the handwritten note. *We regret that through an oversight you were not invited to the vertical tasting of Château Latour this evening at 20:00 hours at L'Ambroise. You would do us honor by coming, and you may, of course, bring a guest.*

It was signed, *Hubert.*

Under any other circumstances Nadim would have eagerly accepted, though he didn't believe for an instant that there had been an oversight. They must have had a last-minute cancellation. That didn't bother Nadim. What did concern him was that he was so engrossed in planning the operation with the American pilot. Could he afford to take an evening off? Wanting to attend because it was a plum of an invitation, Nadim rationalized: Once he made his initial calls for the next moves about the pilot, there was little else he could do today.

Another thought popped into his mind: Layla. She was so heavily involved in buying, selling, and financing Bordeaux properties that she was now well connected in the area. There were rumors that Château Latour was considering a major expansion, and her bank was on the short list of possible lenders. With all of that, there was a good chance she might be there at the tasting. Her presence opened up new possibilities. That made the decision for Nadim.

He scribbled a note: *I'll be pleased to come with a guest.*

Then he handed it to his secretary. "Give this to the messenger."

When she was gone, Nadim moved aside the newspaper and glanced down at the photos of the American pilot again. He knew what the next step was for his plan. He picked up the phone to make the first call.

Chapter 18

The cab turned right and entered the Place de Vosges, in one of the oldest sections of Paris, close to the Bastille. *The trouble with Paris traffic,* Jack thought in the backseat, *is that it's totally unpredictable.* Generally, getting down here was a nightmare. This evening they zipped right along.

Jack, who wanted to arrive precisely at eight, found himself exiting the cab a full twenty minutes early. He strolled on the cobblestones around the Place de Vosges, with the grassy Louis XIII square in the center, to pass the time. He stopped in front of the still stately building that had been Victor Hugo's house. Jack wondered what the aristocratic writer would think of his *Les Miserables* becoming culture for the masses.

He cut through the grassy plot in the center. It was a warm and pleasant spring evening. Flowers were in bloom around the fountain. A young man and woman were locked in a passionate embrace on a park bench. Jack was envious. It was springtime in Paris, and what was he doing? Spending one more of an ever declining number of available springtimes chasing killers and terrorists. One thing was different this time, Jack realized. With Daniel Moreau now pursuing him, this would be the last spring he spent in Paris, regardless of what happened with Nadim. There would be killers and terrorists to chase in other places, including Israel, but Jack decided as he glanced back at the young couple kissing that he wouldn't be doing it any longer. This would be it for him. He wasn't Moshe, in the game for a life sentence. He didn't know what he'd do, but the young lovers made up his mind. When this was over, he was finished.

Jack thought about Daniel Moreau. He knew that it was risky coming to a gathering like this. Moreau could have mentioned to one of the other guests that he was looking for Jack Cole, but he had to take the chance. He had to find a way to get to Nadim, to find out what the Syrian was planning.

On the other hand, he doubted if Moreau would recognize him. Denis had done a superb job of remaking Jack's appearance. The dark black toupee, the black contacts behind wire-framed glasses, and the thin mustache would have been enough, but he had shown Jack how to use makeup to soften his nose and eradicate the lines under his eyes. He had also forged a perfect French passport for Jack in the name of Henri Devereaux. Jack would have dearly loved to use the Henri Devereaux name this evening, but that wasn't an option. Hubert had invited Jack Cole because he was in the wine business, and that was the hook to get Nadim.

Jack returned to 9 Place de Vosges. The restaurant, L'Ambroise, was housed in a magnificent and tastefully renovated old stone structure with high ceilings and dim lights. Monsieur Pierre, the sommelier, couldn't believe that he was really Jack Cole. "What have you done to yourself, my friend?"

"I went off to a place in Switzerland for a little touch-up, trying to look younger and more attractive."

Pierre had laughed. "You Americans are all insane about your appearance." As he looked around, Jack saw that the Latour tasting had taken over the entire restaurant. In the first of the three rooms, waiters were passing Dom Pérignon on trays as an aperitif for the reception that preceded the serious dinner and tasting set up in the two farther dining rooms.

Being early, Jack, with a glass of champagne, drifted around the two other dining rooms. At the several tables in both rooms, about sixty places were set. Each had eight Bordeaux glasses. Trying to be unobtrusive, Jack checked the name cards at each place.

Hubert had seated Jack on one side of a round table of ten in the first of the two rooms. Major General Nadim and "Guest of Major General" were seated on the other side of the table, too far away for casual conversation during dinner. *So I'd better get to know him during the reception,* Jack decided. *Then maybe I can arrange to meet him tomorrow to discuss wine.*

The room for the reception was filling up. Jack looked around. No sign of Nadim.

Anxiously Jack watched the front door while he half listened to someone else in the wine export business who was rattling on about the wines of the last couple of years. The next time the door opened, in walked a large-busted blond woman wearing a low-cut magenta dress, whose appearance cried out "bimbo." Jack recognized her from one of the police shows on prime-time television in France. Behind her in his brown military uniform came Nadim.

The picture in the folder Avi had given him didn't do Nadim justice, Jack decided. The Syrian looked suave, sophisticated, and worldly. There was no question that he belonged in this room, at this elaborate evening. Yet there was something about the face of the debonair figure with slicked-down coal-black hair, parted in the center, and a precisely trimmed mustache that told Jack it wasn't surprising that Nadim was known as the Butcher of Beirut.

Jack waited until Nadim and his actress friend had a glass

of champagne in their hands to approach him. The two of them were standing alone. Trying to appear nonchalant, Jack walked up and said to Nadim, "Hello. I'm a wine dealer from New York."

Taking the measure of this brash American whom he had never met before, Nadim shot Jack a piercing look that cut through him. Always a believer in his ability to judge people by snap first impressions, Nadim quickly decided that Jack wasn't worth talking to. He gave Jack a supercilious smile, then said in an arrogant tone, "Well, isn't that nice. Marie is interested in New York. She wants to be a Broadway actress. Why don't you tell her about it?" With that, Nadim turned and stalked away, leaving Jack with the actress.

For now, Jack was willing to live with that. After all, one way of moving in on Nadim was by getting close to the woman he was with. So Jack said, "I've enjoyed your show on television."

She didn't bother to respond. Jack doubted if she had even heard what he had said. She had her eyes on Nadim, who was making a beeline for a chic-looking woman dressed in a smart gray Valentino suit, which she might have worn to the office that day. She exuded confidence as well as elegance. She was about thirty-five, maybe a little older, Jack thought. She reminded him of an investment banker Sam had introduced him to in London last year in the hope she might be a suitable marriage partner for Jack. After two dates, they concluded that they had absolutely nothing in common and Sam must have been "daft," as she had put it, to think this would ever work.

The woman in the gray suit wasn't drop-dead beautiful, Jack decided. But she carried herself with a patent sensuality that made him enjoy looking at her. She repeatedly pushed back her long brown hair from her eyes as Nadim approached her. She was engaged in an animated conversation, gesticulating with her hands, with a man whom Jack recognized as the finance minister in the French government.

Nadim approached the two of them. For a few moments they all spoke together. Then the Frenchman drifted away. Left alone with the woman, Nadim dropped his hand down and gently placed it on her derriere. She swatted it away as if she were dealing with a mosquito, shot him an irritated look, and then stalked away. He tried to stop her by grabbing onto her arm below the elbow, but she was too fast for him. "Keep your fucking hands off me," she spat through clenched teeth. Nadim made no effort to follow her.

Jack turned back to Marie, who had been watching the scene unfold with Nadim, as Jack had. "I don't think she likes your friend," Jack said, trying to find some common ground with the actress.

"Do you know who the bitch is?" Marie asked Jack, while pointing to the woman in the gray suit.

"Never saw her before."

"Well, what do you have to do with Broadway?" she asked.

Jack took a deep breath. "I have some very good friends who produce top shows." He thought he told the lie well, but it was clear from her face that it was a story she had heard too often.

"What you mean to say is that you'd like to get into my pants now, and later you'll try to find someone you know in the theater. You American men are all the same. Interested in one thing." She accompanied her words with a smile to show she wasn't angry, just amused.

Jack looked at her hopefully. "You can't blame a guy for trying. Your friend in the military uniform seemed otherwise occupied."

Her smile disappeared, replaced by a hard, cold stare. "Sorry, you're not my type."

"How can you tell that?"

"I have to pee. Since I'm a lady, I'll add, 'Please excuse me.'"

With that, Marie headed toward the toilet in the front of the restaurant.

Jack decided that he should make another approach to Nadim before the reception ended. When he looked around the room, he couldn't see the Syrian.

Jack glanced into the next room. Acting casually, Nadim was picking up the place card that said "Guest of Major General" in the second room and moving it to a table in the third room. He returned with a different place card, which he set down next to him when he didn't think anyone was looking. Jack's guess was that had to be for the woman in the gray Valentino suit. *Jesus,* Jack thought. *This guy's a piece of work. It's a good thing I'm finished in Paris. I'll never be invited to one of these dinners again.*

Jack waited until Nadim reentered the reception room to approach the Syrian. This time he held out his hand. "Hello. I don't think we've met before. I'm Jack Cole from New York."

That didn't change Nadim's initial impression that Jack wasn't worth talking to. This time Nadim stared coolly into Jack's eyes. "Yes," he simply replied. Then he walked away in the direction of a French general, the only other guest in a military uniform.

Moments later, Hubert announced what the procedure would be for the evening. "With the first course, a foie gras *en croute*, we'll be tasting the best eight vintages of Latour from the 1980s. With the second course, rack of lamb, we'll have the best eight Latours from the 1970s. And with the cheese, six Latour wines from the 1960s, as well as the legendary 1959 and 1949."

This announcement produced a subtle "ah" of appreciation.

"And now the waiters will direct you to your assigned seats."

As Jack moved toward his table, he was anxious to see what happened next with Nadim and the two women. This was playing out like a French farce on the stage. If it weren't so serious with Nadim, it might be funny.

Before the woman in the gray suit moved out of the reception room, her cell phone rang. She went off into a corner to take the call. As she did, Nadim led the actress into the third room and deposited her at the new place he had arranged. She was pouting when he left her there, but he acted as if he didn't care.

A moment later the woman in the gray suit finished her call and put the phone away. By then everyone was on their feet for a toast to the president of France. She glanced around both rooms and saw only one open place, next to Nadim. Scowling and looking annoyed, she moved in that direction.

As dinner began, Jack glanced across the table. Nadim, acting pleasant and charming, was trying to talk to the woman in the gray suit, but she turned to the other side. All of her attention was directed to the French finance minister. A couple of times during the first course, Jack made an effort to call across the table to Nadim to engage him in conversation, but the Syrian ignored Jack. By default, Nadim was talking to the wife of the finance minister, who seemed charmed by the dashing military man from the Middle East speaking perfect French. "Didn't we own Syria once?" Jack heard her ask Nadim.

The Syrian smiled and replied, "Once you owned lots of things."

This is turning out to be a total disaster, Jack thought, feeling despondent. *This evening was a stupid idea. Either that or I'm too much of a dunce to pull it off.* He felt even more miserable when he thought of facing Avi tomorrow and letting him know how hopelessly he had struck out.

He decided to stop eavesdropping, forget about Nadim, enjoy the wines, and talk to the people on either side of him. One was a woman who was a food and wine critic from *Figaro*. The other was a man, based in London, who owned one of the largest wine-importing businesses in the U.K.

There were a series of speeches after each course, and the attendees evaluated the wines on written sheets. In the middle of the speeches after the lamb, the woman in the gray suit got up to go to the ladies' room. Jack watched Nadim leering at her while she turned away from him. Suddenly he had an idea. Nadim obviously wasn't involved with the bimbo. But what about the woman in the gray Valentino suit? There was definitely something between her and Nadim. Whatever it was might hold the key to getting access to Nadim.

Jack waited until she was on her way back to the dining room to make his move. Then he headed toward the men's room, also in front of the restaurant.

His timing was perfect. Their paths crossed at the entrance to the second dining room. He stopped and stared at her, making sure he had her attention.

"Say, don't I know you?" he asked.

She stood still and looked at him. "I don't think so." The aroma of her perfume, lavishly applied, aroused his senses.

"Joy, isn't it?" he asked.

She seemed surprised. "You have a good nose."

"I'd say that's de rigueur for the wine business. Wouldn't you agree?" She smiled. It was a warm smile with a hint of mystery, of the exotic.

"What's so funny?" he asked.

"Only an American would use a term like that in this context."

"Good guess. My being an American," Jack said.

"Actually your accent gave it away."

He shrugged. "I'm not trying to pass for something I'm not."

"But that's not true," she said.

Her words alarmed Jack. How could she know he was lying? "What do you mean?" he asked seriously.

The sparkle in her eyes let him know she was jesting with him. "We're all trying to be someone we're not. Rich. Smart. Honest. Depending on our situation. That's life."

"I'm an American from New York in the wine-export business. Jack's my name," he said. Then he held out his hand.

She made no effort to shake it. Instead she laughed.

"What's so funny?" Jack asked.

"Shaking hands is such an American custom. You're in France now."

"So what should I do?"

She gave him that mysterious smile again. "Kiss me on each cheek."

Jack did as he was told. From the corner of his eye, he saw Nadim glaring at him with jealousy.

"My name's Layla," she said.

She pushed her hair back behind her ear. Then she reached into her small black leather purse and extracted a business card, which she handed to him. She wasn't wearing a wedding ring. He glanced at it. It read: *Layla Gemayel, vice president, Euro Swiss Bank (ESB).*

"That's not a French name. Where are you from?"

"I get to ask the personal questions. I don't answer them."

He raised his eyebrows. "Then tell me what's a bank vice president doing here?"

"My specialty is loans to businesses in the wine industry," she said. As she spoke, she looked directly at him, deep into his eyes, making him feel that he was the only one in the world who mattered. He couldn't recall any other woman doing that. "Lately there's been a great deal of expansion in Bordeaux. We're providing the financing for quite a few of those."

That was the opening Jack wanted.

"I'm thinking of expanding myself. I've already spoken to a couple of lending institutions."

She eyed him suspiciously. "Well, that's quite a coincidence."

Layla was smart. His guess was that she didn't believe him, but he didn't care. It was still a good way to get a foot in the door. He waited to see if she'd slam it.

She didn't. "Give me a call," she said, "if you want to talk." She smiled at him.

God, she has a great smile, he thought. Pure white teeth against light olive skin. Her face reminded him of a fourth-generation Israeli woman he had once dated.

"About money, I mean," she added, letting the ambiguity hang in the air as she moved back to her seat.

Now suddenly Jack had Nadim's attention. The Syrian bored into him with dark brown eyes, a menacing scowl on his face.

Waiters served the cheese course and the third flight of wines. Nadim made another effort to talk to Layla. Jack watched her turn and give Nadim the back of her head.

As soon as the speeches following the cheese course began, Layla stood up. Without saying a word to anyone, she walked swiftly across the two rooms toward the front door. Jack watched Nadim to see if the Syrian tried to cut her off. Jack was planning to block Nadim if he did that.

Nadim never moved. Instead he kept his eyes riveted on Jack. Jack was the one at risk, not Layla.

A minute later, when Nadim turned back to the wife of the French finance minister, Jack considered that his cue. He calmly walked toward the front door, planning to call and thank Hubert and Monsieur Pierre tomorrow.

Stepping outside of the restaurant, Jack looked around. He saw Layla climb into the backseat of a chauffeur-driven black Jaguar. Her skirt had hiked up and he saw lots of very shapely leg. She didn't wave to him. He didn't know whether she saw him or not.

Once the Jaguar pulled away, Jack signaled to a passing cab. At the curb, before getting inside, Jack glanced over his shoulder at the front door of L'Ambroise. He had no intention of being intimidated by Nadim. He was feeling heady and excited from the events of the evening. He would have welcomed the Syrian's racing out of the restaurant to confront him.

It didn't happen. The door remained closed. Jack gave the cabdriver his address.

As the cab raced across the deserted streets of Paris at breakneck speed, Jack didn't feel tired despite the hour and the large quantity of wine he had consumed. The evening had been more stimulating than any he could recall, but it was rapidly becoming a jumble in his mind. Trying to get close to Nadim was a challenge. But Layla was something else: an intelligent, clever, witty woman who would have captivated him even if she weren't a way of getting at Nadim. He would want to know her better regardless of whether Nadim was pursuing her. At least, that was what he had thought in the restaurant. Now, as the scent of her Joy faded, he wasn't sure what he thought.

The taxi dropped Jack in front of his building. Looking up from the street at his apartment on the fourth floor, he pulled back in fear. There were lights on in the front living room. Jack was certain he had turned them all off. He had an uncomfortable feeling in the pit of his stomach.

Had he infuriated Nadim so much that the Syrian had sent some of his men to teach Jack a lesson for interfering with Nadim's effort at a romantic conquest with Layla? That was certainly possible for the Butcher of Beirut. Another possibility was that Daniel Moreau was waiting for Jack with a couple of SDECE agents.

Jack didn't know which of the two possibilities he liked least. One thing was clear: He was very vulnerable. He didn't have a gun or any other weapon.

Jack walked swiftly down the street. At the corner he turned right. Once he was out of sight of anyone looking out of the windows of his apartment, he felt safe. He whipped out his phone and dialed Avi's cell.

"Small problem," he said. "There's someone in my apartment."

Avi laughed. "Yeah, I'm here waiting for you to come home, and I'm damn tired of reading your old magazines."

Jack was furious. "I didn't think that was the plan."

Avi could tell that Jack was angry. He laughed again. "Plans change. I didn't want to have to wait until tomorrow to hear what happened with Nadim. Besides, I haven't broken into an apartment with a sophisticated lock like yours in a long time. I'm so rusty that it was a challenge."

"Oh, fuck you."

"Stop pretending you're angry and c'mon upstairs. You know damn well that in our business there's no such thing as a private life."

By the time he reached the apartment, Jack had cooled down. It was Avi's turn to be surprised. "My God. What did you do to your appearance?"

He told Avi what had happened at his place on Avenue de Messine and about Denis.

"Smart move," Avi said. "Now join me in having a glass of your Armagnac and tell me what happened this evening." While Jack poured a glass, Avi asked anxiously, "How'd you do with Nadim?"

"I made one friend tonight. And one enemy."

Avi locked eyes with Jack. "If you wanted to get my attention, you managed to do that. Tell me about it."

Jack described what happened at L'Ambroise while Avi listened intently to each word. At the end, Jack handed Layla's card to Avi. Then he continued, "So my theory is that I call this Layla in the morning and make a date with her. It may be a way of getting close to Nadim."

As Avi studied the card, deep furrows appeared on his forehead. Tension brought out creases in his face. "You liked this woman, didn't you?"

Jack was defensive. "I don't even know her. Is that what's bothering you?"

"I wish it were. She's Lebanese. That's what's troublesome."

"How do you know that?

"Gemayel is the name of a Christian Maronite family in Lebanon. They were one of the most powerful until the Syrians took over the country. Also, the ESB is the successor to the Beirut European Bank. It was formed when lots of wealthy Lebanese decided the time had come to move their money out of Lebanon and into Switzerland."

"So what's all of that mean?" Jack asked.

Avi shrugged. "I don't know. Maybe nothing." He paused, pondering what to do. He had an idea. "I'll stop at the embassy when I leave here and hook up with someone in Tel Aviv in the Mossad research department. I'll have a bio on her in the morning. Then we can decide whether you should make a call to the woman you described as your new friend."

Jack bristled and raised his voice. "Jesus, Avi, you make it sound like this is about my love life. The only reason I'm doing this is so we can get a hook into Nadim."

Avi, who had listened carefully to Jack's intonations when he gave the report, didn't believe what Jack had just said for a minute. "Are you trying to tell me that? Or your-self?"

"That's not fair."

Avi raised his hand. "Listen, you're a good-looking, single young man." Avi cracked a tiny smile. "Well, you're good-looking and single, anyway. If you think you can have a little fun and still do the job, I'd be the last to object. I just don't want—"

Jack interrupted him. "What's the worst case?"

"The worst case is that you're being set up."

Jack was puzzled. "Run that by me again."

"Suppose what Layla and Nadim did this evening was all an act for your benefit. To suck you in. Suppose she's really working with Nadim. This mysterious invitation for Nadim to the wine dinner arrived out of the blue right after the incident in Syria with Yasef. Nadim's shrewd. Like any good intelligence man, he knows never to believe that anything in life is coincidence. Maybe your friend Hubert even sold you out and told Nadim that you were responsible. Suddenly you're a potentially dangerous fish in the water, which you confirm by making repeated efforts to talk to him at the party. He wants to land you. Layla's the bait. You can't wait to get her in your mouth." Avi stopped to chortle at his choice of words in the metaphor. Then he continued: "Once they reel you in, Nadim will cut you open to see what's inside."

Jack squirmed in his chair. "Do you have to be so graphic?"

"Well, you asked me about the worst case."

He thought about Avi's scenario. "There's one thing wrong with your analysis."

"Yeah. What's that?"

"There's no love lost between the Syrians and the Maronites."

"That's true in general. On a personal level between

Layla and Nadim . . ." Avi shrugged. "Who knows? Where men and women are involved, anything's possible. Besides, Nadim and his people in Lebanon may have some control over Layla's family that'll make her do his bidding. Let's face it, the Syrians are in control in her country. Suppose she does work in Paris for Nadim, and her brethren in Beirut get the payoff."

Avi had made it sound so convincing that Jack couldn't argue. He still didn't want to believe it, but he couldn't be a fool, with what they had at stake. "So what do we do now?"

"You don't do a thing. You go to bed. I'll get the research people moving. I'll tell them that the information's for you. I had lots of friends in the agency, but others didn't like me because I didn't always blindly follow the party line. They'd love nothing better than to go running to Moshe if they saw my name on something."

Jack didn't respond. He couldn't get the picture Avi had drawn out of his mind. Was he just a fish, swimming after Layla until Nadim captured and gutted him?

Chapter 19

That's my way out of here, Robert McCallister decided. He was standing in his room looking out of the window, pretending to be admiring the scenery. In fact, he was watching a dark green van pull up in front of the villa. The driver climbed out and unloaded boxes with food and other supplies.

Behind Robert in the room his two guards sat and smoked. This was a ridiculous assignment. The American wasn't going anywhere. They were bored.

The van had arrived yesterday at about the same time.

Tomorrow, Robert decided, *if I'm outside for exercise at this time, I'll have a chance. Hopefully there will be only two guards watching me.* He strained his eyes, studying the layout. *The driver of the van's not armed. The gates are open at the end of the driveway while he's on the property.*

To avoid arousing the guards' suspicions, Robert moved away from the window. His mind was still racing as he picked up a copy of *Great Expectations.* He sat down in a stiff wooden chair with the book open while developing the plan.

I have to assume that the driver leaves the keys in the van—a big assumption, but not unreasonable. When he's in the villa, all I have to do is overpower these two bozos, jump in the truck, and I'm out of here.

There was one obvious weakness in the plan, Robert realized: He would be unarmed. It wouldn't be easy getting past two soldiers carrying AK-47s.

He thought about it for a few minutes. Surprise was the key. That was one thing he had going for him. Also, there was no real downside. At the Air Force Academy he had been taught to do risk benefit analysis. Here, the picture-taking session persuaded him that somebody wanted to use him as part of an exchange. Dead men didn't have any value. So he didn't have to worry about them killing him if he tried to escape.

Once he made up his mind that he would try to break out tomorrow, the adrenaline began flowing. Robert was no longer at the mercy of these people. He was taking matters into his own hands. It was about time he took control of his own destiny.

Jack was astounded as he read the e-mail Avi had brought with him from the embassy. "I can't believe the research people assembled so much information about Layla in a few short hours."

They were having breakfast in Jack's apartment. He put down the e-mail, got up, and poured them each a cup of coffee. "My God, we practically have a list of every sexual encounter she's ever had."

Avi laughed. "Shows what's on your mind."

"Let's get serious."

"I was."

Jack ignored him and began thinking aloud. "She was a child of privilege. Private school in Switzerland."

"While a civil war raged in her country."

"And smart. Degree in economics from the Sorbonne. MBA from Harvard."

"Why don't you get past the personal stuff and go to page two, lover boy?"

"Knock it off, Avi," Jack said irritably. He flipped over the top sheet and began reading. "Jesus, her bank job's a cover. She's a funnel for money collected from Lebanese expats living around the world, which is being sent back into Lebanon. They're doing what we Jews, the Irish, and lots of other people do."

"Exactly. They're raising money all around Europe, even in the United States. The problem is, we don't know where the money's going in Lebanon. Our research people are trying to get an answer to that question."

"So it could be used to rearm the Christian militias in order to force Syria out of Lebanon. If that's the case, she would never be working for Nadim to set me up."

"Unless, of course, he's holding one of her family members hostage."

As Jack paused to think about that, Avi continued: "Another possibility is that the money she funnels ends up with the Lebanese government, which is controlled by the Syrians. In that case, she's really on Nadim's payroll, for all practical purposes."

"Either way you think I'm being set up by Nadim. So I shouldn't call her."

Avi shook his head. "I didn't say that."

"What do you really think?"

"You don't want to know."

Subconsciously, Jack rolled the e-mail into a tube. He was becoming exasperated. "Yes, I do. Tell me."

Avi sighed. "Okay, you asked for it. I think you should go out and get laid. That's what I think."

Jack's face turned beet red. "Very funny."

"No. I mean it. Go call some Frenchwoman you know, or hire one. After a few hours in the sack, you'll be thinking only with your big head."

Avi's words stung, but Jack kept his anger in check. Perhaps Avi had a point. Jack's attraction for Layla might be coloring his thinking.

Afraid he had gone too far, Avi pulled back. "Listen, Jack, I'm sorry. It's got to be your decision. If you make that call to Layla, you're putting your life on the line. We can't be sure either way. I just want to make certain you're focused. We laugh all the time about guys who get caught in the honey pot, but it's not always that easy to see it coming."

Jack got up and paced around the small kitchen, weighing the factors. Avi didn't say a word.

After several minutes Jack stopped moving and turned to him. "Okay. Here's how I look at it. If I call Layla, my life will be on the line, but it's likely that a lot of Israelis will be in danger as a result of whatever plot Nadim is hatching. As long as there's a chance that we can gain some information to foil Nadim's plan, I've got to call her. How can I afford not to?"

Avi smiled. He had known that would be Jack's decision. "Besides, look at the fun you might have."

"Oh, fuck you."

Jack picked up the phone on the kitchen wall, glanced down at Layla's card, and punched in the number of her office.

A woman answered in a very official-sounding French-accented voice. "Madame Gemayel's office."

"I'd like to speak with her please. It's Jack Cole."

"Just a minute. I'll see if she's available."

While he stared at the silent phone, Jack thought, *You know that she's available. What you mean is that you'll find out whether she'll talk to me.* Suppose Layla didn't take the call after all that he and Avi had gone through? Jack cracked a tiny smile. That would be a scream.

While Avi pretended to be reading a copy of *Haaretz* he had picked up at the embassy, he was in fact watching Jack carefully. *I'm not onstage for you,* Jack thought. He turned in his chair and faced the wall.

"Ah, Jack Cole," Layla said with enthusiasm. "How nice to hear from you."

"So what did you think of the wines?" Jack asked, deciding to warm up with small talk.

"The 'eighty-two, 'fifty-nine and 'sixty-one were phenomenal," she said with enthusiasm. "The 'seventy disappointed me, as it always does."

Jack was amused. "Don't hold back; express your opinion freely."

"And you?"

"The 'fifty-nine was beyond belief. I would add the 'eighty-five and 'seventy-eight to your list of top ones, but I'm partial to those years in general. All in all, an incredible performance."

"I agree with that. So what can I do for you?"

"I'd like to take you up on your offer," he said with confidence. "To talk about a loan. Maybe we can get together today."

"Let me check the schedule on my computer." Her tone was now brusque and businesslike. He felt as if he had chilled her by turning to business. She must have been hoping for a personal call from him. That was a good sign—unless Avi was right that she was working for Nadim.

"Three o'clock, I can do," she said. "My office."

"Let me look."

Jack glanced at the sweep of the black second hand on the white face of the kitchen clock. Thirty seconds would be long enough to pretend he was consulting his calendar. "Three will be tough for me. But, hey, I've got an idea," Jack said, trying to sound spontaneous. "How about if we talk over dinner?"

Her initial reaction was silence, which didn't surprise Jack. He had momentarily confused her by shifting back to the personal, which was exactly what he had wanted to do. He wanted her to know he was interested in her for something other than business.

A long silence hung in the air as she made him wait for his answer.

"That I can do," she finally said, still sounding as if she were setting a business meeting.

"How about nine o'clock at Guy Savoy?" he asked.

"Good choice. Guy is a friend. I'll be there."

Jack put the phone down and turned back toward Avi. "A success," he said with pride.

"For you or for Nadim?" Avi replied.

Jack felt as if someone had just tossed a bucket of ice water over his head.

Avi was getting ready to leave the apartment when Jack's cell phone rang. "This is Jack."

In response he heard Moshe's voice. The Mossad director was shouting loud enough that Avi heard him across the room. "What in the world is going on?"

"What do you mean?"

"Don't play games with me!" Jack had never heard Moshe sound so angry. "I learned from our research people that Avi Sassoon put in a request in your name for a bio on a Lebanese woman. Yesterday they downloaded the file on someone else for him in Paris."

Avi gave Jack a thumbs-up sign. "Don't let him intimidate you," Avi whispered.

Jack decided to hold his ground. "You told me that you didn't want to be involved in—"

Moshe cut him off midsentence. "Don't talk on this phone. Get over to the embassy right now and use a secure phone. If that joker is with you, bring him."

"You mean Avi?"

Moshe snarled. "No, Napoleon Bonaparte. Of course Avi."

*   *   *

They were in a tiny, metal-lined, poorly ventilated room in the Israeli embassy in Paris. A black phone sat on a battered wooden table in the speaker mode so both Jack and Avi could listen and speak.

Moshe began. "Jack, I assume this is all about the American pilot, Robert McCallister."

"That's right."

"Tell me everything that you've done since you left my office, and I mean everything."

Jack began with his call to Avi.

"You had no business recruiting him on your own," Moshe thundered. "For your sake, I hope that your wine business is self-sufficient, because I intend to cut off your monthly payments."

That threat didn't alarm Jack. He could operate on his own now if he had to. With Daniel Moreau on his tail, once this was over he'd be moving his European headquarters to Barcelona or Milan, either of which was less expensive, no matter how it came out.

"So what did you and the indomitable Mr. Sassoon do?"

Standing next to the phone with his hands in his pockets, Avi grinned broadly at the reference to him.

"We took a trip to Syria," Jack said calmly.

"You want to tell me why?"

"That's where they're holding Robert McCallister."

"Are you two out of your minds?"

Jack described what prompted them to go to Syria and what happened there.

"So you already killed a man," Moshe said.

Avi couldn't resist the temptation to needle his former boss. "You can call it a rogue operation like Kemal's. Off the books. Which this one was. As opposed to one in Aqaba last year."

"Very funny."

Jack signaled Avi to stop talking. They wouldn't gain

anything by goading Moshe. He picked up and described what they'd been doing since they arrived in Paris. He was getting ready to tell Moshe about his date that night with Layla, when the director interrupted.

"Now let me tell you two something," Moshe said. Apprehension had replaced hostility in his voice. "I've received an unconfirmed report from a source in Turkey that the Syrians are trying to lure Kemal into a plot that involves the American pilot."

That was valuable confirmation, which Jack was relieved to hear. "So we're on the right track."

"Incredibly, you two geniuses stumbled onto something big. If the Syrians are players, we have to assume that we're the target, not merely the United States."

Jack held his breath, hoping that Moshe wouldn't tell them to back off in favor of regular, full-time Mossad agents. To his pleasant surprise, Moshe said, "What's your next move?" The director had reverted to his normal tone. The anger from not being kept in the loop was gone. There was too much at stake. Moshe was ready to deal with the issue on its merits.

"This evening I'm having dinner with Layla Gemayel," Jack said. "It's a way of getting close to Nadim."

"I don't like that," Moshe said.

"Why not?"

"It's also a way of getting yourself killed. You're playing with fire. Nadim's a tough customer."

Jack refused to yield. "Right now Layla's our only way of getting to Nadim, and we don't have much time."

"Are you sure you want to do this, Jack?" Moshe said. "Is it something Avi's manipulating you to do?"

Avi laughed. "It was his idea. He likes the girl."

Jack shot him a dirty look.

"Oy . . . oy . . . oy," Moshe said.

Now Avi was on Jack's side. "Layla could be just what we need to get to Nadim."

Moshe gave a deep sigh. "You two have pushed this so far already that I can't yank you, which is what I'd like to do. I guess that was your plan all along."

Jack winked at Avi, who was smiling.

Moshe continued: "Keep pursuing Nadim, with Layla or any other way. But report to me from now on—early and often. And I'm not kidding about that. I have to know what's happening. Whenever Avi's involved, things get out of control."

Chapter 20

Ali Hashim was nervous, as he always was when he had a meeting with the ayatollah, who served as the Iranian foreign minister. Hashim might have been the head of the Iranian Intelligence Agency, but he never forgot that he was still a layperson in a theocracy run by zealots whose goal was to turn the clock back ten centuries and for whom arbitrary action was the norm. One mistake and the executioner's razor-sharp sword would come down on his neck.

Today Hashim was even more apprehensive than usual. The minute he began reporting on his conversation with Nadim in Paris he knew that he had something to worry about. He understood quite clearly from body language what the ayatollah's reaction was to Nadim's plan.

At the end, the ayatollah was looking at him in mute rage. Hashim realized then that he had made a serious mistake by not simply telling Nadim no, and not even reporting on their meeting to the ayatollah. It was too late for that now.

"I don't want to hear any more about it," the ayatollah said in a low grumble. "Only a fool would suggest that we do anything cooperatively with those heathens in Turkey. Ahmed and the Syrians aren't much better."

The ayatollah waved his right hand toward the door,

which Hashim took as the signal he was being dismissed. "Others will come and talk to you later," the ayatollah said.

"Talk to me about what?" Hashim asked nervously.

"Your reasons for advocating a plan like this. It raises questions about your loyalty to the republic."

Hashim cringed. That was what he was afraid the ayatollah might think.

"I saw it as a way to obtain valuable American technology."

The ayatollah wasn't persuaded. "Computers aren't necessary to run the Islamic republic we want. The Americans can choke on their technology."

Hashim realized that he had been a fool to think that gaining American technology would be enough of an incentive to overcome the ayatollah's hatred for the Turks and his unwillingness to work cooperatively with them. Full of despair, his back to the wall, Hashim suddenly thought of a way to save his neck. "Suppose," he said tentatively, "we pretend to be going along with Nadim and Kemal, but at the end we seize everything for ourselves . . . the pilot and everything else. And we leave them with nothing. How about that?"

The ayatollah was cunning. He was now fascinated by what Hashim had suggested. "Is that possible?" he asked.

"Of course. Everything has to move through our territory before it gets to Turkey and Syria. Suppose we simply keep it all and double-cross them. We'll get everything, including the American pilot. We can trade him for American technology or kill him. That'll be our decision."

The ayatollah put both hands on the desk and intertwined his fingers. "Are you certain that this pilot is alive and well? That they really have him?"

"Nadim showed me a picture."

"Did he give it to you?"

Hashim shook his head. He didn't want to admit he had refused it.

"Go meet with Nadim again. This time make him give you the picture. I'll need it in order to get the approvals here. They'll want to see that proof. I know how they think."

Visibly relieved, Hashim rose to leave on unsteady legs.

The ayatollah was smiling. "It will serve them right," he said, "those infidels in Turkey and Syria. They should come up with sand in their hands. That's what they deserve."

Knowing that his French wine business was on hold regardless of what happened, Jack decided to clean up one final loose end. It took him three calls on his cell phone to find the special cuvee Chateauneuf du Pape that Ed Sands had ordered. He arranged to ship it to Washington.

Seconds after Jack hung up, the phone rang. Very few people had the number. With everything that was happening with Nadim, it jarred him in a way it never had before.

He decided to listen, holding his breath, before identifying himself.

"Jack," he heard a woman say. He thought he recognized her voice, even after all of these years. *Oh, hell, it can't be. I don't need this now.* But it was.

"Jack, it's Sarah McCallister."

The phone fell out of his hand and onto the desk. When he picked it up, he heard her say, "Sam gave me your cell phone number. I hope you don't mind my calling."

"No, of course not," he said in a flat, unemotional tone.

"My brother told me about your son, Robert. It's horrible. I feel bad for you."

"Thanks, Jack. It's been hell for all of us."

"I can imagine."

"Actually, you can't," Sarah said sadly.

It hit Jack that Sarah, because of Terry's relationship with President Kendall, might have some information about

Robert that would be useful to him and Avi. "Any news about his release?"

"I wish there were."

"I'm sorry."

"I know you are, Jack, but you're not willing to do anything to help."

So this was the point of the call. "I'm flattered that you think I could do anything, but I'm sure that Sam explained to you I'm in the wine business. I'm not a soldier or a spy."

"You know people in Israel who could help. Don't you?"

Good old Sarah. Always blunt and direct. Never one to mince her words. Jack didn't respond.

"I want to come to Israel or Paris or wherever you are and talk to you about it," she said.

Thanks a lot, Sam, he thought. "I'm afraid now's not a good time."

She ignored his words. "Buy me lunch tomorrow, Jack. I'm in London. You tell me where and when. Anywhere in the world. I'll be there. Bobby's my child. My only son." Her voice was cracking with emotion. "You can't deny me that."

"But I just said—"

"With our history you can't possibly say no."

What he wanted to say was, *Precisely because of our history, I can say no.* But he couldn't do that. The desperation in her voice tugged at his heartstrings.

Jack softened. "Take the train down to Paris in the morning. Meet me in the lobby of the Hotel Bristol at one. We'll go from there."

"Thank you, Jack," she said, sounding relieved.

Sharp spasms of pain shot through Margaret Joyner's back. She stood up from her desk chair and walked around the office, holding an electric heating pad with a long extension cord against her lower back and cursing. Not wanting to risk dulling her mind, she refused to take painkillers. With surgery out of the question, the heating pad, standing, and muttering obscenities were her only relief. Until about fifteen minutes ago her back hadn't been bothering her for the first time in several days. Then Michael's report of his visit to Volgograd arrived with the photographs. As she began reading it, the pains returned.

The situation was treacherous. Her briefing yesterday with the president, one-on-one, based on Michael's oral report, had been a waste of time. Kendall had refused to focus on the issue. All he could talk about was Robert McCallister and Turkey. It had become an obsession with him.

Joyner refused to be blocked by the paralysis at the White House. She would respond to Michael and tell him to step up his vigilance on Suslov in Moscow and at the warehouse in Volgograd. She would move other CIA agents to Moscow if he needed more resources. She swallowed hard. She would also notify her Pentagon liaison that American troops at nearby locations should be on alert for possible assistance. This was dicey, because her request could find its way to Chip Morton and then to the White House. She'd have hell to pay for acting on her own, but she was willing to take the risk.

Satisfied with this approach, she returned to her desk to call in Carol and dictate the messages. Before she had a chance, the red phone rang.

"It's a gorgeous spring day in Jerusalem," Moshe said when she picked up.

She took a deep breath. This had to be more bad news. "You didn't call to give me a weather report."

"But I did. Because it's so nice my window was open, and a little birdie flew into the office."

"And?" Joyner said, holding her breath.

"The birdie told me that Robert McCallister has been moved to Syria."

Joyner couldn't get angry at Moshe. The news he was giving her was too important for that. "I thought you weren't going to get involved."

"Not a single Mossad employee has had anything to do with this. I can assure you of that."

Joyner was perplexed. "Why Syria? How reliable is your birdie?"

"Very. Two people almost lost their lives confirming it."

"Where in Syria are they holding him?"

"The birdie didn't know."

"Do you think it's just the Syrians helping out the Turks by providing a secure place for McCallister outside of their country?" She paused. "Or do you think there's some kind of joint Turkish/Syrian plot being hatched?"

Moshe hesitated before answering. He was afraid to tell Joyner everything he knew, which pointed toward Nadim's involvement with Kemal, who was acting on his own. First of all, nothing in detail had been established. Second, he didn't want to risk having Kendall order the Israeli prime minister to shut down Jack's operation with Avi. It was too critical to Israel's self-interest. So he equivocated. "I can't give you any hard information yet. You now have all I can pass along, which isn't an awful lot."

Joyner was thinking about her options. "I appreciate the call. Really I do, but now . . ." She hesitated.

"You don't know what to do with the info. Right?"

"Precisely."

"I'd say you're like the rabbi who skipped synagogue on Saturday to play golf and made a hole in one."

"Seriously, though, Moshe. Thanks for the information. Let me know if any other birdies fly into your office."

Joyner hung up the phone and called Mary Beth Reynolds on her cell phone. The vice president was in a car on Pennsylvania Avenue. "We have to talk," Joyner said.

"How about my office up on the Hill in thirty minutes? I

may be a little late if I have to vote to break a tie on the health-care bill."

"Doesn't matter. I'll wait."

The vice president had an office on the Senate side of the capitol. That was where Joyner found Reynolds when she arrived.

"No vote," the vice president said. "The Democrats are playing parliamentary games. So what else is new? But none of that's important. I gather from your voice that something's happened."

Joyner told her about Moshe's call. "What do we do now?" she asked Reynolds at the end.

"We go over and tell Kendall."

"He'll bust a gut because I'm working with the Israelis."

Reynolds was never one to shy away from a battle. "It's the right thing to do . . . for the good of the country. We'll give Kendall the info. He can do what he wants with it."

"He might ask for my resignation."

Reynolds looked over at Joyner, shifting in her chair to find a more comfortable position. "At this point, do you care?"

"Are you kidding?"

"Good. I'll call and tell him we're coming."

As Reynolds picked up the phone, Joyner said, "Tell him we want to meet with him alone. I've had enough of Jimmy Grange for one lifetime."

"Amen."

Joyner got her wish. Kendall was the only one in the Oval Office when she arrived with the vice president.

"I'm making the Japanese prime minister wait so I can meet with you," Kendall said, not bothering to conceal the animosity he felt for his vice president. "You said it was urgent."

"It is," Reynolds replied in a firm voice, refusing to be intimidated. She looked at Joyner. "Tell him what you learned."

The back spasms returned. Joyner stood up and walked around, holding her back as she prepared to speak.

"Can't you see a doctor and take care of that?" Kendall said testily. "It's driving me crazy."

"What do you think it's doing to me?" she fired back, then returned to the issue at hand. "The director general of the Mossad called today. The Israelis have learned that Robert McCallister has been moved from Turkey to Syria."

She watched Kendall's face turn bright red as he digested her words. The veins were throbbing in his neck. *I hope to hell he took his blood-pressure medicine this morning,* Joyner thought.

"Dammit, Margaret," he said pounding his fist on the desk. "I told you several times to keep them out of it."

Joyner moved in close to Kendall with her hands on her hips. "I didn't involve them," she said emphatically. "I have no idea how they got the information. I thought you should know about it. If you want me to resign, that's okay with me. I gave you an undated letter when you appointed me. Add today's date and release it to the press. I promise you I'll go quietly without making any statements. I'll say I want to pursue other interests. It's your choice."

The last thing Kendall needed right now was a media circus concerning Joyner's resignation. He may have wanted it, but it wasn't an option. "They're wrong," he said with conviction.

"Who's wrong?"

"The Israelis."

"How do you know that?" Mary Beth asked.

"General Childress received a report from the DIA earlier today. The Turks are holding Lieutenant McCallister in an underground bunker beneath a hospital in Van. I've personally told their ambassador that if they don't turn him over to us in the next three days, when the ultimatum expires, I intend to suspend all aid to Turkey and give the order for a limited bombing of one Turkish air base. At that point, General Childress will put a special-operations unit on the ground to go in and get him out. Childress and Chip haven't exactly been sitting on their hands for the past few days."

"What's the source of the DIA information?"

Kendall had no idea. He was annoyed by the question. "What makes you think the Israelis are always right?"

Joyner began walking around the office again with her hands on her lower back. "They're not," she said, "but it's their neighborhood. We have to consider what they tell us."

"I'm considering it, but rejecting it," Kendall snapped. His voice had a hard edge and the ring of finality.

The prison in Marseilles was one big cesspool. Daniel Moreau was confident that after two days in the hole, and the threat that he might spend the rest of his life there, Edouard Laval would be ready to tell Moreau everything he knew.

Waiting for them to bring the prisoner, Moreau reread the file. Laval was a petty thief who had three prior arrests. Trained as an auto mechanic, he had turned to crime in order to support his wife and two children when he was fired for stealing a car phone. All three of his priors were for stealing cars. He was part of a gang that snatched them from the streets in the Marseilles area, then drove them through Spain into Morocco, where they were stripped down for parts or sold on the black market.

In total, Laval had spent a year and a half in jail. Not long enough for what he had done, Moreau decided, but sufficient time to know that he didn't want to spend the rest of his life that way.

Moreau had kept in close touch with the Marseilles police ever since the Khalifa murder. Once he heard they had ar-

rested Laval, he dropped everything and flew down from
Paris.

Moreau was surprised when they brought in Laval. He
had been expecting a big, strapping auto mechanic who re-
sembled a football player. Instead he saw a thin, waiflike,
terrified creature shuffling into the room in handcuffs. Laval
was only twenty-eight, but already his light brown hair
barely covered his head. His face was pockmarked. Generally, he looked so terrible that Moreau thought his picture
could appear on posters that read, *Crime doesn't pay.*

The two armed guards accompanying Laval roughly
pushed him into a battered wooden chair, then moved to the
side of the room, where they could watch him without being
in the way.

Moreau saw no point playing games with this punk. "For
murder you spend the rest of your life in jail. You know
that."

Laval tried to show a false bravado. "I didn't murder nobody."

"The police have the evidence. The records that you
bought the explosives that blew up Khalifa's car when he
started the engine." Moreau shook his head in disbelief.
"Not too smart on your part, eh?"

Laval didn't respond. He looked down at his hands. Shit,
he had really done it this time. He'd never see his wife and
kids again. Never be able to spend all that money the
stranger had paid him that was in a locker at the train station.

"And that's not all," Moreau added. "The police found
the key to the locker in your apartment. They've got the
money. All ten thousand Euros."

Jesus, how'd they get that? Only Clara knew where it
was. The wench must have blabbed to the cops.

"So if you have all of that," Laval said, "what do you
want with me?"

"I want information."

Laval was watching him closely. "Are you a cop?"

"I'm working with the police."

"What's in it for me?"

"You tell me what I want, and they'll agree to limit your jail time to two years."

Laval smiled, showing badly discolored teeth and a couple of spaces in his mouth. At first the offer sounded good. Then he thought about it some more. "How do you know the judge will do what you say?"

Moreau gave him a copy of an agreement a magistrate had signed. The local prosecutor had initially objected, but a call from the justice minister in Paris had settled the issue.

Laval read the document slowly. Satisfied, he clutched the paper tightly in his hand. "What do you want to know?"

Before responding, Moreau took a small cassette recorder out of his briefcase and put it on the table in front of Laval. He pressed a button. The sprockets began turning.

"Who paid you to kill Khalifa?"

"You mean the Arab terrorist?"

Moreau hit the stop switch. "You don't know he was a terrorist."

"Everybody in our part of town knew it. When he got drunk he bragged about how many Israeli civilians he had killed by arranging those suicide attacks. Here he was safe. He knew the French government would never send him to Israel."

"I don't want to hear any more about that," Moreau said testily.

"Yeah, then what?"

Moreau rewound the tape to the beginning and hit the record button. "I want to know who paid you to kill Khalifa."

Laval didn't like being a stool pigeon, but he had to save his own ass. "A guy came down from Paris."

"What was his name?"

Laval held out his hands, palms facing up. "He didn't tell me."

"How did he hook up with you?"

"He said he got my name from some guys at a bar. I don't know. He stopped me on the street when I was leaving my house one morning. So he knew where I lived."

"What did he ask you to do?"

Laval looked around nervously. In his world, stoolies had their tongues cut out. But the man who hired him wasn't from his world. "He wanted me to plant a bomb in Khalifa's car that would blow up when the Arab started the engine."

"You did that. Didn't you?" Laval nodded. "Speak up," Moreau said sharply.

"Yeah. I did it."

"And the man paid you ten thousand Euros for the job. Didn't he?"

"Yeah. Five before. Five after. And my expenses to buy the shit. You know. But I'm not a murderer."

"That's what it sounds like to me."

Laval pulled back. "Hey, this Arab was scum." He sounded proud of what he had done. "It's not like I was killing a decent guy."

Moreau snarled. "I didn't realize that you were God. That you decided who lives and who dies."

"Well, I'm not. I don't like the Jews, but killing people in a restaurant with suicide bombs. Man, that—"

"I told you, I don't want to hear that. Stick to what you did, or you'll lose your deal."

Laval squeezed his hand against the paper. "Okay. Okay. I got it. What else do you want to know?"

Moreau reached into his briefcase and extracted a picture of Jack Cole, which he handed to Laval. "Is this the man who paid you to kill Khalifa?"

Laval nodded. "He's the one."

"You might have to testify against him in Paris in order to keep your deal."

"Yeah," Laval said, and he nodded. "I guess I'll have to do whatever you want."

Moreau was pleased. He not only had Jack Cole nailed for espionage in connection with Osirak, but for the murder of Khalifa. For the second crime, he now had a witness. Jack Cole would rot in a prison like this for the rest of his life.

Chapter 21

Seated alone at a table at Guy Savoy, Jack felt as if everyone were staring at him. *She changed her mind. I'm being stood up.*

He looked around the small room, one of three with only six tables each, that made up the restaurant. Modern paintings hung on the walls of what was otherwise an austere white interior.

Suddenly he heard a commotion at the front door, followed by the maître d's words, "Ah, Mademoiselle Gemayel. So good to see you again."

As she approached, Jack felt an excitement, surging through his body. Layla was radiant. She looked stunning in a sea-foam-green chiffon dress from Valentino with spaghetti straps. A matching scarf trailed over her shoulders. She wasn't wearing a bra. She looked as if she had just gotten her hair done. Again she brought with her the scent of Joy.

He stood up and kissed her on each cheek.

In response she touched his shoulder affectionately and winked at him. "No handshake?"

"I'm a fast learner."

"Sorry I was late. Traffic was impossible."

And the hairstylist must have been running behind, he thought.

A waiter came by. "Aperitif?" he asked.

"Champagne," she replied.

"The same for me."

Jack decided to begin with business, which, after all, was supposed to be the point of the dinner. "I've never heard of your bank," he said, trying to sound like a potential borrower. "Is it a new one?"

"Forty years ago it began as the Swiss branch of a Beirut bank. Now most of our operations are in Europe."

"And what do you do there? I mean you personally."

The glasses of champagne arrived. Jack raised his. "To making new friends." They clinked together.

"The wine industry is one of my specialties," she said, "which is why I was at the Latour tasting. We finance all aspects of the industry." She gave him that warm, mysterious smile, while looking right at him. "So you would be in experienced hands if you decided to finance with us."

He nodded. "That's what I was hoping to hear."

"And what exactly does your company do?" she asked in a way that made him think she had some doubt about what he had told her last evening. Or contrary information from Nadim.

Fortunately for Jack, at that moment Guy Savoy came out of the kitchen to greet Layla. She rose at the table as the gray-and-black-haired, bushy-bearded chef in his white apron kissed her on each cheek.

The headwaiter then came with menus and a wine list.

First they settled on the food. They were both starting with scallops with truffles cut into the center, followed by a *cote de veau* for two.

The sommelier handed him the wine list. "No. No," Jack protested. "We pick together." He placed it in front of Layla.

She opened up the thick booklet. "What do you think about white Burgundy?" she said. "Followed by red Bordeaux?"

"Sounds great."

As they both scanned the pages, she found a 1995 Batard Montrachet by Etienne Sauzet. Jack pointed to a 1985 Chateau L'Evangile. "Since the 'eighty-five was so good last evening. Fabulous," he said. She looked amused. "What's so funny?"

"You are. You've got an exuberance about you. Like a kid."

He shrugged. "There's nothing wrong with being enthusiastic."

She touched his arm and rested her hand there for a minute. "I meant that as a compliment. Maybe it's because you're American. Frenchmen are more staid."

"So when you're not eating here, where do you like to dine in Paris?" Jack asked, hoping to draw the conversation away from himself.

She wasn't having any of it. "You're not interested in borrowing money from my bank, are you?"

Jack had to drop the ploy. She was too intelligent to be fooled. "You're right, of course. I just wanted to see you again."

She was amused. "You could have simply asked me out. No need to go through this phony loan story. I thought you were pleasant enough for an American. I would have accepted. Besides, I'm willing to try one evening that includes great food and wine with just about anybody."

Jack thought he saw an opportunity. "Well, I noticed somebody else at the dinner last evening trying to get friendly with you, and—"

"The one in the military uniform?"

Jack nodded. A dark look of horror covered her face. "I don't want to talk about Nadim."

"I'm sorry." He retreated quickly. "The truth is, I found you attractive. I'm going to be in France for a while, and I thought . . ."

Their first courses arrived. Jack tasted the Batard Montrachet and nodded.

"How long have you lived in Paris?" he asked.

"Actually, I went to school at the Sorbonne for a few years. Then I got an MBA at Harvard."

"When was that?"

She gave him the mysterious smile and shook her head. "If I answered that question, you'd know how old I am. You're clever. I'll have to watch you."

Was she being witty, or toying with him? "Okay, what happened after Harvard, which I assume was two years ago?"

She laughed. "I went to Beirut to live."

Jack feigned surprise. "Lebanon?"

"That's where I was born. My family has deep roots in the country. I wanted to go back and help rebuild the economy. After two years I realized it was hopeless."

"Why?" Jack asked, trying to sound like someone who knew very little about the situation in Lebanon.

She paused to eat some food and sip the wine. "A good choice," she said to Jack, pointing to the glass.

"Thanks. So why was it hopeless in Beirut?"

"The Syrians wouldn't let it happen. They were determined to keep our country under their control. And the Israelis didn't help. The two of them decided to play their war games in our land. Actually, my uncle Bashir tried to make peace with the Israelis, which could have improved the situation in the region."

"It cost him his life."

She raised her eyebrows, making Jack sorry he had said it to show off his knowledge. He tried to recover. "We do have newspapers in the United States."

"Touché. I was just surprised. Not many Americans have the vaguest idea of anything that's happened in Lebanon. For them it's just one of those Arab states over there. They don't realize that it was once the Switzerland of the Middle East, a great commercial center where Arabs from all over came to deposit their money, and a vacation playground. My country was a jewel in those days, an oasis in the turbulent Middle East, with incredible beauty at the crossroads between East and West. Not so long ago we had everything: mountains, the sea, entertainment and culture—even a political balance between Christians and Muslims, who existed in a partnership, and then . . ." She looked glum. "Egged on by the Syrians, the Muslims demanded more power, and they launched a civil war to get it."

"Must have been a frightening place to live in those days."

"It was." She paused to smooth down the tablecloth, while she remembered scenes from her daily life. "Going to the store for a bottle of milk meant putting your life at risk. You could get caught in a cross fire at any time."

"So did the Syrians bring an end to the civil war?"

"At the price of our freedom. I couldn't live that way. That's why I returned to Paris, where I proceeded to meet a French lawyer whom I married and divorced. I hate all lawyers. Scourge of humanity. If you were a lawyer, I wouldn't go out with you."

Jack laughed.

She anticipated his next question. "No children, and here I am."

During the main course she asked Jack about himself. He took his time responding, pretending he was chewing the tender veal. He liked her a lot. Suddenly he wanted to tell her the truth, but he heard Avi's words from last evening echoing in his brain: *You're being set up.*

Avi was objective, and Avi was his friend. He couldn't take the chance. His life was on the line. So he reinvented Jack Cole, telling Layla that he had been born in New York. He had married a woman named Sarah after attending the

University of Michigan. He moved back to New York, where he took over his father's wine-importing business, Calvert Wine Importers. "Sarah died five years ago. I have a son and daughter, both grown, and here I am," he said, mimicking her final words.

They talked easily about Paris and other European cities. She shared his love for music. By the time the cheese course was over, they had finished the 1985 L'Evangile, which was spectacular. Everything about the evening was special, Jack decided. He couldn't remember anyone he had enjoyed talking with as much. He was convinced that she really liked him. From time to time she touched him, placing her hand on top of his. And he felt the same way about her. Then he heard Avi's words pounding in his mind again. He cringed.

During dessert, a rich chocolate tart, he decided to return to the subject of Nadim. Hoping the wine would loosen her tongue, Jack said, "I didn't like that military guy who was hitting on you last night. He gave me the creeps."

She had been smiling. With Jack's words, her face turned somber. "You want to keep away from him."

"Sounds as if you're talking from personal experience."

She glanced around nervously to make certain no one could hear them. By now, only one of the other tables in the room was occupied, and that by a French couple at the far end. "My family had been part of the ruling class in Lebanon for centuries," she said. "We owned land. We had great wealth, as did most of the other powerful Maronite families. Even during the long civil war and the last big Arab–Israeli war, we hung on."

"How'd Nadim become involved?"

She pushed some hair behind her ear. "That was when my uncle Bashir thought he saw a way out of the nightmare by making peace with Israel. Nadim engineered his execution and installed my other uncle, Amin, as the ruler. Once he got away with that, Nadim gave the order to assassinate Maronite leaders who wanted to make peace with Israel or re-sist Syrian control. My father is a banker. He's still alive in large part because he's stayed out of politics. It isn't easy. Even within the Maronite community, people are split on every issue." She sighed. "It's a real mess."

"From what you've said, that sounds like an understate-ment." Jack tried to appear sympathetic.

"Now you see why I wouldn't talk to Nadim last evening," Layla told him.

Jack looked at her and nodded. "Absolutely."

"For some time he's been pursuing me. Nadim's used to getting what he wants, and he wants me. In his bed. He's made that clear. As long as I have it in my power to deny him that, by God, I will." Her eyes blazed with determina-tion to confirm her words.

Casually, a waiter deposited the check on the table. It was time to leave. Jack gave him a credit card. She pulled one of her own out of her black leather purse. "Please split the check," she told the waiter over Jack's protests. "I'm an in-dependent woman," she declared.

Jack laughed. "I don't doubt that for a minute."

As they exited the restaurant, she said, "Do you have a car?"

"I came in a cab."

"Where do you live?"

When Jack told her the neighborhood, she said, "I have a car waiting. Jean Claude will take you home. If you don't mind, he'll drop me first. I'm on the way."

"Thanks. I appreciate it." In the back of the black Jaguar, she snuggled up next to him. Her apartment was in a high-rent area along the Seine near the Place de l'Alma, close to the Plaza Athenee and Avenue Montaigne, which housed the world's most expensive boutiques. "Well, here we are," she said, as the car slowed to a stop.

Jack got out first and held the car door for her. Once they

were on the sidewalk, he said, "I love how you get in and out of a car. You show lots of gorgeous leg."

She fluttered her eyes. "Really. I never noticed."

Jack offered to walk her to her door. "Just to make sure you get in okay."

She gave him that warm smile of hers. At the door to 6B, the penthouse, she took the key out of her bag and put it in the lock. Then she turned to Jack, lifting her face up toward his. Her coat was open in the front. As he kissed her, she pressed her body close to his. They stayed that way for several minutes.

Jack was incredibly aroused and caressing her back under her coat. He ran one hand along her leg.

He pulled his face away and whispered in her ear, "I could come in for a little while."

She kissed him lightly on each cheek. "I don't do sex on the first date."

Disappointed, Jack watched her turn the key and open the door. "What are you doing tomorrow night?"

"Having dinner with you, of course."

"Great. Taillevent at nine. I'll somehow manage to get a reservation."

"I'll be there."

"It'll be our second date."

His eyes followed her until the door was closed.

Riding down six flights in the elevator, Jack tried to calm himself. He couldn't remember being so excited by a woman in years.

He stepped out of the front of her building and looked around. The sidewalk was deserted. Still thinking about Layla, he walked toward the waiting Jaguar. Suddenly he heard a rustling behind him and to the left. He wheeled around and stared in that direction. Lurking in the shadows, in the doorway of the next building, was a swarthy-looking man in a leather coat with a thick black mustache. He was watching Jack in a menacing way. Nadim must have sent him, Jack decided.

Though he was unarmed, Jack stopped moving and stood still, locking eyes with the man, challenging him to attack. When the man made no effort to move, Jack calmly walked toward the Jaguar and climbed into the back. "I'm ready to go, Jean Claude," he said.

"We scored big," Avi said as soon as Jack entered his apartment, sounding excited.

He didn't feel as if he had scored big, but he didn't tell Avi that. Instead he asked, "What happened?"

"I heard from Yudi at the embassy a couple of hours ago."

I must have had too much wine, Jack decided. He couldn't place Yudi in his mind.

Sensing his bewilderment, Avi explained. "He's my guy at the embassy checking airplane manifests and reservations in and out of Paris for any mention of Nadim."

Jack remembered what Layla had said about the Syrian. "Where's the bastard going?"

"Moscow, early tomorrow morning on Air France."

Jack was startled. "Moscow?"

"Yeah."

"What do you make of it?"

Avi shrugged. "It can't be good for us."

"Have you told Moshe?"

Avi nodded. "I called him from the embassy. He'll have a couple of people at the airport to follow Nadim from the time he arrives."

Jack had been in Moscow last year when Chava had played Katerina in Shostakovich's *Lady Macbeth of Mtsensk*. He had been astounded by the traffic and chaos on the roads. "Have you been to Moscow recently?" he asked Avi. "It won't be easy."

"Shlomo's in charge. He's very good."

Jack was still worried. "He'll have to be. Getting around in that city's a nightmare. Trying to follow someone will be even worse."

"Shlomo was born and lived the first twenty years of his life in Moscow. Moshe stationed him there a year ago. Believe me, he knows the city." Avi pointed to the Armagnac. "You want some?"

A yawn forced itself out of Jack's mouth. "More alcohol's the last thing I need right now."

"What happened with you?"

Jack described his evening with Layla and what she said about Nadim. He decided to omit any mention of the man lurking in the shadows next to Layla's building, because he didn't want Avi to discourage him from seeing Layla tomorrow. Also, he rationalized that he was being paranoid. The man had never even tried to approach him. His initial instinct that Nadim had sent the man may have been wrong.

At the end of his report, Jack said, "So I don't think she's in cahoots with Nadim, trying to set me up. I've established that much."

Avi's face registered doubt. "You don't know that."

"C'mon, Nadim's responsible for the death of her uncle Bashir and lots of her Maronite brethren. That's how he earned the title of Butcher of Beirut."

"True, but he also installed her other uncle, Amin, as the ruler, and he's let her father live. If she doesn't do what Nadim wants, all he has to do is pick up the phone and have someone kill her father. I'm sure that thought has crossed Layla's brilliant little mind."

Jack was becoming exasperated. "She detests Nadim. She's made that clear to me sixteen different ways. Why would she be working with him?"

"Suppose it's all an act," Avi said. "Suppose she's willing to tolerate him, but she hates the Israelis. She sees us as her enemy, the people who destroyed her country."

"But we didn't," Jack protested.

"People believe what they want to believe. Maybe Nadim's in Layla's bed fucking her right now. Meantime, she's trying to con you, to suck you in."

"Why?" Jack was raising his voice. "Why would she possibly be doing that?"

"Suppose Nadim knows you were one of the Israeli spies in Damascus with Yasef. He wants to find out what you learned, and what we're planning to do to block his plan. He figures that if Layla gets close enough to you, then you'll talk to her, because after all she's convinced you that she can't stand Nadim. How's that?"

When Jack didn't respond, Avi added, "And one more thing. Nadim may be called the Butcher of Beirut, but the man's not just a violent psychopath. He's also extremely smart, shrewd, clever, cunning, or whatever similar adjective you want to use. He spent years being taught by the spymasters in the KGB. They pulled shit like this all of the time. The Americans and the British often fell for it, which is why the Russians knew so much about what the West was doing."

Avi's words rocked Jack back on his heels. His face registered amazement and incredulity.

Avi picked up on it. "Look, my friend, we're on the same side. I'm trying to help you. Besides, I'd just as soon not have to report your demise to Moshe."

Wide-eyed, Jack stared at Avi. "Jesus, you don't trust anyone. Do you?"

"That's why I'm still alive, but none of this matters any longer. Layla's in your past. Forget about her. We'll move on with the Moscow trip. Now we have something real and tangible."

Jack took a deep breath. "I'm seeing her tomorrow night."

Avi wrinkled up his face. "You've got to be kidding."

"We may still be able to use her," Jack said stubbornly.

"I'll give it to you straight, my friend. You don't believe that for a minute. You're being led around by your dick. She's working for Nadim and using you. When they're finished with you, they'll chew you up and spit you out."

Chapter 22

Robert McCallister was despondent. All dressed up with no place to go. He had revved himself up emotionally for the escape attempt. His timing was perfect. Immediately after breakfast he had asked if he could exercise.

Judging from the location of the sun it was about the same time as the last two days when the dark green van had come with the food delivery.

Under the watchful eye of two guards gripping their AK-47s and moving with him, Robert jogged around the property just inside the heavy stone wall that surrounded the villa.

After running almost an hour, he gave up. The van wasn't coming.

Breathing heavily, he stopped running and picked up a bottle of water from a bucket of ice on the porch of the villa. He took one more look around. "Ah, shit," he muttered under his breath. With the two guards behind him, he trudged into the house. Tomorrow was another day. Maybe the van would come then, and he could escape.

Shlomo decided on three teams of two each. Almost as important as following Nadim was avoiding detection. All six Israelis had Nadim's picture.

Nadim's plane arrived on time at Moscow's Sheremetyevo Airport. As the Syrian emerged from the customs area and cut swiftly through the arrival hall, two Israelis were walking behind him.

One of them, Gadi, was on his cell phone, in constant contact with the other teams. "Subject is headed toward the exit for chauffeur-driven cars."

That was precisely what Shlomo had guessed. He and Eytan were parked in a black Mercedes in a row of waiting limos. Eytan was behind the wheel in a chauffeur's uniform. Shlomo was in the backseat.

"Subject is getting into a gray Mercedes parked near exit door number four," Gadi said. "License plate 167492."

Shlomo leaned forward in the seat and strained his eyes, watching the other limos. A gray Mercedes pulled away from the curb. Shlomo grabbed his small binoculars from the car seat. The license plate was 167492. "Let's go," he barked to Eytan. "That's the car."

Shlomo picked up his cell phone. "We're moving. Proceeding toward the highway for Moscow Center. Are you in place, Judah?"

"Ready to enter the highway at Exit Two when you give the word."

Eytan followed the gray Mercedes until they reached Exit Two, then he signaled to turn off. "Go," Shlomo told Judah. "Now."

Judah's Volvo, with a beat-up body and a new engine, moved onto the highway two cars behind the gray Mercedes. "Got him," Judah said.

Eytan made a loop around the highway exit and returned to the road now well back of the gray Mercedes, moving in the flow of traffic. Team three arrived on the scene in a taxi that had been borrowed for a hefty fee and was speeding down the left side of the highway. It overtook the gray Mercedes. All three of the Israelis' cars were now on the road.

At the exit for Moscow Center, Nadim's gray Mercedes

turned off the highway. The Volvo was still two cars behind, Shlomo's black Mercedes half a mile back.

For the next ten minutes they moved in that pattern, with the Volvo dropping back a little and moving up. "Let's switch," Shlomo said to Judah. "You turn right and reenter the road in a couple of minutes. We'll move up."

"Done."

Shlomo and Eytan were now three car lengths behind Nadim. They rode like that for five more minutes until Nadim's car pulled off the road and parked in front of a grim-looking four-story gray stone building. A high black wrought-iron fence with loops of barbed wire on top encircled the property. Antennae sprouted from the roof like wildflowers in a spring meadow. Half a dozen armed guards, two with German shepherds, patrolled the grounds.

In the back of the black car, Shlomo trembled. In front of the building, on the fence near the guardhouse, were two small black plaques with gold lettering. One identified the former occupant of the building, the other the current one.

From the road Shlomo couldn't read the words. He didn't have to. He knew exactly where Nadim was going, and he didn't like it one bit.

"Hold here," Shlomo said to Eytan. From a distance of forty yards he watched Nadim get out of his car. The Syrian gave a quick look around, then moved with fast, determined steps toward the entrance gate, where they were expecting him. He was passed straight through. Shlomo watched Nadim enter the building. Then he told Eytan, "Drive over to that café on the corner and park."

While Eytan followed the order, Shlomo told the other two units where they were.

With Eytan in tow, Shlomo walked into the Philadelphia Café, which had only a couple of patrons. They sat down at a table next to the window. Unobtrusively, Shlomo parted the grimy black-and-white-checked curtains in order to have a clear view of the entrance to the building with the fence and the gray Mercedes.

In perfect Russian, because he was a native, he ordered two coffees and some babka.

Eytan, who had been in Moscow only a month, asked softly, "Do you know what building that is?"

Shlomo's facial muscles were taut. "Formerly the operations center for KGB special projects. That's a polite way of saying they interrogated people in the basement. It consumed huge quantities of electricity."

Eytan grimaced. "And now?"

"Headquarters for Dmitri Suslov Enterprises."

"I've read about him. He's one of the new Russian big shot industrialists. Isn't he?"

"More precisely, a thug parading as a big businessman. Isn't Russia a wonderful place?"

Shlomo whipped out his cell phone and scrolled through the directory until he found what he wanted—the cell phone number of Michael Hanley. The top officials in Jerusalem and Washington could play whatever political games they wanted, but the Israeli and American agents in the field knew they could gain from cooperation. Shlomo regularly had dinner with key CIA agents in Moscow during which they exchanged information about current projects. He knew that Dmitri Suslov was the top priority for Michael.

"It's Shlomo," he said tersely. "We're in the Philadelphia Café. We've been following a subject who just went into your favorite building across the street. My guess is that he's visiting one of your best friends."

Michael was excited. This could be Suslov's next sale. "I'll drop everything and be there in twenty minutes. Less if I fly. Order me a coffee. It won't have time to get cold."

Fifteen minutes later Michael arrived. The coffee was waiting for him on the table. He sat down and whispered to

Shlomo, "Subject still in there?" Shlomo nodded. "Who is he?" Michael held his breath.

"Major General Nadim. Deputy director of Syrian intelligence."

Michael gave a long, low whistle as he remembered his visit to Volgograd with Perikov. He hoped to hell there was no relationship between the two—that Syria wasn't trying to obtain nuclear arms from Suslov. "Why are you following Nadim?"

"Moshe didn't tell me," Shlomo replied. "Since the old man is personally involved, it has to be top-level stuff. You've been watching Suslov. . . . Have any ideas?"

"One that you won't like," Michael said. A picture of the warehouse in Volgograd popped into his mind. "You'll wish you never asked. You won't sleep tonight. And if I'm right, you won't sleep any other night until this is over."

After Michael explained why he had been pursuing Suslov and what he had seen in Volgograd, the three of them sat in glum silence trying to imagine how dreadful it would be for Israel, the Middle East, and the world if the Syrians or one of their allies obtained nuclear weapons.

"Perhaps Nadim came for some other reason," Eytan said hopefully.

"It can't be for a chess match. Suslov doesn't play." Michael shook his head. "There's one foolish optimist in every crowd."

"How can we find out for sure?" Shlomo asked.

Michael hadn't seen Irina since they had gone to the inn together overnight. She was his only chance. "I'll do what I can," he said. "Meantime, let's wait and see where Nadim goes from here."

Jack got to the Bristol early. He went into the men's room, removed his toupee, glasses, contacts, and mustache, and placed them into his briefcase. He couldn't risk Sarah telling Sam how different he looked. His brother was smart. He might guess why Jack felt it necessary to assume a disguise. Then Jack returned to the lobby and waited. Ten minutes later he watched a sad-looking woman with puffy eyes come through the glass revolving doors. From his distance of twenty yards, he immediately recognized Sarah.

After thirty years, the bright flower of spring had faded. Some men would have found her attractive, but Jack remembered something else.

Her brown hair was streaked with gray. She still had a shapely figure, but instead of the explosive colors and tight-fitting clothes she had once worn to show it off, she was dressed in a nondescript wrinkled beige suit and practical pumps. In the old days had once refused to wear makeup, laughing at women who did. Today it was caked on her face.

The sad-looking woman turned to a bellman inside the door and said, "I'm meeting someone." She spotted Jack moving forward and forced a smile.

As long as he was having lunch with her, Jack had made up his mind to be polite. "You look just the same, Sarah."

She gave a short, nervous laugh and touched his arm. "You can't mean that. Or you've lost your sight. But you're nice to say it."

"I thought we'd eat here," Jack said, pointing to the luxurious wood-paneled dining room just off the lobby of the Bristol.

"Wonderful. We always stay here in Paris. I like the dining room."

We obviously meant she and Terry. Jack guessed that she didn't want to mention his name.

When the waiter asked if they wanted an aperitif, Sarah said, "A scotch on the rocks would be nice." Jack settled for a glass of white wine.

"To better days," she said, raising her glass.

After they ordered lunch, she told him, "You're in the wine business, Jack. Pick something good for us."

Jack selected a simple Mersault with the grilled turbot they were having.

He let her lead the discussion. For a while she talked about Ann and Sam. "They're so good together," she said. "Right for each other. I couldn't hope for anything better."

Then she moved to the usual "Let's catch up on our lives." She was tense and nervous as she began, gulping down the Mersault. "A wonderful wine," she said.

"You obviously like it," he responded.

She let that pass. "I spend a great deal of my time helping people as a volunteer. I'm the director of an organization that runs shelters for the homeless, and another one that dispenses food to the poor. I'm on the foundation board of a large public hospital. Nothing glitzy. No opera or symphony boards. I'm not an officer of the country club in Winnetka, though of course we belong and I've learned to play a decent game of golf."

She was waiting for some words of approval from Jack. When they weren't forthcoming, she added, "Not much different from the old Sarah in the soup kitchen at Ann Arbor."

He watched her picking at her food as she drank more and more wine. What was running through his mind was, *How could I have been such an ass, remembering those golden days of our youth?* Like the high school football hero, Sarah had peaked at eighteen. He could tell that she was desperate for him to like her. He realized that she had been unhappy long before Robert's plane was shot down.

"What about you, Jack? Sam says you've built a good business."

Jack laughed. "That's my brother. Always focused on the bottom line."

"Well, you've had your dream of living in Israel. Has it turned out the way you wanted?"

"I wouldn't live anywhere else, but the country and I grew up together. The dreams of the early days have given way to some harsh realities. It's a hard, tough life, and I don't just mean economically."

"You mean the wars and the terrorist attacks?"

He nodded. "That's part of it. Anytime you go to a restaurant or walk on the street, you know there's always the possibility of an attack by a suicide bomber. But even more than that, we're constantly under siege from the Palestinians and our neighbors one way or another."

He thought about his discussion with Layla last evening. "The Syrians are the worst."

"Are you married? Any children?"

"I was married once for a short time. No children. Didn't work out," he said curtly. She wasn't entitled to an explanation.

"Then I guess I sort of messed things up for both of us," she said.

Looking at her, he thought, *Only for you, my dear. Only for you.* Instead of responding, he signaled the waiter to clear the dishes from their main course.

"The past few days have been hell for me," she said, "since my Bobby's plane was shot down."

"I truly feel sorry about that." Jack sounded sincere. He meant it.

"Bobby reminds me of you in a lot of ways. He's a nice guy. Gets along with people. A good student. A real decent human being."

She paused to wipe some tears from her eyes with a napkin. "My Bobby had dreams of going to medical school, but Terry insisted on his attending the Air Force Academy. Terry wants him to be president one day."

"If that's what Bobby wants, I hope he gets it," Jack said, trying to sound as if her son had a future.

"We've gone everywhere. Done everything. Been to the

White House. Met with the president and his top advisers, both senators from Illinois, everyone. It's all so hopeless and frustrating." She began sobbing. Tears were running down her face, causing her mascara to run.

Jack removed a handkerchief from his pocket and handed it to her. She wiped her eyes and blew her nose. "I'm sorry. I'll pull together. I came to see you because the Israelis are good at this sort of thing."

"You know I would do anything I could to help. The reality is that I'm not in the government, Sarah."

"But you always had a good way with people. You could get them to do things."

"I'm sure that the American government has asked the Israelis to help. That means more than my calling somebody I met once at a party."

"He told the president not to involve the Israelis. I was there when he said it."

The *he* was obviously Terry. Jack was thinking, *The old anti-Semite couldn't stand the idea of Jews rescuing his son,* but he didn't say that. Instead he replied, "With all due respect, Sarah, the American government will do whatever makes sense regardless of what a hostage's father says. No matter how important the person is."

Jack's words put a ray of hope on her face. "Do you really think so?"

He nodded. He decided to probe for information. "Surely the American military is planning a rescue operation?"

She got a pained expression on her face. "They tried one somewhere in southeast Turkey, but they were too late. By the time they got to the jail where they were holding Bobby, the Turks had moved him. Terry said he's in the town of Van now in an underground bunker. They'll never get him out of there."

Jack wondered whether Moshe had decided not to tell the Americans about Robert's present location, or whether

Kendall and his people were keeping Terry in the dark. He wanted to say, *Bobby's been moved to Syria. He's probably safe because they're planning to use him in some bigger deal.* But he couldn't do that. He fiddled with a cuff link. If her information was current, then he and Avi were ahead of the Americans. He would have to report that to Moshe.

She was staring at him before making another try. "You must be able to do something. You've lived in Israel so long. You have to know people who could help." The niceness was gone. In her desperation, fueled by alcohol, she sounded ugly.

"Shh. Keep your voice down."

She got herself under control. "I'm pleading with you to consider what you can do to help. That's all I'm asking."

Jack looked away from her down at the table. "I'll do what I can, Sarah," he said softly. "I can't promise anything."

She reached over to touch his hand, but he pulled away. "Please, that's all I ask."

Jack stole a glance at his watch. It had been the longest hour he could ever remember. He would have preferred to get the check and wrap it up when the waiter came by. She ordered a cognac in lieu of dessert. Jack had a cappuccino.

As long as he had to stay, Jack made up his mind to ask her the one question he had always wondered about. "How did the head of the New Left student association become a right-wing Republican?"

"Ah, the great metamorphosis of Terry McCallister," she said bitterly. He nodded. "We were living in a commune near Big Sur, farming and smoking pot. Ann was four and Robert was two when Terry's father died. He hadn't spoken to his dad for years, though he'd stayed in touch with his mother, which was more than I did with mine," she said sadly. "So we came back to Chicago for the funeral. His father had a large real estate business, but his affairs were in shambles. The day after the funeral Terry and I went with his mother to the family lawyer's office, Edward M. Jones the Third. We were in dirty jeans and sandals—to prove a point, I guess. The kids were barefoot. What we found was a roomful of blue-suited lawyers and bankers ready to pounce like vultures on a fresh carcass. Mr. Jones, as the old stuffy bat insisted on being called, explained that the chances of his holding the creditors at bay and leaving Terry's mother with even the house were between slim and none.

"Something happened that day to Terry. Maybe he was tired of the life we had. Maybe he loved his mother. Or maybe he wanted to prove something to his recently departed father. But Terry made up his mind to do battle with the vultures.

"He fired Mr. Jones and hired Del Prescott, a high school buddy of his, who was a lawyer with one of the big La Salle Street firms. We moved into his parents' house with his mother and cleaned up, so to speak. Actually, Mrs. McCallister was a very nice woman. First she scrubbed the kids. Then she tidied me up. She was doing all of this while she was still shaken over her husband's death and the financial mess. I remember she even tried to call my parents. I knew that would be hopeless.

"Funny thing was, Terry had a good head for business, and he could be charming when he wanted to be. In about twelve months he and Del sold off enough property and had a large enough nest egg to start a venture-capital firm, one of the first in Chicago. They took early large stakes in Microsoft and Intel and soon had high-tech start-ups beating a path to their door. Timing in life is everything. They cashed in most of their chips before the bubble burst. By then Terry was spending about half his time contributing and raising money for Republican candidates. They were all sucking up to him for money, mostly on the right. He was loving every minute of it. I wanted him to set up a charitable foundation, but he wouldn't do that. It had to be the Republican party. Terry saw himself as a kingmaker and Bobby as his future. Believe it or not, Joe Kennedy was his model. Does that answer your question?"

"I think it does." Jack signaled the waiter for the check.

She looked at Jack, and her eyes filled up again with tears. "I'm sorry for what I did to us. I really am. You've got to believe that. I was young then. If I could take it all back, I would do it differently." Her words were slurred.

Feeling disgust for her, he replied in a sharp tone, "We were all young."

"I had more than myself to think about at the time."

He didn't respond. He knew that she had been pregnant when she married Terry. His parents had told him in August of the year he had gone to Israel about the Goodmans' anguish at not attending their daughter's wedding. "We know how much she hurt you," his mother had said. Seven months later his mother had been in tears when she called to tell him that Sarah had had a baby girl, and the Goodmans had vowed they would never see their granddaughter.

Jack tossed a credit card on the silver tray with the check. The waiter discreetly picked it up.

Sarah was looking at him beseechingly. "Terry and I have nothing. I know that we can't go back thirty years in time, but maybe you and I can start from this point and create something new."

Her offer was absurd. He wanted to laugh. "You can't turn the clock back," he said as gently as he could manage.

"You're right." She was trying to get a grip on herself. It was a matter of pride. It was obvious what he thought of her. She refused to humiliate herself any further.

As she rose from her chair, her knees were wobbling. She steadied herself by gripping the table. "After you think about it, if you can do anything to help my Bobby," she said, trying to mask the desperation she was feeling, "I would appreciate it. That's all I came to tell you today."

He helped her find a cab; then he returned to the men's room in the Bristol to put his disguise back on. He decided to walk for a while on the Rue St. Honore to clear his brain after lunch with Sarah. He didn't have a good record with women.

Avi was right: He should break it off with Layla before it was too late. They didn't need Layla any longer to get at Nadim. That was the sensible thing to do, and it would avoid the great risk to himself. His head told him that.

He was a mature man now, not a college student, but he couldn't help himself. He was intoxicated with Layla.

For more than two hours, Shlomo, Eytan, and Michael sat in the Philadelphia Café drinking coffee, smoking cigarettes, and taking turns glancing out of the opening in the dirty, thin curtains at the front of the entrance to Suslov's building.

Suddenly Eytan said, "Nadim's on the way out."

"With whom?" Shlomo asked nervously.

"Alone. Headed toward his car."

Shlomo and Eytan bolted for the door. With his cell phone, Shlomo notified the other two teams.

A minute later all six Israelis were on the move in their three cars along with Nadim's gray Mercedes. They headed in a direction that led back to the airport.

In the café, Michael remained behind and took out his cell phone. He knew that calling Irina at her office was dangerous, but he had no choice. "I have to see you," he said as soon as he heard her voice.

"I can't talk now, Mother," she replied, trying to sound annoyed that her mother had called. But he also detected panic in her voice.

"Call me when you can. On my cell," Michael said, and hung up quickly.

What had happened? he wondered. He wanted to believe that Suslov or one of his people was close by when Michael had called. That was all. But the sound of her voice told him it might be more than that.

What was his next move? Michael wondered. Report to Joyner, or wait awhile to see if Irina called?

Wait, he finally decided. At this point he didn't have any hard information that Nadim's visit was related to Suslov's sale of nuclear arms.

At Sheremetyevo Airport two Israeli teams followed Nadim into the terminal. The third remained parked in the limo lot in case the Syrian went back to his car for a quick getaway.

Shlomo watched Nadim get in line at Alitalia. The Israeli queued up in the adjoining line. When Nadim reached the ticket counter first, Shlomo strained his ears to listen.

"Space has been reserved for me on flight four-fifty-three to Rome today," Nadim said, "and on your flight tomorrow at sixteen-thirty from Rome to Paris. Both in first class."

Having gotten the information he wanted, Shlomo drifted away from the ticket counter and headed toward the terminal exit. Eytan was a short distance away, watching Nadim. He continued doing that until Nadim walked through passport control, on the way to the boarding area. Then he joined Shlomo at the terminal exit.

He gave Shlomo a thumbs-up, which evoked a smile. They had accomplished their mission without a hitch. Nadim was gone. They could relax. But first Eytan drove Shlomo to the Israeli embassy so he could report to Moshe on a secure phone.

Shlomo had expected the director to chew him out for involving the Americans without approval from Jerusalem. To his pleasant surprise, Moshe responded, "Washington may be able to help us. Stick close to Michael Hanley. Also, try to find out what connection Suslov has to Rome. Meantime I'll alert Benny in Rome. He'll pick up Nadim at Fiumicino."

"What do you think is happening?"

Moshe's mind was processing what Shlomo had told him. "Every bit of information you gave me raised more questions." He decided not to tell Shlomo about the possible connection of any of this to Robert McCallister, particularly because he couldn't put the pieces together himself.

Ten minutes later Joyner listened to Moshe's report of what happened in Moscow with alarm. She didn't want to believe that the erratic and irrational Syrian government, blinded by its hatred for Israel, would be acquiring nuclear arms. An even worse scenario was that Nadim was somehow acting in coordination with the renegade Turks, and they would both be receiving the arms Suslov was selling. That meant they were planning some type of nuclear blackmail. Robert McCallister was a pawn in their scheme.

At the end of his report, Moshe put Joyner's fears into his own blunt words: "Suslov's nuclear arms will be moving to Syria and Turkey."

"You haven't established that," a grim Joyner responded, wanting to believe Moshe was wrong.

"You're deluding yourself if you don't accept it. And by the way, you'd better face the fact that your American pilot, Robert McCallister, has been tossed in the middle of this dangerous mix. That's why they moved him to Syria."

"You made a huge leap to get there."

"I may have, but I can't take a chance on that scenario. I intend to act on the assumption I'm right and do everything possible to block them."

Moshe's words further alarmed Joyner. She had set up, with painstaking care for several months, Michael Hanley's

project in Russia. Assuming there was a transaction involving Suslov, Turkey, and Syria, the only way it could be
blocked was if they caught Suslov in the act and Kendall
went to Drozny, the Russian president.

"I'll be blunt," Joyner said in a harsh voice. "Your people
stumbled onto Suslov by accident. We've been watching
him for some time. We're now in the delicate final stages of
a sting operation and—"

Moshe cut her off. "The answer's no." His voice was
firm. "We won't back off and let you handle it alone. Once
the Arabs get nuclear arms, the very existence of the state of
Israel is at risk. You have no right to ask me to step aside and
place our fate in the hands of your President Kendall."

His response was understandable as well as predictable.
Joyner didn't argue. "At least keep me informed. Let me
know before you make your next move."

"We'll coordinate with you in Russia," he replied tersely.
He had omitted from his report to Joyner the fact that Nadim
was now en route to Rome and what the Israelis planned to
do there.

Joyner put the phone down and immediately called
Michael Hanley on his cell phone. "Can you get to the embassy? We have to talk."

Twenty minutes later he called her back.

"The Israelis told me about Nadim's meeting with
Suslov."

Michael was furious at himself for letting her find out
from another source. "I waited to call you until I had more
information. It was a mistake. I'm sorry."

Joyner didn't chastise him. There was no point. "In the
future, call me immediately if anything happens."

"Absolutely, Ms. Joyner."

"Now the question is, Do you have any facts, reliable and
confirmed, other than that Nadim met with Suslov, or more
precisely someone in Suslov's building? Because that's as

much as I got from the Israelis. As far as I'm concerned, everything else about the sale of nuclear arms and so forth is speculation."

"I'm working on it," he said tersely.

"What's that mean?" Joyner demanded to know.

"My contact called me a few minutes ago. We're meeting tonight."

"Irina?"

"Yeah," he said sheepishly. "I'm going to push her hard to find out what the deal is between Suslov and Nadim."

"Be careful, Michael," she said. "I want to find out, but I don't want to lose you."

Chapter 23

Jack knew there was a problem as soon as he saw Layla's face. She was following Monsieur Vrinat, the venerable proprietor of Taillevent, into the wood-paneled front room of the restaurant. Her broad smile from last evening was replaced by a tightly drawn mouth. The warm, twinkling eyes were shooting looks that stung. Today there had been no last-minute visit to the hairstylist. She had even omitted the perfume.

Jack stood up as a waiter pulled the table back so she could sit next to him with their backs against the wall on the red-cushioned banquette. He leaned forward to kiss her cheeks, but she pulled away, leaving him with air.

Once seated, she said coolly, "I almost didn't come."

"Why not?" He tried to sound innocent, but he could guess what happened.

"I don't like men who lie to me."

Before Jack could respond, Jean Marie, the black jacket clad maître d' in the front room, approached the table and asked, "An aperitif?"

"Champagne, please," Jack responded.

"And for the lady?"

"Whatever the liar says."

Jean Marie, who had witnessed every conceivable domestic scene in his many years at Taillevent, gave a tiny smile, raised his finger, and pointed it at Jack. "I think you're in big trouble. I take her side."

"You're a smart man," Layla snapped. "You can't believe a word he tells you."

When Jean Marie left, Jack whispered, "Calm down, please."

"Don't tell me that. I hate it when anybody tells me that."

Jack didn't know what to say. His mind was racing, but so far without success. If there was a chance Avi was right, and she was doing Nadim's work, Jack couldn't possibly tell her the truth. Across the room, Monsieur Vrinat was leading a Frenchman in a military uniform to a table. Jack decided to try to toss the ball into her court.

Once their glasses of champagne arrived, he said, "Tell me what's bothering you. There may be an explanation."

"I doubt it."

"Well, at least give me a chance. I'm entitled to that much."

"Wrong. You're not entitled to anything." She raised her glass and said, "To honest men."

Jack sat in stoic silence, maintaining his composure. After several minutes she said, "Computers are wonderful things. And I have an effective research department."

She reached into her black leather bag and pulled out an e-mail from someone in her bank's research department, which she handed to him. "Here. You can see for yourself."

Jack let his breath out slowly as he read. *There is no New York business named Calvert Wine Importers. Jack Cole is an Israeli citizen with Israeli and U.S. passports. He is the president of a company based in Tel Aviv, with offices in Paris, Milan and Barcelona, by the name of Mediterranean Wine Exports. Paris telephone number 1-23-43-68-68. Divorced. No children. Current banking connections are Bank Leumi in Tel Aviv and Credit Lyonais in Paris.*

He handed it back to her without saying a word.

"That doesn't sound like the New York widower with motherless children I had dinner with last night at Guy Savoy. Does it?"

Jack swallowed hard, thinking. Finally he saw a way out. "There's so much animosity between Arabs and Israelis," he said. "If I had told you who I was, you'd never have gone out with me. I didn't want that. You're simply the most beautiful, the most sexually attractive woman I ever met in my life."

"It's amazing that you could discern all of that from a one minute conversation at the Latour tasting."

"Sometimes I form snap judgments about people."

She wasn't buying it. She looked into his eyes and shook her head. "I'm terribly disappointed. We had such a great time last evening. We clicked. I can't ever remember feeling that way about a man, and then bam, I find out that I had no idea whom I was even with."

Her face remained tight and drawn. Jack had only one more card to play. It was a dangerous one, because she was smart. She would know that he was in the intelligence game. But if Avi was right, and she was working for Nadim, that wouldn't be news to her.

He leaned in close. "Complete disclosure runs two ways," he said in a low conspiratorial voice. You didn't tell me that you were funneling money raised from Lebanese around the world back to Beirut. Did you?"

Layla looked as if she had been slapped in the face. Her head snapped back. "How did you find that out?"

"I, too, have friends who have computers."

"That's not on the Internet," she whispered through clenched teeth.

Before Jack could respond, she pulled a BlackBerry out of her bag, typed something on the screen, and showed it to him. It said, *Mossad.*

Jack stared at the gray screen without saying a word. She deleted it.

"I think we'd better order," he said.

"For two cents, I'd walk out."

Jack knew she was on the verge of doing that. "At least stay for dinner." He was pleading with her with his eyes. "Let's try to talk about it."

"Fine, then you pick for me. You seem to be calling the shots here."

"I'll do the food. You select the wines." He handed her the list. "Tonight I won't say a word. You're on your own."

Jack watched her looking at the wine list. He could see that she was deep in thought, and it wasn't about which wines to select.

Once the waiter was gone, she turned to him, visibly upset, with an intently serious gaze. "Listen, Jack," she said in a halting voice. "What you told me a minute ago about funneling money to Lebanon?"

"Yeah?"

"Please don't mention that to anyone. I'm not sure how much you know, but you would be signing an execution order for me and my family."

He reached over and touched her arm. "I would never do that. I would never do anything to harm you. I promise you that."

That seemed to satisfy her. "Then tell me what you want with me. It has to be something political."

He sighed deeply. This might be quicksand, but he was ready to wade in. "Initially, I did have an ulterior motive in wanting to meet you. I'm sorry about that, but it's true. Last night changed all of that for me. I had the type of evening I've dreamed about having with a woman, but it's never worked out. You're a very special person. We're good together." Jack saw from her face that she was softening. "I want to spend more time with you. And not for any other reason. I hope you'll believe me."

Watching him as he spoke, Layla was convinced he was telling her the truth. Under the table, she put her hand in his. "I do believe you," she said, "but you are engaged in some type of espionage activity for the Mossad that involves my country . . . right now in Paris. Aren't you?"

Jack looked away from her, toward the entrance to the room, where waiters were carrying in trays with quiet efficiency. He didn't want to lie to her anymore. "Not your country."

Suddenly she discreetly pointed toward the French military officer seated against the far wall. "That's it, isn't it?"

"What do you mean?" He was puzzled.

"You were so interested in Nadim at the wine dinner at L'Ambroise. He's the reason you asked me out. You were hoping I could help you get at Nadim. That's right. Isn't it?"

Jack gulped hard. He would never underestimate her again. "Originally I did call you because I thought it was a way of getting to Nadim, but that changed last evening."

"You're taking a horrible chance by seeing me." Jack could see that she was frightened. "Nadim's called me every day for the last week to go out with him. I keep turning him down. Today he asked me if I'm seeing that American, Jack Cole. I'm terrified of him."

He put his arm around her for reassurance. "Don't worry. I'll be able to deal with him."

She shook her head. "You're kidding yourself. Being naive. You can't imagine how horrible Nadim is. I despise that man more than I thought it was possible to hate anyone or anything. From what I told you last evening, you know that I'm justified." Jack nodded. "I also hate the Syrians and what they did to my family. To my country."

"You don't like the Israelis much either."

"You're right there." She made no effort to conceal her

animosity. "It's close. But I dislike the Syrians more. At least your people aren't occupying my country any longer. There's an old Arab expression: The enemy of my enemy is my friend. So I guess what I'm saying is that for all of these reasons I'd like to help you in whatever you're doing. If you tell me about it, maybe there's something I can do."

Well, there it was, Jack thought. She had played her cards exactly how Avi predicted if she were working with Nadim. But Avi was wrong. Jack was a good judge of people. He knew that she wasn't Nadim's agent. "Thanks for your offer," he said, "but I don't want to involve you. That would mean putting you at risk, which is something I won't do."

She looked into his eyes and decided he meant what he had just said. She was ready to move on. "Sorry I came on so strong when I arrived at the restaurant this evening. It's just that—"

He leaned over and kissed her on the lips. "You don't have to apologize. I had no right misleading you like that. Can we start over?" He held out his hand and said, "Hi, I'm Jack Cole."

She laughed. "Shaking hands is such an American custom. You're in France now. Kiss me on each cheek."

He obliged, just as the waiter arrived with their first courses, lobster sausage for Layla and ravioli with morel mushrooms for Jack, accompanied by a Corton-Charlemagne. From across the room, Jean Marie was watching them and smiling. The lovers had made up.

She took a bite and nodded. "Good choice," she said, pointing to the plate.

"Thanks. I've eaten here a few times over the years."

"This evening I want to learn about you," Layla said. "Not your involvement in the stuff we talked about earlier, but the rest of Jack Cole. To the extent you can talk about it."

He was pleased that he had salvaged his relationship with

her. "You'll learn that I'm a lot older than you are," Jack said.

She gave him that warm, mysterious smile. "Maybe yes, and maybe no. I'll never tell."

He described for her what it was like growing up in Chicago. About political and racial unrest in the United States in the sixties and the seventies, and about his desire to live in Israel.

"What is it about you Jews and your almost mystical attachment to Israel?"

Jack could feel his hackles rising.

She sensed it. "I didn't mean that as an insult. I've never spent any significant time with anyone Jewish before, much less dated a Jew. I want to understand it. There are millions of proud Lebanese around the world who don't yearn to live in Beirut. What is it?"

He thought about her question for a long minute. It was a difficult one. "I could say the same thing. There are millions of Jews who don't want to live in Israel. Some don't even want to have any connection . . . but for others, there is a great attachment to the people and the Jewish homeland."

She paused to ponder his words as the sommelier poured the 1990 Premier Cru Vosne-Romanee from Meo Camuzet. Monsieur Vrinat came by, looked at Jack, and said, "An excellent selection."

Jack pointed to Layla. "It was hers. I had nothing to do with it."

"Then you're a lucky man."

"I think so, too."

When Vrinat departed and an incredibly tender rack of lamb arrived, Layla asked Jack, "Where do you live in Israel?"

He told her about his apartment in Tel Aviv and about his wine business.

"Did you ever fight in my country?" she said, tensing her back.

"Never. Not even in the reserves. In the 'seventy-three war I fought in the Golan against the Syrians."

"I hope you killed a lot of those bastards."

"Several in a huge battle. I also took a bullet in the side," he said, pointing to a spot below his belt. "Fortunately, they got me to Hadassah Hospital. It took a while, but they fixed me up."

"Do you have a nasty scar?"

"It's fading."

"I want to see it," she said.

He looked horrified. "Now?"

"Not now, you idiot. Later." Concealed by the tablecloth, she rested her hand between his legs for an instant to let him know what she was thinking. "My, my." She laughed. "Your horse is ready to run."

For dessert she had a mango mousse and he had a rich chocolate gâteau. Then they slowly sipped a complimentary glass of cognac.

She pushed back her hair and said, "I'm glad I came this evening."

"I feel exactly the same way. Tonight confirmed what I thought the first time I saw you at the wine tasting. There's something about you that makes me want to forget everything and run off to a romantic island."

Layla's Jaguar was waiting on Rue Lamennais when they left the restaurant. Jean Claude pulled up under the blue awning. On the way to Layla's apartment, the Paris skies opened up with a spring thundershower. It was a deluge that soaked Avenue George V. Jack and Layla weren't paying attention to it. He had his arms around her and was kissing her passionately in the backseat.

The car came to a stop in front of her building. "No need

to wait for me this evening," Jack told the driver. "I'll take a cab."

They were the only ones in the elevator. As it rose, they picked up where they had left off in the car. Jack moved her back against the wall and continued kissing her while he slipped his hand under her skirt and caressed her thigh.

At the front door, she was so excited that she fumbled with the key while Jack kissed her on the back of the neck. "You're not helping," she said, laughing.

From behind he cupped his arms around her breasts. "How's this for assistance?"

Once she had the door open and they were inside, Jack tried to embrace her, but she slipped out of his grasp, heading toward the bedroom.

He followed her and stopped in the doorway to look around.

The room was dominated by a king-size bed. She paused to light an aromatic candle, which provided the only light. It was enough for Jack to watch her slip out of her dress. All she was wearing was a pale yellow silk bra and panties trimmed with lace and her shoes.

She stood against the wall and held out her arms to him.

Jack hugged her tightly and kissed her. She was pressing her body against him. Jack unsnapped her bra and stroked her breasts, playing with the nipples.

"Suck them," she said.

He leaned down and took one in his mouth and then the other while she moaned softly.

Jack dropped his hand down and pressed it against the moist bottom of her silk pants. He left it there, cupping her vagina in his hand, while she put her tongue into his mouth.

She reached down and unzipped his pants, then grabbed his erect penis and pulled it out of his blue boxer shorts. "You're so hard," she whispered as she clutched his shaft tightly. "Come to bed," she said. "I want you now."

He pulled down her panties. "In a minute. First I want to see you."

She kicked off her pants and tossed her loosened bra on a chair. Then she stood like that, wearing only her three-inch stiletto heels.

He stared at her in wonderment. "You're so beautiful," he said.

"Do you really think so?"

"More beautiful than any woman I've ever seen."

And she was. Her long legs were perfectly proportioned, coming together at her gorgeous brown bush. Her breasts, not large, were round and firm, the nipples jutting out from her olive skin.

She undressed him and then led him over to the bed.

"On your back," she ordered him.

"Whatever you say. You're in charge."

When he was stretched out that way with his head on the pillows, she dropped to her knees and lowered her vagina down toward his mouth. She didn't say a word. She didn't have to. Jack toyed with her clit with his tongue until she cried, "There! Oh, yes! There. Right *there*. That feels so good." Then she lowered herself all the way onto his face, and he took her pleasure spot into his mouth, sucking it hard.

"My breasts, Jack," she cried. "Play with my breasts."

He cupped one in each hand and he held her like that as she pressed down with an urgency against his mouth. Her whole body began shaking. She screamed out, "Oh, yes! Oh, God, *yes!*"

He expected her to roll off, but she didn't. She reached one hand behind her and grabbed his cock. She stroked it a few times; then she moved back and slid him inside of her, while grabbing it tightly at the base to keep him from coming, to prolong their pleasure while she moved up and down.

"It feels so good," he said. "It's like a dream."

"I wanted you so much, Jack. From the first time I saw you."

Finally she took her hands away from him and put them behind her on the bed as an anchor. She was moving rapidly, breathing heavily, her forehead dotted with perspiration. She bit down hard on her lower lip, her face contorted in pleasure. "I'm coming, Jack!" she screamed. He was right with her, and he screamed too as he exploded inside of her.

As she rolled off, Jack said, "It's never been like that for me. And I mean *never*. Not with anybody."

"Really," she said. "I do this every night."

For an instant he thought she was serious and he looked despondent. She laughed. "You're a funny man, Jack Cole. I like you. Of course I don't do this every night." She laughed again. "In fact, it's been a whole week."

Playfully, she ran her hand through his hair. That loosened his black toupee and it slid partially off. Even in the dim light of the candle, Layla noticed it and bolted upright in bed. She turned on a light on an end table.

"You're full of surprises," she said, flabbergasted.

"I'm in a dangerous business."

"I've come to realize that. How about showing me what the real Jack Cole looks like?"

Having gone this far, Jack didn't think it would matter. He went into the bathroom and took off the wig, mustache, and makeup. Then he emerged—and held up his arms. "The real Jack in the flesh."

"This one's much better-looking. Now get your ass back into bed."

When he stretched out, she ran her hand over the indentation in his skin on his right side. "Your scar from the bullet wound you told me about?" she said.

"Yeah. That's it."

"Does it hurt when I touch it?"

"Naw, it's been too long for that."

She leaned down and kissed his scar. Before long she was using her tongue over his entire body. She took him into her mouth, playing with his balls, finding a sensitive pleasure spot in the sac between them. When he was hard again, she rolled over onto her back. As Jack entered her, she raised her legs high so he could penetrate deeper. After they both came this time, and Jack rolled over onto his side, she snuggled up beside him pressing her breasts against his back.

"Stay the night, Jack," she said.

He was totally exhausted. He had neither the desire nor the energy to move. He was ready to say, "Of course I will," but then he remembered Avi, whom he had totally forgotten about.

He peeked at the digital radio alarm. It was already 12:48. Avi had been at his apartment the last two nights. Maybe he was there tonight with some news about Nadim, or something Jack had to do.

"Unfortunately, I have an early business appointment tomorrow."

"Cancel it," she mumbled, only half-awake.

He turned around and kissed her. "I'm sorry, I can't," he whispered. "But I promise I'll never make another one on a morning after we go out. How's that?"

She was satisfied. "Let yourself out," she said as she closed her eyes.

He looked at Layla and thought about what they had done. *Unbelievable*, he decided. *Absolutely unbelievable.*

As he gathered up his wrinkled clothes from the floor, he realized that he reeked of sex. Avi might be in his apartment. He couldn't walk in this way. He took a cold shower, which woke him up. Then he put back on the wig, mustache, and glasses. Satisfied that he had restored his appearance, he dressed.

Before leaving the apartment, he looked out of the living room window at the sidewalk below. There were two men loitering in front of Layla's building: burly, swarthy men in black leather jackets. One of them had been there last evening.

Jack went into Layla's kitchen and grabbed a sharp boning knife. He held it concealed under the front of his jacket.

He took the stairs down in case they planned to surprise him when the elevator doors opened. The lobby was deserted.

Before walking out of the building, Jack looked through the glass front entrance, surveying the sidewalk while gripping the knife handle tightly in the palm of his right hand. He couldn't see the men. Maybe they were gone—or they had never come for him. He took his glasses off and stuffed them into his pocket, calmly walked outside, and turned left. It was only a couple of blocks to the Place de l'Alma. He'd be able to find a cab there, even this late at night.

As Jack passed the open space between Layla's building and a four-story office building, one of the two men sprang out. He came at Jack from the rear, looping a powerful arm around his neck. He pulled Jack into the concrete pavement between the buildings, hissing into his ear. "Major General Nadim has a message for you. Keep away from the girl."

Jack felt the man loosen his grip when he delivered the message. That was the opening he wanted. Jack drove his left elbow hard into the man's ribs. As pain shot through the assailant's body and he tumbled to the ground, Jack slipped out of his grasp. He looked up to see the second man with a large wooden club raised high in the air. His jacket was unzipped and open in the front.

"You're dead meat," he shouted at Jack, brandishing his club. From the look in his eyes, Jack had no doubt that he intended to beat Jack to death.

"I don't think so," Jack said defiantly.

The man was coming at Jack fast, planning to smash his head with the club, when Jack whipped out the knife. In a single swift motion, he flung it at his assailant. The knife stuck in the man's chest. He screamed and collapsed onto his back while the club fell to the ground.

In a rage, Jack pounced on him and put his hands around the

man's throat, while cursing, "You bastard . . . you *bastard*." At the same time the man was fighting back, grabbing for Jack's face and eyes, punching and scratching. Jack tasted blood running into his mouth. He kept squeezing until the man stopped moving.

By now the first one had recovered and was charging Jack with a knife of his own. Jack was too fast for him. He grabbed the wooden club and smashed it against the man's side. He could hear the sound of ribs breaking like dry twigs on a cold day. When the assailant let go of the knife and collapsed to his knees, Jack began pummeling the man's face with his fists. After several blows, the man fell on the ground with blood flowing from his nose and mouth.

"This is the message you take back to Nadim," Jack said. His breath was coming in short bursts. "What we say in Chicago is go *fuck* yourself."

Jack removed the knife from the dead man so it couldn't be traced to Layla. Lights were being turned on in Layla's building. People must have heard the commotion, Jack decided. He moved fast and began walking along the sidewalk toward Place de l'Alma, hoping nobody had seen him. When he was almost there, two police cars with their sirens blaring were driving the other way, toward the scene of the attack.

Jack signaled to a waiting cab. In the backseat he collapsed. Totally drained, he closed his eyes on the ride home.

The lights were on in his apartment. Hopefully it was just Avi. Facing him would be bad enough. Dealing with other goons of Nadim or Moreau might be more than he could handle. Jack was glad he still had the knife from Layla's kitchen.

When he cautiously opened the door and looked around, he gave a sigh of relief. The apartment was empty.

Jack went into the bedroom and looked in a mirror. His face was all battered and bruised. Blood was caked on his nose and cheek. One eye was puffy and half-closed.

On the bed behind him he saw some papers. Jack crossed

the room and examined them. There was a note from Avi: *We're on a six A.M. plane to Rome. Here's your ticket. It's in the name of Henri Devereaux.*

"Just what I need." Jack groaned.

Since he was leaving Paris in the morning, Jack decided he'd better have someone look at his face. There was an Israeli doctor, Mordecai, temporarily in France, whom the embassy used. He was on call twenty-four hours a day.

"I'll come to your place," Mordecai said when Jack woke him up.

Exhausted, Jack was tempted to say, "Thank you. I'll be here." Then it hit him: he couldn't stay in this apartment tonight. Nadim might have had someone follow him here. Perhaps there was a third man, who had watched what happened from a parked car. After what Jack did to Nadim's thugs, the Syrian would try to kill him for sure.

He told Mordecai he'd take a cab to the doctor's apartment. He'd be able to sleep there for an hour before going to the airport.

Once Mordecai cleaned him up, Jack dialed Layla's home number and let it ring and ring until she finally woke to answer.

He told her what happened with the two men and explained that he had to leave for Paris for a day or so for business. "You have to go to a hotel right now," he said. "Nadim could send people to attack you."

"I can take care of myself," she said.

"Are you sure? You're the one who told me how dangerous he is."

"I've got a gun. Don't worry about me."

Jack put the phone down and shook his head in bewilderment. She should have been terrified by what he had told her. He felt a cold chill.

Chapter 24

Bulgakov was a dimly lit, intimate club in the heart of Moscow. Prices were twice what they were at comparable places in London or New York, but it was mobbed inside, with a long waiting line on the sidewalk. Most would never get in. It was ultrachic and trendy. The doormen admitted only movers and shakers.

Irina had become a regular during her modeling days. Women in that business were passed right in. Since she had introduced Michael a month ago, he now got the VIP treatment as well.

He was sipping slivovitz, waiting for her on a couch in the corner, as far from the combo and the noisy bar as possible. He didn't like meeting her in public places.

"It's too dangerous," he had told her when she called him back this afternoon and suggested it.

She had brushed aside his concern. "Don't be a killjoy. I haven't been to Bulgakov in days. I'll die if I don't get there soon."

So he had acquiesced because he was desperate to see her after Nadim's visit to Suslov.

She arrived wearing sunglasses, as if they could ensure her anonymity. It had the opposite effect. Several men looked up to see who this blond bombshell was in the Versace shades. Two old friends kissed her on the cheek as she made her way to Michael in the corner.

She slid down next to him on the couch and kissed him on the lips. "Ah, you taste so good," she said, then giggled.

A waiter immediately hustled over with a bottle of Dom Pérignon and a plate with caviar. He knew what the lady liked.

"You sounded upset when I called you today," Michael said. "I was worried."

She paused to sip some champagne. "We had an important visitor. Some big-shot Arab. Security in the building was unbelievable. The guards tried to keep everybody away from Dmitri's office. Nobody was supposed to see this Arab."

Michael's mind was churning. This was consistent with the idea that Suslov was about to do a deal with Nadim for nuclear weapons in Volgograd.

He tried not to appear too interested. "But you, my dear, were busy typing outside of Dmitri's office. So they couldn't interfere with you."

"It didn't matter. Dmitri shut the door as soon as the Arab went in. Guards outside his office were leering at me the whole time. This one guy got so excited I thought he was going to start jerking off." She laughed. "So I handed him a few tissues from the box on my desk. He was too stupid to get it."

Michael decided to change the subject. "How's your mother?"

"Ach. The same. She's sick. She whines."

"Does she need money?"

"For a vacation. I think it will do her good."

"Later tonight I'll give you some."

She reached over and kissed him. "You're a sweetie. Now you have to feed me. I'm hungry."

They ordered steaks. She devoured hers along with two

more glasses of champagne and the caviar. Michael was too nervous to do anything more than pick at his food.

When she was finished eating, she said, "I called my girl-friend Natasha."

"The good-looking brunette you used to model with?"

Pangs of jealousy shot through Irina. She didn't want Michael to think any other woman was good-looking. "Actually, she's a cow. Her tits are too large. But you men like that."

He smiled and rubbed his hand over her breasts. "I think these are just the right size. They fit into my mouth perfectly."

That satisfied her. "She said we could use her apartment tonight for a couple of hours."

"That's great."

"I told her that you'd leave her a little money to help her out. She's not working so much these days."

"Sure, my little bird. Whatever you want."

Michael was relieved that Joyner had told him to forward his expense reports directly to her. Nobody else in Langley would believe what he spent his money on.

He wanted to take a cab to Natasha's and meet Irina there. But she insisted on having him ride in the Mercedes with her. He didn't argue. Otherwise she would have pouted. Tonight he wanted to keep her in good humor. He had something important to ask her.

As they pulled away from the club, a dark blue BMW, with one of Suslov's security men at the wheel, fell in behind Irina's Mercedes. Michael kept glancing back to see if they were being followed, but in the Moscow night traffic with all the lights, it was impossible to tell.

He waited until they had finished making love to tell her want he wanted. They were naked, lying in bed. She was on her back, smoking a cigarette, her breasts rising and falling with each breath.

"If you ever hear anything more about this Arab who came today, and his business with Dmitri, please let me know. It could be important to my oil business."

A horrified expression appeared on her face. "You want me to spy on Dmitri for you?"

"Not spy," Michael said, selecting his words carefully, because she was smarter than the airhead she liked to portray. "Help me because you love me."

Not certain that love alone could do it, he climbed out of bed, reached into his pants pocket, took out a huge roll of dollars, and put it on her purse.

She said. "I could never do anything like that for money. Only because I love you."

Michael reached for the bills to take them back. "Sorry, I didn't mean to offend you."

She smiled. "You can leave them there." A worried expression suddenly appeared on her face. "I could get into trouble for doing this. Dmitri's a dangerous man."

"If you're careful, he'll never find out."

"And if he does?"

"You don't have to worry. I want to take you to the United States."

She was elated. "Really, you mean that?"

"Absolutely."

"To live there with you?"

He turned away, not wanting to look at her when he lied. He would do everything he could to get her safely out of Russia once his operation with Suslov ended, but he wasn't in love with her. He had no intention of being with her in the United States, regardless of how good their sex was.

Irina couldn't believe her ears. She would have a life like one of those women in a Hollywood movie. "Can we have a big house with a swimming pool in Beverly Hills?"

"If that's what you want. And you can shop on Rodeo Drive."

She moved over and gave him a big kiss. "I'll do whatever you want. Even spy on Dmitri."

When Michael left her at Natasha's, he went to the American embassy. He wanted to call Joyner and tell her that Irina would try to get the information. By then a different security man of Suslov's was following his taxi in a blue SAAB. The man was good. Michael never spotted him.

Chapter 25

"My God, you look like hell," Avi said as Jack slid into his seat on the airplane two minutes before the doors were scheduled to close. "You've given a new meaning to the term 'rough sex.'"

Unwilling to share his misgivings about Layla, Jack said, "Not funny, wise guy. So tell me, why are we going to Rome?"

The business cabin was only half-full. Avi looked around and decided it was safe to talk as long as they kept their voices down and didn't use any names. Besides, the chances of anyone on this airplane understanding Hebrew were slim. "The good news is that it won't involve any reading on your part, because you have only one eye that's open. So what happened?"

"I ran into a door."

"Was she that good?"

Jack was willing to play Avi's game. He tried to smile, but his face hurt too much for that. "Actually, she was."

"That's great, because people used to say, No pain, no gain. In your case, I hope it's lots of pain, lots of gain."

Jack sighed. "Now that you've had your fun, would you please tell me what we're doing on this plane?"

The engines started. They were moving away from the gate.

"I think you'd better go first with the latest version of the soap opera. It could affect what we do in Rome."

When Jack didn't respond, Avi waited until they were up in the air to take his own stab at what happened. "So the Butcher found out that you were moving in on his girlfriend, and he didn't like it."

Jack waited until a flight attendant gave them each a tray with coffee, a very hard roll, and some fruit before giving Avi a report from the time of Layla's angry entry into the restaurant. Avi sipped coffee and listened carefully with a deadpan expression. "When we left Taillevent, we went back to her place."

"Where Nadim had some thugs waiting for you."

Jack shook his head. "That came later, when I left her apartment." He then described what happened on the street.

"So I know she can't be working for Nadim," Jack said. "She can't be that good an actress to say she found out about me. She was angry, and she still came to dinner. If she were working with Nadim, why wouldn't she have just come without that whole routine?"

Avi smiled. "To gain your confidence and throw you off guard, which is what she did."

"Jesus. You—"

"The important thing is that she wanted to know your plans vis-à-vis Nadim. Didn't she?"

"She wanted to help me."

Avi let out a long, low whistle. "You are being led around by your dick, my friend."

Jack didn't say anything. Avi couldn't possibly be right. No woman could have done what she did with him last night at the same time she was setting him up.

"And the beating," Avi added, "was brilliant. A great way

to get you to have even more trust in her, to confide in her what we know about Nadim's operation."

"C'mon. The Maronites hate the Syrians."

"But they hate us even more."

Jack tore off a piece of the roll, lifted it to his mouth, and then tossed it back on the tray. "Give it up, Avi. I know what I'm doing. Now tell me about Rome."

"Your friend the Butcher is there right now."

"He must be a busy man, what with masterminding the attack on me by remote control. I don't imagine that he enjoyed getting the call telling him what happened to his goons."

Avi's expression turned grim. "Hell, I was so busy worrying about you and the girl, I never even focused on what you did to those two guys. Once Daniel Moreau gets wind of it, he'll know you're in Paris."

Jack was flabbergasted. "It's a routine police matter. It'll never get to Moreau."

"It will if they were Syrian nationals, which is likely. Then Daniel Moreau will know that Mackie's back in town."

"I'm sorry, Avi," Jack said, sounding contrite. "It was self-defense."

"I'm not blaming you. Shit happens. It's just one more thing we have to worry about."

Jack was staring into space, furious at himself for messing things up.

"Tell you what," Avi said. "Take a nap. You need it. We'll talk about Rome when we're on the ground. Moshe has one of our boys meeting the plane."

Robert McCallister jogged around the inside perimeter of the stone wall surrounding the house where he was being held. He was wearing cotton khaki slacks and a gray T-shirt. Two guards carrying automatic weapons, dressed in military uniforms, jogged behind him. On the other side of that wall lay freedom, he told himself. If he could break out, he'd find someone willing to help him.

He glanced over his shoulder. The two guards were perspiring profusely. Robert had barely broken a sweat. *Even after being cooped up as a prisoner, I'm in so much better shape than those guys,* he decided. *Once I cut loose and sprint, they've got no chance of catching me.*

If the green van was coming today, it should be here before long, he figured. And if it didn't come . . . He eyed the wall longingly. There were crevices at various spots throughout. Getting up and over would be difficult, but it was doable. He had climbed harder walls at the academy. The only problem was these two bozo guards. He'd have to get enough of a jump on them to go over before they could shoot him.

Dummy, he chastised himself. *What are you worried about? You've got very little downside. They can't kill you. They need you alive to work whatever deal they're planning. The most that you'll get is a superficial wound.*

Buoyed by that thought, he decided to go for it today. One way or the other, van or no van, he had to try to escape. If he didn't, it meant either that the president would have to make a national sacrifice to trade for him, or that he'd be in prison forever. Both of those options were unacceptable.

Two more loops past the front entrance, he decided. If the van wasn't there by then, he'd make his move. On the first loop around, the wrought-iron gate was closed. There was no sign of the green van. *Okay, one more.*

He looked back at the guards. One was cursing, but keeping the pace. The other was lagging behind.

On the next loop he saw the dark green van passing through the gate and parking in front of the villa. He slowed to see what happened. The driver was unloading boxes from the back. He had left the keys in the ignition. The black wrought-iron gate remained open.

Robert decided to make one more loop to give the driver time to go inside the villa. Halfway around, Robert put his head down and broke into a sprint.

For an instant, the two guards were confused. "Hey, slow down!" one of them shouted.

Then the other one figured out what was happening. But he had been lagging behind and was well off the pace. His legs were heavy and tired. Fear propelled his body. He was terrified of the thought of what would happen to him if this American escaped.

They were out of sight when Robert turned the corner of the villa. He saw the driver yakking away with two other guards standing at the front entrance, smoking cigarettes. In his arms the driver held a bushel of produce. He had left the front door of the van open on the driver's side. Robert could have kissed the man.

With a final acceleration, Robert covered the last few yards faster than he had ever run before. He jumped into the van, slammed the door with his left hand, and cranked the ignition with his right.

There was no time to turn around inside the compound, so he shoved the gearshift in reverse and floored it. The van shook and sputtered for an instant. Then it responded, propelling him backward through the wrought-iron gate.

One of the guards in front reacted fast. He tossed his cigarette on the ground and grabbed the rifle at his feet. Running after the van, he fired a warning shot into the air. Robert had no intention of stopping.

Once the van was through the gate, Robert kicked it into first and shot around in a 180-degree turn. He was on gravel, and the tires were worn. The van bucked and skidded when Robert floored it. "C'mon, baby," he shouted. The van responded. He was off, heading down a long dirt road. His plan was to find a place to hide out, then at night look for someone to help him.

The guard who was giving chase dropped to one knee and aimed for the left rear tire, praying to Allah that he wouldn't hit the fuel tank, which would cause an explosion and kill the prisoner.

He was a superb marksman. The first shot was right on target. The tire blew out and the van spun out of control, despite Robert's efforts to keep the steering wheel straight.

The van slid off the right side of the road, rolled over once onto the roof, and would have kept rolling except it crashed into an olive tree. The impact dazed Robert. He was groggy, but still conscious.

With a struggle, he climbed out of the open window of the van. Disoriented for an instant, he rubbed his eyes. A bullet went whizzing by. That was all it took to get him started again. He staggered down the hill toward a stream at the bottom swollen with spring rain and runoff from snowpack in the mountains. *If I can just make it to the stream,* Robert thought, *I'll be okay. I can dive in and swim. I'll lose them that way.*

Two armed guards were now in pursuit. More warning shots, accompanied by a shouted order in English— "Halt!"—flew over Robert's head.

When that didn't do the trick, the marksman knew he had no choice. He couldn't let Robert get into that stream. Waving off his colleague, he dropped to one knee and aimed for Robert's right shoulder. His first shot, a little too far to the right, narrowly missed the pilot. The second shot was perfect, just grazing the shoulder.

Robert let out a bloodcurdling scream, lost his footing, and tumbled to the ground. Before he could get to his feet to resume running, the two guards pounced on him.

Blood was oozing from his shoulder, which hurt like hell.

What pained Robert more than that was the realization that he'd never escape now.

Eppy, as Ephraim liked to be called, had spent the last two years in Rome for Moshe with the title of cultural attaché at the Israeli embassy. Behind the wheel of his Fiat, he took to heart the expression, *When in Rome, do as the Romans do.* He tore across the roads at breakneck speed, honking his horn, furious when another driver threatened to cut in front from a different lane, waving his arm wildly, and shouting out of the window if someone was going too slowly.

In the backseat, Avi, the daring air force pilot, was loving every minute of the ride. Sitting next to the driver, Jack was convinced he'd seen the last of Layla for sure. Dead men didn't date.

"Let's talk about the plan for today," Avi said to Jack, who was gripping the door handle to keep from sliding around.

"First, tell me what Nadim's doing in Rome."

"You cut right to the heart of the matter. That's what we have to find out." Avi then reviewed for Jack what had happened yesterday in Moscow.

"Jesus," Jack said. "That's worse than I ever imagined." What was running through his mind was that while he was having a great time with Layla, a diabolical plan by Israel's worst enemy to acquire nuclear weapons was advancing.

He no longer felt tired. His eye, the scratches and bruises on his face, no longer hurt. The adrenaline was surging through his body. He was ready for action. "What happened when Nadim reached Rome?"

"We followed him from Fiumicino to the Hassler Hotel, where he checked in. Then we struck a deal with an assistant manager. In return for a hefty supplement to his retirement fund and those of a couple of his colleagues, we can have free rein within reason. We promised him nobody gets hurt on hotel property."

"Then what?" Jack said anxiously.

"I talked to one of our guys on the scene before I got on the plane this morning. Nadim ordered room service for dinner. When the waiter was in the room, he pretended to be stocking the minibar and stuck a bug on the side of the little refrig."

"What'd we pick up?"

"Your friend the Butcher made two calls: one for a lady of the night who came to service him, which didn't go too well."

"What's that mean?"

"He had a little trouble getting it up. He told her it was his prostate misbehaving."

Jack burst out laughing.

"You obviously didn't have that problem."

"This isn't about me. I'll bet our friend beat the girl up."

"He didn't have to. She earned her money. She finally got him off."

"I'm so pleased to hear that. What was his other call?"

"To Ali Hashim, the head of Iranian intelligence."

Jack was stunned. "Whoa. What the hell is this? An alliance of all the people who hate us the most?"

"Sounds like it."

Jack shook his head. "Having the Iranians in this mess makes everything so much worse, particularly because nuclear weapons are involved. The Iranians have money and resources the Syrians can only dream about. They've been financing both Hezbollah and Hamas."

"I'm well aware of what the Iranians want to do to us."

"So what did Nadim and Hashim talk about?"

"They set a meeting. Lunch today at one on the Hassler patio. Nadim wanted to meet earlier, but Hashim's playing hard to get."

Chapter 26

Nadim was white with rage. He shook his head in disbelief as he listened on a cell phone in his hotel suite at the Hassler to the report of Robert McCallister's attempted escape. He couldn't believe that officers in the Syrian army could be so incompetent.

"The pilot's perfectly all right now," the terrified commander of the unit guarding McCallister tried to reassure Nadim. "I had two of the best surgeons in Damascus flown up here by helicopter to look at him. They said it's a superficial shoulder wound. 'Superficial' was their word. The bullet exited his body. They're certain of that. They applied ointments and rebandaged it. They have him on a sedative and painkillers. He's in his bed sleeping now. I ordered one of the surgeons to remain here around the clock."

Nadim decided that he couldn't believe the commander. "Who are the surgeons?" he asked. He recognized the name of one of them, the chief surgeon at the largest hospital in Damascus. Nadim asked to talk to him.

"Not a big deal," the doctor said calmly. He then repeated what the commander had told Nadim.

Satisfied, Nadim resumed talking to the commander of the unit. "It's inexcusable that your two men who were supposed to be watching the pilot let him escape. I mean the two who were jogging with him." Nadim's tone was fierce and brittle.

The commander was shaking as he listened. "I know that, sir. They've been reprimanded."

"That's not enough."

"I'll strip them of their rank and post them to a hardship assignment."

Nadim snarled. He was on his way to being president of the country. Soldiers had to understand that they couldn't fail to carry out an assignment because of stupidity. His orders had to be followed to the letter. News always spread through the army like wildfire. How he handled this situation would be a valuable lesson for the entire military. If Ahmed had dealt with the Hama situation firmly in the beginning, the destruction of the town would not have been necessary. "I want both soldiers shot," Nadim said. "In the courtyard of the military school."

"Shot?" the disbelieving commander said.

"You heard me. Executed by a firing squad."

"Both of them?"

"You think that's not enough? Perhaps I should include their commander as well."

"No. No," the commander protested as the muscles tightened up in his stomach so badly that he practically doubled up in pain. "You order will be carried out," he managed to get out of his mouth through clenched teeth.

"Shot," Jack said to Avi. "He's going to have both guards shot."

They were in the penthouse suite of the Hassler listening to conversations emanating from Nadim's room.

"Why are you surprised? I gave you the bio. Hama. Beirut. God only knows how many people he's had killed over the years."

"He's not someone we want to make a mistake with."

Avi gave Jack a wry smile. "Don't look at me. I'm not dating his girlfriend."

"She's not his girlfriend."

"I hope you're right. Meantime, at least we know Robert McCallister is alive and well, more or less."

"But we still don't know what they're planning to do with him and when."

Avi glanced at his watch. It was almost noon. "One hour to showtime. Hopefully we're going to get the answers to those questions then."

Jack looked out of the window at the patio restaurant below. "I wasn't my sharpest this morning. Run it by me again."

"We've planted a bug in the bowl of flowers on the table, which the maître d' has reserved for Nadim and Hashim." Avi pointed to the sound equipment on the desk in the suite. "We'll be able to hear and record every word they say. Finally we're going to find out what Nadim's planning."

"What if Nadim or Hashim asks for a different table?"

"The maître d' will tell them to wait a minute while he finishes setting it. He'll move the flower bowl. Also we'll have a photographer up here in our suite with a telephoto lens to take a picture of them during the meeting so we can have visual confirmation."

Avi could tell that Jack wasn't satisfied. "What do you think I missed?"

Jack shrugged. "I don't know. I just don't have a good feeling about this. Something's going to go wrong. I know it."

"You're worrying too much."

"I hope you're right."

At the table in the Hassler's patio restaurant, Nadim looked at his watch and cursed under his breath. It was already ten minutes past one. Ali Hashim was playing a game by being late—the same game he had been playing when he insisted that he was too busy for a meeting this morning. *He's trying to show me that I need him more than he needs me.*

To calm himself, Nadim ordered a bottle of Vernaccia di San Gimignano. As he sipped the chilled white wine, Nadim looked around the restaurant, which was still only sparsely filled. Italians ate late. That was why he had wanted to meet earlier, when there would be less chance of someone recognizing them. In fact, Nadim had wanted to meet in his suite. Hashim had insisted on the restaurant. *Probably doesn't trust me alone in a hotel room,* Nadim decided.

The patio was surrounded by a garden and a low wall. A light breeze rippled through the trees. It was a magnificent spring day, peaceful on the patio. The smell of fragrant flowers was in the air. They were everywhere in bloom around the patio and in the beautiful compact little centerpiece on each table.

On the other side of that wall, it was a different world. Horns honked vociferously. Cars racing by the Spanish Steps spewed noxious exhaust fumes. Vendors hawked gelato to the tourists, busy snapping pictures.

Twenty-five minutes late, Ali Hashim arrived. He offered no apologies. He declined any wine. "It's forbidden by our religion. Maybe you don't know that," he told the Syrian with contempt.

Nadim would have liked nothing better than to pour the rest of the wine and the ice bucket it was resting in over Hashim's bald head, but that wouldn't get him what he wanted. So he squeezed his fists together tightly under the table and said to Hashim, "Let's order lunch first. Then we'll talk."

The Iranian nodded. Once the waiter departed, Nadim couldn't wait any longer to launch into the discussion. First he glanced around the restaurant to make certain there was no one he recognized and that no one was watching. Then he began speaking softly.

"Is your country in or out?"

Hashim's expression was noncommittal. Inside, he was smiling. Nadim was a brutal killer, but he was a poor negotiator. Everything that he did signaled how much he wanted the deal. By doing that, he lost his bargaining leverage.

"We have some problems with the proposal you presented," Hashim said calmly.

"Problems?" Nadim asked. "What problems?"

"We're willing to give you the five million dollars you want in a Swiss bank account, but we refuse to make an identical payment to Kemal, the infidel."

Nadim didn't like what he was hearing. "Without Kemal, we would never have had the pilot."

"But we have him now. We don't need Kemal any longer."

Nadim realized that he was between a rock and a hard place. If he didn't get the cash payment he had promised Kemal, then the Turk would balk, and under Nadim's plan his participation was still critical. "But we do need him," Nadim said. "The last time we were together you said you had a keen sense of the geography. The only way we can bypass Turkey is by moving through Iraqi territory. That's obviously not a possibility."

Hashim pressed his fat lips together. "Five million for Kemal is too much. A half a million is enough."

I feel like I'm in a bazaar, Nadim thought. "I could persuade Kemal to take two."

"I'll tell you what I'll do," Hashim said slowly, "and this is my final offer. I'll pay six million altogether. I'll tell my people that you needed another million for baksheesh. We're not paying Kemal anything. You can split it with him however you like. That's your business."

"Done," Nadim said, relieved to be finished with this

point. "Now let's talk about the rest of it. Here's my proposal for a time and place for the exchange. . . ."

In the penthouse suite, Jack and Avi were in a panic. An Israeli technician wearing heavy black glasses with thick lenses and earphones who was operating the sound equipment was shaking his head grimly and saying, "Nothing . . . nothing . . . nothing."

"What do you mean, nothing?" Jack shouted at the man.

He took off the earphones and put them down carefully on a table.

"I mean zero. I mean I haven't heard one word that Nadim or Hashim said since they ordered lunch."

"Then you're not recording."

What a stupid comment, the technician thought. He looked annoyed. "We can't record what we don't hear."

Jack threw up his hands in the air in frustration. "Before Hashim arrived, when Nadim ordered the wine, you heard it all clearly. Even the year."

"True."

"So what happened?"

The technician shrugged. "We're dealing with micro components. An insect could have blocked a critical orifice. Or the tiny microphone could have fallen out of the flowers and into the water. Even with state-of-the-art technology, equipment malfunctions."

Jack watched Avi pacing around the living room of the suite, frustrated, red in the face, shaking his head, seeming as if he would explode. Glumly Jack stared out of the window, through a crack in the curtains, at Nadim and Hashim now locked in intense conversation, and considered their options. Even if the technician had an extra microphone, they could hardly have a waiter rush down and change the flowers. Nadim and Hashim were too smart for that.

As he looked at the two of them deep in conversation,

leaning forward, their faces just over that flower bowl centerpiece with its dead microphone, he knew that they were now discussing the very facts that he and Avi desperately needed.

Jack looked at the photographer with his long telephoto lens who was waiting for an instruction from Jack or Avi to take a picture of the two men. Jack thought they should still do it, but without a tape of the conversation, it meant nothing. So what if Nadim and Hashim had lunch in Rome? Big deal.

Jack watched a waiter put two salads down on the table. Nadim and Hashim stopped talking until he was gone. They ignored the food and resumed their conversation.

Suddenly Nadim reached down into the brown leather briefcase resting on the tile floor at his feet. Jack turned to the photographer. "Now. Use your highest magnification. They're going to look at something. Take a picture of it. Be quick."

Jack knew there was a risk of Nadim or Hashim noticing the lens sticking out of an open hotel window through a crack in the curtains, but he had to take that chance. Besides, the two of them were so engrossed in their conversation they might not glance up.

Jack saw Nadim take what looked like a small piece of paper from his briefcase. As he held it out to Hashim, the photographer was clicking away. Hashim was studying the piece of paper. The photographer kept shooting. *Will we be able to see the writing on the document?* Jack wondered.

Avi was standing behind Jack, looking over his shoulder.

"Make sure you get both of them in some of the pictures," Jack said to the photographer.

"Will do."

Hashim slipped the piece of paper into his pocket. Now they turned to their salads.

Jack looked at the photographer. "How soon will you have prints for us?"

"Go take a leak. By the time you get back, I'll have them."

The photographer was as good as his word.

In the best picture, Nadim and Hashim were looking at a photograph of a man holding a newspaper. Around his neck hung a sign. The words were difficult to read. With a magnifying glass, which the photographer supplied, they unmistakably read, *Lt. Robert McCallister.* The newspaper was the *Herald Tribune* from a few days ago.

"Well, that's sure something," Jack exclaimed with joy.

"But it's not nearly enough," Avi said. All we've done is confirm that Robert McCallister is part of the deal. Unless and until we know the rest of it—the time and place of the exchange—we're nowhere. Fucking sound equipment. If it hadn't malfunctioned, we could have—"

Jack interrupted him. "Would have, could have. It doesn't count. We have to find another way to get what we want."

For the next three hours Jack and Avi remained in their suite at the Hassler trying to decide how they could move up on Nadim and get the information they wanted.

Then Eppy called from Fiumicino. "Nadim's on the four-thirty Air France to Paris," he told Avi.

"How's he seem?" Avi asked.

"He's smiling. He looks happy."

Oh, shit, Avi thought. Nadim had gotten what he wanted from Hashim.

By the time Avi hung up, Jack was already studying an airline schedule. "Let's go," he said. "If we hustle, we can get back to Paris on Alitalia at seven."

Eppy was right: Nadim was a happy man. He took a sip of wine and leaned back in his first-class seat en route to

Paris. It had been a tough negotiating session, but he had brought Hashim around.

Everything was falling into place now.

In another five days it would all be over. The deal would be done. He'd have everything he wanted. Well, almost everything. He still had to do something about Jack Cole. And of course, there was Layla.

Chapter 27

Security was tight, as always around the Israeli embassy in Paris. That didn't surprise Jack when the cab dropped him and Avi at the corner of Avenue Matignon and Rue de Panthieu, where French police put them through a metal detector. What did stun Jack and almost cause him to run the other way was the picture of Jack Cole posted on the side of the police van. After clearing the metal detector, he waited to see what happened next. The police were bored with this assignment. No one stared at the two men. No one asked for their IDs or said a word. That would be the job of the receptionist inside the embassy in the middle of the block, and she had Henri Devereaux on her approved list as visiting with Avi Sassoon.

In the embassy they were led to a communications room to place the call to Jerusalem. As soon as she heard Jack's voice, Moshe's secretary, following strict orders, said, "I'll get him out of a meeting."

The closed room was tiny. Avi paced with his hands in his pockets for the several minutes it took Jack to report to Moshe what had happened in Rome.

At the end, Moshe vented his disappointment at the failure of the recording equipment. "Ach, modern technology is the eleventh plague," he muttered. "I can't even blame you two geniuses. Shoot me the picture immediately. The embassy has fax machines that are especially good for photographs."

"Will do."

There was a long pause. Moshe was thinking aloud. "We still have the problem of finding out exactly what the exchange is, where and when it's going down. We have lots of pieces, but we need the rest of them to put the puzzle together."

"That pretty well sums it up," Jack said.

"What about our assets in Turkey?" Avi asked.

"They haven't been able to come up with a thing. Kemal's playing this very close to the vest. Nobody's talking. Nadim's our only chance. You two have to figure out a way to get the info from him."

"That's easier said than done," Jack replied.

"Don't tell me you can't do it," Moshe said forcefully. "With what's at stake, you have to find a way. We can't let those people get nuclear weapons."

Moshe waited five minutes to place the call to Joyner. Long enough to receive the fax of the picture of Nadim passing McCallister's photograph to Hashim.

"The good news, Margaret, is that your pilot is alive and in good condition, although he received a superficial shoulder wound trying to escape. The bad news is that he's part of the deal Nadim's putting together. There's no doubt about that."

He then told her about the picture and how it was obtained, as well as about Nadim's conversation with the commander of the unit guarding McCallister. "As soon as I hang up, the picture will go on the wire to you."

"I appreciate that, Moshe."

"Now I want something in return."

Joyner was wary. "Yeah, what?"

"I want to know what demands have been made on your government for the pilot's release."

"Up to this point, we haven't heard from anyone."

"I find that hard to believe."

She bristled. "You're not accusing me of lying, are you?"

They were both tense. Moshe didn't want to destroy a close and valuable relationship. He retreated. "No, no, of course not," he said, sounding conciliatory. "I was wondering if someone in your government had heard something, and it hadn't been shared, so to speak. Unfortunately, that kind of thing happens here all the time."

She thought of Doerr, Morton, and Grange. Anything was possible with those three. "I don't think so, but I'll confirm that shortly. Once I get the photo I intend to have Kendall call a meeting of the Crisis Task Force. If I learn anything, I'll let you know."

Moshe was satisfied.

It was a couple of miles from the Israeli embassy to Jack's apartment. "Let's walk," Jack said. "It'll clear our heads. Maybe we'll get a brainstorm."

They headed up the Champs Elysées toward the Arc de Triomphe. It was a magnificent spring evening in Paris. The sidewalk was mobbed with people anxious to get outside after the long winter. Open-air restaurants were crowded. Everywhere lights sparkled, making the wide boulevard seem like midday rather than late evening.

For several minutes they walked in silence, each of them trying to find a solution to what seemed like an insoluble problem. Just as they reached the top of the boulevard and turned left toward Avenue Victor Hugo, Avi said with a burst of enthusiasm, "I have an idea."

"What is it?" Jack said, jumping on it.

"You're not going to like it. I'm not even sure I do."

They turned on the Avenue Victor Hugo, crowded with

expensive boutiques and a smattering of upscale restaurants. "Run it by me anyhow," Jack said. "We're desperate."

"Okay, here goes. Remember, you asked for it."

Jack was tired and irritable. "Just tell me."

Avi looked around to make sure no one could hear them. "You know how it seems as if Nadim is anxious to go out with Layla, and—"

Jack's whole body tensed. "You're right. I don't like it."

"At least let me finish."

"I know where you're going with this."

Avi put a hand on Jack's arm. "C'mon, hear me out. It'll have a benefit for you. You'll know where you stand with her."

"I already know." Jack could see Avi wouldn't quit. He hesitated, then said, "Okay, spit it out."

"Let's assume that Layla's being straight with you. Nadim's anxious to date her. Suppose she calls him and arranges to go out with him tomorrow night. You give her a bug or two to plant. That's it."

Jack remembered telling Layla last evening that he would never do anything to harm her. "No way," he said. "We'd be putting her at terrible risk. Nadim's one of the most dangerous people in the world. You know what he'd do to her if he found out."

"We can tell her how to play it. He won't find out, and nothing will happen to her."

"Forget it," he said firmly. "Besides, why would she do it? She doesn't love the Israelis."

"Yeah, but if she's telling you the truth, she hates the Syrians more than us. She hates Nadim, and she's enamored with you."

"The answer's no. Now drop it."

Avi ignored Jack's words. He stopped and moved into the doorway of a women's shoe store. He whipped the cell phone out of his pocket and called Eli in the Mossad research department in Tel Aviv. "Did you get the information I wanted on the banker's fund-raising activities?" he asked Eli.

"Just this afternoon."

"Thanks for telling me," Avi snapped.

Jack was standing next to Avi, listening carefully.

"I wanted to do a little more checking," the man in Tel Aviv said. "I planned to call tomorrow."

"I told you this was moving fast."

"Do you want to know or not?" The man sounded annoyed.

"Well?" Avi demanded. "What's the answer?"

"The money's being funneled to Maronite Christian militias in east Beirut. They're using it to purchase arms in order to drive Syria out of the country."

"That's just what I need."

Avi hung up and reported what he had learned to Jack. They weren't moving, just standing in the doorway. Jack was relieved to hear the answer. It confirmed that Layla wasn't in cahoots with Nadim.

"That's the hook we need," Avi said emphatically. "We tell Layla either she does what we want, or we'll disclose her fund-raising activities to the Lebanese government, which is Syria's puppet."

"You'd be signing her death warrant. Nadim will have her killed for sure. And members of her family."

Avi raised his hand. "We wouldn't actually tell anyone. We'd just threaten her with that."

Jack grew irate. "That stinks. There's no way I'll do that."

"C'mon, Jack, there's more at stake than your little fling. Like the future of the state of Israel."

Jack was pondering Avi's words. He had a point about involving Layla, but the idea of blackmailing her was too awful for Jack to contemplate. "Tell you what," Jack finally said. "I'll call Layla and set a meeting for the three of us.

Right now, if I can get her. I'll pitch it to her in terms of not wanting Syria to get nuclear weapons. That should be enough."

Avi had an impish look. "I may casually mention to her that we know she's funneling money to the Maronites so they can buy guns."

Jack looked hard at him. "Absolutely not."

"Okay. But don't forget, this woman's no babe in the woods. At the very least, she's involved in espionage herself."

Jack took the cell phone from his pocket and started to punch in numbers.

Avi grabbed his hand. "Where do you want her to meet us?"

"My apartment down the street."

Avi shook his head. "Too risky. Nadim doesn't know about it. If she's with him, then he will."

"Jesus, you don't quit, do you?" Jack was tired of arguing with Avi on the subject. He thought of a neighborhood brasserie that was open late and rarely had more than a couple of patrons at this hour. He called Layla. "I just got back to Paris," he said. "Are you okay?"

"Me? I'm fine."

"Nobody bothered you?"

"Not at all."

Jack was relieved. "But what about you?" Layla asked. "I was so worried after your call last night."

"I'm all right, but I have to talk to you."

"You want to come here?"

"Too dangerous after what happened." He gave her the address of the brasserie.

"I'll be there as soon as I can," she said.

He swallowed hard. He had to say it. "Make sure you're not being followed."

That didn't alarm her. "I'll locate Jean Claude and use

him. It'll take me longer to get there than if I just grab a cab, but he's good at that sort of thing."

Joyner decided to do something intelligent: She called General Childress as soon as the meeting of the Crisis Task Force was set. "I'll swing by the Pentagon on my way into town and pick you up," she told Childress.

In the back of the car as they exited the Pentagon parking lot, Joyner showed Childress the photograph of McCallister, which raised his hackles. She told him everything she knew from her reports from Moshe and Michael. Then she stopped talking and waited for him to come on his own to the conclusion she wanted. She felt confident he would. Childress was a professional soldier and a bright, decent man. Despite Morton's efforts to dominate him, she was certain that Childress would want to do what was right for the country.

He did. "With this information, we certainly can't take military action against Turkey or Syria at this point," he said. "I know that's what Morton and Grange want, and they're planning to lobby the president at the meeting today. As far as I'm concerned, that's no longer an option."

Inwardly, Joyner was pleased. She wanted the idea to come from him. She showed nothing on her face. "Will you say that at the meeting?"

"Absolutely. It's the right decision." Childress continued: "We've got to push our deadline back and run out the string on this. It's more important to block the transfer of these nuclear weapons."

"Do you really think so?" Joyner asked, trying to be careful not to overplay her hand.

"Absolutely."

The car stopped for a traffic light. Childress handed her back the photograph, which she returned to her briefcase.

"Since it's your idea," she said, "I don't want to take

credit for it. I'll give the report from Michael and Moshe. You can propose the bombing delay."

"That's okay with me," Childress said, pleased that Joyner wasn't one of those people who tried to take credit for someone else's idea.

The meeting in the cabinet room played out exactly as Joyner had anticipated.

Following her report, there was a long heavy silence. Tension was thick in the air.

Kendall was so stunned by the photograph and what Moshe had reported that he didn't even chastise Joyner for talking to the Israelis. The president didn't know what to do. As for Chip Morton, Joyner's report of the Nadim–Suslov meeting nearly blew him away. He said it would be horrible if "those countries," as he normally referred to the Islamic nations in the Middle East, obtained nuclear weapons. Jimmy Grange looked confused. He hadn't figured on this. Joyner was glad Doerr was in London to see how the British viewed the McCallister situation. The secretary of state might have come up with some cockamamie proposal. Reynolds passed Joyner a note that read, *C'mon, boys, get a grip. Let's figure out how to deal with this.* Joyner had all she could do to avoid a smile.

General Childress could have been an actor, Joyner decided. He waited precisely the right amount of time to toss out his idea for a deferral of any consideration of bombing Turkey or Syria or anyone else until "we see how this all plays out." When Kendall didn't immediately embrace the general's recommendation, Grange took that as his cue to say, "I told Terry McCallister we would begin bombing in two days. He's been calling me nonstop, night and day."

Grange had finally gone too far. Kendall gave him a sharp look. "You had no business telling him that. I never made a decision to go to war over the release of a pilot."

Grange was defensive. "But in the initial note you authorized to Turkey, it said that they would face serious consequences. I thought—"

"Then you thought wrong. We're not running this government for Terry McCallister. I don't care how much money he gives or raises," the president said emphatically. "Of course I want to rescue his son, as I would any American pilot, but we're going to do what makes sense for the country."

Grange dropped lower in his chair. "I don't know how I'll tell Terry," he mumbled.

Kendall turned away from Grange toward Joyner.

"Margaret," Kendall said, now sounding respectful to his CIA director, "stay close to Moshe on this and that kid you have in Moscow. What'd you say his name was?"

"Michael Hanley."

"Yeah, Hanley. Keep me and General Childress informed. The three of us will talk again when you think it makes sense."

Joyner had now gotten another benefit she hadn't expected: It was the end of the crisis team. There was to be no more government by committee, which she hated. Now it was just down to her, Childress, and Kendall. That was efficient. She would keep Reynolds in the loop, which she wanted to do.

What Jimmy Grange didn't tell the president was that going into this meeting he had been so confident that the decision would be made to begin bombing that he had asked Terry McCallister to come to Grange's office in the west wing and wait there for an immediate report.

On the lonely walk back to his office, Grange decided that his loyalties lay with Kendall and not with McCallister. He couldn't risk losing the support and friendship of Kendall, which was, after all, his ticket to the White House and all the perks that went along with being the president's confidant. He decided to put a positive spin on what had happened.

Dressed in a starched white shirt and navy suspenders, Terry was on the phone shouting about the terms of a business transaction when Grange walked in. Terry immediately hung up and looked at Grange expectantly. "When will the bombing start?"

Grange coughed and cleared his throat. "There have been some new positive developments. We're now on a course for obtaining Robert's release. Bombing would jeopardize that."

Terry was taken aback. "What developments?"

"We learned from the Israelis that Robert has been moved to Syria."

"The Israelis? I told you that I didn't want them to be involved."

"Well, we can't always control events. They've actually been quite helpful."

"Are the Syrians willing to release him?"

"Not quite yet, I'm afraid."

"Then let's bomb the hell out of them until they do. Syria is an even easier target than Turkey."

Grange sighed. "The president is considering all of his options in light of this information."

This was too much for Terry. His face turned beet red and he pounded on Grange's desk. "This is nothing but mumbo jumbo. You guys have no idea what the hell you're doing, and Kendall doesn't have the balls to start bombing, which is the only way to get my son back."

"I'm sorry, Terry, that you feel—"

"I don't give a shit what you think. You're worthless. Get me a meeting with Kendall. I'll tell him myself."

Grange was horrified at the request. Kendall had too

much on his mind to deal with Terry personally. That had been Grange's assignment.

When Grange didn't respond, Terry pointed to the phone. "Pick up the goddamn thing and call downstairs. Get me the meeting with Kendall."

Grange had no idea what Kendall was doing now, so he lied. "The president's gone into another conference . . . with congressional leaders. It will run for quite a while."

Terry was adamant. "If he can't meet me now, it sure as hell had better be soon."

"I'll work on it," Grange said weakly. "I promise."

"You'd better do more than work on it!" Terry shouted. Saliva was coming out of his mouth. "If I don't get that meeting, I'll never give Kendall or the party another cent. I not only won't raise money for him, but I'll make sure all of my contributors find another candidate. Now, do you understand that, or do you want me to draw you a picture?"

Layla walked into the brasserie, took one look at Jack sitting at a table across from Avi in the back, and stopped dead. "Oh, my God," she said, as she saw what he looked like. His face had large black-and-blue blotches. There were scratches on one cheek. His left eye was half-closed, red, and puffy. She put a hand over her mouth. Then she raced over to the table. She ignored the man he was with and put her arms around Jack when he stood up. "I'm so sorry. I'm responsible."

"You didn't do a thing."

"But it's my fault. Nadim wants me. That's why he attacked you."

As Avi watched and listened, he found himself softening a little. He hated to admit it, but he thought she was sincere. Still, it was too early to tell for sure.

Jack introduced Avi as "a friend of mine from Israel."

"We're drinking bad Armagnac," Avi said. "You want one?"

When she nodded, he signaled to the waiter, who hustled over with another glass.

Layla looked at Jack again, shuddered, and gulped some down. She was sitting opposite Jack at the square table. Avi was off to the side.

"So what do we do now?" she asked.

Avi looked at Jack, waiting for him to respond. He was the one who was involved with Layla. It was his show.

It occurred to Jack that this would be easier if Avi weren't there, but it was too late for that. "You asked me at Taillevent," Jack began, "what I was doing with Nadim."

She nodded.

"And you offered to help."

"I meant it," she said with a burst of enthusiasm. "Even more, now that I see what he did to you."

Avi broke in. "If you did, it would mean you'd be helping Israel. I doubt if you like us either."

The instant he opened his mouth, Layla decided she didn't like Jack's friend. She told him bluntly, "It's true I don't like you Israelis, but the Syrians I like less for what they've done to my country. Jack, I like. You, I don't."

"We know that you're not a big fan of Syria," Avi said. "That's why the money you're sending to Beirut is going to arm the Christian militia."

Her whole body shook. "How'd you find that out?"

Jack glared at Avi, willing him to keep quiet before he lost Layla. Then he took control. "None of that's relevant," Jack said, looking straight at Layla, making her feel she was the only person who mattered, which was what she did with him.

Layla was losing patience with Jack. "Would you mind telling me what's going on?"

He took a deep breath and spat it out. "Nadim has concocted some type of plan to acquire nuclear weapons from a Russian source. We know that—"

She interrupted him in midsentence. "Mother of God," she said with a horrified expression on her face. "Nuclear weapons . . ."

"They will unless we can stop them."

"So you're both with the Mossad?"

Avi opened his mouth to respond. Jack cut him off. "Yeah, that's right."

"Mother of God," she repeated. "You've got to stop him."

"We need your help."

"What can I do?"

Jack hesitated. He hated putting Layla's life on the line. "I'll only ask you once," he said. "We've got no threats or inducements for you. If it's something you want to do, that's great. If not, you and I will be friends and go back to where we were last night."

She ran her hand over Jack's bruised face. "We can't just go back to where we were now that we know they could get nuclear weapons in Damascus."

"That's true, but I don't want you to feel any pressure to do what I'm asking."

She nodded. "Tell me then."

"Suppose," he said softly, "you were to call Nadim tomorrow."

Her whole body shook with revulsion at the sound of the man's name and the idea of approaching him.

Watching her reaction, Jack waited a moment before continuing. "Suppose you were to go out with him tomorrow night." Jack paused to look at Layla.

She was up on the edge of her chair, her face as white as chalk. "What do you want me to do with him?"

"Somehow plant a bug or two that we will give you so we can listen in on conversations the next day that he—"

Layla cut Jack off. "There's only one way to do that.

You're asking me to sleep with Nadim." She looked repulsed.

Jack was upset. He was sorry he had agreed to ask her. "I didn't say that. I figured that you'd find a way to plant them. Maybe at dinner."

"Nadim's not a gentleman like you, Jack. You can imagine his reaction when I tell him I don't do sex on a first date. He won't take no for an answer."

Jack sighed. "I guess you're right. I didn't think it through. I'm sorry. Forget we ever had this discussion."

Jack knew that Avi wanted to jump in with his blackmail threat on the Maronite gun money. With his eyes, he persuaded Avi to keep quiet.

Nobody said a word for three whole minutes. Jack could tell Layla was thinking about the proposal. She finished her drink. He couldn't read her face.

"I'll do it," she said reluctantly. "Because I hate Nadim and Syria. For what he did to my family. For my uncle Bashir and the others he killed. But also for you."

"Thank you," he said softly. Jack reached across the table and clutched her hand. *I've got to come up with a foolproof plan to protect her,* he decided.

"I'll only talk to you. Your friend here . . ." She pointed to Avi. "Doesn't trust me."

Avi didn't argue with her. He had gotten what he wanted. Besides, she was right. He didn't trust her, but he wanted her to know her condition was acceptable. He turned to Jack. "I'll get the electronic equipment for you in the morning. You can give it to her in the afternoon."

There was a long, awkward pause. The discussion was over. Jack looked at Avi. He got the picture. "I'm bushed," Avi said. "You guys mind if I bail out on you?"

"See you tomorrow," Jack said.

Layla didn't even nod when Avi left.

Jack still couldn't believe she had agreed to do what he

had asked. He wanted nothing more right now than to take her off to bed and pick up where they left off last night. But where to go? Her place was out of the question. Nadim might have two better thugs waiting this evening. A hotel seemed so tawdry. He decided to take her to his apartment a few blocks away off Avenue Victor Hugo. To hell with Avi's doubts about whether she was working with Nadim. She'd never give away the address.

Chapter 28

The phone rang in Nadim's office at ten in the morning. He let his secretary take it.

"A Daniel Moreau from the SDECE is calling," she said. "He wants to know if he can come and see you in an hour."

Nadim wondered what was going on. "Did he give you any reason for the meeting?"

"Nothing."

"Tell him to come."

Nadim leaned back in his desk chair and thought about Moreau's visit. He hoped that Jack Cole hadn't turned Moreau on to Nadim to try to disrupt his plan. No, that was ridiculous. Nadim had spent enough time over the years at diplomatic receptions and the like with Moreau to know that the Frenchman was no friend of the Israelis. Quite the contrary, on a couple of instances when the Americans were considering economic reprisals against Syria for actions against Israel, Moreau had heard about the Americans' plans and tipped off Nadim.

The phone rang again. "There's a woman named Layla Gemayel on line one," Nadim's secretary said on the intercom. "Are you in or out?"

Nadim bolted upright in his chair. "I'll take the call."

Picking up, he said, "Well, well. This is a pleasant surprise. To what do I owe the honor?"

"Things have gotten out of control between us."

"I don't know what you mean."

"The dinner at L'Ambroise. The men you had outside of my building and what happened with a man I dated two nights ago."

Where was she going with this? He decided to hold back and let her keep talking.

"I don't like being harassed by you, and I don't want to go to the police."

"They would never get involved."

"You're right," she said, sounding upset. "But this has to end. Suppose we sit down and talk about it. Maybe we can reach an understanding."

"I'm all in favor of talking."

"It'll have to be in a public place."

"You don't trust me, do you?"

"You're right about that. Maybe a small brasserie for coffee this afternoon."

"Let's talk over dinner," he said boldly.

When she didn't respond, he smiled sadistically while trying to sound pleasant. "You'll find that I'm not a monster."

She hesitated. "I don't know about dinner. It's not what I had in mind."

He decided to press ahead, believing that he could persuade her. "What could happen to you at a public restaurant?"

"Nothing, but—"

"Good. Carré des Feuillants at nine o'clock this evening."

He could tell she was uncertain, but he was manipulating her. Once he had her at dinner, he had no doubt that he'd charm her sufficiently to get her into his bed—the prize he had been seeking for months. He got excited thinking about it.

"If I agree to come," she said in a stammering voice, "then I want you to promise that you'll never harass me again. Just this one date and that's it."

"Absolutely. After this one evening, it'll be whatever you want. We'll meet at the restaurant," he said, and held his breath as a heavy silence settled over the line.

Finally she said, "I'll be there."

When she hung up, he stared at the phone for several seconds. The timing of the call—coming now—bothered him. Was the reason she gave honest? She could be sufficiently frightened by what had happened to Jack Cole outside of her apartment the other night to want to find a way of reaching an understanding with him. But there was another equally plausible alternative—Jack Cole was working for the Israelis, and he wanted her to pry information out of Nadim.

That latter possibility put a smirk on his face. If that was her game, she was doomed to failure. Unlike many men, it didn't matter how much he drank. He never lost control of his tongue. If he ever found out that was what she was doing, he would make her pay for it in ways she couldn't even imagine. His mind was racing trying to formulate them.

In the meantime, though he'd be vigilant, he was prepared to take her at her word. It wasn't just that he wanted to get into her pants and into that moist pussy of hers. That was only part of it. The other part was that having Bashir and Amin Gemayel's niece meant for Nadim extending to the utmost his subjugation of the Lebanese people and those stubborn Maronites. Layla was the prize in more ways than one.

Nadim was so engrossed in thinking about Layla that it took persistent knocking by his secretary on the closed wooden door to gain his attention. "Yes," he called when he finally heard her.

She opened the door and said, "Daniel Moreau is down in the reception area."

"Good, bring him up and offer him some coffee."

Moreau didn't want anything to drink. The Frenchman wasn't in a friendly mood, Nadim noticed as the sour-looking man entered his office. Nadim pointed to a sofa against the wall. He waited for Moreau to sit down before taking a chair facing him.

"It's always a pleasure to see you, Daniel," he said, trying to appear nonchalant.

"Not this time, I'm afraid."

Nadim sucked in his breath. "What happened?"

"You know damn well what's going on. I don't like you Arabs and Israelis playing your deadly little games on French soil. Save them for your own backyards."

Nadim didn't know what had occurred that could be traced to him. "I honestly don't know what you're talking about."

Moreau looked angry. "I hate being lied to."

"I wouldn't do that."

"Well, you are now." His face was flushed with anger and the hairs rose on the back of his neck. "The police picked up two men night before last near Place de l'Alma. One was dead. One was badly beaten. Both had Syrian embassy IDs."

Nadim cursed under his breath. *Those incompetent fools.* He had told both of them to carry fake Saudi identification in case they were caught. The French were too frightened about their oil supplies to do anything against Saudi nationals.

"There must be a mistake."

"There's no mistake, but I will tell you that you trained the one who's alive very well. So far he has refused to talk. We're continuing to work on him."

Nadim knew it would be counterproductive to persist with the denial. "What do you want from me?" he asked.

"Stop the war games in France. Right now."

"It will be done," Nadim said.

"Good."

Suddenly Nadim had an idea: Maybe he could use Moreau for information. "Does the name Jack Cole mean anything to you?"

The man's sour expression gave way to a face aglow with intensity. Moreau leaned forward on the sofa. "How do you know him?"

"He's an American. He's been pursuing me. Makes me think he may be an Israeli agent."

"He is," Moreau said flatly.

Well, well, isn't that nice to know, Nadim thought. "Why are you interested in him?"

"I want him for two crimes. Tell me where I can find him . . . I'll owe you a big favor in return."

Nadim frowned and tapped his fingers on the side of his chair. This was now getting tricky. He thought again about Layla's call. Jack Cole had tried to use Layla and failed, or he was in fact using her. Regardless, he wanted Jack Cole out of circulation, but he didn't want Moreau roughing up Layla to get at Jack.

"I don't know where to find Cole," Nadim said.

Moreau sputtered. "You're lying again."

"Actually, this time I'm not lying. But I can offer you a suggestion."

"What?" Moreau asked anxiously. From Moreau's tone and demeanor, Nadim could tell how much Moreau wanted Cole.

"It's possible," Nadim said slowly, watching Moreau hang on each word, "that those two men who were beaten up the other night near Place de l'Alma may have encountered Cole in the area." Nadim shrugged before continuing.

"Maybe he lives near there or has a friend close by. If I were in your shoes, I would station police or my men on that street with Jack Cole's picture."

Moreau narrowed his eyes. "You know something you're not telling me."

Nadim ducked the implied question. "I've just helped you out a great deal. Patience, my friend. Jack Cole will return to that location." *Damn right he will, as long as he continues to see Layla,* Nadim thought. "You can nab him then."

"I just heard from Stefan," Perikov said to Michael in a grim voice.

Michael pressed the cell phone to his ear. "Who's Stefan?"

"Remember when we finished our visit to the warehouse, you asked me to send one of the people on my staff down to Volgograd to pretend to be a tourist to keep his eye on those weapons?"

"Of course I remember that."

"Well, Stefan's the man."

"Sorry, I didn't know the name. What's he say?"

"Grab on to something and hold it tight."

God, this must be awful, Michael thought. Perikov wasn't prone to dramatic gestures.

"As of an hour ago," Perikov said in a rapid staccato manner, "nuclear weapons are moving out of Volgograd. At the warehouse they were loaded in the backs of four tractor-trailer trucks, buried under fruits and vegetables."

He wasn't exaggerating, Michael thought: This was terrible. "How reliable is Stefan's information?"

Perikov was offended. "He was hiding in another building on the abandoned plant side watching the operation through binoculars."

"Does he have any idea of their destination?"

"They began moving in a southerly direction. That's all he knows. The roads have been closed to other traffic.

Detour and Road Construction signs have been posted. He can't follow them. It's now up to you and your government."

Michael thanked him, then clicked off. He had to call Joyner ASAP. He thought of doing it on the special so-called secure cell phone the Company had given him, but worried about it. The Russians had gotten better at picking up communications coming in and out, especially from the United States. An hour wouldn't matter. He decided it would be safer to make the call to Joyner from the embassy.

Margaret Joyner's secretary pulled her out of a meeting in her office with the head of the FBI about homeland security to take the call from Michael. Her face turned pale as she listened to the report of his conversation with Perikov.

"Are you certain of this information?"

"Perikov has never been wrong yet."

Joyner should have been happy with Michael's information. After all, the reason she had set up his operation was to catch Suslov in the act of doing precisely what he was doing now. The difficulty was that the idea of nuclear arms on their way to renegades in Iran, Turkey, or Syria, or some combination of the three, was too horrible to contemplate. Those shipments had to be stopped, regardless of the cost.

"We need to know where those weapons are going, when the exchange is scheduled to take place, and what the rest of the deal is."

"Absolutely. I couldn't agree more. But Russia's a large country. They could be going anywhere."

It was a stupid comment. Michael had been thinking aloud. He wanted to take it back. It was too late.

"I know it's a big country," she snapped. "I need answers from you any way you can get them. Meantime, I'm on my way to the White House to brief the president."

Michael put the phone down and stared at the metal walls of the tiny cubicle of an office he was in, devoid of furniture except for a table, two chairs, and this magic phone. He felt as if he were in a prison cell.

Joyner wanted answers. Michael had only one way to get them. He glanced at his watch. It was almost eight thirty in the evening. Irina was probably out at one of the trendy clubs with Natasha or some other girlfriend, or on a date with Suslov.

He called her home. No answer. The same on her cell. He wasn't surprised. She rarely kept it on when she was out for the evening. Said it spoiled her fun. He didn't leave a message. He'd keep trying. Eventually she had to go home.

"I don't think you should do this," Jack said to Layla.

The two of them were back at last night's brasserie in the neighborhood of Jack's apartment.

Her eyes were blazing with hatred. "I want to do it. More than ever," she insisted. "You should have heard the arrogance in the bastard's voice. I could imagine the smirk on his face. The great lover thinks he's about to score one more conquest that's eluded him." She could see the reluctance on Jack's face. "It's ironic that you suggested it to me. And you're the one who's getting cold feet." She reached over and put her hand on his.

"He's too dangerous. I'm afraid you'll get hurt. Call it off now before it's too late."

She smiled. "You're a smart man, Jack, but I've been in greater danger before. Do you know what it was like living in Beirut during the civil war? We knew that the Muslims saw each of us as a potential target. I've never used the knowledge, but I learned how to fire a gun."

She paused and patted her leather Gucci purse. "Since Nadim had those men attack you, I've kept one with me at all times."

"I'm not surprised. I would never underestimate you."

"Now let's talk about logistics."

He couldn't believe the discussion. She wasn't at all hesitant. She was a very unusual person. He reached into his pocket and slipped out a small plastic bag. Inside were two tiny round objects resembling black buttons. He held the bag under the table. She took it from him and stuffed it in her purse.

"Each one's a powerful electronic transmitter," he said softly.

"Bugs."

"Precisely. They'll transmit to a receiver we've installed in a sound lab not far from the Syrian embassy and Nadim's apartment on the Left Bank. Peel the paper off the bottom of the button and there's a sticky base."

"Where do you want me to plant them?"

He shrugged. "It's your call. See how the evening goes. If he has a briefcase with him, that's a good possibility if the button blends in. If you end up in his apartment . . ." He hesitated.

"And hopefully I will," she said.

"Then under a desk in a study or some other piece of furniture would be good. Remember, we're looking for places where it'll pick up his voice on the phone or in a meeting."

She nodded.

He reached back into his pocket and pulled out a wristwatch with a burgundy leather strap and handed it to her. There was a tiny diamond in the center of the small gold face under the word *Piaget*.

"A Lady Protocol. Jack, I've always wanted one of those. It particularly means a great deal coming from you right now. I take it as a vote of confidence."

He couldn't decide if she was putting him on. "It's not what it seems, although it does keep time. Pushing the stem activates a two-way panic button. I'll be following you around . . . outside whatever building you're in. It'll set off a buzzer on a receiver in my pocket. I'll come running."

She looked concerned. "If Nadim spots you, that'll blow the whole thing."

"Don't worry. He won't."

"I can really do this myself," she insisted. "I don't need you shadowing me around like some schoolgirl who—"

He cut her off. "We're doing this my way."

Chapter 29

Layla became frightened. The minutes of the afternoon passed slowly. The movement of the Piaget watch advanced grimly, as if heading toward the hour of her execution. The bravado she had expressed with Jack faded. Nadim was a horrible, cruel man. A killer. By doing this she was putting her life on the line.

She took her time getting dressed for her date with Nadim. Wearing a pale pink silk bra and panties, she eyed longingly a bottle of scotch that was standing on the bar. She would have dearly liked one stiff drink to steel her courage. A bad idea, she decided. She'd have to drink enough tonight as it was. She needed to keep her wits as best she could.

One floor below, Daniel Moreau was knocking on the door of the owner of the apartment just beneath Layla's. Moreau had taken Nadim's advice and put several men on the street in the area where the two Syrians had been attacked. He and another one of his people were going door to door in the several closest buildings with Jack Cole's picture, trying to find out whom Jack had been with that evening. In this building it was easy. There were only two apartments to the floor.

Moreau rang the bell to 5B and waited several minutes. When he rang it again and there was still no answer, he slipped a note under the door for the occupant to call him. Then he trudged up the stairs to the top floor.

The owner of 6A, Oliver, was a screenwriter. He resented the intrusion, which came just as he was drafting a critical section of a police action thriller. Besides, Oliver had no desire to cooperate with the police or the SDECE. He made a very good living writing about them, but he had come to despise their brutality in real life.

"I've never seen the man," Oliver said tersely when Moreau showed him Jack Cole's picture.

Moreau wasn't convinced. "I could take you to the center for questioning."

"Not unless you'd like to see yourself on the front page of *Figaro*," Oliver said.

"Who are you?"

"Go see *Cops on the Loose*. I wrote it."

Moreau stepped back and Oliver slammed the door.

Across the hall was 6B. On the mailbox downstairs, the occupant was identified as L. G. Moreau rang the bell.

"Who's there?" a woman called from behind the door.

"Police. SDECE," he said.

Not many people knew about the counterespionage agency, but Layla did. Between her fund-raising work for Christians in Lebanon and her involvement with Jack, Layla was apprehensive. She had Jack's cell phone number. For a moment she considered calling him. No, she decided. There was no need to panic. *Play it cool and you can get rid of this guy.*

"I'll open the door a crack with the chain on," she said, sounding like a careful woman who lived alone. "Show me your ID."

Moreau took it out of his pocket and held it up to the crack in the door. At the same time she was looking at it, he was sizing her up. *Foxy woman*, he concluded. *Wearing a*

white terry-cloth bathrobe, makeup partially on her face.
Must be getting ready to go out for the evening.

She opened the door and gave Daniel Moreau a warm
smile with a hint of mystery. "What can I do for you, Monsieur Moreau?"

He took out Jack Cole's picture and handed it to her.

As she studied the photograph, her robe loosened a little
on top. Moreau found his eyes being drawn to the cleavage
between her shapely breasts. *Sexy woman.* After this was
over, maybe he'd come back and get acquainted.

"I'm sorry, Daniel," she said politely. "I've never seen the
man before. Did he do something wrong?"

"He killed someone in the neighborhood."

Layla looked astonished, which was genuine. She knew
that Jack had been attacked by some of Nadim's thugs. She
didn't know how it had ended. Moreau's words made her
feel better about the protection Jack would be providing this
evening.

"Do you think he'll come back this way?" She was sorry
that she kept talking. *Don't say too much,* she chided herself.
Break it off with him.

He handed her his card. "If you see him on the street,
please call me." He wanted to add, *or if you want company,*
but he didn't.

"I'll do that, Daniel."

"Good, well, thanks for your time," he said, and was
gone.

She was ready to leave the apartment when the doorbell
rang again. *Oh, hell,* she thought. Moreau must have gotten
new information and decided to come back. She looked
through the peephole and held her breath. No, it was only
Oliver, her neighbor. They had developed a friendly relationship over the years—not romantic, as he was interested
in men, but they got together for drinks or coffee every
month or so.

When she opened the door, Oliver saw she was dressed to go out. "Sorry to bother you," he said. "Did that asshole Moreau from the SDECE grill you too?"

"Yeah," she said trying to sound irate.

"Why the hell's he looking for this Jack Cole?"

She shrugged and Oliver left.

Michael dialed Irina at home and on her cell phone every half hour, getting only an answering machine. Finally, at eleven-thirty, she picked up, sounding groggy.

"You woke me," she said. "I just got in a few minutes ago. I went right to sleep."

"Well, where were you? With Suslov? I've been calling all evening."

That annoyed her. "You're not my boss, you know."

Though he wasn't in love with her, Michael still didn't like the idea of her being with Suslov, but he brushed all of that aside. Those four trucks with nuclear weapons were moving south from Volgograd. Michael desperately needed her help to stop them from falling into the hands of lunatics. Right now that was all that counted. He tried a conciliatory approach. "I'm sorry, my little bird, it's just that last night with you was so great."

She laughed. "I know. Poor Micki. So jealous. I wasn't out with Dmitri. You don't have to worry. For me, last night was great, too. This evening I was with Natasha at the Territoria. A boring scene. Nobody was there."

"But lots of men hit on you, I'll bet."

"All babies. I've got my Micki, and he's taking me to Beverly Hills to live."

"I was making plans for us today."

Her face was flushed with excitement. "Wow, really? When are we going?"

"Once this project of mine is finished. If you can help me out, I'll get done faster."

Michael rationalized that what he was telling her was mostly true. When he didn't need her for information on this exchange any longer, he intended to take her to safety in the United States. He'd help her resettle in California before he left her and went back to the Company. Okay, she wouldn't be living in Beverly Hills at first. Maybe she'd start out in Venice or Santa Monica, but he'd help her get a job modeling. Those rich Hollywood guys would eat her up. In a year, two at the most, he was confident that she'd be ensconced in a house in Beverly Hills as some hotshot producer's trophy wife or mistress.

"Tell me what I can do," she said.

"Tomorrow try to find out what you can about the deal Suslov is working on with the Arab who visited him a couple of days ago."

"The one they had all the secrecy about?"

"Yeah. That one. Anything at all."

"I'll do my best. I promise." She sounded sincere and determined.

"That's all I ask, my little bird. I'll keep my cell phone on. Call me anytime."

As she exited her apartment and climbed into the waiting Jaguar, Layla noticed the two men in suits and ties standing at either end of the block trying to blend in with the scenery. Frenchmen. Not Arabs. Chances were they didn't belong to Nadim. Daniel Moreau must have set a trap for Jack. She'd have to warn him not to come back here.

The restaurant, Carré des Feuillants, was in an old section of Paris, on Rue Castiglione, close to the Ritz Hotel and the Opera. When they were two blocks away, the skies opened with a sudden spring downpour.

Climbing out of the car and under Jean Claude's waiting umbrella, Layla thought about what Jack had told her on their first date: *I love how you get in and out of a car. You show lots of gorgeous leg.* Where was Jack now? she wondered. Already in the area of the restaurant, or would he come later? She looked around quickly. No sign of Jack. That didn't surprise her. She expected him to be concealed.

"I won't need you any more this evening," she said to Jean Claude.

He knew her well enough to sense the tension in her voice and in her movements. "Are you certain? It's not a problem."

"No, I'll be okay," she said, displaying a confidence she didn't feel.

He was reluctant to leave her, but she dismissed him with a wave of her hand. "Really. I'll be fine."

Her knees were knocking as she proceeded down the small covered path that led to the entrance to the restaurant. *Get hold of yourself; you have a chance for revenge. Don't mess it up.*

By the time she passed through the door held by the maître d's assistant, she was walking gracefully and calmly, carrying the black bag with her loaded gun inside. Dressed in a simple mauve sheath, which was a little provocative, she turned men's heads in the small restaurant when she followed the proprietor to a corner table. Nadim was waiting with a glass of champagne in front of him.

He smiled as she approached, then rose smartly. He was wearing a freshly pressed double-breasted pin-striped Armani suit.

He leaned forward to kiss each of her cheeks. She let him, swallowing hard the whole time.

"You look fabulous, my dear," he said.

"And for you, no military uniform this evening."

"I'm decidedly off duty . . . trying to make a fresh start with you. I figure a different image might help. Try to think of me as a fellow banker."

But you still have the blood of my people on your hands, she thought.

"Champagne?" Nadim asked.

"But of course."

He nodded to a waiter, who hustled over to pour another glass from the bottle of Grande Dame that Nadim had selected.

After they had ordered, Nadim said, "I know I have been a bit persistent in chasing you."

"That's an understatement. You've been horrible."

"But if something's worth having, I'll do everything humanly possible to get it. You should take my behavior as a compliment."

She forced a smile. "Let's ignore all of that. I agreed to one dinner. In return, you promised to stop harassing me. That was our deal."

"Fair enough. We'll also forget our respective politics for this evening. Who knows? You may not even think I'm so bad."

"I doubt it," she said, gritting her teeth. "But promise me one thing."

He raised his eyebrows. "What's that?"

"That you'll stick with what you said. If, at the end of this evening, I'm not interested in dating you anymore, you'll leave me alone." For a few seconds he fiddled with a spoon, trying to frame his response. That was too long for her. Abruptly she rose from her seat and grabbed her purse. "If you don't confirm that right now, then I'm out of here."

God, she has a hot temper, Nadim thought. *I'll bet she's wild in bed.* Her condition didn't trouble him. He was confident that she would fall for him. He broke into a wide smile. "You have my word on that."

"Good," she said. "Then let's drop it."

When Joyner arrived at the White House for a meeting to brief the president on the call from Michael and Perikov's news, Kendall's secretary said to her, "I'm supposed to tell you you'll have to wait ten minutes at most. Mr. Grange and a Mr. McCallister just arrived."

The secretary had pronounced McCallister's name with an expression fitting for someone who had just bitten into an extremely sour lemon.

Joyner smiled. Terry McCallister must have been his usual odious self.

Behind the door to the Oval Office, Kendall was in no mood to pamper Terry McCallister.

Grange had tried to open the meeting on a conciliatory note, saying, "Terry has some concerns about—"

But Terry didn't need Grange speaking for him. "Listen, Calvin," he began, which infuriated Kendall. He should have been addressed by McCallister as Mr. President, and nobody told the president of the United States to listen. Grange, who could sense Kendall's reaction, was horrified and cringing as McCallister continued: "Jimmy told me that you changed your mind on the bombing."

Kendall was ready for him. "There must be a misunderstanding on your part. No decision was ever made on the bombing."

"That's not what Jimmy told me. He said you would bomb them back to the Stone Age unless and until they released Robert."

Kendall glared at Grange, who tried to defend himself. "That's not exactly what I—"

Kendall cut him off. "All of that's beside the point." He wanted to sound presidential. "The fact of the matter is that I'm dealing with a complex situation. Your son's release is important, but it's only one part of the equation."

McCallister was trying to keep himself in check. "If you won't bomb, what exactly are you doing to get Robert out of that cesspool?"

"I'm afraid I can't give you any specifics. Our plans are highly classified."

McCallister ran his hands through his hair in frustration. "Oh, that's bullshit." He was raising his voice now. "Why don't you admit you're not doing a damn thing?"

Kendall was on the verge of terminating the meeting. Out of gratitude for what McCallister had done for him, and wanting to cut a distraught father some slack, he decided to make one more stab at bringing Terry around. "I can understand how you feel, Terry," he said in a soft voice, wanting to lower the decibel level. "And your son's life is important, but the welfare of his country, our country, is more important. When he joined the air force he knew that there would be a possibility of being captured or even killed. All military men know this. It's particularly true for pilots. Yet this is what your son wanted to do, and I admire him for that."

Kendall's words stung McCallister, who had coerced Robert into attending the Air Force Academy.

Kendall continued. "But please believe me when I say that it's my decision, and I'll do what I can to get Robert out of there consistent with my obligation to the country."

That didn't satisfy McCallister. "I'm not some ordinary Tom, Dick, or Harry. You're forgetting how much money I contributed and raised for—"

Kendall had enough. "This meeting's over."

When McCallister didn't move toward the door, Kendall looked at Grange. "The two of you leave now, or I'll call the Secret Service men outside this door."

McCallister knew he had no choice. Grange took him by the arm and said, "Let's go, Terry." McCallister lowered his head in abject resignation and turned around.

As the door opened, Joyner watched Grange and McCallister leaving the Oval Office. Instantly she knew how the meeting had gone.

"Okay," Kendall told her when Grange and McCallister

were out of sight. "Let's do something constructive. Where's General Childress?"

"He should be here momentarily."

Behind her she heard Childress's booming voice. "Present and ready for action."

Kendall smiled. "The only action in this room is people flapping their mouths."

They all laughed to cut the tension.

"Margaret," Kendall said, "give us the latest news."

She repeated what Michael had said verbatim. At the end she added, "I think you should call the Russian president."

"Drozny was rude and arrogant when we met at the U.N. last September. I don't like the man. I don't want to ask him for anything. Can't we find another way to stop this deal from taking place?"

Joyner sucked in her breath and looked at General Childress for support.

"She's right," the general said, taking his cue. "There is no other way to stop this short of putting U.S. troops on Russian soil, and I doubt if—"

Kendall raised his hand, signaling Childress to stop. "You know how to convince a guy, don't you?" Kendall turned to Joyner. "What time is it now in Moscow?"

She glanced at her watch. "Almost nine in the morning."

Kendall hit the intercom. "Kathy," he said to his secretary, "I need President Drozny in Moscow on the phone. But first you'd better get that Russian translator, Vince whatever-his-name-is, in the west wing over here to interpret."

Twenty minutes later Vince was in place and Drozny was on the line with his own interpreter. It quickly became apparent to Joyner during the strained and forced exchange of greetings that the Russian president had an equal disdain for Kendall. "That's the trouble with summits," one pundit had observed after their meeting at the U.N. last September. "When leaders don't get along, great damage can be done."

Drozny spoke virtually no English. Following Kendall's words, "Good morning, Mr. President," the interpreters took over. Joyner hated operating that way. Without seeing Drozny's face or hearing the inflection in his voice, she knew she was missing a great deal. However, in this situation they had no choice.

Kendall let Joyner explain what they had learned about the nuclear weapons moving south from Volgograd.

There was a pause. Vince Kuzinski, the interpreter in the Oval Office, translated Joyner's words, followed by a long silence.

At the end of it, three short sentences came back from Drozny's interpreter. "What you say is very unlikely. We will investigate. Thank you for your interest."

Then the phone went dead.

That infuriated Kendall. The fucker hung up on me," he said. "I told you he was a rude son of a bitch."

Joyner tried to soften his reaction. There was enough going on here without adding personal pique to the mix. "I'm sure he thought the conversation was over."

"Well, he'd better cooperate, or . . ." Even in his pique, Kendall couldn't force himself to say that he'd send American troops into Russia to do the job. But what other choices would he have?

Reluctantly, Layla had to admit that for the two hours during dinner Nadim exhibited a charm that frightened her. He spoke about his years in the United States at the Syrian embassy, and he asked about hers at Harvard. He made clever and witty comments about phonies and hypocrites he had met in the French and American governments over the years. He talked to her about Paris restaurants she liked and skiing in the Alps, for which they shared a passion. He even got her talking about the boarding school she had attended in Switzerland.

She found it terrifying that this monster, the Butcher of Beirut, could turn himself into a wholly different personality as easily as he had shed the military uniform for the double-breasted suit. She had never known anyone like him. He wasn't merely duplicitous and a charlatan. He had some type of mental disorder, the split personality she had read about in school, but she couldn't recall the psychiatric term. What she had to keep reminding herself was not to forget how dangerous he really was and the risks to her tonight.

All the while they talked and ate, the wine flowed. Following the champagne, he had chosen a Puligny-Montrachet and an 'eighty-five Haut Brion. With dessert he ordered a half bottle of Château d'Yquem. The whole time she was trying to drink as little as possible, but that was difficult. The sommelier kept refilling her glass.

Nadim admired her wristwatch, the one Jack had given her. She blushed and said, "Thank you." Then she put her hand under the table before he studied it carefully. After dessert and coffee, he ordered them each a glass of cognac. When he went to the bathroom, she dumped most of hers into her coffee cup.

Outside, Jack sat in the backseat of a dull gray nondescript Renault sedan parked across the street, twenty yards away from the entrance to the restaurant. Behind the wheel was Gal from Haifa, a twenty-five-year-old who was working part-time at the Israeli embassy in Paris while he studied at the University of Paris. After three years in the city, Gal knew the streets well. The rain was finally letting up. Jack had a clear view of the front of the restaurant. The instant he saw Layla and Nadim emerge, he planned to stretch out on the backseat so they couldn't see him. It would be up to Gal to follow them wherever they were headed.

Jack looked at his watch nervously. *Jesus, it's almost eleven-thirty. She's been in there with him a long time. Suppose she likes him. Then what?* Another equally sickening thought was that the restaurant had a rear entrance. What if Nadim had hustled Layla out that way? When Jack had checked this afternoon, he saw only one entrance. Still, there could be a service door where supplies were delivered. *Dummy*. He blamed himself for not thinking of that. All restaurants had separate doors for vendors, didn't they? Too late now.

Suddenly he saw Layla walking down the path from the front of the restaurant with Nadim beside her. "There they are," Jack said to Gal. He ducked down and stretched out on the seat.

When the car didn't move, Jack called out anxiously to the driver, "What's going on?"

Gal strained his eyes to see. "He's waving for a cab. He has an arm around the girl. He's kissing her."

"Jesus, don't tell me that."

"But you asked."

"Now what?"

"They're getting into a cab together."

Jack raised his head enough to see the cab in front of the restaurant begin moving. "Go now. Follow them. . . . You'd better not lose them."

He ducked back down. Two minutes later, Jack snapped at Gal, "Tell me where you're going."

"Toward the river."

"Which bridge?"

"The Pont Neuf."

Layla's place was the other direction. There were hotels close to the restaurant. They wouldn't be driving so far if that was where Nadim was taking her. They must be going to Nadim's apartment, Jack decided. That was good for planting the bugs, but bad for what could happen to Layla. He was sorry he had done this.

In the back of the cab Nadim, without any warning, pushed his hand under Layla's skirt. He had a wild, animal-like look in his eyes. His garlicky, alcohol-laden breath was in her face as he tried to kiss her. So close to the object of his desire, he abandoned the charm. She wondered if he planned to have sex with her in the cab.

Layla was ready for him. Without panicking, she clamped her legs together. "Please wait," she said. "We'll both enjoy it so much more when we get to your apartment."

He pulled his head away from her. The urgency was gone. "Just a tiny touch. Down there. A preview," he said. He was coaxing, not demanding.

This guy's technique leaves a lot to be desired, she thought. *He's obviously used to taking what he wants from women.* She spread her legs a little and his hand was in her panties. He was forcing two fingers inside of her.

She pulled them away and said, "That's the preview."

He didn't argue.

The cabdriver smiled, enjoying the performance.

"I'll undress you," Nadim said once they were inside his apartment.

"No. No," she protested. "I have to use the bathroom first. I'll strip in there. You take your clothes off out here. I'll meet you in bed. Two naked bodies."

That satisfied him. In the bathroom she looked at herself in the mirror. *Oh, God, how am I going to go through with this?* Then she thought about all of the people he had killed—family members and others. More than avenging their deaths was at stake. She couldn't let this madman get his hands on nuclear weapons. *You're going to close your eyes and do it,* she vowed.

She slipped out of her clothes and let them fall to the white-tiled floor. Then she reached into her purse and yanked out a bottle of body lotion and a condom. "No way am I going to have this monster's stuff inside me," she muttered to herself.

When she stepped out of the bathroom, she saw Nadim naked in bed, lying on his back stroking himself. "Sometimes he needs a little help," he said.

"That's my job," Layla replied, now sounding self-confident and in control. "First I want to give you a massage."

"I am your slave," Nadim said.

Slowly, with probing fingers, she massaged his shoulders and the back of his neck using the body lotion. He gave himself over to her fully, moaning with pleasure.

What I should really do right now, she thought, *is get the gun in my purse and kill the bastard.* It was tempting, and it took all of her control to resist. That wouldn't get Jack what he needed.

She had Nadim so relaxed that she was hoping he might fall asleep this way. Then she could plant the bugs and get the hell out of there. No such luck. He began talking again. "You have great hands."

She closed her eyes and tried to imagine she was alone on a beach in Beirut when the city was still beautiful, before all of the wars.

"Now the front," Nadim said as he flipped over. "Down there."

She went to work with her hands on his penis and his balls, stroking lightly with the tops of her fingers the way Enrico, an Italian from Verona she had been in love with a few years ago, had taught her. She wasn't that experienced, but the couple of other times she had tried it with men, it always brought them to a state of arousal in a matter of seconds.

Nothing was happening with Nadim. He remained soft and limp.

"Sometimes it takes me a little longer," he said. "Just work with me."

"That's nothing to worry about," she said. "It happens to

everybody, especially when they drink a lot." He reached for her breasts, but she twisted away.

Now something else began bothering her. She had read that some men become abusive toward the woman they were with if they had this problem and couldn't get an erection. She had left her bag in the bathroom. She knew precisely where it was: on the sink. At the first sign of that kind of behavior, she'd get her gun and shoot him.

"Put it in your mouth," he said. "That always works."

Before he knew what was happening, she slipped the condom on him, which wasn't easy given his lack of arousal. Then she took him into her mouth, but that still didn't do a thing. She decided this must be a recurring problem with him from the way he was sounding. So much for Nadim's being a great lover.

She was racking her brain, trying to decide what she could do to prevent this from turning into a total disaster. Then an idea popped into her head. She knew how she could save herself and Jack's mission. In Nadim's diminished state as a result of all the wine he had, and with his massive ego, she might get away with it.

He was still on his back. She rolled on top of him.

"You're nice and hard now," she said, trying to make the lie sound convincing. "I want you inside of me."

She pressed her breasts against his chest. Then she reached down and grabbed his flaccid member. With her hand cupped tightly around it, she began thrusting herself against him and crying out, "Oh, it's good. It feels so good. . . . I'm coming. . . . Oh, God, I'm coming. You too."

She kept tugging and pulling on him until his body gave a shudder. She felt warm, sticky fluid in her hand as it spilled out of the condom.

With that, he turned over on his side and fell asleep.

Layla moved fast. Resisting the urge to throw up, she washed her hands and splashed cold water on her face. Then she reached into her purse and took out the two bugs Jack had given her.

One she fastened under the center of the tablelike desk in the study. On the floor was the briefcase Nadim had taken to the restaurant with him. Her guess was that he carried it everywhere. She attached the second bug to the bottom of the briefcase.

She took a pen and paper from the center desk drawer. Praying that he wouldn't wake up, she quickly scribbled a note. *You're a fabulous lover. I had a great evening. Hope to see you again soon. . . . L*

She left it on the other pillow, next to him in bed, trying to be as quiet as possible. She was tiptoeing around the bedroom as he snored loudly. *Another minute. That's all I need.* She dressed so quickly in the bathroom that she put her panties on backward. She didn't care. She raced toward the front door, closed it softly, and got out of that damn apartment.

Her clothes were disheveled. Her entire body was trembling as she walked out of Nadim's building into the chilly night air. The instant Jack saw her, he climbed out of Gal's car and raced over. "Are you all right?" he asked anxiously.

"I planted the bugs," she said in a voice filled with self-loathing and disgust. "Isn't that what you care about? One under his desk. One attached to his briefcase. It's done." She couldn't get her body to stop convulsing.

"What's wrong?" he asked.

"What the hell do you think's wrong?" she cried out. "I feel like a whore."

Jack was distraught. "This afternoon I told you not to do it."

"Yeah, you did," she said. "I can't blame you. I should have listened to you, but I didn't and . . ."

Suddenly she felt horribly sick. She staggered over to the gutter along the curb, leaned over, and threw up her entire dinner. Tears were running down her cheeks. Jack handed her a handkerchief and put an arm around her. She was sobbing and shaking her head.

"It's over now," he said. "I have a man waiting in a car across the street. We'll take you home."

She pulled away from him. "You can't. Some cop, Daniel Moreau, is looking for you on my street, going door to door with your picture. He has men stationed there."

"Jesus, since when?"

"This evening."

"Then come to my place."

She stared at him with dead, cold eyes. There was no hint of a mysterious smile on her sad face. "I just want to go home alone. Please, Jack. Right now I hate myself. I want to spend about an hour in the shower and get rid of his smell. That's what I want."

An empty taxi was passing. Layla raised her hand.

She didn't even look at Jack as she got in the cab.

Jack climbed back into Gal's car. His mind was a jumble. Concern for Layla and guilt for what had happened were threatening to cloud his mind and muddle his judgment. He couldn't let that happen.

He had already seen the poster of himself on the police van near the Israeli embassy. Now Layla had said Moreau was searching for him near her apartment. The Frenchman was closing in on him.

Out of an abundance of caution, Jack asked Gal to leave him off at Place Victor Hugo, four blocks away from his apartment. "I'll be okay from here," he told the young Israeli. Then he set off on foot, following a circuitous route along narrow back streets until he reached a corner that he could peek around and have an unobstructed view of his apartment building. It took Jack only one quick glance to spot the police car parked immediately in front of his building. Next to the car, on the sidewalk, two blue-uniformed gendarmes were standing, smoking cigarettes and chatting. Jack realized that Moreau must have penetrated his carefully constructed layers of dummy companies to find out about the apartment.

Oh, shit, he thought. *I can't go back there.* He didn't want to stay with Avi. They had to remain apart, at least at night, so Moreau couldn't capture them both together. The Hotel Bristol was close to the Israeli embassy. He decided to stay there, using his Henri Deveraux identity to register.

Jack retreated, staying on side streets, heading toward the Bristol on foot. After ten minutes he pulled out his cell phone and woke Avi up at the Hotel Pyrenees. "Don't call me anymore at my apartment. Just use the cell."

"Your place has gotten hot?"

"Moreau is tightening the noose. We don't have much time."

Chapter 30

Nadim woke up and reached across the bed for Layla. All he found was a piece of paper on the pillow.

He grabbed it and bolted upright in bed. His head was pounding, and he felt washed-out from all the alcohol last evening. Finishing that large glass of cognac had been a mistake. There wasn't much he remembered in detail of what had happened after they had left the restaurant. He and Layla had come here. After that everything was fuzzy.

Then he read the note. And he read it again. A broad smile lit his face. There was no question about how he had performed. He'd see more of her in the next couple of days and while he was still in Paris. Once the deal with McCallister was complete and he seized control of the Syrian government from Ahmed, he'd bring her back to Damascus to live in the presidential palace with him. He was confident that she'd come. Her note told him as much.

What really pleased him was that he had beaten out Jack Cole, that Israeli spy, where it mattered most: between the sheets.

Carrying his briefcase, Nadim was whistling a tune as he entered the embassy. Not only was the deal for the American pilot coming together, but he had Layla now as well.

His good mood ended once he walked into the reception area

of the Syrian embassy and saw General Kemal waiting for him. The Turk should have called first rather than making a sudden surprise visit to Paris, but he could understand Kemal's anxiety. To be fair to the man, Nadim had not kept him informed of developments. Kemal couldn't risk calling or sending a message from Turkey. He had to assume that the Americans were now using every conceivable electronic device to pick up any communications coming in and out of the country.

Nadim hustled Kemal up to his office. He put his briefcase down on the table next to his desk and turned to his visitor. "The Iranians are on board," Nadim said with pride.

"Thanks for telling me when it happened."

What Nadim wanted to say was, *Look, asshole, if it weren't for me and my plan, you'd be rotting in a Turkish prison for the rest of your life.* But he didn't do that, of course. The road from Iran to Syria ran through Turkey. So he sucked it up and calmly said, "It just happened yesterday. I had planned to call and invite you to Paris today to give you that report, but you beat me to it. You're a very smart man, as always, General Kemal."

And you're full of shit, as always, Kemal was thinking.

"There is one small adjustment to our original plan," Nadim said.

"Yeah. What?" Kemal asked warily.

"Ali Hashim won't pay us what I asked."

Kemal looked indignant. "Then to hell with him. We'll cut Iran out."

It's not possible, you imbecile, Nadim thought. *Do you have any brains at all?* "I settled for a million dollars for each of us, to be deposited in a Swiss bank account."

Kemal grumbled. "It has to be two. That's the least I'll accept."

Nadim thought about reducing his own five-million-dollar share as a way of getting two for Kemal, but he quickly rejected that possibility. "Listen, my friend, today is already Tuesday. The exchange takes place on Friday. That's only three days from now. We don't have the luxury of time to continue negotiating. A million dollars is a lot of money. I'm satisfied with it. I think you should be too."

"Bastards. They claim to be so righteous, and they always swindle us."

Nadim tried to sound sympathetic. "I know how you feel. I was plenty angry at him myself. I did the best I could."

Kemal was squirming in his chair. He hadn't anticipated this development. How could he be certain that Nadim wasn't skimming some of Kemal's money for himself?

Nadim wanted to wrap this up already. He was tired of haggling with both Hashim and Kemal. He decided to press Kemal. "The train's leaving the station. It's now or never."

Kemal fumed in abject resignation. He knew that he had no choice about the money. "I want to talk about the details of the exchange."

What now? Nadim wondered. "I'm listening."

Kemal had his back up. "When we made the deal, you told me that I would have control over the American pilot again before the exchange takes place."

"And you will," Nadim said. "I promise you that you will be the one who brings the pilot to the exchange. To set it all up, I want you to fly to Adana in southern Turkey today. Have one of your troops, someone you can trust, meet you there."

Kemal decided that he'd call Abdullah.

Nadim continued. "I have your cell phone number. Tomorrow evening I will call you and tell you where and when on Thursday we'll turn the pilot over to you. Friday at first light is the time for the exchange."

Jack was relieved. The bugs Layla had planted were working. He and Avi were in the sound lab with a technician. They had heard every word Nadim and Kemal said.

Jack now knew that the exchange would take place Friday morning. Nadim, Kemal, and the Iranians would all be involved. Kemal would be bringing Robert McCallister to the site. He still didn't know where that was, or what the terms of the exchange were, but they were getting close. Jack had to stay out of Moreau's clutches long enough to obtain that information, then develop a plan to rescue Robert and block the exchange.

Thinking about the pilot reminded Jack of that awful meeting he had in Tel Aviv—the last time he had seen his brother. Between Nadim and Moreau there was too much of a chance Jack might never make it out of this alive. He couldn't bear the thought of leaving his relationship with Sam the way it now was with their argument in Tel Aviv, if he never saw his brother again. Though it involved some risk, he had to take it. He picked up the phone and called Sam at his office in London. "I have to see you in Paris today," he said. "It's quite important."

"Is this about Robert?"

"Please, no questions, and don't tell Ann or Sarah."

Jack heard a shuffling of papers as Sam either checked his calendar or the train schedule.

"I can get to Gare du Nord at five o'clock this afternoon."

"Good. When you arrive, take a cab to a little brasserie at number Thirteen Rue Marbeuf. There's a section in the back, up a few steps. Sit at a table up there. Order something and wait for me."

Nadim returned to his office and picked up the phone. He called Layla at the bank.

"What a nice note you left," he said.

Her stomach churned as she heard the sound of his voice. This wasn't something she had figured on. It took her a few seconds to recover her composure. "It was a special evening. One I'll never forget," she said, forcing the words out, while all she could think of was throwing up in the gutter outside of his apartment.

"Let's do it again this evening," he said, sounding euphoric.

She couldn't possibly relive that nightmare. But it was unlikely Jack had gotten the information he needed. She couldn't destroy everything she had put in place.

Playing for time, she said, "Let me check my calendar."

She thought of putting him on hold and calling Jack on the other line, but there wasn't time for that. Nadim was too smart. He would grow suspicious. She came up with a plausible story. "I have a dinner meeting with key officials at the bank. I can't break it."

"What about afterward?"

"These sessions run late." To give herself credibility, she added, "Let's do it tomorrow."

Nadim was thinking that tomorrow was already Wednesday. He had planned to fly to Baku Wednesday evening. He hesitated. . . . Thursday morning would be soon enough. Not only would it be another great evening with her, but he was anxious to solidify their relationship. "Tomorrow, then," he said. "Apicius at nine."

"I'll be there."

Her hands were shaking so badly she could hardly hang up the phone. *What am I going to do? I'll never go to bed with that monster again.* She picked up the phone and called Jack on his cell. "I have to talk to you."

Jack was too distraught and worried about Layla to be thinking clearly.

"Why did you tell Nadim you'd see him again?" he blurted out as soon as Layla entered the sound lab.

She was stunned. "How do you know about it?"

"The bugs you planted are working perfectly."

It never occurred to her that Jack would have heard

Nadim's side of the conversation. Of course, he could easily have pieced together what she had said.

"I don't know what you were thinking."

His words and tone reminded her of her father when she was a young girl and he disapproved of something she had done. The situation was all too much for her. She lost it.

Ignoring both Avi and the sound technician, she railed at Jack. "Don't be so stupid! I didn't have a choice."

"I can't stand the thought of your being in his bed again."

She moved in close to him. "*You* can't stand it!" she shouted. "How do you think *I* feel? I'd rather die than do that again."

"Then you should have—"

Avi cut him off. He realized that Jack's concern for Layla was clouding his judgment. "She's right," Avi said. "She had no choice. If she refused to meet him, he'd know something was wrong. Delaying him a day was a brilliant move on her part."

Avi's words brought Jack back to reality. He didn't like it, but he had to admit they were both right. Once you put a ball in play, you couldn't always tell which way it would bounce. Nor could you stop the game in the middle.

In frustration, he slammed his fist into the palm of his other hand. All of this was his own damn fault. He was in love with her, which was crazy, with what was happening. He should have followed Avi's advice in the beginning and never gotten involved with her. Once he did, he should never have suggested that she call Nadim. There had to be a way out of this morass. God, she had looked so awful leaning over the gutter and retching in front of Nadim's building. He couldn't let her go through that again. Then it hit him: There was a solution.

"You won't have to sleep with him again," Jack said. "I have an idea."

Layla and Avi both looked at Jack expectantly.

"You're safe at the restaurant, right?"

She nodded.

"Suppose we give you something to take with dinner, to slip into your wine or food, that'll make you throw up. One of those drugs they give kids when they ingest poison and you want them to get rid of it. You'll be so sick you wouldn't be any fun for him. He'll have to let you go home."

Layla wrinkled up her nose while she thought about what he had proposed. "That should work," she said. "I can do that."

Avi wasn't as enthusiastic, but he decided to keep his nagging doubts to himself. There wasn't anything he could point to. He was just worried that something unexpected would occur. They would never be able to control Nadim so easily.

The four trucks in the nuclear convoy were barely moving.

A snowstorm had struck the greater Caucasus Mountains. In near-blizzard conditions, they were still on the Russian side of the border with Azerbaijan.

The head of the convoy, Nikolai, knew very well what the weather could be like. His grandfather had survived the battle of Stalingrad but was left without fingers or toes as a result of frostbite. He was one of the lucky ones. The Russian winter had done what its soldiers couldn't do: destroyed Hitler's army. Nikolai had come prepared. Each of the trailer trucks had chains for the tires in their cabins. Once the snow started coming down, he had ordered all of the drivers to stop and install the chains.

Nikolai had a razor-sharp mind that functioned like a computer, which was one reason that Suslov, his commander in Afghanistan, gave him this assignment. Nikolai knew precisely how many more miles they had to cover.

As long as they continued moving, albeit at this snail's

pace, they would make it to the destination in time. Once they crossed the mountains conditions would improve.

Nikolai forced the men to keep driving regardless of the conditions. He was aware of the precious cargo they were transporting. The possibility of a truck rolling off the highway and crashing down the rocky, mountainous terrain sent a wave of fear up and down Nikolai's spine. Still, he refused to order the convoy to stop moving on the deserted road and wait out the storm.

Suslov had impressed him with the absolute necessity of getting to the destination on time. He had given Nikolai an incentive: The former Russian army captain would have enough money that he would never have to work again a day in his life.

"Keep moving," he repeatedly shouted into the communications system that linked the convoy. "We don't stop. Under any circumstances."

The drivers could barely see, but the trucks kept lumbering up the mountain.

In his Henri Devereaux disguise, Jack, with a .38 in the pocket of his black leather jacket, waited around the corner from the brasserie on Rue Marbeauf, continually glancing out, looking for a cab to pull up in front.

Thirty minutes after Sam's train was scheduled to arrive, a green Citroën taxi slammed to a stop in front of the brasserie. Jack watched Sam pay the driver, climb out, and go inside carrying a briefcase.

He waited a full ten minutes to see if Sam had been followed. During that time Jack weighed in his mind what he was doing. Talking to Sam did have some risks, but he was confident he could trust his brother. At any rate, he wouldn't give Sam any hard information. All he wanted to do was make peace with his brother. If this was the end for Jack, he couldn't leave Sam with the guilt and pain he would have because of their last meeting.

Satisfied that no one had followed Sam, Jack walked into the brasserie. The air in front was heavy with cigarette smoke. At the bar a couple of workmen on their way home were sipping beer. A lottery machine was punching out tickets. Jack stopped at the bar and picked up an espresso. Then he made his way toward the stairs leading to the back section, which was deserted except for Sam, sipping a Coke and staring at some legal documents.

As Jack approached, Sam looked up, didn't recognize his brother, and turned back to the papers. When he got to the table, Jack said softly. "Don't say a word. It's me."

Recognizing Jack's voice, Sam nearly dropped his drink. Jack slid into a chair at the table next to Sam, but in a position where he could still watch the front of the restaurant.

"Oh, my God. It *is* you. I saw posters at the train station. The police are looking for you. . . . That must be why you're wearing the disguise." Sam looked around the room nervously.

"There are some things I want you to know," Jack said. "I'll trust you not to mention a word of this to anyone. Not even Ann or Sarah."

"You don't have to worry. They think I'm in Brussels on firm business. I swear I won't tell a soul."

"Good. When we were last together in Tel Aviv, you asked me to help get Robert released. You said I must know people in the Israeli government. People who could help rescue Robert."

"Uh-huh."

"Well, I do know people like that. I've known them very well for a long time."

"Jesus. You've been working with the Mossad all these years?"

"Shhh," Jack admonished. "Whisper, please." Sam was a

quick study. Jack was glad he didn't have to spell it out. "Let's just say that I've served Israel in any way I could."

"What's the situation with Robert?"

"All I can tell you is that people are working hard for his release. Good people in Israel and in the United States."

"I hope your life's not in danger because I asked you to get involved in helping Robert."

The horrified look that Jack saw on his brother's face underscored how much Sam meant what he had just said. "There is danger, and that's one reason I had to see you: to tell you not to feel guilty if something does happen to me. What's at stake is now much bigger than Robert McCallister's release. I can't say any more than that. But regardless of what happens, I am grateful to you for getting me involved. Otherwise things might have happened—terrible things for Israel and the world."

"But why the posters at the train station? Why are the French police looking for you?"

Jack gave him a sardonic smile. "C'mon, Sam. You know the politics of this part of the world."

Sam grimaced. "Yeah, that was a stupid comment. I'm really glad that you called me over to tell me this."

"There's something else I want you to know."

With tears in his eyes, Sam put his hand on Jack's arm, dreading what was coming next.

"My work here for the government of Israel is the reason I wasn't in Chicago more when Mother and Father were dying. I was involved then in something equally important."

Sam looked chagrined. "I'm so sorry. All these years I busted your chops over that. Please forgive me."

"Don't worry. You didn't know. I couldn't tell you. In your situation I would have done the same."

"Will this be over soon?"

"In a matter of days. One way or the other."

Chapter 31

Major General Nadim leaned forward in the chair and studied the map of the former USSR spread out on the breakfast table in his apartment. He took a sip of coffee, then extended his finger and traced a line south from Volgograd, trying to estimate where the nuclear convoy was right now.

Nadim was ecstatic. Everything was going so well. He was close to his goal of becoming the Syrian leader, a player in world politics with Layla at his side.

Then his balloon burst with a vengeance.

The telephone jarred him. Nadim jumped up to answer. It was his secretary at the embassy. In a halting voice she said, "President Ahmed is calling you from Damascus. His assistant says it's a matter of extreme urgency."

Nadim cursed under his breath. The last thing he needed right now was for that imbecile Ahmed to disrupt his plans.

It took several more minutes before Ahmed was on the phone.

"Good morning, Mr. President," Nadim said, using the form of address Ahmed preferred and trying to sound obsequious.

"There's nothing at all good about it," Ahmed fired back. "I'm furious at you." He sounded like a stern teacher addressing a student who had been caught cheating.

One thought kept running through Nadim's mind: *Uh-oh, he knows about the pilot. He found out.* Nadim sat down to steady himself and took deep breaths, gulping for air. One good thing about being unmarried was that there was no wife and children back in Damascus for Ahmed to hold hostage and torture.

Nadim decided to tough it out. "I'm sorry, sir. What did I do?"

Ahmed was shouting now. "You know damn well what you did. You had no business letting the Turks hide the American pilot in Syrian territory without my knowledge and agreement. It was only because of a comment my physician made—that he had been called north to treat a bullet wound of the pilot—that I managed to find out. Have you lost your mind?"

Nadim didn't like the idea of having this conversation on an unsecured phone. "We should talk later," he said. "When I get to the embassy. We have a special phone that—"

Ahmed was in too much of a rage to listen. "You have a choice," he said. "You can talk to me right now. Tell me what's happening . . . Or you can fly home and explain it to a board of inquiry at your treason trial."

"But—"

"No buts. Those are your choices."

Nadim swallowed hard. There was only one thing he could do to save his own life: level with Ahmed now. Well, at least partially.

"I have been working on a plan, Mr. President," Nadim said, returning to his subservient voice. "I didn't want to bother you until I knew I could get it all together. I expect that to be later today. Then I had planned to call you and seek your approval before moving forward."

"A plan to do what?" Ahmed said, still sounding hostile.

Well, here goes. If he doesn't understand it and buy in,

I'm a dead man. Speak slowly, Nadim cautioned himself. *The man's not the sharpest blade in the knife drawer.*

"Acquire nuclear weapons for our military . . . Put Israel on the defensive . . . Change the entire political landscape of the Middle East."

"That's quite an objective, isn't it?"

Nadim could sense Ahmed's wrath abating as his curiosity took over. "It's easily attainable. . . . But the American pilot is a critical component. I had to gain temporary control over him until the rest came together." Nadim knew how much Ahmed despised the Turks. He decided to play on that. "They're such fools in Ankara. You know that."

Ahmed laughed. "Very well."

"They might have done something stupid, like killing him, and then we would have lost our bargaining chip."

Ahmed was now intrigued. "What is it you're trading him for?"

Nadim hesitated for an instant, wanting to select his words carefully, making certain to conceal his disgust for this fool Ahmed. The plan was complicated, but Ahmed had to understand each and every term. Only if he appreciated the great benefit of what Nadim had conceived would he remove the death sentence that was hanging over Nadim.

"It goes like this, Mr. President," Nadim said. "Early on Friday morning, at first light, which will be five A.M., an exchange will take place at a truck stop at a key crossroads fifty miles northwest of Baku in Azerbaijan. A former Russian general, Dmitri Suslov, will be bringing to the meeting four trucks loaded with nuclear weapons from the former USSR arsenal."

"Nuclear weapons. Are you serious?" Ahmed was becoming excited. "With nuclear weapons we could become a real power. A match for the Israelis."

Nadim smiled. He now had Ahmed where he wanted him.

"I have it all worked out with Dmitri Suslov, a powerful economic figure in Moscow."

"How do we know we can trust this Suslov? My father always said, 'You can't trust the Russians.'"

"Suslov won't get his money until he turns over the weapons."

Ahmed was outraged. "You stole money from our limited reserves for this without my approval?" The president sounded belligerent.

Nadim pounced. "We don't have to put up a cent. That's the beauty of my plan. The Iranians have agreed to finance the entire transaction. One point two billion dollars for Suslov."

There was a heavy silence while Ahmed absorbed what Nadim had said.

"Why don't we get any money?" he finally asked.

"We get two of the truckloads of nuclear weapons. Iran gets one. General Kemal in Turkey gets the other to threaten the Kurds with. The idea is that after the exchange, the convoy will move south into Iran. One truckload stays there. The other three move west into Turkey. One stops there. The final two move south into Syria."

Ahmed still wasn't satisfied. "The Turks will cheat us and keep all three."

"I don't think so. General Kemal is operating without his government's knowledge, and he is also receiving a personal payment from the Iranians. I made it clear to him that if he doesn't follow the plan, I will make certain word reaches his prime minister that he took a bribe in an important government matter. Their prime minister has sworn to clean up corruption. Kemal's life will be worth less than dog shit."

"What happens to the American pilot under this great plan of yours?"

"The Iranians will take him back to Tehran from Baku. They can use him in a quiet trade with the Americans to obtain sophisticated technology that the Americans have prohibited them from acquiring. The same way that Iran has made other secret exchanges with Washington over the years."

"So everybody gets something," Ahmed said, thinking aloud as he weighed Nadim's words.

"I think so, Mr. President. Except the Israelis, of course. After this exchange, they will find two of their most mortal enemies armed with nuclear weapons."

"What are you missing to move forward?"

"Only your approval, Mr. President. As I said, I had planned to seek it this afternoon, but since you called, I wish to ask for it now."

Nadim held his breath. *God, please don't let that moron call it off.*

"You have it," Ahmed said, although he sounded tentative, worrying whether there was some downside he had missed. "If you pull this off, I'll present you with the Presidential Medal."

And if I fail, you'll put me before a firing squad, provided you can catch me. But don't spend much time worrying about that possibility, because I will succeed. Then I'll be generous after I seize control from you. I'll present you with a choice of death by a firing squad or a hangman's noose. You'll pay for the humiliating way you've treated me, he silently vowed.

Jack Cole could not believe what he had just heard. He was in the lab with a technician. Every word that Nadim had said to Ahmed had been broadcast directly to Jack via both transmitters, which meant that Nadim was still at home. The sound had been clear. Nadim's words had been recorded and were now on a tape that was perfect.

Unlike the botched operation at the Hassler, this time the technology had worked. Jack now knew exactly what

Nadim's plan was. It was more diabolical than he had ever imagined. He had to find a way of blocking it.

Jack's first call was to Avi, who was at his hotel. "Get over here fast," was all Jack said.

"I'm on my way," Avi replied, without asking any questions.

Then Jack called Layla at her office at the bank.

"You may have saved the world," Jack said, his voice ringing with excitement.

It took her a minute to absorb what he said. "Sounds like you heard what you were looking for."

"Exactly."

"What happens now?"

"There's no need for you to meet Nadim tonight or any other time,"

She gave a deep sigh of relief.

"Call his office," Jack continued. "Don't talk to him, but leave a message with his secretary that something came up, and you can't make dinner this evening. Tell him you're free tomorrow, so he won't become suspicious."

Layla was confused. "But you said—"

"You don't have to worry. He'll never be able to meet you tomorrow. He has to be somewhere far from Paris."

"I'll do what you said," she replied softly.

"Good. Then come to the sound lab after work. I'll fill you in."

With mounting concern, Avi listened to the tape of Nadim's call with Ahmed. At the end he asked Jack, "Why Baku?"

"Think about the geography. It's between Russia and the other countries involved. It means Suslov doesn't have to do the deal on Russian soil. He also must have powerful friends in Azerbaijan."

Avi mulled it over and nodded. "Layla did great work. I

was wrong about her. . . . But how are we going to stop the shipment?"

"I have an idea," Jack said. "I can pitch it, but Moshe has to implement it. I'll go to the embassy and call him. You stay here with the sound technician." The receiver was broadcasting what was being picked up by the bugs Layla had planted. There was no way of knowing what further gems Nadim might give them. "Call me if you hear anything important."

During Jack's monologue about what Nadim had planned, the Mossad director gave grunts, followed by a long sigh. At the end, Jack said, "I want to fly with Avi to Baku tomorrow. We'll try to locate the meeting site when we arrive. The question is, Can you arrange to send in some commandos so we can block this exchange from taking place? I know I'm not giving you much time. It's all happening Friday morning. That's less than forty-eight hours from now."

There was a long silence while Moshe digested Jack's words. "I like your proposal," he finally said. "But I'll need the prime minister's approval. If he gives me a green light, I'll fly commandos into Baku. We've got to block that exchange. It's a grave threat to our national security."

"You have to make the prime minister go along."

"With politicians you never know, but I'll present it in a way that he has no choice. Meantime, make sure either Avi or you are at the embassy. I'll call as soon as I have the answer."

Something else was troubling Jack. "What about the government of Azerbaijan? Do you think they'd help us? After all, they can't be in favor of the spread of nuclear weapons so close to their border."

Moshe didn't hesitate before answering. "Don't waste a minute thinking about it. Their president is a former KGB general and big deal in the Communist party. He's not exactly known for his integrity. We have to assume that Suslov has paid him off to keep his troops out of the area. We'd better spend our time worrying about . . ."

Jack completed Moshe's sentence for him. "Washington."

"You guessed it. That, my friend, will be a tougher sell, but it won't hold us up. The time for playing games is over. We have to act to protect our own interests, regardless of what Washington says."

Chapter 32

Margaret Joyner was worried. Everything was spiraling out of control, and she didn't know what to do about it. Her late husband, Ken, was fond of the expression, "He popped his cork," when someone got really angry.

Watching Kendall during the report she gave to the president and General Childress in the Oval Office, she thought those words fit the situation.

"I can't believe that the Mossad director told you his government would do whatever it had to do, regardless of how we decide the issue."

Joyner had been infuriated by Moshe's words as well, and by his unwillingness to tell her whether the Israelis were planning to send troops to Baku in response to her direct question. Still, she found herself once more defending the Mossad director. "Israel has a great deal at risk. Moshe didn't take the hard line with me until I said that I couldn't assure him that we would send American troops to block the exchange."

That didn't mollify Kendall. "Well, I sure as hell don't want to send our boys uninvited onto Russian soil unless it's absolutely necessary."

Gingerly, Joyner corrected the president. "Baku's not Russian soil. It's in Azerbaijan."

Kendall turned as red as his necktie. "Of course, I know that, Margaret."

She wasn't certain whether he did until he added, "My point is that since it's one of those countries that used to be in the USSR, the Russians figure they can exert control."

"Fair enough."

Kendall reached for the phone. "What I should really do is call the Israeli prime minister, raise hell with him, and get them to back off."

Joyner looked at General Childress, who was undecided on the issue. On the one hand, he sided with Joyner. He wanted to do everything possible now to block Turkey, Syria, and Iran from acquiring nuclear weapons, rather than having to commence an operation later where they threatened to use them. On the other hand, the idea of American military action that close to Russian soil could lead to a nuclear war. Childress was grasping for a way out of the dilemma. "Suppose you call back President Drozny," the general said. "Maybe he's moving up on the issue. If he can stop the convoy of nuclear weapons before it leaves Russia, that'll make everything a lot easier."

Kendall looked at Joyner. "What do you think?"

She shrugged. "Can't hurt."

Kendall summoned Vince, the interpreter, before placing the call. Again, Kendall got nowhere with Drozny. "We're still investigating this matter," the Russian president said in a kiss-off. "If it's necessary to act, we'll do what's appropriate." The implication was clear: *This is a matter within the Russian sphere of influence. Keep out.*

Drozny's response further infuriated the president. "He's giving me the runaround," Kendall said when he hung up the phone. "No-good Russian fuck."

Joyner tried to seize the initiative. "Let's get a special-operations unit out of Afghanistan, or on the base in Uzbekistan. They could be ready to move into Baku quickly."

Kendall had practiced law with a large New York firm for a decade before going into politics. His legal education and training had taught him to avoid making a decision whenever possible. To those outside the legal profession, this was perceived as being indecisive. Now he frowned and pursed his lips. At this point he wasn't willing to take the step urged by Joyner. "It's only Wednesday. We have two more days. If I did that and Drozny found out about it, he'd view it as a hostile act. Besides, if we move too soon, we'll get Robert McCallister killed."

Kendall rapped his hand on the table, trying to appear as if he were taking control of the situation, while he was in fact doing precisely the opposite. "We can move rapidly later on, if we have to. Can't we, General Childress?"

"It will be more difficult, Mr. President."

That didn't deter Kendall. He was always capable of hearing what he wanted to hear. "But you can do it."

Childress nodded. Inside he was feeling uncomfortable. It took time to mount an operation like this. Civilian leaders never had a grasp of military logistics.

Kendall had one other justification for his inaction. "Hell, Nadim may have been giving Ahmed misinformation. Perhaps Baku's not the meeting point at all."

Joyner jumped on Kendall's words. "I'll get satellites focused on the area. We'll find the convoy and track its movement."

Kendall liked that idea, which eliminated the necessity for an immediate decision.

The minute she got back to her office, Joyner made a call to the satellite command center. Implementation was immediate. Her next call was to Michael in Russia.

She found him sitting in the American embassy in Moscow, where he'd been staring glumly at his cell phone waiting for Irina to call with information about Suslov's operation with Nadim. Once they switched to a secure phone, she told him, "The Israelis got what we needed."

She then described what Moshe had reported.

"I'm sorry. I let you down," he said, sounding dejected.

She was puzzled. "What did you do?"

"I couldn't come up with the Suslov/Nadim plan myself. You had to find it out from the Israelis."

Joyner didn't have patience for this nonsense. "It's not about credit. You're the one who learned about the warehouse in Volgograd. I don't care who found out what. The point is that now we all know what's happening."

"What do we intend to do about it?"

Joyner took a deep breath and blew it out in a whoosh. "That, Michael, is up to our distinguished president." She made no effort to conceal her frustration at Kendall's indecisiveness and unwillingness to act.

"We have to send a significant number of troops," Michael said firmly. "We can't let that exchange take place. Those weapons are so potent. They could—"

She didn't need Michael to tell her what she already knew. "You're preaching to the choir. Kendall has asked Drozny to stop it."

"What's he smoking?"

Joyner laughed "That's not a very respectful way to refer to our leader."

"Yeah, I know, but Suslov's paid off so many people. Their troops will never act, regardless of what Drozny says."

"What can you find out about Drozny's intentions at your end?"

"I'll call Perikov and ask him to find out what's happening."

She liked that idea. "Do it. Regardless of what he says, I want you to fly down to Baku by midday tomorrow. You've got to be on scene."

"Will do."

"Oh, and Michael, one more thing," Joyner said shifting from a spymaster's voice to her motherly tone. "Let me give you some advice."

"What's that?"

"Things could get dicey for Suslov. The time's come for you to hustle Irina out of the country if you don't want to risk her becoming a casualty."

"The same thought was running through my mind." He stopped there, not wanting to tell Joyner that he had already promised Irina asylum. "How do you want me to handle it logistically?"

"Deliver her to our embassy and turn her over to Bill Worth. I'll take it from there."

"I appreciate it."

"It's the right thing to do. Regardless of what motivated Irina, she's put her life on the line for us."

Michael hung up with Joyner and dialed Irina at the office. "Can you talk?" he said.

"Not now, Mother. I'll call you on your cell phone when I get a chance."

The line went dead. Michael stared at the phone for several minutes. It may have been his imagination, but he thought she sounded even more nervous than usual when she spoke to him from the office.

Rather than waste more time thinking about Irina, Michael decided to drive to the Philadelphia restaurant across from Suslov's office. When she called, he'd tell her to finish out her workday as if nothing unusual were happening. Then she should walk over to the Philadelphia. He'd take her from there straight to the American embassy.

Major General Nadim arrived at his office carrying his briefcase, cursing and sputtering aloud. His secretary retreated to a room across the hall, where she pretended to be filing. He had been clever enough to survive Ahmed's onslaught this morning, but that wasn't the point.

"The man's an idiot," Nadim cried out. "The only reason he's running the country is because his father was the president. That's a piss-poor reason. If he had been anyone else's son, he'd still be a mediocre optometrist or dentist or whatever the hell he had been." Nadim was seeing so many shades of red right now that he couldn't even remember what Ahmed's occupation had been. What particularly infuriated him was the way in which Ahmed had dressed him down, talking to him as if he were a schoolboy or worse. For everything he had done for the country over the years, he was entitled to respect. He demanded it. And once he took over the country, the optometrist would be begging for mercy.

Nadim was so enraged that the minute he stopped ranting and raving, he raised his arm and flung his briefcase with all the force he could muster against a bulky white marble pedestal in one corner of his office.

The pedestal didn't move when the briefcase smashed into it. However, the force of the blow dislodged from the leather a tiny round black object resembling a button. Nadim watched it fall through the air and come to rest on the polished wooden floor.

"What the hell?" he muttered aloud. He raced over and picked it up. With his intelligence background, it took Nadim only a second to determine that he was holding the microphone of a sophisticated eavesdropping device. He immediately thought about the two spies in Syria carrying phony Italian passports, and Daniel Moreau's confirmation that Jack Cole was an Israeli agent. It all added up to a single conclusion: Cole had used someone to plant this bug.

"I'll kill that fucking Cole," he vowed.

Nadim put the black object back down on the floor. He

jerked up his leg and smashed the heel of his shoe down hard, pulverizing it into little pieces.

"That's what I'll do to you when I catch you, Israeli spy."

Once Jack returned to the sound lab, Avi left for the embassy to await the call back from Moshe.

Jack was studying airplane schedules to Baku when he heard the sound technician cry out in dismay. "No . . . oh, no . . ."

Jack was alarmed. "What happened?"

The man didn't respond. He was too busy pushing buttons and staring at an oscilloscope with a worried expression on his face.

He ripped off the earphones and placed them down on the table.

"For God's sake," Jack said anxiously. "Tell me what's going on."

"All of the sound just stopped on the second transmitter."

"The one on his briefcase?"

"Yeah. I was picking up the noise of traffic when he rode to the embassy, people greeting him and Nadim hollering about Ahmed. Then suddenly everything went dead."

Jack didn't know why this should be so startling. "Perhaps he left the briefcase in his office. Then he went to a meeting somewhere else in the building. There were no sounds to pick up."

The technician pointed to the flat white line moving across the green screen. "Not when you get this," he said with conviction.

Jack, who always counted on Mossad people to supply the technological help, had no idea what the man was talking about. "That doesn't mean squat to me. What's it tell you?"

"We've got a dead transmitter."

Jack threw his hands up in the air in exasperation. "Oh,

great, another technical fuckup. First the Hassler flower
bowl, now this. You guys are two for two."

The technician shook his head. "That's not it. This system
had a severe shock."

"What's that mean?"

"From everything I've seen, I'd bet my next month's
salary that Nadim found the bug on his briefcase and violently destroyed it."

"Oh, shit." Layla was in trouble. Jack grabbed his cell
phone and called her at the bank.

"Layla," he said without trying to mask the anxiety in his
voice.

"What's wrong?" she asked, picking up on it.

"You'd better get over to the sound lab as soon as possible. Make sure nobody's following you."

She understood the urgency. There was only one possible
explanation—Nadim had found the bug. He would be smart
enough to deduce who had planted it.

"I'm leaving now," she said grimly.

"Keep checking behind you. If you think somebody's
tailing you, don't try to lose them. Go into a public place. A
restaurant . . . a hotel . . . or somewhere like that. Stay close
to other people and call me."

Chapter 33

Nadim was boiling over with anger. He decided that Jack Cole must have overheard his conversation with Ahmed and reported all of the details of his plan for the pilot's exchange to his Israeli spymasters, which meant the Americans knew it as well. That had to be the fact. The briefcase had been at home, close to him, when he had had the telephone conversation with Ahmed. Thinking about it made him groan. If that dumb fucker Ahmed had not demanded answers on the phone call, none of this would have happened.

But it did. And now two questions were running through Nadim's mind: How did Jack Cole manage to plant the bug, and what could Nadim now do to avoid the impending disaster? He wanted to give all of his attention to the first one, figure out who the culprits were and take revenge. But he was a good enough intelligence man to put aside his personal pique and the accompanying vendetta until he had taken appropriate action to get the operation back on course.

With quick long strides, Nadim left his office and went up to the embassy telecommunications room. After directing one of the staff to sweep it for bugs, he tossed everyone out and called Moscow on the most secure phone the embassy had.

"Mr. Suslov's office," a woman said. Nadim recognized her voice. That was Irina, the well-built dish sitting outside of Dmitri's office. When Nadim had leered at her on his visit the other day, Suslov had said, "Don't even dream about it. She's my property."

Nadim had laughed. "But I thought you might want to offer her to me as a way of sealing our bargain."

To Suslov, that wasn't funny. "If the two of you end up in bed together, I'll tie you both to the mattress myself, then set it on fire."

Nadim had responded, "It was just a joke."

"And a bad one at that."

Now, when Irina answered, Nadim barked, "It's Nadim. I have to talk to Suslov. Tell him it's urgent."

As he waited for the Russian to come to the phone, Nadim's lower lip began quivering. He didn't know whether it was from fear of Suslov's reaction to his news or outrage at having to make this call. All the years the Russians were Syria's benefactor, they had treated Syrian officials as if they were morons and incompetents. What Nadim was about to tell Suslov would confirm that view, but he had no choice.

Suslov picked up the phone and shouted to his secretary, "Irina, close the door and make sure nobody bothers me."

Then he turned his attention to the phone. "She said it was urgent." Suslov's tone was surly. "What happened?"

Listening to the sound of Suslov's voice made the decision for Nadim about how to play the call. He had to tell the Russian what the Israelis and Americans knew, but he certainly didn't have to tell him how they found out. That might lead to Suslov's calling off the operation or arranging to assassinate Nadim. Neither was a very attractive alternative. Nadim decided on the perfect lie for Suslov. "I've developed a relationship with a Lebanese woman who's dating an Israeli agent in Paris by the name of Jack Cole. The woman just told me that the Israelis know all about our plan for the exchange Friday morning in Baku."

Suslov was flabbergasted. "How could they have found out?"

"I pressed her hard on that issue, but she couldn't tell me anything that was the least bit helpful." Nadim paused before turning the tables on the Russian. "I hate to suggest it, but the Israelis or the Americans might have a mole at your end."

Before the words were out of Nadim's mouth, one thought popped into Suslov's head: Irina. He knew she was seeing the American Michael Hanley. The bitch must have overheard more than he had thought when Nadim was here; then she reported it to the American. Or even worse, she had planted a bug in his office. So he had to assume that the Americans knew as well, which meant they might be calling Drozny. It was his own fault. He should have killed her the minute he had found out she was seeing the CIA agent. He thought he could use her relationship with Michael to his own advantage by watching her and having someone listen in on her phone calls to find out what the American wanted. It hadn't yielded a thing until now, which was too late.

In hindsight, he should have killed her. But it didn't matter. Suslov had the situation under control. By spreading enough money around to the right people, he had eliminated any chance of the Russian or Azerbaijani governments acting to block the exchange. Moscow didn't have much incentive in any event. The arms wouldn't be used against Russia. The American president could be a problem, but Suslov was willing to bet he'd never have the guts to send troops to the area. And as for the Israelis, even if they ferried in one of their elite commando units, Suslov could defeat them with superior firepower. He'd increase the number of troops from his private militia that he was sending to Baku. Suslov was salivating at the prospect of a battle like that with the Israelis or even the Americans. The last two times he had been in battle were in Afghanistan and Chechnya, both disasters due to political constraints, as far as he was concerned. Here there were none. Suslov could press his troops to pull out all the stops. This time they would fight to win.

"I'm willing to take any steps you believe appropriate," Nadim said.

Suslov was no longer interested in what the Syrian had to say, and he had no intention of sharing his thoughts with Nadim. "We proceed as planned. I'll take care of it."

Nadim was relieved. "I'm flying to Baku tomorrow morning," he said.

Suslov was surprised he was waiting that long. "Tonight would be better. You want to make certain everything is in place on your end."

Nadim was unwilling to commit to going then. He had to find out who had planted the bug and deal with them before he left Paris. "I have one important loose end to complete here before I can leave, but my presence is not critical. Everything's on automatic pilot from my side at this point."

"It had better be," Suslov said in a stern voice.

"There is one other thing," Nadim said. "I'll fax you a picture of the Israeli agent in Paris, Jack Cole." Nadim was confident that Daniel Moreau would give him one. "Cole will probably be in Baku on Friday. Distribute his picture among your troops. He's working against us. He has to die."

"I'll make sure it happens."

Satisfied, Nadim put down the phone and turned his attention to the other question: How had Jack Cole managed to plant the bug? It took him less than a minute to come up with the answer. Layla. Of course Jack Cole had used Layla to attach it to his briefcase. She had done a first-rate acting job to convince him that she wanted to go out with him. Jack Cole had put her up to the whole thing. And he had believed her because he wanted to believe her. They had set him up perfectly.

Two nights ago, after their dinner when he fell asleep, she had access to his briefcase. No one else did.

Nadim pounded his fist on the table. Cole would pay for it with his life on Friday. As for Layla, Nadim would get his revenge before he left Paris for Baku.

First the operation, though. He called General Kemal and told the Turk to fly to an air force base in Syria in the morning with his aide. From there, a Syrian plane would fly the two of them to Baku with the American pilot.

Then he turned his thoughts back to Layla. This explained her message canceling dinner. There was no point for her to see him again. Jack Cole had gotten the information he needed from the bugs.

Nadim called Layla's office. The secretary said, "Ms. Gemayel is out. I don't know when she'll return."

He phoned her apartment. No answer. That didn't bother Nadim. He was a patient man. He had another twenty-four hours before he had to leave for Baku. Plenty of time to deal with Layla.

Suslov had worked closely with the KGB over the years. He had seen repeated examples of the benefits of their misinformation. Now he decided to resort to that technique himself. First he casually opened the door to his office. After making certain that Irina was at her desk just outside, he picked up the phone, pretended to dial a number, and began speaking loudly enough for her to hear him. "Listen, Major General Nadim, we're all set for the exchange early Friday morning in Baku. . . . No, I'm not bringing any troops with me . . . just a single bodyguard. . . . There's no reason to do more than that. . . . No one will be able to interfere with us."

Next, Suslov left his office so Irina would think that she was free to call her American lover. He went to the telephone control room on the first floor of the building. He intended to listen himself.

Suslov had to wait only three minutes. Through earphones, he heard her place the call. She was talking softly, but sounded excited.

"Micki, it's me. I've got the news you wanted."

"What did you find, my little bird?" The American's voice was muted.

"The exchange with the Syrian will take place early Friday morning in Baku. Wherever that is . . ."

"Don't worry. I know where it is." Michael was excited. She might have some valuable information that the Israelis hadn't been able to obtain. "What else did you hear?"

"Dmitri's going there with only a single bodyguard. He's not bringing any other troops."

Oh, dammit, Michael thought. Suslov had found out about Irina. He tried to conceal his anxiety and sound upbeat. "Oh, really?"

"Did I help you?"

"So much, my little bird." He was terrified for Irina. *I have to get her out of that building alive.* "Now I want to take you to the United States, as we discussed."

Suslov stiffened. How could the little wench and the American be so stupid as to think they could leave the country?

"That's what I want. To live with you in Beverly Hills."

"Then do this," Michael commanded. "Stay till the end of your regular working day. I don't want anyone to get suspicious. When you walk outside, cross the road to the Philadelphia restaurant. I'll be waiting there."

"I have to stop at home and pack before I can go anywhere."

"Don't worry about that."

"Really, Micki." She sounded irritated. "Don't be silly. I can't leave all of my beautiful clothes."

Suslov was breathing fire. He had paid for them.

"Okay. Don't worry. We'll stop for them. See you in a couple of hours."

As soon as Michael hung up the phone with Irina, he knew that he had to call Joyner and report what had happened. Suslov couldn't possibly be bringing a single bodyguard with a convoy of four trucks loaded with nuclear weapons. He must have a contingent of troops. So there was only one explanation for what Suslov had permitted Irina to overhear: misinformation to keep down the size of any force the United States sent, if it decided to send troops. That meant Suslov knew about Irina's relationship with Michael. Why else was he using her to pass false information? Michael was in a panic. He desperately wanted to get to the embassy to call Joyner, then return to the Philadelphia before Irina left Suslov's building. For several minutes he vacillated about what to do while he ran his hands through his hair. He went to the bathroom and relieved himself. Finally he decided to call Joyner on the same cell phone Irina had called him on. It was risky, but it was the best of the alternatives. He stepped outside the Philadelphia restaurant, found a deserted spot on the sidewalk, and dialed Joyner in Washington.

Inside the building across from the Philadelphia, Suslov was in a blind rage. From the first floor he put his head down and charged up four flights of stairs as fast as he could with one gimpy leg. Terrified secretaries and clerks who saw him ran the other way. They hid behind desks to avoid being swept up in the coming explosion.

From a distance of twenty yards, Irina saw him limping toward her, breathing fire. That menacing look on his face, the hatred shining in his eyes, told her that Suslov had found out about her and Micki. She stuffed the cell phone into her purse and ran in the opposite direction.

The building had a rear staircase. *If I can just make it down to the ground floor,* Irina thought, *I can race out of the building and across the street to the Philadelphia. I'll hide there until Micki comes. I'll be safe.*

Suslov saw that she had a good jump on him. Running fast wasn't something he could do after the injury in Afghanistan. So he took the easy way out. He slammed his hand against the large red button on the wall, a holdover from the days the KGB occupied the building. It activated a loud, piercing security alarm. That not only shook all of the people inside the building to their core, it also meant that every door to the building automatically closed and locked. Six armed guards on the ground floor started upstairs, gripping automatic weapons.

Irina had forgotten about the alarm until she heard it.

Getting out of the building at this point was hopeless. *I know what I'll do. I'll hide. They'll never find me.* She exited the staircase on the second floor, ran five yards down the corridor, and ducked into a closet that housed office supplies. It had a small dead-bolt lock, which she set. Hopefully they wouldn't find her until she called Micki. He could come and get her out.

Irina sat down on top of a brown cardboard box of computer paper and whipped the cell phone out of her purse. Her hand was trembling so badly it fell to the ground. Once she retrieved it, she frantically punched in the numbers of Micki's cell.

The busy signal she heard was like a death sentence.

Get off the damn phone, Micki. She hung up and tried again. Still busy. *Oh, no. What do I do now?*

Fear threatened to paralyze her body and her mind. *Think,* she told herself. *You must be able to do something.* She dialed her friend Natasha.

No answer. The machine kicked on.

Feeling helpless and hopeless, she mumbled into the machine, leaving Natasha a message. Someone had to know what was happening. Maybe Natasha could get to Micki.

"It's Irina. I'm locked in a closet in the office. Dmitri

found out about me and Micki. He's going to kill me. Micki's on his phone. I can't get through to him. I want you to—"

Irina heard a pounding on the door. Suslov was shouting, "Open up. Right now."

Irina realized it was futile. At least she could help Micki before Suslov killed her. She continued her message to Natasha: "Tell Micki that Dimitri tricked me. The information he gave me about a single bodyguard has to be false. And tell him I love him."

On the other side of the door, a soldier aimed his gun and blasted away the lock. Suslov kicked open the door. Saliva was dripping from his mouth as he glared at her.

Irina hit the power button, turning off her phone. Then she tossed it at him. Suslov batted it down with his left hand and sent it crashing against the hard cement floor. With his right, a huge, powerful meaty claw, Suslov grabbed her around the neck, pulling her to her feet. She tried to punch him, but her tiny fists didn't even make him flinch when they struck his chest.

"I was so good to you . . . you ungrateful little bitch."

She spat at him, right in the eye.

Suslov gripped her neck with both of his hands.

"My little bird," he said in a mocking tone. He laughed sadistically. "You won't be going to Beverly Hills."

He squeezed tighter and tighter. A gurgling noise came out of her mouth. Her eyes bulged. Her body tensed, then grew limp in his hands. As all of the life oozed out of her body, his face lit up with a sweet smile of revenge.

When she was dead, he turned to one of the guards standing in the doorway and said, "Take her to the basement downstairs. Hack her up. Then put her in the old KGB burial chamber. There's room for one more body."

Chapter 34

Layla closed her eyes and sat back in the cab on her way to the sound lab, analyzing the situation. She was no longer terrified by Nadim and the prospect that he knew she had planted the bugs.

Plenty of her relatives in Lebanon had died fighting Nadim and the Syrians. The brave ones went down with a struggle after taking Syrians with them. The cowards suffered in their humiliation as well as in their death.

She knew which group she wanted to be in. She was calm and cool when she walked into the sound lab.

Not Jack. He was frightened about what might happen to her. "You've got to leave Paris right now. Nadim knows about the bug you planted." A bundle of nerves, Jack was talking fast. "I've got a car waiting at our embassy to drive you to Amsterdam. You're booked on the ten-o'clock El Al flight tonight to Israel."

Layla gave Jack that mysterious smile of hers. "I'm not going."

"You have to. He'll kill you."

"Maybe he will, and maybe he won't." She pulled the gun out of her purse and held it up. "And I know how to use it."

Jack was exasperated. "Do you know what you're up against?"

She smiled again. "Unfortunately, much better than you do. Let him try. It's time somebody stood up to the bastard."

Avi walked into the sound lab. For the entire five minutes it took Jack to explain what was happening with Nadim, Avi looked at Layla with admiration. "Boy, was I wrong about you," Avi told her. "You're a feisty woman."

"Nadim killed my uncle Bashir for what I'm doing now. It's time somebody got even."

"It's okay with me."

"But not with me," Jack said to Avi. "You don't care for her the way I do."

"Back off, Jack," Layla said. "I'm a big girl."

Avi found himself in the bizarre situation of supporting Layla against Jack. He'd like nothing better than for Layla to get rid of their old nemesis Nadim. "She has a right to decide for herself."

"You were the one who didn't trust her," Jack told him.

"That was before I saw what she could do."

It amused Layla that they were having this discussion as if she weren't in the room.

Despairing, Jack realized it didn't matter what he said. He hadn't known Layla a long time, but he was well aware of how strong-willed she was. She was determined to square off with Nadim. He gave a long sigh of resignation. "I'll stick with you and provide protection until Nadim leaves Paris."

"That may not be possible," Avi interjected. "Moshe wants you and me on the first plane to Baku in the morning. It's at seven A.M. on Turkish Air out of Orly via Istanbul. He's got approval from the prime minister for your action plan to block the exchange."

Jack locked eyes with Layla. "Please change your mind about leaving Paris," he said, knowing his words were in vain.

"I'm staying," she said with a ring of finality. "A person has to confront her demons. Mine is in this city right now."

"Tell you what," Jack said, "at least let me offer you a little help. First of all, I'd like you to stay at the Bristol with me tonight until . . . I have to leave in the morning."

Avi was looking at her. She blushed. "I'm okay with that," she said.

"Second," Jack continued, "when I was involved in a recent operation"—even though he trusted her, instinctively he couldn't bring himself to tell her he was responsible for Khalifa's assassination—"I learned about this device the techies have over at the embassy. It's a special doorknob. I want to have it installed to replace the doorknob leading from the living room of your apartment to the bedroom. Hopefully Nadim will already be gone from Paris when we split in the morning, but maybe he won't." He paused and took a deep breath, gulping for air. "If Nadim tries to attack you in your apartment, you'll race into the bedroom, slam the door, and flip a special switch on the wall that resembles a light switch. It'll activate an electrical charge on the doorknob. When Nadim grabs it, he'll get one hell of a shock, literally and figuratively."

Avi wasn't familiar with the device. "Will it kill him?"

Jack shrugged. "It's about fifty-fifty."

Layla interjected, "I'd like better odds than that."

Jack cracked a smile. He never wanted to cross this woman. "Let's put it this way: At the very least, he'll be knocked out for a while, long enough for you to call somebody at our embassy who can hustle you up to Amsterdam by car and on the first plane out to Israel."

"David Navon," Avi said. "That's the man she should call. I'll set it up." He scribbled a number on a piece of paper and handed it to her. "I'll also make the arrangements for the doorknob."

"Sounds like a plan," Layla said. She took out a key to her apartment and offered it to Avi.

He waved her away and smiled. "Our people don't need keys."

Jack looked grim. "If you have to use this doorknob, let's just hope it functions better than a certain recording device in a bowl of flowers in Rome."

Layla didn't know what happened in Rome, but she had a pretty good idea. The tension in the room was thick. Avi decided to cut it. "I think I'll get out of here and leave you two kids for the night. Meet you at the airport tomorrow morning, Jack."

"Kids?" Jack said to Avi. "I'm older than you are."

"Well, I'm certainly not," Layla said.

They all laughed nervously.

President Kendall wanted to believe what Irina had heard Suslov say. If Suslov was bringing only a single bodyguard, then Kendall didn't have to confront the question of whether to send a sizable contingency of American troops. "The information you just received from Michael Hanley changes the dynamics," President Kendall said, sounding relieved as he looked at Joyner and General Childress seated with him at a conference table in the Oval Office.

Joyner knew where Kendall was headed, and she didn't like it.

"Let's assume that what Irina told Hanley is correct," Kendall continued. "Then we won't need a large contingent of troops to break this up and rescue our pilot. So we can give Drozny more time to act. If he doesn't, we move in with a small group of commandos and surgically do the job. That way we'll minimize the damage to our relations with Russia and the chances that this could escalate. What do you two think?"

With her eyes and a nod of her head Joyner tossed the question to Childress.

"The problem, Mr. President," Childress said, coughing to clear his throat, "is that I don't believe that Suslov will have only a single bodyguard or anything like that."

"I agree," Joyner said

Kendall's eyes went from Childress to Joyner and back again. "What makes you two so sure?"

Joyner picked it up. "Michael Hanley is on the scene in Moscow. He knows the players, and he has no doubt Suslov was feeding his contact misinformation."

Childress gave the president a few seconds to absorb that before adding, "Suslov's background with the Russian army confirms Margaret's conclusion. In Chechnya, Suslov always used plenty of brute force to accomplish any task."

"But suppose . . . let's just suppose . . ." Kendall said stubbornly.

Joyner shook her head in dismay. Kendall was a smart man, but that didn't prevent him from seeing things the way he wanted to in a complex situation.

"Suppose," Kendall repeated, staring at Childress, "we continue to work with Drozny and we don't make the type of troop movements that would alarm him. At the same time, you send Major Davis with his six-man group to Baku quietly, maybe even dressed in civilian clothes. Give Davis a chance to redeem himself from the earlier abortive effort. Let him and his men get themselves into the area. We'll all stay close to the situation. If it turns out that Drozny won't act or we get some independent information that Suslov's sending a large force, then we bring in an increased group of our own to offset Suslov's troops."

Childress was cringing. "The problem with that, Mr. President, is that it takes time to move in troops and their arms. Baku's not an easy place to get to."

Kendall dismissed the objection with a wave of his hand. "Ah, c'mon. We have so many troops and weapons around the whole Middle East area and in Asia. You can shuttle some in on short notice."

Childress didn't argue. His commander in chief had made a decision. For her part, Joyner kept still. She knew Kendall well enough to realize that once he had taken a position, further opposition was useless. It would simply force him to dig in further.

"Six special-ops troops?" Moshe said to Joyner in disbelief. "Has Kendall lost his mind?"

Regardless of how Joyner viewed the decision, she felt the need to defend the president to the Israeli. "He's relying on information from what's been a reliable source in the past. We're trying to balance the need to block this exchange with the delicacy of American–Russian relations. If we receive different information in the future, we'll readjust. It's a fluid situation."

"Hmph," Moshe said. "I think it's a ridiculous way to go."

"You have to appreciate that our relationship with Moscow is always sensitive."

"But the exchange is taking place in Azerbaijan. Not Russia."

"Which used to be a part of the USSR. Moscow views it as within Russia's sphere of influence."

"We don't. I just want you to know that. We'll take whatever action we believe is in our best interests."

"C'mon, Moshe, at least you've got to give Drozny time to act. To stop the nuclear convoy."

"You undoubtedly have satellite photos, Margaret. We've done the calculations. We figure that the convoy will be across the Russian border into Azerbaijan in another couple of hours, at most. If Drozny hasn't acted by then, he's not going to."

Joyner couldn't argue with that logic. She decided to shift her approach. "If you act too soon with too large an armed contingent, you run the risk of the convoy turning around and heading back to Russia. The next time—and there will be a next time—we'll never have as good a chance of stopping them."

"I've discussed that with the prime minister," Moshe said. "That's a risk we're prepared to take," The Israeli sounded implacable and unyielding. His voice was tinged with a sharp tone of righteousness.

"You'll also get our pilot, Robert McCallister, killed," Joyner protested.

Moshe's voice softened. "You can be sure that we'll take every step humanly possible to save young McCallister's life."

"God, you're stubborn," Joyner said.

"Coming from you, I take that as a compliment."

"You would."

"Don't forget what the Bible says—we're a stiff-necked people."

Joyner took a deep breath and exhaled. "Whoever wrote that knew what he was talking about."

"No, seriously, Margaret, I know we disagree from time to time, but . . ."

She wanted to be conciliatory as well. She liked Moshe. Israel was an important and valuable ally. "I recognize that your country sometimes has different interests from ours. That causes the disagreements."

"That's certainly true. Last night I dreamed about you."

Joyner wondered where this was going. "Yeah?"

"Well, anyhow, I dreamed that you and I had died. We were up in heaven arguing with each other. First it was about David and Sagit and the Saudi Arabians. Then it was about Jack Cole and Michael Hanley and the Russians and Syrians in this mess."

She laughed. "Do you think we're going to make it to heaven? I mean you and I?"

Moshe shrugged. "God needs people to direct his intelligence agents, but who can know for sure? At least we have a lot better chance than Nadim and Suslov."

"In English, we call that damning by faint praise."

Given her disagreement with Kendall, Joyner couldn't tell Moshe, but she was changing her mind. The longer she thought about it the happier she was that Israel was sending a contingent of troops to Baku. "Do what you have to do," she said. "I'll still work with you in the next world."

The proprietor of the Philadelphia restaurant came over to Michael. It was almost midnight, and the American had been sitting at a table sipping stale coffee and looking out of the restaurant's window at the headquarters of Suslov Enterprises for almost nine hours.

"I'm sorry, but we're closing now," he said to the visibly distraught young man in a kind tone.

Wise to the ways of the world and having operated the restaurant when the KGB had used the building across the street, the proprietor recognized this as a familiar scene. He realized that Michael was conducting a vigil, waiting for someone who would never come out. Probably a woman, judging from Michael's face.

"Perhaps she's decided to spend the night," he said. "I'm sure she'll be out in the morning."

The man was being kind. Michael tried to force a smile. He couldn't even do that. He had only one more possible move.

With wobbly legs he left the restaurant. Trying to appear bold, Michael walked across the square and straight up to one of the two guards in front of Suslov's building who was gripping an AK-47.

"I want to speak to Irina Ivanova," Michael said in his best Russian.

Without consulting any list, the man responded, "There is no one inside by that name."

Michael pointed to the phone attached to a concrete post. "Would you please call and ask?"

The guard looked at Michael with mean, cold eyes. "There is no one inside by that name," he repeated.

Michael considered pushing aside the guard and rushing to the front door. Sensing this, the other guard trundled over. He aimed his gun at Michael. "Move on," he barked.

Michael's guess was that Suslov had left a specific order that they were supposed to shoot to kill if he tried to break in. He looked from one battle-hardened Slavic face to the other. Neither of them flinched.

Filled with guilt and remorse, Michael turned and walked away.

Daniel Moreau was persistent. He sat in his office and went back over all of the notes he and his colleagues had made in their interviews of people around Place de l'Alma in the search for Jack Cole.

He lit up a cigarette and scratched his head. There had to be a lead somewhere he was missing.

When he came to the notes of his own interview with the woman in apartment 6B with the initials L. G., he remembered how good she looked, and he smiled.

As he smoked, blowing circles in the air, he continued thinking about her. The smile turned to a sullen, grim expression. He began kicking himself. It wasn't just that he had been sloppy. Replaying the interview in his mind, he became convinced that she was conning him, using her sexual appeal to distract him. And he had fallen for it like some rookie, rather than the seasoned operator he was.

You're a man, and you're only human, he told himself, trying to rationalize. That didn't cut it. There was no excuse for how he'd behaved.

Think about the facts, he told himself. *The woman in 6B*

has olive skin. Definitely could be Middle Eastern. He didn't have her name. Just the initials L. G.

He snuffed out the cigarette and picked up the phone on his desk. It was almost one in the morning. He didn't care. He'd call Charles, the superintendent of her building.

"This is Daniel Moreau," he said to the groggy Charles, who woke out of a deep sleep to answer the phone.

"It's very late, monsieur. No?"

"No," Moreau barked. "The woman in six-B. What's her name?"

There was a shuffling of papers by Charles. Then the answer: "Layla Gemayel."

"Oh, Christ," Moreau shouted. "How fucking stupid can you be?"

Thinking that the cursing was intended for him, Charles was terrified. "But monsieur—"

Moreau hung up. He was furious at himself. He knew damn well that Gemayel was a Maronite Lebanese name. That made her the enemy of Major General Nadim. The Arabs had a saying: The enemy of my enemy is my friend. That made Layla Jack Cole's friend. But Moreau was still mystified as to why Nadim was covering for her. Why didn't Nadim just give Moreau Layla's name? He would have known how to interrogate her to learn where he could find Cole. That didn't make sense. Maybe she wasn't the right one. He shook his head in bewilderment. Nothing made sense.

Calling Layla and asking her about Cole over the phone was a waste of time. He'd have to confront her in person.

He got up from his desk, grabbed his gun, and headed for the door. *I'm going to wake you up, Layla, and see what you can tell me.*

Fifteen minutes later Moreau impatiently rang the doorbell to apartment 6B several times. When no one answered, he woke Charles again to get a key.

He searched the apartment but found nothing of interest, other than the fact that she worked at a bank. *She's probably out on an overnight,* he decided. *Maybe with Jack Cole.*

He yawned. Tired himself, he decided to go home and sleep. He'd return early tomorrow morning. No banker ever went to work at the crack of dawn. That would be a great time to question her.

Chapter 35

It took Nadim two minutes to pick the lock to Layla's door. Once he was inside her apartment, he moved on tiptoe toward the bedroom. He hoped to find her asleep in bed. His guess was that she slept naked between expensive silk sheets.

For much of the day Nadim had thought about what he should do to her. Finally he made up his mind. It was absolutely perfect. Before he told her what it was, he intended to have her again with brute force. He'd let her know who her master was from this point on. Thinking about it made his sexual desire temporarily push the anger to the back of his mind.

Tonight he hadn't had a single drop of alcohol. He wanted his mind to be sharp. All parts of his body were functioning like a well-oiled machine. As he cut across the Oriental carpet in her living room, he unzipped his pants, reached his hand inside, and stroked himself, wanting to be ready for her.

The bedroom door was ajar. He didn't hear any sounds. The scent of Layla and her perfume lingered in the air.

He crossed the threshold and looked at the king-size bed. Empty!

He checked the rest of the apartment. No Layla. So she must be spending the night with Jack Cole somewhere in

Paris before he left for Baku. *Well, he's never coming back from there, sweetheart. You, on the other hand, have to come home after your date with the Israeli spy.*

Nadim had memorized the schedule of airplanes from Paris to Baku. His guess was that Cole was on the early one via Istanbul. That meant Layla would be home before long. Who knew, he might get lucky. Cole might even walk into the apartment with her. Then he could take care of both of them.

For this, Nadim had patience. He wouldn't lose anything by taking a later plane.

He decided to sit down and wait for Layla. Eventually she'd walk in the front door.

It was the middle of the night, and Robert McCallister's shoulder was throbbing under the heavy bandage. He was scared that the doctors who had treated his wound had inadequate training and lacked experience. Certainly the way in which they had milled around anxiously talking to each other before they gave him an anesthetic evoked little confidence.

All of that left him with the feeling that if the president made a deal for him, and he managed to make it home, it would be a miracle if he ended up with two fully functioning arms.

The idea of ever returning to the United States seemed so preposterous that Robert nearly burst out laughing. Since his failed attempt at escape and the treatment of his wound, he had been confined to bed with both legs tied to the bedposts. The restraints had been loosened only when he had to use the bathroom. Then two armed guards watched him every second.

Robert closed his eyes, trying to sleep, but the pain in his shoulder and the uncomfortable position of being on his back, unable to turn over, precluded that.

He glanced over at one of the guards sitting in a chair, fully awake, aiming his AK-47 at Robert. The man was staring at the prisoner. He saw no need to look away.

Robert thought about Ann and his mother. He didn't want to die. He wanted to see them again.

Since the abortive escape effort, he no longer had the mood swings he had felt earlier in his captivity, alternating between optimism and despair. Now it was all black. It was as if a huge curtain of depression had settled over him.

His room was on the second floor of the villa. Judging from the tiny crack of daylight in the eastern sky, he guessed that it was now around four in the morning. The villa was deathly still.

Suddenly, through an open window, he heard the sound of vehicles approaching the villa. It sounded to him like two or three cars or trucks. He couldn't tell. Headlights from outside illuminated one wall of his room.

It's all over, he decided. *Kendall refused to accept their terms for an agreement. They're going to kill me now. I'm just one small, expendable grunt down in the trenches of a larger war.* The term *cannon fodder* popped into his mind.

The courage he had felt before was gone. He was afraid of dying. He began to cry.

He heard voices downstairs inside the front of the villa. A door slammed. More people.

There were heavy boots on the stairs. Men were coming to get him—his executioners. He didn't care how they killed him as long as he didn't suffer. He tried to recall a psalm he had once heard. "The lord is my shepherd. I shall not want. He maketh me to—"

Four heavily armed soldiers burst into his room, followed by two men in doctors' white gowns. Lights were turned on. Robert recognized one of the men in white as the physician who had been present when they treated his shoulder. Another man, unarmed and wearing a different uniform from the others, appeared in the doorway. Robert recognized Abdullah, the cruel and sadistic officer from the beginning of his captivity. For sure they had now come to kill him, he decided.

"So we meet again," Abdullah said. "For the final time."

Robert tensed in bed. He was right. This was the end for him.

Abdullah glowered at Robert, sorry he hadn't had the opportunity to interrogate the American pilot. "You're going home soon," he said to Robert. "You're going home."

Tiny buds of hope stirred in Robert. He didn't let them grow. Believing it was only a cruel joke by Abdullah, who intended to send his dead body home in a wooden box, he squashed his hope quickly.

"First you have to sleep," Abdullah said.

Robert didn't resist when one of the medics crossed the room with a syringe in his hand. The American was prepared to accept the notion that he would never wake up. At least death by lethal injection would be pain-free.

The shot was a powerful anesthetic. Once Robert was asleep, two soldiers lifted his body out of the bed. They carried him on their shoulders downstairs and outside of the villa. One of the vehicles that had arrived was an ambulance. They loaded him onto a gurney in the back and strapped him in. A medic hooked up leads to monitor his vital signs.

"Ready to go," the medic called to Abdullah, who was waiting outside the ambulance.

"The plane's on standby at the airport," Abdullah said. "We have a place like this to hold him once we land in Baku."

Jack and Layla walked out of the Bristol onto Rue St. Honore and into the gloom of predawn in Paris. The hour belonged to laborers struggling to make a living getting an early start, women of the night on the way home after tumbling out of their last client's bed, and writers desperately afraid of shutting down their computers for fear that a new bout of writer's block might overtake them. Side by side they moved slowly to the curb, not wanting to leave each other, knowing that one or both of them might not survive the next couple of days.

Jack put his arm around her. "I think you're insane not to take a cab to the Israeli embassy right now and let David Navon get you out of Paris."

She leaned over and kissed him gently. "We've been through that a thousand times."

"Then at least let me ride home with you to make sure Nadim's not waiting at your apartment."

"I know you want to help me, Jack, but you have a plane to catch. Besides, Moreau's men may still be on my street."

She was right, of course. He had forgotten about Moreau. He didn't argue with her.

Layla spotted a cab. She raised her hand. The old Peugot's brakes squealed. It stopped in front of them.

"You take it," Jack said. "I'll get the next one."

As he opened the door for her, Layla flashed the mysterious smile that had captivated him the first time he met her at the wine dinner. "Will I ever see you again?" she asked.

Jack knew that the answer called for was, "You're damn right," but he was too honest for that. He thought about the dangers they were each confronting. He forced a smile and said, "I sure hope so."

That was good enough for Layla. She hugged him, kissed him quickly, and climbed into the cab.

Exhausted from making love most of the night, she dozed until the cab pulled up in front of her apartment. Paying the driver, she thought about what Jack had said, that Nadim might be waiting in her apartment. She dismissed that with a wave of one hand, while at the same time clutching tightly the black leather bag that held her loaded gun.

As the elevator rose to the sixth floor, she thought about Jack. He was different from any other man she had ever met. More sensitive. More caring. But they were an odd couple, the two of them. A common enemy, Nadim, had united them. When this was all over, if they both made it out alive, would there be a future for them?

She yawned and checked her watch. *What I need right now,* she chided herself, *is a bath, two hours of sleep, and about three cups of strong black coffee before I go to work at the bank.*

Exiting the elevator, she yanked the gun out of her purse and gripped it tightly. She turned the key in the lock to her apartment door, pushed it open, and looked around. She didn't see anybody. The apartment looked normal to her.

She started across the Oriental carpet in the living room and kicked the door shut behind her. Just as she did, Nadim, who had been hiding between the open door and the wall, jumped out. Before she had a chance to react, he raised his right hand and brought it down with a hard chop on the wrist of her arm holding the gun. She lost control of her hand, and the gun fell out. Helplessly she watched it skidding across the floor.

"Get out of here," she screamed, steeling her courage. "Or I'll call the police."

Coldly, he stared into her eyes. Then, without any warning, he raised his right hand, which had a large gold ring, swung it hard, and smashed the back of it against the side of her face. The force of the blow knocked her off her feet.

He looked down at her and shook his head grimly. "You're not giving me any orders."

Tasting blood, she staggered to her feet and positioned herself between Nadim and the bedroom. "What do you want with me?"

"You spied on me for the Israelis. You'll pay for that."

"I did what I had to do for my own people."

"I'm your people. Not the Jews."

Trying to be unobtrusive, she backpedaled a couple of steps toward the bedroom. "You killed more of my people than the Israelis did."

He raised his hand and pointed a finger. "I won't kill you for what you did. That would be too easy."

With loathing, she glared at him, terrified, trying to imagine what his evil mind had fashioned for her.

"I'll give you the choice," he said, savoring each word. "Once I return from Baku—where, incidentally, I intend to kill Jack Cole—you will become my mistress, available for me whenever I want you."

"Never," she said, spitting blood out of her mouth onto the carpet.

"You can take that position if you'd like, but then I will arrange to have one member of your family in Beirut killed every day, starting with your dear father, until you change your mind."

Her body trembled with fear. She knew he meant it.

"Of course," he continued, "you have one other way out. You can simply kill yourself. Then you won't know how many members of your family I'll murder. The choice is yours." He stopped to gaze at her. "Although it would be a crime to destroy such a beautiful body." When she didn't respond, he said, "You don't have to decide right now. You have until I return from Baku."

"You're a monster," she blurted out.

He laughed. "I've been accused of worse, but being my mistress won't be so bad. You'll enjoy the wonderful sex with me."

He took off the jacket of his military uniform and tossed it onto the couch. Then he began unbuttoning his shirt. "I'll show you right now how much you'll enjoy it. In case your memory of the other night is short."

It was Layla's turn to laugh. "I lied in my note. You

weren't man enough to do anything. You couldn't even get it up. At least with Jack Cole I get a hard prick."

Nadim's body froze. "You're lying, you stupid cunt."

She continued in a mocking voice: "Perhaps you were tired and it was late. Maybe you had too much to drink." She shrugged. "Who knows."

She picked her skirt up, flashing her sheer white panties and showing off her thick brown bush. "Let's see if you're man enough to do anything this time."

Then she turned and ran toward the bedroom.

For an instant Nadim was too stunned to move. No one had ever dared to insult his sexual prowess. By the time he recovered, she had slammed the bedroom door. He unzipped his pants. As soon as he reached inside and stroked it a couple of times, his member sprang out, rock-hard, red, and veiny. With fire in his eyes, he vowed that he'd make her pay for her words.

The couple of seconds was all Layla needed. She just hoped Jack's friends had done what he promised. Her terrified eyes quickly scanned the wall near the door. She saw an electrical switch that had never been there before. With moist, shaking hands she tossed the switch upward. Then she moved into the bathroom and grabbed a pair of scissors, her only other possible weapon.

The scissors were in her hand, raised high above her head. She held her breath, waiting for Nadim to grab the doorknob.

First she heard a crackling sound, then a piercing scream from Nadim, finally the sound of Nadim's body collapsing to the floor.

She dropped the scissors, turned off the current, and cautiously opened the door.

At the same time that her eyes saw Nadim crumpled up and unconscious on the floor, her nose detected the dreadful odor of seared human flesh.

It was almost too much for Layla to bear. She couldn't bring herself to get near Nadim's body, even to look at it to see if he was dead or alive. The fact that he had been responsible for the deaths of hundreds of innocent people—her people—gave her no joy. Her knees tottered. She was afraid they would buckle and she would end up on the floor next to Nadim.

She had to get out of the apartment fast. Rallying all of her remaining strength, she staggered across the living room and picked up her gun from the floor. All the while she was muttering to herself, "Please God, let him be dead . . . please, God." She closed the door behind her and grabbed the metal banister.

Her breath was coming in short spurts. If Nadim was dead, she'd be charged with murder. There was no way she'd ever be able to convince the French police that it had been self-defense. She knew what she had to do: Get out of this building, grab a cab, and leave the area—then call David Navon at the Israeli embassy. He would be able to get her out of France.

She stumbled down one flight of stairs, clutching the banister. On the next landing she got a sick feeling in the pit of her stomach. Jack had said that the chances of Nadim's being killed by the electrical device were only fifty-fifty. But what if Nadim survived? Even if the Israelis helped her escape, the killing and mayhem he would inflict on her family was too terrible to imagine. She couldn't take that chance. No matter how horrible it was, she had to go back into that awful apartment, determine whether Nadim was dead, and if not, finish the job. She had no choice, regardless of how awful it would be.

She turned around and started up the stairs. As she did, she heard voices coming from the ground floor. Two men were talking, and one of them was Daniel Moreau, the SDECE agent who had been looking for Jack. He had to be returning to talk to her. Going back into her own apartment was hopeless. He would find her there with Nadim's body.

She listened carefully. They were coming up the stairs. She could try for the elevator and hope to avoid them, but it was too slow. God only knew when it would come.

Think, she told herself. *Think*. There had to be a way out of this quagmire. Then it hit her: Oliver, the screenwriter who lived across the hall. She just had to hope he was at home and not asleep, because then he might not get to the door in time.

She charged up the flight of stairs, then pressed hard on Oliver's bell, ringing it again and again.

"Okay. Okay. I'm coming," he called from inside. He looked through the peephole, saw it was Layla, and opened the door. She stumbled inside and closed it quickly.

"Hey, what's going on?" the startled Oliver asked.

She pushed a finger up to her lips. "Shhh. Be quiet."

Oliver, with two days' growth of a beard, bags under his eyes, and dressed in old jeans and a faded gray sweatshirt, led her away from the door.

"You look like hell," he whispered.

"You don't look so hot yourself."

"I've been up for forty-eight straight hours rewriting my screenplay, because some asshole producer thinks he's more creative than I am, and the director's too much of a wimp to take my side. What's your excuse?"

"It's better if you don't know."

"It's that SDECE guy, Moreau. Isn't it?"

She nodded weakly.

"He's coming for you?"

They heard a commotion outside. "Don't open the door," she said. "Just look through the peephole."

He crossed the room toward the door. As he did, he called over his shoulder, "Go hide in my bedroom."

She followed his advice, reaching into her purse on the

way and grabbing the .38. She clutched it tightly in her hand.

What Oliver saw was Moreau accompanied by one of his goons pounding hard and angrily on the door to Layla's apartment.

"Open up, bitch," he shouted. "Open up now."

When nothing happened, Moreau reached into his pocket, took out the key that Charles, the building manager, had furnished, and unlocked the door.

From habit, Moreau grabbed his gun and stepped into the room slowly. You never knew what might be waiting for you. His assistant, also armed, stood in the doorway and covered Moreau.

First the horrible stench of charred skin hit Moreau in the face. Then he saw Nadim. "You poor bastard," Moreau cried out.

Moreau crossed the room and touched the pulse in the unconscious Nadim's wrist. "Jesus, he's still alive. This guy's one tough bird." Nadim's pants were unzipped. Moreau could guess what he had in mind. Nadim wasn't on his way to the bathroom to take a leak.

"Call for an ambulance," Moreau barked to his assistant.

While they waited, Moreau studied the doorknob. Pretty clever device. Moreau had seen one of these before—state of the art. Had to be the Mossad—Jack Cole using Layla and her honey pot to lure Nadim and kill him.

Moreau was furious that the Israelis and Arabs were playing their war games on French soil. He was determined to put an end to it once and for all. But without Layla he didn't have enough evidence for his government even to file a protest with the Israelis, much less charge Cole.

He needed Layla, and he needed her now. The trouble was, she wouldn't be hanging around Paris after this. She was probably on her way back to Beirut and the safety of her family. He searched the apartment and found lots of expensive jewelry in a brown wooden box. That told him she had left in a hurry.

With one call to headquarters, Moreau had her name flashed to security at both airports in Paris. He was convinced that this had happened only an hour or so earlier. He was confident that security agents would nab her at passport control or getting on a plane.

"Well, what's happening?" Layla called frantically to Oliver from across the room. He was looking out through the peephole in his front door.

"Nothing yet," he said. "The medics went in with a stretcher and all their equipment."

"What the hell's taking so long? If he's dead, they should put him in a bag and take him away."

"Don't keep asking," Oliver responded. His own nerves were frayed. Not only had he drunk umpteen cups of coffee in the last forty-eight hours, but now he had become an accessory after the fact to murder, or at least attempted murder, if they caught Layla and she couldn't make her self-defense story stick. He thought she should be able to, from what she had told him, but lots of French hated Arabs, so they rarely got a fair shake in the French judicial system.

Oliver was willing to take the risk. He liked Layla, thought she was right, and hated cops like Moreau. Besides, he had read extensively about events in Lebanon in recent years. He knew how Nadim had earned his nickname, the Butcher of Beirut. *So I'm not just doing this to get material for a new screenplay,* he told himself.

"Something's happening now," he said to Layla without turning around.

"What?" she asked anxiously.

"They're carrying Nadim's body out on a stretcher. They have oxygen hooked up to his mouth."

"Oh, no," she wailed. "He's still alive."

When everyone had left the apartment and was on the stairs, out of sight, Oliver opened his door a crack to hear what he could. "They're taking Nadim to University Hospital," Oliver said.

"My family's all as good as dead," she moaned.

Oliver felt sorry for her. He couldn't let that happen. "I've got an idea for you," he said, "from a scene I used in one of my screenplays. When I write, I do thorough research. I can help you."

Chapter 36

Turkish Air flight 17 was in the final stages of boarding at Orly. In the gate area, Jack pulled Avi by the arm off to a deserted corner and whispered, "I've got to call and find out if Layla's okay."

He pulled out his cell phone and dialed frantically. There was no answer at her apartment. The message machine kicked on.

"She must have gone to work early," Avi said, trying to sound optimistic. He didn't want to tell Jack how much he, too, was worried about Layla. "Or turned off the phone to get some sleep."

"Maybe," Jack said, unconvinced.

Avi grabbed Jack by the arm and herded him onto the plane.

In his seat, Jack was staring blankly into space. Once the engines started he turned to Avi. "Regardless of how this plays out, I can't go back to Paris. Not with Daniel Moreau so close. Before long he'll discover where I'm living. . . . Will you call someone and have them clean out my apartment? When Moreau turns up, I want him to find an empty place."

"Good idea," Avi said.

Jack realized that a part of his life was over.

The minute Michael woke up in his Moscow apartment, he called Irina at home. All he got was the answering machine.

He was furious at himself for not whisking Irina over to the American embassy and out of the country yesterday. He had already put most of the pieces together with Perikov's help and their visit to the warehouse in Volgograd. The Israelis had supplied the other critical details. He had been greedy to try to use Irina for additional information. Suslov was a shrewd man. It was only a question of time until he found out about Irina and Michael. In the Company's training program, they emphasized how important it was to pull a source from the field before it was too late. But there were no rules, just an agent's gut instinct. His had failed him. Irina had paid the price.

He tried her telephone number at Suslov Enterprises. The call rolled over to the control operator.

"I want to speak to Irina Ivanova," Michael said politely. The phone went dead.

In frustration, he pounded his fist against the wall. His stomach ached. His body was racked with guilt. A heavy stone settled into his heart.

He hadn't loved Irina, but she had trusted him, tied her life to his. And what had he done? Cut the cord and sent her into a free fall to her death. He should have gotten her out a day earlier.

He glanced anxiously at his watch. He should be dressing to leave for the airport. Grief and guilt threatened to paralyze him.

The sound of pounding on the door of his apartment jarred Michael out of his stupor. *Jesus, that could be some of Suslov's goons coming to kill me,* Michael thought. He grabbed his gun. Clutching it tightly, he walked over to the front window, which had a view of the entrance, then looked out through a crack in the curtains. It was only Perikov. He relaxed and opened the door.

"I didn't want to do this over the phone," the Russian scientist said.

Looking at Perikov's glum face, Michael was confident this wouldn't be good news.

"Drozny refused to act while the convoy was in Russian territory." Perikov sounded dejected. "He won't do a thing now that they've crossed into Azerbaijan."

"What happened?"

There was a long silence. Perikov was hesitating.

Michael could guess what was involved. He had spent enough time in Russia to understand how rampant corruption was at all levels of the government. "If you tell me to keep something to myself, I will. You know that."

Perikov sighed. "Okay, Suslov not only paid off people close to Drozny, but a Swiss bank account's been opened for the Russian president."

Michael shook his head sadly. This was even worse than he had figured. "How do you know this?"

"I have friends in high places, but that's not important. What matters is that you must tell Washington immediately that Drozny won't do anything to block the transaction." Perikov was worried he had said too much. "Please don't mention anything about the Swiss bank account. I don't want my friends to lose their lives."

"You don't have to worry about that." For reassurance, he placed his hand on Perikov's shoulder. "I would never betray your confidence."

That satisfied Perikov. "The rationalization for looking the other way is that these arms will never be used against Russia. None of the people involved care what the Arabs do to the Israelis."

"That's a responsible attitude."

Perikov dropped his head in despair. "When has my government ever been responsible?" The words came out in a hoarse, barely audible whisper.

Michael decided to try another tack. "Do you think there's any chance of Kendall turning Drozny around?"

"Never." Perikov shook his head forcefully for emphasis. "Drozny thinks Kendall's ignorant and arrogant."

"Great."

"Besides, it'll be easy for Drozny to resist Kendall's request now that the weapons aren't on Russian soil any longer."

In agony, Michael ran his hand through his hair. Suslov was beating them. There was no chance of the government of Azerbaijan acting to block this exchange from taking place. Suslov's MO foreclosed that possibility. No doubt he had paid people in Baku to look the other way, or he would never have set the meeting there. *Jesus, what a fucking mess.*

"It's up to your government now," Perikov said. "They have to stop this travesty from occurring."

Michael knew that getting Washington to act was easier said than done. Joyner would be all for it, but she wasn't the president. Kendall was another matter. "I'll do what I can," Michael said softly.

When Perikov left, Michael decided that it would be close, but if he hurried, he had time to stop at the embassy and call Washington before heading to the airport.

Joyner was dismayed to hear from Michael that Drozny wouldn't act. "Satellite photos show that the convoy's already in Azerbaijan," she said tersely.

"That's what Perikov said." Michael sounded beaten.

Joyner sighed and rubbed her back, which was killing her. "What do we do now?" Michael asked.

"You get your butt on a plane to Baku. I'm going over to the White House. The time for mincing words is over," she said sharply. "I'm sure as hell going to get some action from Kendall."

Michael was taken aback. This wasn't a tone he had ever heard from Joyner in discussing the president.

Joyner's mind was racing. One way or another she would compel Kendall to give the order to substantially increase the size of the American force. The question was whether there was enough time to do that. Had Kendall's indecision cost them a chance to block the exchange and rescue Robert McCallister? She didn't share any of those concerns with Michael. "Your job is to be there on the scene."

"Yes, ma'am. I'm on my way as soon as I finish this call."

Joyner shifted to her concerned voice, which always reminded Michael of his mother when she was worried about him. She and Mrs. Joyner were about the same age. "What happened with Irina?"

"I was too late," he said glumly.

She had figured as much from the way he sounded. "I'm sorry, Michael. Really, I am." There was no hint of, "I told you not to get involved with her."

"I know that and I appreciate it."

"Tomorrow this should be over, one way or another. I don't want to tell you what to do, but afterward you might want to take some time off."

"That's a good idea."

"Meantime"—she was back to being the CIA director—"I spoke to the head of the Mossad. Whatever the Israelis do in Baku—"

"Which is what?"

"At this point, I don't know. Moshe and I have been dancing around with each other, as we sometimes do. Eventually it may shake out to full disclosure, but we're not there yet. He did tell me that his leads in Baku will be two guys, Jack Cole and Avi Sassoon. They'll be at the Hyatt Regency in Baku tonight. Get close to them if you can and work together. Moshe and I both want that."

"Meaning that somebody else doesn't."

She laughed. Michael was smart. She liked him and didn't want to lose him. She hoped he wouldn't go into a tailspin over Irina when this was over. "Yeah, the politicians."

"Morons."

"You said it. Not me."

"Now I'd better get going."

"There is one other thing," Joyner said with such severity that Michael knew he wouldn't like what was coming next.

"What's that?" he asked.

"Chances are that Suslov's going to be in Baku."

Involuntarily, Michael stiffened. "I'm sure of that."

"Just remember," Joyner continued, "and this is an order—your first objective is to stop those nuclear weapons from getting into the hands of the Turks, Iranians, and Syrians. Second, you are to bring Robert McCallister home alive. This isn't the time or the place to conduct a personal vendetta against Dmitri Suslov."

Michael touched the hard, cold steel of the .45-caliber pistol in his pocket.

When he didn't respond, she added, "Am I making myself clear?"

Michael knew better than to argue with her. She had the option of sending someone else to Baku in his place. "You always make yourself clear," he said, sounding respectful. He was determined to carry out his assignment in Baku. At the same time, he planned to kill Suslov.

Joyner's eyes were blazing when she put down the phone. Her first call was to General Childress. "How soon can you get to the White House?" she shouted.

"What happened now?"

"Drozny won't lift a finger. The trucks have moved across the Russian border. The time for playing games with Kendall is over."

"Whoa. That's a mouthful. I'd say you blew your cool, Margaret."

"Damn right. How about fifteen minutes?"

"I'll be there."

Her second call was to the president's secretary. "This is Margaret Joyner. Is the president in his office?"

"He is, but he has—"

Joyner cut her off. "Tell him that General Childress and I will be there in fifteen minutes. This is more important than anything else he's doing."

Unaccustomed to being spoken to in this manner, the flustered secretary stammered, "Please hold for a minute, Mrs. Joyner. I'll see if—"

"I won't hold, and you won't see anything. Tell him we're coming."

Joyner slammed the phone down and grabbed her briefcase.

The treasury secretary and three aides with thick notebooks of economic data were hustled out when Joyner and Childress arrived.

She slapped a map down on the president's desk. In a voice cracking with emotion, she told Kendall what she had learned from Michael and the satellites, and where the convoy was now.

She was prepared to lean on Kendall with every bit of strength she had in her body until he gave the order to increase U.S. forces and block this exchange from taking place. It didn't take much. By the time she finished her presentation, the sheepish and abashed look on Kendall's face told her that the president now realized he had played this poorly. He should have left intelligence and military matters to her and Childress. She wondered if this was how Kennedy had felt when he had personally micromanaged and mismanaged the Bay of Pigs invasion.

Kendall was now willing to get out of the way and let the professionals take over. "Do the best you can," he said to General Childress. "Keep me posted."

"Will do, sir . . ."

Kendall was looking at him with a shell-shocked expression.

The general continued in a businesslike tone: "I would like your approval, Mr. President, to coordinate our activities with the Israelis. They're probably ahead of us here. They can help us play catch-up."

Joyner was looking at the president, ready to pounce if he turned Childress down. The president glanced from Childress to Joyner and back again, then swallowed hard. He didn't like the proposal, but he had no choice. "Whatever you think makes sense under the circumstances."

Joyner suppressed the urge to smile.

Then Kendall continued: "There is one condition, though. The Israelis have to understand that we take possession of the nuclear weapons and sort out with the Russians what their disposition is. They don't get control of those. Can you sell that to your buddy in Jerusalem, Margaret?"

"Moshe will agree to it," Joyner said without hesitation. "According to our intelligence, they've got an adequate stockpile of their own, although they'll never admit it."

Kendall stood up. The craggy lines in his face had deepened with worry. "Okay, you two, go and get the job done."

Outside the Oval Office, when they were alone, Joyner said to Childress, "I marveled at your self-control. I'm sure you wanted to tell him that he's the one who buried you in a sand trap. Now he wants you to make an eagle."

Childress laughed. "Did you ever play golf, Margaret?"

"Never in my life."

"That's what I figured. Well, I play, and you just came up with a terrible metaphor. There's almost no chance anyone, even Tiger Woods, could make an eagle on a hole in which he's been buried in a sand trap."

Joyner gave him a wry, intelligent smile. "That's precisely why it's a good metaphor."

Childress winced at her. "Except for one fact."

"What's that?"

"I've had marine units and helicopter gunships at Karshi-Kanabad in Uzbekistan on alert. I figured it would come down to this. So we're not buried in a sand trap. We might just make that eagle. On the other hand, Baku's not an easy place for our troops to reach without getting shot down by hostile forces."

Chapter 37

Oliver guided Layla each step of the way. He took her into a shop on Avenue Bosque that sold nurse uniforms. He picked up an empty brown paper shopping bag from a fruit vendor and told her to stuff the uniform inside. Pretending to be a member of the Syrian embassy staff, Oliver learned that Nadim was in room 321 at the hospital.

Their last stop was the pharmacy at Hospital St. Lazare, across town. Oliver had forged the papers Layla needed to emerge from the shop with a bag of potassium chloride solution and a syringe.

"You don't have to worry," he said. "When I was writing the scene for *Cops on the Loose*, I had the lead actress actually run through it incognito at another hospital. It worked like a charm. Security at hospitals in this city is a joke."

Finally, when he pulled into the parking garage for University Hospital, Oliver said to Layla, "Okay. Showtime. I'll be waiting here for you."

"I'm not sure I can do this," she said.

He reached over and squeezed her arm for encouragement. "Of course you can. Go get him."

As Layla left the car, holding the nurse uniform in the brown bag in her hand, her mind was focused on Nadim and how horrible he was. By the time she walked through the front door of the hospital, she was determined to succeed. The righteousness of her cause gave her strength.

Nadim was responsible for the deaths of hundreds, even thousands of people—her people. What she was doing was totally justified.

She had wondered what security would be like in the reception area of the hospital. There was none. The young woman behind the desk was engrossed in a personal call. *Walk as if you belong,* Oliver had told her. *As if you know where you're going.*

She saw a sign for elevators that pointed to the right.

Clutching the brown bag tightly, she took that path, rounding a corner out of sight of the young woman. Opposite the elevator doors were toilets.

Layla ducked inside and looked around. The room was deserted. Before anyone else could enter, she went into a stall. Quickly she pulled off her clothes and put on the nurse uniform. She slipped the syringe and the potassium chloride into her pocket. Once she put her own clothes into the shopping bag, she looked in the mirror. *Not bad,* she thought. She started toward the door; then it hit her: Nurses on duty didn't carry shopping bags. She had to stash it somewhere until she was finished with Nadim and ready to leave the hospital. But where?

She spotted a trash bin open on top in a corner of the rest room. She'd have to take a chance that it wouldn't be cleaned out before she returned. Unable to think of a better solution, she stuffed the brown shopping bag with her clothes into the bin. She straightened up her uniform and walked outside into the corridor.

In the elevator there were visitors for patients, as well as doctors and nurses. Two exhausted-looking residents with bloodshot eyes were discussing how many admissions they had gotten last night. As they yawned, she wondered how such tired doctors could care for their patients. Nobody stared at her, as she had thought they would. Layla was relieved that she didn't stand out, but she knew the tough part was still ahead. What if a doctor or a nurse stopped and asked her to assist in treating a patient? What would she do then?

Layla exited the elevator on the third floor and followed the signs leading her to room 321.

I can't believe I'm doing this, she thought, but then she remembered everything else that had happened to her in the last couple of days since she had met Jack at the wine dinner at L'Ambroise.

Announcements were continually blasting over the loudspeaker: "Code blue, room two-ten" . . . "Dr. Benoit, call two-four-six-seven." Nurses scurried down the hall and nodded to her. A patient on a gurney went whizzing by, surrounded by four urgent-looking medical personnel.

She was looking at the room numbers as she passed. Room 321 should be around the next corner to the right. She was about to make the turn when she heard Moreau's booming voice coming from that direction. "Listen, Doctor, I want you to call me when he regains consciousness. I'll be right over. I have to talk to him."

Oh, my God, he's coming this way, Layla thought. *I have to get out of this corridor, and fast.* She looked around, on the verge of panic. There were a couple of patient rooms on the left. She could head for one of those, but the doors were open. She would be visible to Moreau from the corridor. On the left she spotted a door marked, *Linen Room.* She ran that way and grabbed the doorknob. *Please let it be unlocked.* It was.

Inside the darkened room, she collapsed onto a pile of clean sheets and tried to listen through the closed door. A few seconds later she heard the sound of Moreau's voice—albeit softly, muffled by the wooden door—as the SDECE agent passed by.

Layla breathed a sigh of relief. She decided that she'd better wait a couple more minutes before exiting the closet.

To her horror, the door opened. A medical orderly, a young man, dark complexioned with curly black hair, entered the room and turned on the light. He saw Layla and gasped. "What are you doing in here in the dark?"

Layla stood up and took a deep breath. "Just resting for a couple of minutes. I worked a double shift. I'm exhausted."

"You okay? Should you see a doctor?"

"I just have to finish up, go home, and get some sleep. I'll be okay."

He bought her story. "The administration's so fucked-up here. They know they need more nurses, and they refuse to hire them. This place is run by imbeciles."

Layla smiled. "You can say that again."

She decided to exit quickly, lest he try to draw her into a more detailed discussion.

Out in the corridor she rounded the corner. Room 321 was on the right. Before entering, she peeked in. As she had hoped, Nadim was alone. He was in bed with monitors hooked up to his body. His burned hand was wrapped in layers of sterile white gauze. His wrists were restrained to the bed. He had a central line in his right subclavian vein. From one of the ports he was getting fluids. The other two ports were clamped. *Perfect*, she thought. That was exactly the way Oliver had described it to her.

Nadim's eyes were closed. Judging from what Moreau had said, he was still unconscious. That was too bad. She wanted him to see her, to know what was happening.

Approaching the bed, she stared at his face. Waves of revulsion surged through her body as she thought about that dreadful evening with him in his apartment and everything he represented.

When she reached into her pocket for the syringe, her

hands began shaking. *Stay focused,* she admonished herself. *In another minute it will all be over.*

She moved close to him with the needle in her hand. Suddenly his eyes fluttered open. He was moving into that foggy state of semiconsciousness, gradually emerging into the realm of the conscious.

He recognized her. Her name emerged in a low murmur from his lips: "Lay-la."

His eyes were pleading with her. He feebly attempted to jerk his wrists forward to free himself, but the restraints held him back. She stifled a scream. Then, acting on instinct, with sure, deft fingers she unclamped a port with one hand, while she injected the potassium chloride through the port into his vein with the other. Oliver had told her this would go straight to his heart and kill him.

From his eyes, she knew that he realized what was happening, but he was powerless to do more than raise his head slightly.

"You won't be able to harm me or anyone else," she said in a quiet whisper.

She replaced the empty syringe in her pocket and reclamped the port. She wanted to bolt from the room before someone came, but she willed herself to stay. She had failed to kill him once. She wouldn't fail this time. Calmly she stood, staring into his face with one hand on his pulse, until his heart stopped beating.

Then she moved quickly, exiting the room. Her clothes were waiting in the trash bin on the ground floor. Once she was in Oliver's car, she made a call to David Navon at the Israeli embassy. "This is Layla Gemayel. Please help me."

Michael's cell phone began ringing fifteen minutes after his plane touched down in Baku. He was still in the terminal when he heard the familiar *beep . . . beep . . . beep.* He whipped it out of his jacket pocket, hoping that, however improbable, Irina was calling.

She wasn't. Rather it was her good friend Natasha. He began walking toward a deserted area of the terminal as he listened.

"Have you heard from Irina?" she asked with panic in her voice.

"No, and I'm concerned." Rather than tell her any more, he decided to stop talking and hear what Natasha had to say.

"I think we have something to worry about."

"What happened?" he asked anxiously.

"I was out all night with one of my men. When I got home this morning I had a message on my machine from Irina."

"When did she call?" Michael asked frantically. He was hoping that Irina had found a way to escape. Maybe there was a secret tunnel out of the building.

"Yesterday afternoon."

"Oh," Michael said. He felt like a balloon that had just deflated.

"Yeah, on the message she said that she had tried to call you, but your cell phone was busy."

"Damn," Michael cursed. "What was the message?" he asked. He was dreading what was coming next.

"Oh, my God, it's awful." Natasha started to cry.

"Tell me, please."

"You don't want to know."

"Natasha, please, tell me already."

Natasha blew her nose, then continued while sobbing. "She said that she was locked in a closet in the office. Suslov had found out about her and you. She said he was going to kill her." Natasha's cries became louder. "It's so horrible."

Michael's heart was pounding with anger and grief. "Did she say anything else?" he asked weakly.

"Just one thing I didn't understand. So I listened to it three times . . . and wrote down her words."

"What'd she say?" Michael had the phone plastered against his ear, not wanting to miss a word.

Natasha picked up the paper and began reading. "Tell Micki that Dimitri tricked me. The information he gave me about a single bodyguard has to be false. And tell him I love him."

Michael was touched that Irina had used her last breath of life to try to help him. She wasn't just the vapid airhead that she had seemed. The call made him hate Suslov even more. No way would that Russian bastard leave Baku alive. Even more important, the message confirmed how right he and Joyner had been to treat Suslov's words as misinformation. Suslov would be coming to Baku in force.

Chapter 38

Jack stood at the window of the suite in the Hyatt Regency and looked down eight stories at the old town of Baku. The city lay on the south coast of the Abseron Peninsula, which reminded him of a hook extending out into the Caspian Sea from the western shore.

Standing out among the winding narrow cobblestone alleys of the old town with its mosques and monuments was the Maiden's Tower, a massive stone lookout post built in the seventh century. Behind it were stately buildings and tree-lined streets from the first oil boom, a hundred years ago. Still farther were the industrial monstrosities erected during the Soviet rule, when the land and its resources were plundered and looted. Oil-drilling rigs were everywhere. Huge, ugly, block-style apartments for the workers stood one next to the other—a testimony to the Communists' indifference to aesthetics.

Jack raised his eyes over the polluted landscape marked by oil slicks and factories with uncontrolled emissions, to the lush countryside beyond and the high mountains of the eastern Caucasus, its peaks still snow-packed, leading to Russia in the north. The route of the convoy of nuclear weapons from Volgograd was over those mountains.

Jack wheeled around and looked at Avi, who was examining a map of the area.

"When does Igor get to the hotel?" Jack asked him anxiously.

Avi checked his watch. "In about an hour."

"Good. It's a real break for us that Moshe found an Israeli who was born and lived in Baku before emigrating to Israel . . . once the USSR collapsed and the gates opened for the Jews to get out."

"What did he tell you about Igor?"

"In Moshe's typical way, not much. He said that Igor's an engineer. A virgin—no prior Mossad work. Knows nothing about the assignment except that he's driving for us. Moshe told him it's important for the state. That was all it took."

An hour later they met Igor in the lobby of the hotel. He was a big, strapping man, six-foot-four with a bulging gut, beefy arms, and a large, round face with a reddish glow.

"I rented a car at the airport," Igor said. "It's parked in front."

"Good, let's take a drive," Jack told him.

Once the three of them piled into the Lada, Jack, who was in the front, explained to Igor what they had heard on the recording of Nadim's conversation with Ahmed. "We're looking for a truck stop at a key crossroads fifty miles northwest of Baku. Can you find that for us?"

Igor gripped his chin in a large palm and pondered the question for a couple of minutes. Finally he said, "I have an idea, but we have to take a look. A lot could have changed in the ten years since I left."

"Ever been back?" Jack asked.

"Are you kidding? My whole family left with me. Why would I possibly return? The locals were nice, but when the Russians ruled they were such bastards to everybody, particularly the Jews. I don't have good memories."

Igor turned over the engine. For the next half hour they

drove west to the end of the peninsula through an industrial cesspool worse than anything Jack could have imagined. Oil derricks, chemical plants, and decrepit buildings littered the landscape, polluting the air and the ground with chemical waste that flowed into the Caspian.

"Fucking Russians," Igor cursed. "This was a beautiful place. They took the oil and left this crap behind. The area's one big sewer."

From the backseat, Avi interjected, "Now that Azerbaijan is independent, are they trying to clean it up?"

Igor held out his hand and rubbed his thumb against two fingers. "There's no money."

"Where did you work when you lived here?" Jack asked.

"For an oil company in exploration. It was a cinch. Everywhere we drilled, we found black gold." Igor shook his head. "The problem is, we couldn't move it out of here fast enough."

As they rode away from the sea, crude-oil factories on the landscape gave way to green fields. Farmers were plowing, buds were breaking out on the trees, baby birds were in their nests.

Approaching an intersection, Igor braked and pulled over to the side of the road. "This is the one I thought of," he said. "But the truck stop that used to be here is gone." He pointed to a three-story gray cinder-block structure. "That apartment building is on the space."

From the backseat, Avi looked at Jack. "Are you sure Nadim said the exchange will take place at a truck stop?"

Tired and irritable, Jack didn't like being questioned on such a basic issue. "Positive," he said in a sharp tone.

"Okay, just checking. Don't blow your top."

Ignoring the two of them, Igor pulled a map out of the glove compartment. Again with his chin in his hand, and furrows on his wide forehead, he studied it. "There's another location," he said, and shifted the car into gear. "Let's try it."

Jack was very happy Moshe had sent Igor.

Twenty minutes later they pulled into the parking lot of a truck stop at the intersection of two main roads. There was a restaurant and gas station with a large oil-coated dirt area for truckers who wanted to sleep for a few hours on a long haul.

"This has to be it," Igor said.

"Are there any other possibilities?" Jack asked.

"Not within a fifty-mile radius."

"We'll go inside the restaurant," Avi said. "See what we're dealing with."

"You two do that," Jack told him. "I want to walk around out here and check out the area."

Jack climbed out of the car, stretched his legs, and surveyed the scene. The truck stop was on the northwest corner of the intersection. On the diagonal across from it was a combination office building and workshop that belonged to Spartan Oil, an American company based in Houston. On the third corner fruit and vegetable vendors were hawking their wares. The fourth one was the site of some type of building under construction, with much of the concrete structure in place.

Jack crossed the two roads and pretended to be casually walking past the two-story gray stone Spartan Oil building while he studied it. There were people in the office. Outside in the yard in the rear, mechanics were working with pipe and repairing machines. *This should be perfect for us,* Jack thought.

Walking back to the truck stop, Jack thought about Layla. Where was she now? He hoped they had been able to get her out of France.

When they were back in the car and Igor was driving toward town, Avi said, "A nice woman and her husband run the joint. They open at four in the morning. Most of their customers are people making deliveries of equipment for companies in the oil industry."

"You think they're on the take from Suslov?" Jack asked.

"What's your opinion, Igor?" Avi asked.

"I doubt it."

"What about the cops and the army?"

"In Azerbaijan, they're mostly honest and honorable people. They hate the Russians, who have been trying to control them for thousands of years." Igor took his eyes off the road for a second and looked thoughtfully at Jack. "Still, like people everywhere, there will be some who are corrupt if the price is right. That's the way of the world."

"So we have to assume," Jack said, "when we square off with Suslov and his troops tomorrow, that the cops and army won't be anywhere nearby."

Avi agreed. "A fair assumption."

Igor was beginning to catch on to some of what was happening. "The woman who runs the restaurant and her husband won't become casualties, will they?"

"I hope not," Jack said.

"Let me come with you. I'll look out for them."

Avi responded, "But Moshe said—"

"I don't work for Moshe," Igor told him.

Avi smiled and said to Jack, "I like this man. Let's bring him with us."

Back in Baku, Igor suggested the place for their meeting with Michael Hanley. "Dinner at the Mugam Club in the old town. They have private dining rooms. You can talk."

"Maybe the hotel's better," Jack said. "We'll stand out in the town."

Igor shook his head. "You don't have to worry. There are lots of foreigners all the time. People are decent here. They like visitors. They'll assume you're from the oil industry. Besides, the food's good."

Looking at Igor, Jack decided, *He's someone who likes to eat.*

"Okay, we'll do it."

Jack wasn't worried that Suslov would try to attack them tonight. Even if the Russian knew they were here, he wouldn't do anything now for fear of jeopardizing tomorrow morning's exchange. Once that took place, all bets were off.

As a precaution, Jack and Avi were both armed. Also, ten Israeli commandos dressed in plain clothes had arrived and were staying at the Hyatt, posing as members of an Israeli oil exploration team who had flown in a private plane, which permitted them to bring their arms with them. Jack asked four of them to come along to the restaurant.

On foot, Jack, Avi, and Igor walked along the winding cobblestone streets, up and down steps, past the Maiden's Tower, with four Israeli commandos following behind, until they reached the Mugam Club. Michael was waiting for them at the entrance to the restaurant.

As Igor talked to the proprietor, Jack watched him hand the man some of the American dollars Moshe had given him for the trip. With that they were led to a private room in the back of the restaurant separated from the other tables by a heavy brown curtain.

The commandos were seated out front, at a table near the door.

Jack felt as if he were playing a part in one of the old Western or gangster movies he used to see as a child in Chicago. At this point, what usually happened was a group of gunmen burst into the restaurant and began firing. He hoped that didn't happen tonight.

They drank bottled water and local wine while a waitress kept bringing food: salads and dolma, peppers, tomatoes, and eggplant stuffed with minced lamb.

"Tell me about Dmitri Suslov," Jack said to Michael.

"He's the devil's alter ego in Russia," Michael began. He

then recited in a soft voice the presentation about Suslov he had given Joyner that morning at her office, which now seemed so long ago. As he neared the end, Avi's cell phone rang.

"With those things, they can always find you," Michael said.

Jack was too worried about Layla to banter. Anxiously, he watched Avi move away from the table with his back to them to take the call.

Jack looked at Avi apprehensively when he returned a minute later. Suddenly Avi broke into a smile and gave Jack a thumbs-up. "They got Layla out via Amsterdam. She's on a plane now. She's safe."

"That's great news," Jack said in a burst of joy.

Michael became very quiet and still. *I should have done that for Irina,* he berated himself. His face was ashen.

Alarmed, Jack looked over at Michael. "Are you all right?"

"Yeah. I was just thinking about someone," Michael said wistfully. Then he snapped out of it. He was mindful of Joyner's admonition. He wouldn't forget about their objective, but he sure as hell intended to kill Suslov before this was all over.

Jack pulled the map Igor had used out of his pocket and pointed to the intersection with the truck stop. He kept his voice down to a whisper. Anyone who looked at them in this place would think that they were oil company representatives discussing a site for exploration.

Jack marked an X on the intersection and described for Michael what was on each of the four corners. "Now here's what we need from you," Jack told him.

Jack stopped talking when the curtains to their room abruptly opened. In the entranceway stood a man with a musical pipe, accompanied by a woman clad in a flaming red halter top with sparkling sequins and transparent pink cotton trousers, with a brief bottom underneath that matched the top. "You want music?" the man asked. "She's good belly dancer."

Responding to the cue, the woman, who was big busted and seemed to be of an indeterminate age somewhere north of thirty, swayed her broad hips and breasts. Igor looked at Jack, who shook his head. Concealing his disappointment, Igor got up, walked over, and handed the couple American money. "Not tonight," he said. The money made them happy. Smiling, they waved to everyone, closed the curtain, and left.

Jack returned to the map. Michael was now on the edge of his chair, waiting to hear what Jack said.

"It's still early in the day in Washington," Jack said. "Have someone at your agency get to a key official at Spartan Oil. I know it's an American-based firm. We're going to use their building as a command center and staging area from about midnight tonight. Make sure all of their people stay away until this is over. Hopefully they'll have a building to return to."

Michael leaned back in his chair and closed his eyes, trying to visualize what the intersection looked like, because Joyner was certain to ask him that. He turned back to Jack. "You're planning to lay your ambush there."

"Exactly. But I prefer to think of it as *our* ambush. When will the American troops arrive? How many are coming?"

Michael hesitated.

"Well?" Jack pressed.

Michael took a deep breath. What he was about to say wouldn't endear him to the two Israelis. "Washington has told me that at this point we have six men in the area. A special-operations force headed by Major Davis, who's quite experienced, will be joining me tonight at the Radisson."

Avi sprang to his feet. "Six!" Avi said in disbelief. "That's all? Suslov's sure to have at least a hundred men guarding those four trucks. The way I do the math right now, we have ten Israeli commandos, six special-operations troops, and the three of us. We'll be dead meat. What are they thinking in Washington?"

Michael agreed with Avi. He felt no need to defend his government. "You're preaching to the choir. I've been arguing for much more firepower. I'm told the logistics will take time. Hopefully they'll arrive before the convoy."

"What the hell took them so long to get the process started?"

Michael held out his hands. "You know. The usual political stuff and indecision in Washington. They were worried about American–Russian relations and all that."

Jack was shaking his head in disbelief.

"Oh, that's bullshit," Avi said with a scowl.

"Look, don't shoot the messenger," Michael pleaded. "I'm as frustrated as you are."

Avi was preparing to fire back a brutal retort when Jack stood up and put his hand on Avi's shoulder to calm his colleague. "There's no point beating up on Michael. We'll have to make do with what we have."

"That's just great," Avi moaned.

Jack was becoming irritated by Avi's carping. The situation was what it was. He was anxious to move on and decide what to do, make the best of it. "We have the element of surprise on our side. It's up to us to come up with a plan that takes advantage of that. We don't have a choice. The objective is to block the exchange from taking place. That means we keep fighting until the rest of the American troops get here."

Sixty miles west of Baku, Suslov was ensconced in the commander's villa of a former Russian military base near the village of Samaxi. The barracks were occupied by his troops, former Russian army officers, eighty in all.

It was time to check on each of his partners.

Suslov took out his cell phone and dialed Nikolai, the head of the truck convoy with the nuclear weapons. "Position and status?" Suslov barked.

"We're in place. Parked twenty miles north of the meeting point. All drivers are sleeping a couple of hours before the final push. Armed soldiers are surrounding each truck. We'll arrive at five hundred hours, as you ordered."

Suslov's next call was to the Irshad Hotel, where Nadim was supposed to be staying. The operator told him, "Mr. Nadim is expected, but hasn't arrived yet."

Suslov frowned, wondering what happened to Nadim, but he wasn't alarmed. Nadim had told him where the other players would be. The Syrian had better be right, or Suslov would kill him.

He moved on to Ali Hashim, the Iranian intelligence chief, who was critical. Suslov was relieved to reach him at the Caspian Great House Hotel in Baku, where he was staying with a high-ranking Iranian treasury official and two bodyguards.

Nervously, Suslov asked, "Do you have the one-point-two billion dollars?"

Ali Hashim calmly replied, "My colleague from Treasury has his laptop."

Suslov didn't like that answer, and he didn't hide his displeasure. "What does that mean?"

The Iranian chuckled. "You didn't expect me to bring cash in a suitcase, did you?"

"Stop playing games with me."

Hashim knew instantly that this Suslov was a despicable man, someone he would never have chosen to do business with. But at this point there was no turning back.

"Once I give my colleague the order, he'll use his laptop to transfer the funds to your numbered Swiss bank account."

"And how will I know it gets there?"

"I assume you'll have a cell phone with you. Use it to call

your banker in Geneva. It takes less than a minute for the transfer to go through."

Suslov's final call was to Kemal, who was at an air force base in northern Syria, which had been arranged by Nadim. "How's the patient?" Suslov asked.

"Properly sedated and looking forward to his ride to Baku. Don't worry; we'll be on time. At the airport we have an ambulance waiting. We paid a local company a great deal to let us borrow it. They have no idea what we want with it."

Suslov put down the phone and smiled with satisfaction. Everything was now in place except for Nadim, and he was redundant. Suslov permitted himself the luxury of only a small slivovitz, wanting to keep his mind sharp.

He was now confident that the exchange would go smoothly. He had two other missions tomorrow. One was for himself: to deal with Michael Hanley. The great American lover had to suffer for what he had done with Irina. And one was for Nadim: to kill Jack Cole, who must be responsible for the Syrian's absence. Nadim had put this together. He owed it to Nadim to kill the Israeli spy.

All of that was easily doable, Suslov decided. He was neither nervous nor worried. His entire life he had loved nothing better than combat. Other men shied away from battle, but not Suslov. When he had resigned from the disintegrating Russian army, he thought he had directed troops in battle for the last time. Happily now he had another chance. The adrenaline was flowing. But that didn't stop him from lying down in bed and sleeping like a baby. He needed his rest and energy. Bullets would be flying tomorrow.

Chapter 39

Jack checked his watch. It was ten minutes past four in the morning. The lights were on in the truck stop on the other side of the intersection. The café was open for business.

In contrast, the Spartan Oil building was dark. To anyone looking at it from the outside under the full moon, it seemed deserted, which was precisely what Jack wanted.

In a second-floor office, in the front of the building that faced the intersection, Jack and Avi stood at adjacent windows, each with a pair of night-vision binoculars glued to his eyes, surveying the roads leading to the intersection and the truck stop. Behind them, Igor was sitting at a desk, chain-smoking cigarettes, while Michael paced nervously back and forth across the room. Jack, Avi, and Michael were all armed with pistols and Uzis.

Downstairs, two Israeli commandos and two members of Major Davis's special-ops force were ready to go. Each had a powerful pistol and a submachine gun. The rest of the Israelis and Americans were spread out among the other three corners of the intersection. A few were concealed in the concrete frame of the building under construction. Some were hiding behind the shuttered stalls of the produce vendors. The remainder were crouched down behind parked trucks in the parking area of the truck stop.

The ambush was set.

Outside, the wind started to kick up, blowing dust around the intersection, just as Igor had predicted. "Mornings are windy this time of year almost every day."

"Dust is good for us," Jack said to Avi. "That's one break we have."

"Yeah, why is that?"

"Because we're outnumbered. They won't be able to spot our people."

"Gee, that makes me feel so much better."

Michael stopped pacing and yanked the cell phone out of his pocket. It was his third call to Joyner in the last two hours. "What's the latest word on the additional troops?"

"Six Blackhawk helicopters armed with Hellfire missiles are in the air right now, en route to your location. The choppers are ferrying marines, eighty-four in all."

"What's their ETA?" Michael asked anxiously.

"Five-forty-five."

Michael groaned. "That's an hour and a half from now."

"General Childress did the best he could under the circumstances," Joyner said testily. "Lots of places in the region are off-limits to the American military. We couldn't take a direct route from the base."

"Okay. Okay. I'm sorry."

Jack and Avi had been watching Michael and listening to him during his exchange with Joyner.

"Not good?" Jack asked when Michael hung up.

"We have to make it through the next hour and a half on our own."

"Oh, great," Avi spat. "What are—"

Jack cut him off. "Don't worry about it." He was trying to display a confidence he didn't feel. "We have a good plan. We may not have the numbers, but all our troops here are tough and seasoned. If they have to do it alone, they'll get the job done."

Avi, a hero of Entebbe, wasn't so sure. There they had faced Idi Amin's poorly equipped ragtag army. Here, they would be going up against battle-hardened Russian soldiers who had no doubt served in Afghanistan and Chechnya.

Downstairs, Major Davis and Capt. Ben Zvi were poring over a piece of paper on a table in the coffee lounge on the ground floor. On it Davis had sketched a map of the intersection. The truck stop was on the northwest corner. Their Spartan Oil building was on the southeast.

"From everything we know, the convoy will be coming from the north," Davis said. He drew four rectangles north of the intersection and penciled in a series of X's on each side of the rectangles. "Suslov's troops."

Ben Zvi nodded. "The initial objective has to be to halt the movement of the four trucks—whatever it takes. Those nuclear weapons can't leave the area."

Davis was in complete agreement. The veins on his neck were protruding with the tension. "And I have a secondary objective. When they bring our pilot, Lieutenant McCallister—and God only knows when they're getting him here—I have to rescue him."

"We'll give you whatever help we can on that."

"Good. I appreciate it. Let's just hope that the Azerbaijan police and army stay away. They could only complicate matters."

"I was told by headquarters we can assume that."

Davis hoped Ben Zvi was right. Washington was thinking the same way. "Even without them, we've got a big job ahead of us."

Major Davis and Captain Ben Zvi climbed up the stairs to the office where Jack and the others were. It began functioning as a command center.

Twenty minutes later Jack strained his eyes looking

through the binoculars. "Large car coming from the east. Appears to be a BMW sedan."

"I can see it," Avi said.

They watched the BMW slow down as it passed the front of Spartan Oil, then cross the intersection and ease into the parking lot for the truck stop. The car doors opened, and four men got out, dressed in dark suits and ties. One was carrying a bag for a laptop computer. Two looked around nervously, as if they were ready to go for their guns. All four walked into the café.

"Ali Hashim," Jack said to Michael. "The Iranian intelligence chief."

"Then the two goons must be bodyguards. Do you recognize the fourth? The guy with the computer bag?"

Jack shook his head and turned to Avi.

"Never saw him before . . . My guess is he's the moneyman."

"You're right," Jack interjected. "He'll use his laptop to wire the money to Suslov."

"The age of high-tech thugs," Avi muttered.

Behind them, Igor put out his cigarette and lit another.

"One piece in place," Jack said. "Which one is next?"

Five minutes later Jack had his answer. Through his powerful binoculars, he saw headlights on the crest of the hill in the distance, approaching from the north. "Has to be the convoy at about two miles." He handed the binoculars to Captain Ben Zvi. Avi handed his to Major Davis.

The two military men confirmed that the four trucks were approaching with heavy escorts. "We'd better remind our men to hold their fire until we give the order," Ben Zvi said to Davis. They both got on their cell phones and barked that directive.

Michael took a position next to Jack at the window. "Now where is Lieutenant McCallister?" he said.

"I wish he were here already. When all hell breaks loose

in a couple of minutes, it may scare away whoever is bringing him."

Michael recoiled at that possibility. "That had better not happen, or they'll fry my ass in Washington. For my bosses, that's what this is all about."

"It may have been once," Jack replied. "But right now it's about a lot more than McCallister."

Igor said, "I'm going into the café to try to protect the owner and his wife."

"Be careful," Jack told him.

Outside, the wind was blowing hard, swirling the dust. Jack stared hard through the binoculars screwed to his eyes. Finally, he saw a large black Mercedes approaching from the west. That must be Suslov, Jack decided. His conclusion was confirmed by the license plate. In Russian letters, the vanity plate spelled out THE BOSS.

The Mercedes eased into the truck stop's parking lot. Michael's heart was pounding as he watched the driver climb out and look around. Then he opened the rear door for Suslov.

Shielding Suslov with his body, the driver led the way into the café. Michael was tempted to raise his machine gun to the open window and mow both of them down. The bastard would be directing the battle from the safety of the café, Michael deduced. Shit.

Jack stared at the headlights approaching from the north and swallowed hard. The tip of the lumbering truck convoy was only a hundred yards from the intersection now. The four trucks were escorted by armored personnel carriers that were loaded with troops. "Ah, hell. How are we going to stop these people?"

Davis and Ben Zvi were looking anxiously at Jack. "I say we start firing now," Ben Zvi said.

Jack held up his hand. "We need McCallister. He's not here yet."

"If you wait much longer, their soldiers will be on the ground. Our job will be much tougher."

Jack knew Ben Zvi was right. He was ready to say, "Give the order," when he scanned the area through his binoculars once more.

Suddenly he saw what he was looking for, approaching from the east. With the sun now rising behind it, a white ambulance was racing toward the intersection. They must have Robert McCallister inside, Jack decided.

"One more minute," he said to Ben Zvi and Davis. Then Jack glanced quickly at his wristwatch. It was just past five A.M. They had to hold out for another forty-five minutes.

Jack watched the ambulance skid to a halt on the side of the road next to the truck stop. Kemal and Abdullah, each holding a gun, quickly climbed out and went into the café. Jack was relieved they must have left McCallister in the ambulance. He'd be easier to rescue that way. Jack would have to get him out before a shell hit the ambulance and blew it apart.

Jack turned to Ben Zvi and Davis. "Now," he said. "Go."

Davis barked into his phone, "Begin firing immediately. Don't hit the ambulance."

They both scrambled down the stairs to get outside and join the fight. Avi was a step behind them.

In seconds flashes of light illuminated the area. Shattering sounds and booming noises filled the air as the Israelis and Americans opened fire at the convoy, which was grinding to a stop. The first volley was aimed at the four trucks. One of Davis's soldiers, hiding in the construction site, fired a grenade, which exploded on the engine of the lead truck. The roar was deafening. A spectacular explosion was followed by flames and then billowing dark clouds from the diesel fuel.

From behind the produce vendors' stalls, an Israeli rolled a grenade under the back of the fourth truck. When it exploded, the back of the truck sagged and dropped to the ground in a disintegrating mess.

The second and third trucks were now hemmed in, but the Americans and Israelis weren't taking any chances. From the construction site, sharpshooters took aim at the tires of the other two trucks and flattened all eight of them on one side of each truck.

In awe, Jack stared out of the window. The good news was that those nuclear weapons weren't going anywhere soon. The bad news was that the battle had just begun. The Russian soldiers were jumping out of their APCs and firing in every direction from which the shots had come.

The *clack clack clack* of automatic weapons filled the air along with flashes of gunfire. A Russian officer was shouting orders to his troops, imposing discipline, trying to get them out of the line of fire to take control of the situation.

The Russians had heavier arms as well. A missile flew out of a mobile launcher and smashed into the entrance of the oil company building, near the large black letters that spelled out SPARTAN OIL. Most of the front windows shattered. The blast took down an Israeli who had been shooting through a downstairs window. Instinctively Jack and Michael hit the floor and covered their heads to avoid being hit by flying glass.

Jack could smell smoke nearby. He felt the floor under him beginning to buckle. "Let's get the hell out of here," he said to Michael.

They sidestepped broken glass and ran down an inside staircase along one side of the building and out into the open air. In the equipment maintenance yard, in the back, they took cover behind a metal toolshed. Jack looked out of one side, Michael from the other.

Heavy black smoke was pouring out of the office building. The wind was fanning the flames. Suddenly the whole structure collapsed. Debris shot up into the air.

Jack watched a fierce firefight raging in all directions around the convoy. The Russian troops had taken cover behind their trucks, firing from there at the Americans and Israelis. He saw at least twenty Russians on the ground, dead or wounded. He desperately wanted to get to McCallister, who had to be in the back of the ambulance, and pull him out before bullets or a missile struck the vehicle, but Jack knew he'd never survive the cross fire. The longer he waited, the greater the risk that Kemal and Abdullah might return to the ambulance and drive McCallister away. So Jack raised his machine gun and shot out two of the tires on the ambulance.

Then he glanced at his watch and turned to Michael. "Thirty more minutes. Our guys are good, but there are too many of the enemy. We're never going to make it. When your troops finally arrive, their only job will be to take away our dead bodies."

"Maybe," Michael said grimly, "but I'm sure going to kill Suslov before that happens. Try to cover me."

While Jack unloaded shot after shot from his Uzi, Michael raced out from behind the shed toward the café, keeping close to the ground and taking refuge behind a couple of cars while bullets flew in every direction.

Shells were now striking the shed with regularity. Jack kept ducking as he heard a *ping . . . ping*. One Russian soldier was hammering away at Jack and the shed. When he stopped to reload, Jack leaned out and mowed him down with a shot to the chest.

He snapped his attention back to the ambulance, waiting for the right moment to try a rescue. A Russian soldier tried to take cover behind the ambulance. Jack gunned him down before he got there.

Inside the café, Suslov, standing next to his driver, locked eyes with Ali Hashim, who was sitting at a table with the other three Iranians.

"I want my money now," Suslov demanded. "Give it to me."

Hashim wasn't intimidated. "Are you crazy? There's a war going on out there."

Suslov, who had been on the phone barking orders to the soldiers, wasn't worried. The vast majority of the weapons were still intact. New trucks could be obtained in the area. Most important, his men had the other side badly outnumbered. It was just a question of time. "Only a little skirmish," he said. "My troops are in control."

Hashim rose to his feet and glared at Suslov. "You don't get your money until the nuclear weapons have been transferred and we have the American pilot in our control."

Suslov, accustomed to having his orders followed, pointed a fleshy finger at the Iranian finance man sitting in front of his laptop and said, "Transfer the money *now*."

The finance man looked up nervously, but kept his hands on the table.

"Are you deaf as well as stupid?" Suslov shouted. His tone was now belligerent.

The two Iranian bodyguards sprang to their feet, ready to go for their guns, which were holstered under their suits.

Watching the scene unfold with increasing horror, the proprietor of the café took cover behind the wooden counter. His wife put down a carafe of boiling water she had been holding to make coffee and ducked down beside him. Igor, pretending to be a customer who happened to be in the café at the wrong time, dove behind the counter to join them. He peered out of one side to see what happened next.

Seething, Suslov clinched his fists tightly to keep from losing control. He knew that the Iranians had outfoxed him for now. If they had brought cash, he could steal it and kill them. But he'd never be able to force them to punch the computer keys that would transfer the money. Only the fi-

nance man could do that. "All right," he said. "We wait until
the firing dies down. Then we'll complete the transaction."

•

Butch Davis was pinned behind a large pine tree. Captain
Ben Zvi was in back of another one six feet away.

Davis was worried. The battle was going the way he expected without the additional support. Of the hundred or so
Russians who had arrived with the convoy, his guess was
that about fifty were left. From the beginning all the Russian
soldiers had taken cover behind the trucks.

His own troops and the Israelis were excellent marksmen,
but there just weren't enough of them. He and Ben Zvi had
started with sixteen. Davis's guess was that they were down
to eight effective combatants.

Suddenly the Russians changed their strategy. The wind
had died down. They decided to use their huge numerical
advantage to take the battle to the enemy.

Davis heard an order shouted by the Russian unit commander. Then the troops fanned out from the trucks, firing
as they raced toward individual soldiers on the other side.

Three of the Russians spotted Ben Zvi and ran toward
him.

The Israeli fired rapidly, hitting one in the chest. The man
went down. Davis got a second one, a head shot. Then Davis
watched bullets tear into the center of Ben Zvi's body. The
Israeli continued firing before he pitched forward onto his
gun. Davis took down the third Russian with a short burst.
He ran over and checked Ben Zvi. The Israeli was dead.
"Shit," Davis muttered.

It's only a matter of time until they get all of us, he thought.

"Fucking helos," he cursed. "Where the fuck are they?"

A bullet sailed over his head. A sniper had taken cover behind a nearby tree. Davis waited for him to lean out before
drilling the man in the side. When he fell against the tree, he
finished the sniper off.

Suddenly the radio on his belt cracked to life. "Major Davis . . . Major Davis."

The same instant he heard that, he saw dark objects approaching in the dawn of what would be a bright, sunny day. *Manna from heaven,* Davis thought. *The goddamn cavalry!* "This is Davis, over."

"Roger that. This is Captain Kelly, U.S. Marines. We're coming up on your position. Six Blackhawks, Chestnut four-one through four-six. Fourteen troops in each. I figure you'll need all of them. From up here it looks like a war zone. Over."

"Roger that. My guys and the Israelis, what's left of us, are all in camo. The Russkies are in brown uniforms and heavily armed. They've fanned out from the trucks. I need you to take out as many as you can. But watch carefully. They could be firing from anywhere. Over."

"Roger. Should be like a turkey shoot. Over."

"I hope you have a lotta fun, but wrap it up fast. We can't hold on much longer. Over."

"Roger that. We're movin' in. Over and out."

Seconds later Davis heard the chop of the rotors from the approaching helos. Two Russians raced toward one of their personnel carriers for cover. Just as they reached it, the lead bird let go with a Hellfire missile that blew up the APC. A third Russian tried to hide in the trees, but gunfire from another chopper cut his legs out from under him.

One of the other Russians loaded up a grenade launcher and aimed at the second helicopter in the formation. The grenade smashed into the main rotor housing. For an instant the helo was suspended in midair while the pilot struggled unsuccessfully to control its movement. It veered wildly out of control, tipped forward, and plunged headfirst into the ground; then it exploded, sending a fiery orange ball into the air.

Davis zeroed in on the Russian with the grenade launcher

in his scope, aimed carefully, and nailed him in the center of his back. The other five Blackhawks landed. Marines poured out, firing as they ran.

When Suslov heard the sound of helicopters overhead, he turned deathly pale. He knew that he hadn't ordered any helicopters. If they were American, his troops would be no match for them. The Iranians would never turn over the money. This was turning into a fucking disaster. "We leave now," he said to his driver.

The driver, who was standing a few feet away from Suslov, took the car keys out of his pocket and held them in his hand. As he and Suslov turned toward the door, it opened from the outside.

Michael was standing there with a gun in his hand.

"You're a dead man, Suslov," he said.

Suslov's driver reached for the gun at his waist. As he did, Igor jumped up, grabbed the carafe of scalding water, and tossed it at the driver's head.

The man screamed. His hands flew to his head and he dropped the keys as well as his gun. It fired. That was enough of a diversion for Suslov to grab his own gun from a shoulder holster. He ran for the back of the counter, ducking while Michael's shots flew over his head. As he landed behind the bar, Suslov swung his arm and pistol-whipped Igor in the face. He grabbed the terrified gray-haired woman in her mid-sixties around the soiled blue apron at her waist. He kicked her husband hard in the head, knocking him out. Then Suslov stood up with the woman in front of him as a shield. He raised his arm, aiming his gun at Michael.

Afraid of hitting the woman and wanting to lure Suslov outside, Michael dashed out of the café.

As Suslov fired, the woman moved, trying to twist free. Her movement jarred his arm, and the shots ricocheted off the wooden doorpost.

Suslov grabbed his driver's keys from the floor and stuffed them into his pocket. With his left arm tight around the woman as a hostage in front of him, and the gun in his right hand, Suslov made his way out of the café.

Crossing the threshold, he looked around. He couldn't see Michael, who had taken cover in a cluster of trees adjacent to the parking lot, twenty yards from the Mercedes.

Michael was watching Suslov carefully as the Russian moved toward the Mercedes S500, no doubt equipped with body armor, ultrathick glass to withstand gunfire, and run-flat tires that he'd never be able to blow out with his pistol. It was a virtual fortress on wheels.

Michael's plan was to stay out of sight. He doubted if Suslov would take the hostage with him, so his guess was that there would be a split second, between the time Suslov let go of the woman and when he climbed into the car, when he would be vulnerable. That was when Michael had to nail Suslov.

Michael had his eyes glued on the Russian. Suslov switched the gun to his other hand, and with his free hand grabbed the car keys from his pocket. He pressed down on the keypad to unlock the car door. Then, with a rough push, he shoved the woman to the ground and opened the driver's-side door. That was when Michael took aim.

But the woman on the ground wasn't content to flee toward the café, as Suslov had expected. Instead she gave the Russian a good swift kick to the balls, which made Suslov lurch his head just as Michael fired. That movement was enough to send the bullet whizzing past the Russian's ear by a matter of inches. Michael's next shots bounced off the car's armor plating.

Suslov spotted Michael now standing, gun in hand, next to a bush. Instinctively Suslov fired a round in Michael's direction, ducking down to take cover behind the armored Mercedes. One of the shots grazed Michael's thigh. Though it was just a flesh wound, it had Michael on the ground writhing in pain, unable to try for another shot at the Russian.

Now the woman was stumbling back toward the café. Suslov pulled the trigger and killed her before she made it.

With Michael's gun silent, Suslov was tempted to race into the bushes and finish off the American, if he wasn't already dead. But he couldn't risk losing precious time to get away.

Instead he climbed into the car and floored the accelerater. With squealing tires and dust flying into the air, the Mercedes shot forward and roared out of the parking lot onto the road, heading west.

Avi ran into the parking lot to find out what was happening. Through an opening in the trees, he saw Michael on the ground moaning. Sizing up the situation, he opened fire on Suslov's retreating car. The shots struck and ricocheted off the thick rear window. He helplessly watched the Russian disappear around a bend in the road.

Michael staggered toward the parking lot, still gripping his gun.

"Let me help you," Avi said.

"Thanks. I'll be okay. It's nothing serious."

As Michael, leaning on Avi for support, moved slowly toward the door of the café, the four Iranians stormed out and headed toward their BMW.

They didn't see Avi until it was too late. The Israeli raised his machine gun and said in Farsi, "Drop your weapons. I'm turning you over to the Americans. They can deal with you for your role in the kidnapping of Robert McCallister."

With blood dripping from his leg, Michael helped Avi herd the Iranians back into the café, all the while biting down on his lip as searing pain shot through his body.

The ambulance still sat on the other side of the building. Jack, who had kept firing at Russians from his position behind the toolshed, had not taken his eyes off the white vehicle.

The firing was dying down as the Americans were gaining the upper hand, but Jack decided to wait until it diminished further to try to rescue Robert. He wanted to minimize the risk of getting them both killed.

Suddenly he saw Kemal and Abdullah leave the café with guns in their hands, running toward the ambulance. His guess was that they planned to escape in the ambulance with McCallister. Of course, they didn't know that two of the tires were flat. Jack waited until they were in an open area midway between the café and the ambulance. He raised his Uzi and aimed at Kemal. A short burst dropped the Turk, but Abdullah sprinted toward the ambulance and darted behind it before Jack could zero in on him. *Okay. One down and one to go,* Jack told himself.

Abdullah began firing an AK-47 that blasted into the toolshed.

Jack couldn't get a clear shot. He was afraid of hitting the ambulance and having a bullet penetrate the exterior. Bullets were flying everywhere around him. The noise was deafening.

Suddenly Jack stopped firing. Pretending to be hit, he yelled for help in Arabic from behind the shed: *"Al-haoonee! Al-haoonee!"*

The trick worked. Abdullah leaned out a tiny bit to see what was happening. That was enough for Jack. His shot tore into the side of Abdullah's head.

With the Uzi still in his hand, Jack dashed toward the back of the ambulance, wondering what condition he'd find Robert in.

He dropped the machine gun on the ground. Slowly he twisted the latch and began pulling open the heavy white metal double doors. As he did he heard a muffled shot ring out from inside the ambulance and one of the rear windows shattered.

Jack instinctively threw himself to the ground. As he dropped down, he grabbed the handle to shut the doors until he was ready to fire back at whoever was in the ambulance.

He was too late. The doors kept opening.

Jack rolled along the ground, hoping to make himself a difficult target.

To Jack's astonishment, a Syrian soldier with an AK-47 on his lap and blood flowing down the side of his face and soaking his shirt pitched forward. He tumbled out of the ambulance, landing next to Jack on the ground.

Jack jumped to his feet, gun in hand. In utter amazement he saw Robert McCallister up on his knees on a gurney. His right arm was bandaged. In his left hand he held a pistol, which was smoking.

In a jerky movement, Robert lowered his arm and aimed the gun at Jack. He had a dazed look on his face, which made Jack think they must have given him a sedative that was just wearing off. He had no idea who Jack was, and he might fire again.

Before Robert had a chance, Jack took the gun out of his hand. "I'm here with the American military," Jack said. "You're safe now. We've got you back."

Tears of joy filled the pilot's eyes. "Oh, my God. I'm really free?"

A bullet blasted into the ground not far from the ambulance. The sound of automatic weapons was close by. "I have to get you under cover," Jack said. "I didn't do all this to lose you now."

Jack helped Robert out of the ambulance and hustled him over to the café.

Though Avi and Michael both had guns trained on the Iranians, they let out a cheer when they saw Jack and Robert.

"Good work," Avi called out.

"It looks like the American troops are mopping up the last few Russians," Jack said. "I'd say this is a complete success."

"Not yet," replied Michael, his leg bandaged with towels from the café. "Suslov escaped. He drove off in his Mercedes."

"We can't let that bastard get away," Jack said. "He's the one who was selling the nuclear weapons to our enemies."

Jack glanced at Avi, who nodded his agreement.

"You two stay here and watch Robert," Jack said. "I'll see if I can find Suslov and give him a little justice, Russian style."

"I'm going with you," Michael said. "I owe him big-time for everything he did to Irina."

Jack was prepared to tell Michael to remain behind and help Avi, when Avi spoke up: "Don't worry. I can handle it all back here. Get moving, you two."

The Americans were racing around picking off the few remaining Russian soldiers. Three threw their arms in the air and surrendered. "The area is now secure," Captain Kelly told Major Davis.

With an Uzi in his hand, Jack ran over to the pilot of one of the choppers. "We need a ride," he said. "The Russian responsible for all of this has taken off, heading west in a Mercedes."

"Climb in," the pilot of Chestnut four-four said. "I'll get my gunner. We'll catch him."

The helo lifted off with Michael belted in on one side, gripping his automatic hard. On the other, Jack was clutching an Uzi in one hand and a support in the other. He always found being in a helicopter with the door open and the wind whipping around to be a surreal experience. He pulled in his feet and legs to avoid falling out.

Ten minutes later they saw Suslov's Mercedes streaking along the open road at well over a hundred miles an hour.

"His car's armor-plated," Michael shouted to the gunner over the roar of the helo.

The gunner laughed. In an accent from the mountains of western North Carolina, he shouted back, "This sucker's equipped with AGM-114 Hellfire laser-guided missiles with enough power to punch through tank armor."

"Yes!" Michael roared.

The gunner gave him a thumbs-up.

In the Mercedes, Suslov watched as the Blackhawk moved in for the kill in his rearview mirror. He expected them to have weapons that would pierce the armor in the car. Thick trees lined the right side of the road. Suddenly Suslov cut a sharp right into the trees and slammed on the brakes. Gun in hand, he jumped out and dashed toward a clump of rocks just as the gunner let go with a missile that took the Mercedes out of the equation. There was a huge fireball and a deafening roar from the explosion.

"He's clear of the car," Jack shouted to the gunner. "Tell the pilot to put it down on the road. We'll chase him on foot." The gunner relayed Jack's request via his intercom headset, and the pilot quickly set his bird down on the road.

Suslov was moving away from the helicopter as fast as he could. Over his shoulder he saw Jack racing after him, while Michael trudged slowly with his bandaged thigh.

With his bum leg, Suslov knew he was no match for Jack. His only hope was to use the thick cover of the woods to circle back and pick off Michael, then surprise Jack from the rear.

But Michael had a pair of binoculars in his pocket. He yanked them out and put them up to his eyes, scanning the area until he saw Suslov. From the Russian's counterclockwise movement, he guessed what Suslov had in mind.

Michael took cover between two large rocks and watched Suslov gradually approaching his position.

Patience, he cautioned himself. *Patience. You already missed twice. Wait for the right shot.*

Michael knew he had it when Suslov stepped into a small clearing, only fifteen feet away from him. Glints of sunlight sliced through the trees. Gun in hand, the Russian looked around, searching for Michael. Michael could see him sweat.

He took aim and then slowly raised himself up behind the rock. Suslov spotted him, but before the Russian had a chance to shoot, Michael pulled the trigger three times in rapid succession. The bullets tore into Suslov's body from abdomen to chest as the gun bucked in Michael's hand. The Russian collapsed to his knees, then onto his back.

Blood and mud covered much of Suslov's body. He struggled to sit up and raise his gun.

Michael was ready for him. "This is for Irina," he said as he pulled the trigger.

Now the gun fell from Suslov's hand as he reared backward with a startled look on his face, as if wondering how this whole episode could have turned to shit so quickly.

Jack walked into the clearing. The Russian was dead. He raised his boot and violently kicked Suslov in the face.

The helo took Jack and Michael back to the parking lot of the truck stop. With the gun still in his hand, Jack trudged wearily into the café.

By now Robert was fully alert. The American pilot looked at him and said, "Hey, I'd like to thank the guy who rescued me. Who are you?"

"I'm Jack Cole. Your future brother in-law."

Epilogue

Politics always follows money, someone told the woman in the gray suit who headed up the Middle East section of Bank Leumi in Tel Aviv. Layla didn't know whether that was correct, but she did know that in the first six months on the job, she had developed a significant portfolio of loans for projects in Morocco, Egypt, and Jordan. The risk for the bank wasn't great. Most had guarantees from the United States, a European country, or a world lending organization. The political benefit from these loans for Israel was significant, as the word spread on the Arab street.

She checked her watch. Running late again. The trip to the hair salon she had hoped for early this evening would have to go.

She left the bank headquarters and jumped into a cab. "The Mann Auditorium, please," she told the driver.

"What are they playing tonight?" the driver asked in Russian-accented Hebrew.

She smiled. No cabdriver in Paris would have ever asked a passenger that. "Yefim Bronfman is playing two Brahms piano concertos, Numbers One and Two."

"Magnificent," the driver responded. "He's one of our best."

Layla shook her head in disbelief. *What a country this Israel is. Everyone's a political analyst and a music critic.*

As the cab slowed to a stop next to the plaza in front of the hall, Layla climbed out. A tall, fit-looking man with thick, wavy, sand-colored hair and sparkling blue eyes was waiting for her.

"Did I ever tell you," he said, "that I love how you get in and out of a car? You always show lots of gorgeous leg."

She smiled. "Yes, I believe you've mentioned it. Sandwich and a glass of wine before the concert?"

"The sandwich I'll buy. The wine I brought." He patted a case he was carrying in his hand. "I can't drink what they're selling here."

Laughing, she leaned up and kissed him. "You're such a snob, Jack. Don't forget you're just a kid from the north side of Chicago."

Acknowledgments

After the successful publication of *Spy Dance*, I breathed a large sigh of relief that events in the Middle East didn't destroy the factual premises for the story, and vowed that I would never write another novel which even tangentially touched upon that turbulent part of the world. With events unfolding at a furious pace in Iraq and the Israeli-Arab conflict, the topic seemed like a minefield. No pun intended.

However, Henry Morrison, my marvelous agent, and Doug Grad, my superb editor, had other ideas. "You know the area," they said. "You can do it again." So it was into the fray one more time. Henry and Doug worked with me and offered valuable insights each step of the way from outline to the final revisions. For that I am extremely grateful.

My wife, Barbara, read each draft and offered constructive suggestions. She particularly helped me shape the female characters. Sarah, Ann, and Layla have all benefited from her sagacity.

Ed Sands at Calvert Woodley in Washington supplied essential information about the intricacies of the wine business. Our daughter, Deborah, was always available to help make the medical issues accurate and coherent.

Finally, the entire team at NAL—John Paine, Adrian Wood, Ron Martirano, Tina Anderson, and everyone in the art and sales departments—were incredibly helpful and amazingly efficient.

Penguin Group (USA) Inc. Online

What will you be reading tomorrow?

Tom Clancy, Patricia Cornwell, W.E.B. Griffin,
Nora Roberts, William Gibson, Robin Cook,
Brian Jacques, Catherine Coulter, Stephen King,
Dean Koontz, Ken Follett, Clive Cussler,
Eric Jerome Dickey, John Sandford,
Terry McMillan…

You'll find them all at
http://www.penguin.com

*Read excerpts and newsletters,
find tour schedules, and enter contests.*

Subscribe to Penguin Group (USA) Inc. Newsletters
and get an exclusive inside look
at exciting new titles and the authors you love
long before everyone else does.